Susan Meier is the author of over fifty books for Mills & Boon. *The Tycoon's Secret Daughter* was a Romance Writers of America RITA® Award finalist, and *Nanny for the Millionaire's Twins* won the Book Buyers' Best award and was a finalist in the National Readers' Choice awards. She is married and has three children. One of eleven children herself, she loves to write about the complexity of families and totally believes in the power of love.

Though her name is frequently on bestseller lists, **Allison Leigh**'s high point as a writer is hearing from readers that they laughed, cried or lost sleep while reading her books. She credits her family with great patience for the time she's parked at her computer, and for blessing her with the kind of love she wants her readers to share with the characters living in the pages of her books. Contact her at allisonleigh.com

Also by Susan Meier

The Spanish Millionaire's Runaway Bride
Carrying the Billionaire's Baby
A Diamond for the Single Mum
Falling for the Pregnant Heiress
Cinderella's Billion-Dollar Christmas
The Bodyguard and the Heiress

Also by Allison Leigh

The BFF Bride
A Child Under His Tree
Yuletide Baby Bargain
Show Me a Hero
The Rancher's Christmas Promise
A Promise to Keep
Fortune's Homecoming
Wild West Fortune
Fortune's Secret Heir
Fortune's Texas Reunion

Discover more at millsandboon.co.uk

HIRED BY THE UNEXPECTED BILLIONAIRE

SUSAN MEIER

LAWFULLY UNWED

ALLISON LEIGH

MILLS & BOON

First Published in Great Britain 2020
by Mills & Boon, an imprint of HarperCollinsPublishers,
1 London Bridge Street, London, SE1 9GF

Hired by the Unexpected Billionaire © 2020 Linda Susan Meier
Lawfully Unwed © 2020 Allison Lee Johnson

ISBN: 978-0-263-27891-0

0820

MIX
Paper from
responsible sources
FSC™ C007454

This book is produced from independently certified FSC™
paper to ensure responsible forest management.

For more information visit: www.harpercollins.co.uk/green

Printed and bound in Spain
by CPI, Barcelona

HIRED BY THE UNEXPECTED BILLIONAIRE

SUSAN MEIER

The most fitting end to a series about family
is to dedicate the final book to mine.
Ten siblings, hundreds (only a slight exaggeration)
of nieces and nephews
and great-nieces and great-nephews.
I love you all.

CHAPTER ONE

A SECRET WAS a funny thing. A person could totally forget the worst part of her past, build a new life and be perfectly content, only to have fear turn her blood to ice water when a memory burst in her brain.

She'd been here before.

Marnie Olsen cautiously stepped into Manhattan's Shutto Building, her heart pounding. Brushed metal handrails enhanced the open stairway on the right. Sleek, sophisticated silver cylinders hung from the high ceiling, lighting the lobby. The dark, delicious scent of coffee floated out from Caffeine Burst, a coffee shop on the left. A doorman in a black sweater over a white shirt and red tie stood by a shiny desk. It was early July, but the air-conditioning was cranked up to high. Probably so he could wear the fancy sweater.

She took a breath, forcing away her fear. It had been ten years. Roger Martin wouldn't be here. Even if his father still worked on the nineteenth floor, Roger should have his own job by now. Hopefully in a building far, far away. Plus, the odds of her seeing him were slim. She'd be in and out of her interview in less than an hour.

Shaky but determined, she strode to the desk and the doorman. "I'm Marnie Olsen. I have an interview with Attorney Manelli at Waters, Waters and Montgomery. He said you'd point me to the private elevator and give me the code."

The older man frowned and walked from behind the desk. "*I'll* punch in the code."

She smiled. "Great."

But her confidence took a direct hit. Danny Manelli had told her the elevator code changed hourly. The doorman could have given it to her and by the time her interview was over, it would be different. But no. He saw her simple summer blazer and scuffed shoes and didn't assume she'd just worked her way through university. He saw trash. A low-class woman trying for a high-class job.

Embarrassment heated her face. She hadn't always been poor. She was the daughter of Eddie Gouse, Manhattan real estate mogul. But he'd packed his things and taken her brother, leaving her mom desperately broke with a twelve-year-old daughter to raise. That, in Marnie's mind, was the real beginning of her secret.

The doorman punched in the code and took another look at her before he sniffed in derision and walked away.

As the elevator door closed, she pulled in a shivery breath. She'd literally thought her life was over, thought there was no way she'd ever pass a company's investigatory process to get a job. Then she'd found nannying. The *service* investigated all their applicants. She'd spilled the details of her life once. They vetted her, discovered her secret and cleared her. As long as she worked for them, no one else had to look into her past. Her secret stayed locked away. And she had a nice, secure job from which she could eventually make a nice, secure life.

There was nothing to worry about.

In seconds, Danny Manelli's private elevator arrived at his office. Before the door opened, Marnie composed herself, prayed to relax and pasted a smile on her face.

The panels slowly slid apart and the office beyond, though decorated with shiny oak furniture, was empty, except for a puppy standing on the chair, his front paws on the desk, his head down as if he were reading the document in front of him.

"Well, Mr. Manelli. You're certainly not what I expected."

"What were you expecting?"

The masculine voice from the left made her jump. She pressed her hand to her chest, not knowing whether to die of embarrassment or laugh because she'd been caught talking to a dog.

She chose dignity and turned, offering her hand. "Mr. Manelli?"

But when she raised her gaze to meet his, her heart stuttered. Tall and slim, with perfectly cut short black hair and piercing dark eyes, he was polished but also sexy and male. She could picture him in a bedroom lit only by a few white candles, pouring wine into expensive flutes, turning lovemaking into an art.

She blinked. *Where the heck had that come from?*

"Yes. I'm Danny Manelli. And you must be Marnie Olsen, my two o'clock nanny interview."

"Yes."

He shook her hand once, a crisp movement, before he released her and walked to his desk. He picked up the puppy. "Oswald, we've talked about this. Your bachelor's degree isn't enough. You have to go to law school and pass the bar before you can edit documents."

His sense of humor surprised her. The puppy wiggled around in his arms until his pink tongue could reach Danny Manelli's face. Then he licked his clean-shaven chin. His tail wagged. His fat tummy jiggled with the frenetic movement. He didn't seem to know what to do with his big paws.

Marnie put her fingers to her lips to hold back a laugh. They were quite a pair. The gorgeous executive and the wiggly puppy. Except—

Oswald? She frowned. He definitely had the dog's name wrong.

"That dog's not an Oswald."

Danny Manelli looked at her as if she'd stolen his last cookie. "Excuse me?"

"He's a Wiggles," she said, walking over to pet the puppy. His ears perked up. His tail wagged wildly. His oversize paws hung over Danny's forearms. Considering their size, Oswald/Wiggles had to be a yellow Lab.

"You're a Wiggles, aren't you, sweetie?" She took the furry ball of energy from his owner, and the dog rewarded her with what felt like eighty rapid-fire chin licks. "Oh, and I see someone hasn't gone to obedience school."

"I had a dog as a child. He never went to obedience school."

"Where'd you live?"

"Upstate."

She winced. "Small-town living is very different than Park Avenue. You'll be taking Wiggles for walks with your little boy. He's going to see other dogs. Run into people he doesn't know. As playful as he is," she said, as the dog enthusiastically squirmed in her arms, "he's going to make contact, and when he does, it might not always end well."

"I thought you were a nanny."

"I am."

"Not a dog expert."

His cool voice sent fear shivering through her again. Danny Manelli was offering three times her usual fee for this job and she needed the money. She also liked the idea that this assignment could turn permanent. She didn't want to lose it over a throwaway comment.

"Lots of the people I worked for were dog owners. That's why I'm familiar with the system."

"Then maybe you should train him?"

The fear rose again. She hated that she was so uncomfortable around new people. She could blame Roger Martin. Let her dread take over and apologetically stumble her way through the interview—

Instead, she forgot all that, raised her chin and looked Danny Manelli in the eye. This was her dream assignment. After a few months of probation, she could have full-time employment. It could mean working with the same child the whole way through his teen years, getting to know him and his family, while making enough money to set some aside. She refused to let it slip through her fingers.

"That's a job for a pro."

"You're telling me I need to hire someone?"

"Or enroll him in a school. There are some excellent choices. I can get you a list."

"I guess I'll have to take you up on that."

Her muscles relaxed. Her breathing returned to normal. For a few seconds, neither spoke. Danny Manelli studied her face as if trying to determine her honesty. Or maybe because nobody had ever told him what to do. Whatever his reason, she stood still under his scrutiny. If he assessed character from a person's face, she would give him time to realize she might be nervous, but she was honest.

Danny reached for the puppy and she handed him over. "Please sit." He pointed to the seat across from his desk. "Excuse my lack of focus. The past few months my life sort of imploded."

"Discovering you're the parent of a two-year-old would be difficult."

"It's more than that." He put the pup on a small dog bed at his feet and gave him a chew toy. "And if you're going to work for me you need to know."

"Okay."

"I was recently told I was adopted."

"Oh."

"I now have a biological father who wants to be in my life, as well as adoptive parents who raised me, who deserve the place my biological father is usurping."

"That's awkward."

"You don't know the half of it." He shook his head. "My biological father is Mark Hinton."

Her mouth fell open. "Mark Hinton? The guy who faked his death?"

"He claims he didn't. That his boat had stalled, and he got himself to safety and never saw the news or went on the internet for the months he was gone."

"Wow."

"Oh, that's just the tip of the iceberg. He's a lot like a tornado. When he comes in, he crashes into everything. And he brings an entourage of bodyguards. Everyone in the family has them now. Nosy and ridiculous as he is, he dug into my personal life, found my son and decided that was reason enough to upend the lives of at least eight people."

Marnie sat back, not knowing what to say. As someone who had worked in other people's homes, seen other people's problems up close and personal without ever getting involved, she would normally answer with something neutral and benign. But this was an interview and, undoubtedly, he wanted her reaction to what he'd said about his father, the *infamous* Mark Hinton.

But for the life of her, she couldn't think of an appropriate response. Her mom was an alcoholic, her dad a real estate mogul accustomed to everyone doing his bidding. When living with her mom had become embarrassing, he'd packed up himself and her brother and gone. He'd wanted Marnie to come with them, but she'd stayed, one more day, unable to leave her unconscious mom for fear she'd die. The next morning when her mom had awakened, still not quite sober, she couldn't reach her husband—who wasn't answering her calls—and she'd shattered into a million tiny pieces. She'd found an A.A. meeting and she'd been sober since.

Yet her dad hadn't come home. He'd also refused to see Marnie or let Marnie see her little brother. He'd called her a defector.

She cleared her throat. "I know a bit about parental drama."

"This isn't drama. This is a man who comes in and takes over people's lives. You'll be dealing with him."

She chuckled. "I'll be fine. Without breaking confidences, I can tell you I've handled a few difficult grandparents. Plus, one of the big perks of being a nanny is that I can always take the child and retreat to the nursery. It's a subtle but effective way of showing an adult like a grandparent that if he missteps, he loses time with the child he came to see."

Danny smiled—his first real smile since she'd entered the room—and it transformed his face, melting the severe lines in his forehead and around his mouth. "That's perfect."

Her heart flipped over in her chest. Attraction rippled through her, surprising her. Though she'd dated on and off in the six years she'd been at university, it had been a long, long time since she'd had an instinctive reaction like this. Part lust. Part longing.

Longing for something she couldn't have.

No. Something she wouldn't *risk*. Not when financial security was at stake.

She schooled her face. Landing this job didn't merely provide room and board. It secured her future. Attraction was nothing but hormones. She knew firsthand the trouble they could cause.

So, no thanks.

"Nannies always do what's best for the child. Including sanctioning their grandparents."

He sniffed a laugh. "It still sounds perfect to me."

"Your little boy will be my responsibility. I don't take that lightly. I also don't let people push me around."

She'd had enough of that to last a lifetime. Running scared. Changing high schools. Using her mom's maiden name—

She stopped her thoughts. She knew her mind kept jerking in the direction of her secret because of the building. The memories it evoked.

She put herself back into interview mode and said, "I can handle anything your new father dishes out."

Danny laughed. Really laughed. For the first time in months, he felt a little bit of the burden that had become his life chip away. Not only did he have full custody of his son, but he was in the process of hiring a nanny who would make their time together a fun experience.

The last woman he'd interviewed had looked so much like Mary Poppins, he'd almost hired her on the spot, especially considering she had a great résumé. To be fair to the other candidates, he hadn't. But the choice was a no-brainer. He was selecting the nanny who knew how to care for his child, so he wouldn't have even one worry. He could simply enjoy raising his son.

Now this woman—Marnie Olsen—was showing him she could do the job too. Despite being so young.

He looked across the desk at her. Average height. Average weight. In an average floral print dress, blazer and black shoes. Her red-brown hair had been pinned into a knot of some sort at her nape. But she couldn't hide or tone down her lush lips, or the vivid green eyes that watched him carefully.

As they should. If she became Rex's nanny, she'd be knee-deep in Hintonville. The crazy world that had taken over his life. Because of Mark, he'd discovered his son, had two half sisters and was about to get a new stepmom when his dad finally married the love of his life.

But also because of his dad, his adoptive parents felt out of place. Though Danny was trying to smooth things over, he was angry with them for never telling him he was adopted, not warning him that he was the child of a crazy billionaire. Or that someday his life could implode.

In case Mary Poppins didn't take the assignment, he had to interview Marnie Olsen as if she would be entering that messed-up chaotic world.

"The agency sent you to me because they believe you are one of three people qualified to do this job."

"Yes. They told me." She smiled. "Typically, though, I just get assignments. I don't go on interviews."

"This is a long-term thing. My son's mother is about to become a vice president for a bank in Europe. It's a huge opportunity for her and we decided that I was the better candidate to have custody of Rex."

"Mrs. Harper said the assignment could turn permanent."

"Is that a problem?"

"No. I've just never worked with the same child for a year, let alone long term." Her lips lifted into a beautiful smile. "I love children. I'm fully capable of stepping back when an assignment is over…but it would be wonderful to help raise a little boy, watch him grow and learn."

Danny's heart took a funny leap. She was gorgeous when she smiled and her green eyes lit up. He knew instinctively that Rex would love her and, truth be told, if Danny had to have another person living in his home it would be nice to have someone so pleasant.

Mary Poppins slipped a bit on the desirability scale.

He cleared his throat. "Tell me a little bit about yourself."

Something flickered across her face. "Myself?"

Confused by her hesitancy, Danny sat forward. "Your past assignments."

Her smile returned. "I put myself through university as a part-time nanny. It was good money and I could refuse assignments when I needed to study for midterms or finals or do a paper." She shrugged. "I've been with all kinds of kids. I've nannied babies and toddlers and children I took to school." She paused for a second. "Never had a teenager though."

"But you have handled toddlers?"

"The terrible twos are nothing to me."

"Terrible twos are scaring me silly," Danny said, wincing. "So far Rex has been a perfect angel. But I know trouble is coming."

"Trouble is in the eye of the beholder. All kids can be naughty. All kids experiment. The real bottom line is how *you* react. For instance, if your little boy unravels all the toilet paper, and you explain to him that you know how much fun it is to spin the whole roll to the floor, but that's wasteful, then he learns something. But if you find him in the bathroom surrounded by white tissue, and you go ballistic, you only confuse him."

Considering how Mark had upset everyone's life, he really liked the idea of his son being raised in a quiet, gentle environment. "I get that. My mom was a learn-your-lesson disciplinarian. My dad was a yeller. I learned so much more from my mom."

"Precisely."

"So, what's your favorite part about being a nanny?"

"The kids. I like to get down on the floor and play. I love when they're talkative because they have such an interesting perspective on life. Everything's new to them."

"Rex would love that."

"It's fun for me too. I have been known to create some really great finger paintings."

He laughed.

"And my mom still puts them on the fridge when I bring them home."

"You sound like someone who should be a teacher."

Her face glowed but she sniffed. "No. I love working one-on-one with the kids I'm nannying. I've been studying the latest research on things like the effect of art in a child's life. Music, painting, sculpture, dance..." She nodded at Oswald. "Even pets. The close relationship of a caregiver gives me the chance to expose a child to all those things and watch him or her grow."

That was *exactly* what he wanted for Rex. With all the money in the world at their disposal, his son could be, have or do anything he wanted. Having someone who would expose him to art, teach him to look around and enjoy, would be amazing.

He fought the urge to change his mind about hiring Mary Poppins, a nice, middle-aged woman who'd raised five kids. Marnie was young and happy. He wasn't saying Mary Poppins had a face like a prune... But there was a certain resemblance. His entire life his son would have anything he wanted. Rex needed someone to teach him to appreciate it.

Danny leaned back, angling his elbow on the arm of his chair and resting his jaw on his closed fist. "I'm doing second interviews...with Rex at my penthouse tonight." He hadn't planned on asking Marnie to come to his penthouse, but something in his gut told him she was the one. It had to be wrong. Mary Poppins had the best résumé. Still...

He didn't remember his instincts ever being this strong.

"I was planning on having all the candidates come to my house tonight." He shook his head, hoping the instinct would go away. It didn't. If anything, it got stronger. Plus, he was working with a service. Not one-on-one with the nannies. If Marnie didn't pan out, he could call her boss and exchange her for Mary Poppins.

"But I don't think there's a need for that. I'd like to hire you."

Her mouth fell open. She gaped at him for a few seconds before she said, "Oh my gosh! That's wonderful!" She bounced up from her seat. "You won't be sorry!"

He hoped he wouldn't be. He waited for a ping of anxiety or a sense that he'd made a mistake, but nothing came. He wrote down the address, then stood and handed it across the desk. "I'll see you tonight at eight."

Her face absolutely glowed. "See you at eight."

He watched her leave, his gut positive he'd done the right thing. While his brain hoped to hell he wasn't turning into an impulsive goofball like his biological dad.

CHAPTER TWO

As MARNIE SAT in the subway train, everything about that day plowed through her brain. Something good had happened. She'd gotten a job. A fabulous job with income enough that she could save for her real goal: to open her own nanny agency.

But it was with the son of Mark Hinton, crazy billionaire. It hadn't seemed like a big deal when Shirley Harper had given her the job specifics or even in Danny Manelli's office during the interview. But walking through the elegant lobby of his building, familiar fear trickled through her. Danny Manelli might not be crazy, but his biological dad was—

Her past bubbled up unbidden. Secrets. Lies. Bullying. Lots of it done on social media—

Under Marnie Gouse. Not Olsen. It would take some searching to connect the dots.

Plus, most people used a nanny service because they knew the person coming into their home had been vetted. Danny Manelli hadn't said anything about checking her references or looking into her past. He probably trusted the service.

Of course, he trusted the service. That's what rich people did.

When she arrived at the little apartment she shared with her mom, she walked into her bedroom. The laptop on her desk lured her over. She turned it on and immediately looked up Mark Hinton—

And groaned.

There had to be at least eighty articles written about the estate looking for three missing heirs in the time Mark was supposed to have been dead. One particularly troubling article spoke of Danny's half-sister Leni Long. Her phone had been cloned, outing her, when she'd been keeping a low profile.

Danny was right. His situation was crazy… But did that really have anything to do with her? What would the press care about a woman whose job was to change diapers, fix breakfast and lunch?

Maybe nothing.

She knew she was rationalizing because she *wanted* this job. Her entire being rebelled at the idea of giving it up because of one stupid incident when she was young and too trusting—

She licked her dry lips. She hadn't searched her name in years. Even if it turned up empty, all a search did was dredge up memories that filled her with shame.

But today, she ran her hand along the smooth edge of the laptop. Her mother had always said, if you hear a noise when you're alone in the apartment, check it out and when you find it's nothing, you'll feel better.

This wasn't a noise. It was a fear about her secret. All along she'd blamed her queasiness on walking into the Shutto Building. What if the instinct was actually a nudge from the universe that Roger Martin had put those pictures online?

Horror tightened her chest, filled her with dread. Her fingers hit the keyboard, as she searched her old name.

Nothing.

She wanted to feel relief, but pictures didn't have to be associated to a name. Somewhere on the dark web the photos he'd taken when she'd fallen asleep after losing her virginity could be up online.

Or not.

She'd spent the last years believing they'd been destroyed. After he'd tried to sell the pictures at school, she'd raced home, filled with shame, and her mom had called the police. In what seemed like minutes, a squad car had been at the school entrance and two uniformed officers had been in front of the principal's desk.

Roger hadn't actually posted the pictures and had carefully disguised the way he offered them for sale on his social media pages. Ten years ago, deleting the pictures from his phone, in front of the police, had satisfied the authorities.

But the shame of it had followed her around. She was bullied at school because her mom had called the police. Because she'd embarrassed Roger. Demonized him.

In her mind, he was a demon. But no one seemed to care about her.

She couldn't think back to that time without feeling trapped, afraid, mortified.

But ten years had gone by. A search had netted nothing. She needed to be brave. Take this job. Enjoy Danny Manelli's little boy. Save for her future.

She turned off her laptop and headed to the closet to get a duffel bag to pack. Changing her name and changing schools had given back her life. But no one could guarantee that Roger Martin didn't have those pictures on a thumb drive.

Or that they wouldn't surface one day.

Still, the older she got, the less she looked like the naive girl in the pictures, and her name was different. Plus, nobody really cared about a nanny. Any household employee was like the woodwork. Present, serving a purpose, but not really interesting.

She took a breath. Maybe the thing to do would be take the job and observe. See if Danny Manelli's life was crazy enough that a reporter might get curious about his nanny.

Even thinking that made her shake her head.

Nobody cared about maids, doormen and nannies!

She forced herself to forget that Roger Martin had been a jackass. A privileged jock. Who'd smirked at her when the police let him leave with a warning and a male bonding slap on the shoulder.

It was that smirk that haunted her—a chilling reminder that he was in charge.

Danny arrived home a little after seven. He walked over to the sofa in his open-plan living space and picked up his son. "How are you doing?"

The yellow-haired two-year-old dressed in bib overalls and a T-shirt said, "Good."

"He had a great time." Danny's half-sister Charlotte rose from the teal sofa. A tall, slim blonde with big blue eyes, she looked comfortable and almost motherly in jeans and a tank top—odd for a woman who'd been more accustomed to a hard hat and construction trailer before she discovered she was a Hinton heir.

"Jace was here for a while and they played tag." She huffed out a sigh. "That kid can run! I thought Jace and I were in good shape, but Rex ran rings around us."

Rex giggled. Charlotte tickled his tummy. "Oh, you won this afternoon but Uncle Jace and I will be back."

"I really appreciate you and Leni watching him today. Having Alisha bring him this morning was a shock. Apparently, her employer wanted her in Spain right away and she had to leave immediately. I'm just glad I already had the nursery set up and essentials bought for the weekends I had visitation. I don't know what I'd have done without you."

"Hey, that's what family does." She laughed. "Or at least that's what I'm told. How do three people who were raised as only children end up siblings?"

"Our dad was a runaround."

She snorted and picked up her big purse. "That should be my line." She leaned in and kissed Rex's cheek, then Danny's. "I've got to go. Let me know if you need help interviewing nannies."

"Actually, I hired one."

Charlotte stopped halfway to the elevator. "Really?"

"I don't have the luxury of time. Rex is here now, and I need help. I called Jace this morning and he suggested an agency. Said it was the best nanny service in the business. They sent over three good candidates. I liked the one who looked a bit like Mary Poppins, but there was another candidate who seemed like she might be better."

"Better how?"

"She's younger." He shook his head. "I don't know… It seems like she has more energy or something."

Charlotte took a step toward him. "After losing three games of tag, I'd say energy is a big plus."

"Yes. And she's already been vetted by the agency. I don't have to do a background check myself or call references. I know she's reputable."

Charlotte's smile unexpectedly drooped. "You're not checking *anything*?"

"That's the whole purpose of going through an agency. Especially this one. Jace says they are the best."

Charlotte laughed. "He does know what he's talking about." She frowned. "It looks like you won't need me anymore."

"Don't be disappointed. I'm sure Marnie will have days off, need personal time, take sick days."

"And I can babysit?"

"You and Leni can split the days."

"And there's the drawback to having siblings." She reached out and lightly pinched Rex's cheek. "I don't want to share this little guy."

"Does that mean I can call you at 2:00 a.m. when he starts wailing?"

She breezed toward the elevator again, slinging her big gray purse over her shoulder. "Not a chance. But I am good for afternoons and weekends." She pressed the button. "Tell your nanny that."

The doors opened and Rex and Danny waved goodbye.

As the elevator door closed behind his sister, he carried Rex to the kitchen. "I'm sure your aunt Charlotte fed you dinner but let's see about a snack."

Generally, he knew what he was doing, but he didn't remember all the specifics about Rex's routine. He reached for the three single-spaced pages of notes Rex's mom, Alisha, had given Danny when she shifted custody that morning.

"It says here you get a snack."

Rex's eyes widened with pleasure. "Snack."

"Before bed," Danny added, finishing the sentence he'd started.

Rex frowned.

"Maybe some juice to tide you over. We don't want you messy when the new nanny gets here."

"Nanny."

Danny laughed. "You have a really interesting repeating words thing going on. I'm guessing that's part of how you learn."

"Learn."

Danny sniffed and kissed Rex's forehead before going to the refrigerator. He pulled out the bottle of apple juice, but it bumped the gallon of milk and knocked it to the floor. Danny jumped out of the way with a gasp, but he didn't make it. When the gallon hit the shiny white tile, it broke and milk sprayed outward and upward, soaking him and Rex.

"I'll bet handling this isn't on your mother's list."

Rex blinked twice, his little face twisted, and he yelped, then began to sob. He was coated in milk. So was Danny, but Danny's shoes were also soaked. He held one up and it dripped liquid.

"Definitely not on your mother's list."

He stood there for a few seconds, shell-shocked, but more confused. There were so many things that needed to be done at once. Everything from changing his clothes and Rex's clothes to cleaning the floor and cabinets and getting a new gallon of milk as soon as possible because Rex always drank some before bed.

But looking at the mess—milk on the floor, dripping from the doors of the lower cabinets and soaking his clothes—his brain froze.

CHAPTER THREE

MARNIE WALKED INTO the building containing Danny Manelli's penthouse, and her eyes widened, her breath stalled. Not because she recognized the building—thank God. But from awe. This lobby looked more like someone's sleek, sophisticated living room with midcentury modern sofas sitting at an angle to a stacked stone fireplace and a view of workout equipment beyond a wall of glass.

It reminded her of the building she and her mom had lived in with her dad. New and filled with amenities. Not that she thought her dad lived *here*. He lived on the Upper East Side. Or had fourteen years ago.

There was nothing to fear from him.

A doorman sat at a desk tucked discreetly in the corner. Wearing a white golf shirt, he watched her closely. Probably because she looked lost, out of place. In a way, she was. She couldn't see the elevator that was supposed to take her to the penthouse.

"Excuse me." She walked over to the doorman. "I'm Danny Manelli's new nanny."

"Oh." He smiled. "He told me he'd hired a nanny when he arrived home tonight." He glanced at a sheet of paper on his desk. "You must be Marnie Olsen."

"Yes." To prove her legitimacy, she showed him her ID. "But I don't see an elevator to get to the penthouse."

The doorman laughed and came from behind the desk. "This way."

He led her around a corner to what looked like an ordinary wood-paneled wall. He pressed a button that Marnie hadn't even seen, and the wall opened.

She gaped at it, her chest tightening as it began to sink in that this was no ordinary building. But she reminded herself she was here on a scouting mission. If anything went sideways or looked like it might cause someone to check into her past, she could quit. The agency would have someone at Danny Manelli's penthouse an hour after she left.

But she wasn't going to be a wimp about this. This job was phase two of her plan. Phase one had been get her degree. Phase two was save money while she learned everything she could, so she could start her own nanny service. She had to check this out.

Still, taking another glance at the upscale surroundings, a building more elegant than the homes of her usual clients, something inside her brain said, "Run."

She ruthlessly stomped it out. *So Danny Manelli was rich? Maybe even a billionaire?* Lots of them led perfectly normal lives. And the paparazzi didn't stalk them like everyone believed. No one had ever been interested in her dad. Just because someone was wealthy, it didn't mean they were a target. Paparazzi liked the crazy people, the ostentatious, the billionaires who put themselves out on social media doing ridiculous things.

True, Mark Hinton was out-there, but Danny, her actual boss, was a sedate lawyer. Clearly a successful one, but not someone who'd raise the media's eyebrows. Just like all her other employers. A new nanny wouldn't even be a blip on anyone's radar. Plus, she'd searched social media to ensure her name didn't come up.

If tonight and tomorrow went okay, she'd be fine. And firmly in phase two of her plan. Firmly in control of her life.

After the doorman punched in the code, she stepped into the elevator, and the little car shot off like a rocket.

The ride to the top floor took mere seconds. The door opened and Marnie gaped. The huge open-plan floor space was decorated with ultramodern furniture and displayed a panoramic view of Manhattan through the back wall of glass. It was so spectacular her breath shimmied.

Warning bells went off in her head. The little voice that

said, "Run," returned full force. People who lived in places like this weren't normal. Even if they tried to be normal, how could they be? If anyone other than Mark Hinton had been lost at sea, he might have been declared dead, but it wouldn't have made the national news. And the three heirs, finally found, wouldn't have become overnight celebrities.

This job was too risky.

She reached to punch the down button on the elevator, but before her finger hit, the cries of a toddler pierced the air.

A sense of duty stopped her hand midair.

She waited a second, and when the cries continued, she exited the elevator and almost stepped on the puppy.

She dropped the duffel bag containing all her necessities and stooped to brush her hand along his back. "Oh my goodness. Wiggles! You're going to have to learn to be more careful around people's feet."

The dog barked once.

She glanced around again. Except for Rex's cries, the place was eerily quiet. Where was Danny Manelli?

She rose, looking around. "Where is everybody?"

He barked again.

The little boy's sobs got louder as she ventured farther into the penthouse. The white kitchen area had black and gray trellis tiles for a backsplash and marble countertops. A teal toaster and coffeemaker brightened the huge space. But those sort of led the eye to the teal sofa with matching paisley chairs, which sat in front of a baby grand piano that sat in front of the amazing view of Manhattan.

The cries got louder.

"Mr. Manelli?" She eased toward the hall that she assumed led to bedrooms. "Danny?"

Nothing.

Following the sound of the baby's sobs, she made her way down the corridor until she reached the door where they were the loudest. She turned the knob to find the most luxurious nursery she'd ever seen.

Everything was blue, silver and white. Except the crib, which was cherrywood. Beside the crib was a changing table, where Danny wrestled with a two-year-old and a diaper.

She called, "I'm here," as she slid the puppy to the floor and entered the room.

Danny glanced over his shoulder at her. "Hey. Sorry about the chaos. I spilled a gallon of milk."

She winced. "Oh, that's not good." The front of his white shirt was soaked. So were the black trousers he'd had on at the office that day. She might not be taking the job, but this guy needed help. She'd tell him after things were settled.

"Okay. How about this? Let me dress Rex while you take off those wet clothes."

He stepped back. "A milk-soaked shirt *is* uncomfortable."

She laughed and walked to the changing table. "Scoot. I'll handle this. We'll meet in the kitchen."

Danny left the nursery and Marnie glanced down at Rex who had quieted once his dad shifted away. Naked, waiting for a fresh diaper, he blinked tear-filled eyes at her.

"Look at all that pretty yellow hair," she said, passing a hand through the curls. Regret that she wouldn't get to know him drifted through her. "And blue eyes. You are adorable! You don't know me, but your daddy hired me to be your nanny," she said, making short order of the diaper. She wasn't exactly lying. His dad had hired her. She'd simply not be taking the job. But she wouldn't leave a single dad in this much trouble.

She looked at the clock. "It's close to eight," she said, one hand on the baby, the other opening the closet door to find a dresser. "So, I'm thinking of putting you into pajamas." Taking a long reach, she found one-piece pj's in the second drawer. She plucked out a pair and slid the bottoms over his feet and legs.

He stared at her.

Her chest tightened. He was the most beautiful child she'd ever seen. "I must be a real curiosity to you, if you've stopped crying." She slid his arms into the top. "Is there broccoli in my teeth?"

One corner of his mouth kicked up as if he understood.

Her heart swelled. In two minutes with this little boy, she was in love. "I knew you liked me."

"He does seem to." Danny's voice came from behind her and sounded greatly relieved.

Marnie's helper gene flushed with pride. She couldn't stay, but she wouldn't leave someone who clearly needed her.

If he'd spilled enough milk, he needed her.

She finished pulling the top of the one-piece pajamas over Rex's shoulders and pulled the zipper over his tummy. "I hope you don't mind. I took the liberty of putting him into pajamas. I assume he'll get a snack and then be off to bed."

"Yes." Danny winced. "I had forgotten his bedtime is between eight and eight-thirty when I asked you to come at eight. I should have said seven."

"No biggie," she said cheerfully, as she lifted the little boy from the changing table and settled him on her arm. Once they got Rex into bed, she'd tell Danny she'd changed her mind, remind him that the agency could send over another nanny and be on her way. "We have a half hour or so to get him a snack, brush his teeth and maybe read him a story."

Danny inched nearer. "He likes stories." When he got close, Rex reached for him.

Marnie handed him over. "He also likes you."

Danny planted a kiss on his cheek. "Hard to believe, since I'm not very good with him yet. But he met me a few months ago. We've had lots of visits."

She remembered him telling her that he hadn't even known he was a father. Yet, here he was not merely pitching in, but obviously determined to be a good dad. "Babies have an instinct about people. And they are patient. If he likes you, he'll cut you lots of slack."

Heading out of the nursery, Danny laughed. "He'd better because he's stuck with me."

Marnie followed him out into the hall and back to the open space. Her breath hitched a bit at the luxury of it all. Shiny and expensive, it had clearly been furnished by a decorator. She'd bet her meager savings the abstract paintings on the wall were originals.

"I'm sure he doesn't consider himself stuck with you. He obviously loves you."

"Yeah. We'll see how he feels tomorrow when there's no milk."

They walked into the kitchen area and around the corner of the huge center island, and there stood Wiggles, lapping up the milk that had spilled when the thin plastic container split.

She grabbed him. "Oh, we can't have that!"

"Really? He seems to like it."

"He's been alone out here for a good ten minutes. Lord only knows how much he drank. Plus, some dogs are lactose intolerant." She smiled at Danny. He looked like sex on a spoon wearing black sweatpants and a big T-shirt. She'd thought he was handsome in a white shirt and tie. In the sweatpants and big T-shirt, he was casual, approachable and so sexy her mouth wanted to water.

"Lactose intolerant?"

"Um. Yes." It took a second to get her bearings. It wasn't like her to react to a good-looking employer. Fathers of toddlers were almost always young and handsome. And she never cared. But her hormones must believe noticing was okay. Since she wasn't keeping the job, it didn't matter how attractive she found him. As soon as everything was cleaned and the baby tucked away, she'd tell him and never see him again.

"But the good news is, you can use this as a test. If Wiggles doesn't have any digestive problems tonight, you can take it as a sign that he can have milk every once in a while."

She surveyed the kitchen until she saw Rex's highchair. "Here's what we'll do. We'll put Rex in his chair with some crackers and a cup of juice. You go to the neighborhood store and get a new gallon of milk while I tackle this mess."

"That's generous, but I didn't hire you to houseclean—"

"No buts. Your son needs milk in the morning, and if we leave this mess too long, trust me, it will smell. This might also be a good time to take the puppy out for his nightly business. I can handle all this while you're gone."

"You're sure?"

For a rich guy, he didn't seem to treat staff with authority. Still, his uncertainty endeared him to her. Mixed with her attraction, it filled her with warmth.

She ignored it. He *was* an extremely handsome guy. His dark eyes were clear and looking into them, she felt like she could see the whole way to his soul. If she thought working for a superrich guy could cause her problems, being attracted to her employer would doubly do so. The press would lap it up the way Wiggles lapped up that milk.

She almost groaned at her thoughts. She wasn't even keeping this job. Stupid to dwell on being attracted to him. Her thoughts had to be running out of control because of proximity. And how sweet he was with his son.

Luckily, he was leaving.

"Yes! I'm fine. Go get the milk."

Danny put a leash on Wiggles, grabbed his wallet from the center island and headed for the door. "You're sure you're okay?"

"Yes!"

"I can send up the doorman."

She laughed. "To do what? Seriously. I'm fine."

* * *

In the elevator, Danny let out a long breath. He'd just left his child with a stranger—

A stranger he'd hired as a nanny, who worked for the service used and recommended by his future brother-in-law, Jace MacDonald, owner of one of the premier security companies in the world.

Rex was fine. *Danny* wasn't.

He'd always seen himself as competent. Sure, he and Rex had had a few odd moments the times he'd visited, but Danny had plowed through. Yet spilled milk had frozen him.

Because too many things needed to be done simultaneously. But Marnie Olsen had surveyed the situation, made a plan and got them all going in the right direction.

Setting Oswald on the sidewalk so he could trot along, Danny decided that proved he'd made the right choice in hiring her. No. That was an oversimplification. He hadn't simply made the right choice. Marnie rocked. Smart and strong, with an organized mind and total grasp of what she was doing, she'd easily righted the chaos.

That weird feeling rolled through him again. Part relief that he genuinely believed Marnie Olsen had been the correct choice for nanny, and part warmth.

Delicious warmth. She was personable, competent, easygoing and—

He winced. Pretty. She was so damned pretty.

Plus, thanks to her yoga pants and pink T-shirt, he also knew she had a smoking hot body.

Which was irrelevant. His world was in turmoil and he wasn't an idiot. He needed someone strong and smart who could handle his crazy life, much more than he needed or even *wanted* a romance. A woman he'd been intimate with had had his child and never told him. He'd only found out a few months ago. His ability to trust would need time to regroup. Romance was the furthest thing from his mind.

And Marnie Olsen was *the nanny he needed*. His gut had not been wrong when he hired her. He wouldn't screw that up by indulging an attraction.

He and Oswald took a side trip to the park for the pup to do his business, then they meandered the few blocks to a small deli, bought milk and headed home. He wouldn't let himself think about how pretty Marnie was anymore. All that was beside the point. He needed a competent nanny.

Arriving at his penthouse, he found her in the kitchen, sitting on a stool beside the highchair, making his son laugh. The milk had been cleaned up. Rex polished off the last of the juice in his sippy cup.

Calm settled over him. The gut instinct returned. He wanted this calm, *needed* this calm.

He'd absolutely made the right choice.

"I don't know what I would have done without your help." The puppy pranced as far as his leash would allow him, then sat, his chest out, his head regal, and stared at Marnie as if showing her he could be a good boy. "I can't thank you enough. You have no idea how happy I am you took this job."

Guilt stricken, Marnie looked over at Danny Manelli as he unfastened Wiggles's leash. The dog immediately raced to her, and she picked him up so he could lick her cheeks. Rex giggled with glee.

Oh Lord. Did he have to be so nice?

His son so adorable.

His puppy so sweet?

Plus, this place might be elegant, but Danny and his son were very normal. The *job* was normal. Add to that that she liked phase two of her plan and the idea of socking away tons of cash so that by the time Rex outgrew her services, she'd have plenty to start her own business.

"As soon as we have Rex settled, I can show you to your quarters." He pointed to the right. "Your room is back there, next to the guest bath and a laundry area and across from the family room."

She debated, but all her doubts and fears seemed tiny compared to how much this little family needed her—

How much she wanted this job—

She cleared her throat.

Don't quit. Be brave. Take the next step. Don't lose this opportunity over something that's probably buried.

She took a slow, strong breath. "Thanks. If you don't mind, I'll unpack and acclimate a bit tonight so I can handle everything in the morning."

"Tomorrow's Saturday and I don't have to go to work. We can run over the important stuff then. Tonight, we'll tackle the musts. Like, I know you're probably wondering why your quarters are so far from the nursery, but the baby monitoring system is elaborate and effective." He laughed. "You'll know when he cries."

She smiled. "Great. I'm familiar with most monitoring systems."

"Good."

There. See? Easy peasy.

Nothing was going to go wrong. Nothing was going to happen. No boogeyman would jump out of a bush and realize who she was.

She was nobody.

And Danny Manelli was just a rich guy, a simple lawyer. Sure, his dad was out there, but she hadn't seen his name in the papers in at least a month. No one would care to poke around in the life of his son's nanny. And even if they did, she hadn't found anything in her search.

She was fine.

Danny Manelli needed her. *Rex* needed her.

And she wanted phase two of her life. If anything *ever* looked like it was going sideways, she could call Shirley at the agency and go back home and be nobody again.

But if things worked out, she'd live in a beautiful home,

raise a beautiful little boy and put away enough cash to start over.

She'd never thought of leaving New York, but what if she took her money and went to another city? A place where no one knew her? A place where the chances of running into Roger Martin were so slim, she'd be free?

She suddenly realized that was her goal. Not merely starting her own agency but doing it in another city.

Chicago. Tampa. Dallas.

The possibilities were endless and along with them came freedom. Real freedom.

But to do that she'd need money. And this job provided plenty of it.

CHAPTER FOUR

ONCE REX WAS SETTLED, Danny showed Marnie her quarters, a suite with a sitting room with a big screen television, a bedroom and bathroom. The color scheme revolved around soft sage mixed with cream and gray in the bathroom and bedroom with a darker sage and gray in the sitting room. Rustic hardwood floors with gray and white area rugs pulled it all together.

She could have spun around with her arms outstretched, taking it all in, but she simply smiled and told Danny it was lovely.

Pleased, he'd nodded. "I want to run through a few more things, then you can unpack, watch TV, do whatever you like."

"Great."

He led her out to the huge open area. As they passed the center island that separated the kitchen from the rest of the space, he grabbed some papers from the marble countertop.

"These are instructions Rex's mom wrote for us. They don't merely set out his routine—Alisha also mentioned a lot of his likes and dislikes." He handed them to her, then sat on one of the paisley chairs.

Lowering herself to the sofa, she scanned them, then glanced up. "This is wonderful, very thorough."

"Rex's mom is one of those overorganized people. She thinks of everything."

"That'll be a big help."

"I know you're probably confused about the arrangement with Rex's mom, so let me just say that she and I had a very short-term relationship. She got pregnant but didn't tell me. My biological dad, who I recently discovered had been monitoring my life, uncovered Rex. In order to tell me about my son, he had to out himself as my father. Anyway, I contacted Alisha, and she and I had been working on visitation when she got a fabulous job opportunity in Spain."

"Spain. Wow."

"I know. She couldn't pass it up. But she also didn't want to take Rex away from everyone. Her parents and two sisters live in Manhattan. I live here. In Spain, Rex would only have her. After some soul-searching, she decided to let me raise Rex. The job in Spain is her dream job, but it comes with tons of responsibility and she'll be working a lot. In the end, she realized it would be better for Rex to be around people who love him. She'll get him for a week or two every summer and one holiday a year. And, of course, she'll come to New York a few times a year to see him."

"That's wonderful for you."

"Yes. It was hard coming to terms with the fact that Alishia hadn't intended to tell me about Rex. But once Mark's private investigators found out about the baby, she was generous. She didn't hedge. She let me see him. A lot. When this job offer came up, she didn't take only herself into consideration, she thought of what was best for Rex. Now here I am, a real father."

He smiled and attraction hit her again. His sweats and oversize T-shirt made him look sexy, especially with his short black hair slightly untidy, his smile quick and genuine. Connection wove through her. The kind of feeling she'd always believed a person would have when they clicked with someone romantically. When they imagined a future with them—

She redirected it. The connection was a result of him being a nice guy, someone who wanted to be a good father. Every nanny in the world could appreciate that. That's why they clicked. As for the future? She wanted to be Rex's nanny for a long time. *That's* what she'd focus on.

"I'm glad everything worked out."

"I am too." He rose from his chair. "Okay. That's it. With Rex in bed, the rest of the evening is yours."

She nodded. "Thanks." She walked to her room, through the sitting room and to the bedroom where her duffel bag lay on the soft sage-colored spread. She took a long breath, as the joy of getting this job hit her fully. She had a gorgeous little boy to care for, a luxurious suite all to herself and would earn enough money that her goal was on track.

And maybe, after all these years, so was her life? For the first time in a decade she hadn't let her fear rule her decision. The sense of taking back her life rolled through her, along with a weird something—

Oh good grief, she felt normal.

Normal.

Who'd have thought experiencing what every other person in the world felt every day would be so empowering, so welcome, so joyous?

Saturday morning, as Marnie finished helping Rex with breakfast, Danny grabbed Wiggles's leash.

Drying her hands in a paper towel, she said, "Are you taking him for his walk?"

Danny laughed. "I'm surprised he waited this long."

Now that she'd acclimated, she'd decided to treat this like any other job. Do all the things she did with the upwardly mobile executives she'd worked for over the years.

"What do you say Rex and I go with you?"

His dark eyes lit. "Go with me?"

"I'd like to get an idea of where Wiggles goes on his walk, and the lay of the land in the neighborhood."

"That makes sense."

He might be clueless about some childcare issues, but he was open-minded. Another thing that would make working for him easy. "Do you have a stroller?"

"A big fancy one and a little thing my mom called an umbrella stroller."

"Let's take the big fancy one."

They loaded Rex in the stroller, leashed Wiggles and rode the elevator to the lobby. Danny pushed the stroller through the revolving door. Marnie followed him out into the almost empty street, typical of early Saturday morning on Park Avenue. The scents of warm pastries and coffee hit her immediately. Her stomach growled.

"We'll pick up something from the bakery down the block when we get back."

She grimaced. "Sorry about that. My stomach usually doesn't growl, but I inadvertently skipped dinner last night."

"You should have said something! There's a whole fridge full of food."

"I seriously forgot." She'd been too busy being confused, then bold, then overwhelmed with how wonderful it was to take what felt like the next step in her life. "But I'm going to hold you to a visit to that bakery."

They strolled down the quiet street. Trees lined the sidewalk in front of buildings that rose to the blue sky. "This is beautiful."

Danny glanced around. "I like it. I didn't think I would, but once I moved in it felt like home."

"I can see why." The area had the mood of a city, but there was a sophisticated hominess about it. The few people milling about wore jeans and T-shirts or yoga pants and tank tops. Sun sneaking through the thick leaves of the trees almost made it look enchanted.

Wiggles found a comfortable tree and did his business. Marnie gave Danny the leash and she took the stroller.

After handling things, Danny said, "And this is about as far as we get every morning."

"We should walk another block or two. Give Rex some outside time."

"You can take him to the park this afternoon after his nap."

She looked around, comfortable with her surroundings and positive she could find her way. "Good idea."

As the words popped out of her mouth, she saw a tall, slim man approaching. Even from a distance she knew who he was. Her stomach knotted. He read a newspaper as he walked, his gait unmistakable.

She stopped. Danny stopped. "What?"

Her dad.

All this time she'd been so worried about Roger that she'd only given a passing thought to her dad because he lived on the Upper East Side. *Not here.*

He walked right by her. She could think he was preoccupied with his newspaper but the truth was, even if he'd looked her in the face, he wouldn't have recognized her. She'd been twelve the last time he'd seen her. He didn't know her as an adult.

Sadness billowed from her stomach to her chest.

"Marnie?"

She shook her head to clear it. This was a plum assignment and she was very lucky to have it. Like it or not, her dad was a wealthy guy. She shouldn't be surprised he'd moved to Park Avenue, probably to a new, fancier building. She'd gotten over his loss years ago. Seeing him had just thrown her, that's all.

Her old fears returned. If she could so easily run into her father, was she tempting fate with Roger Martin? His family was in the same tax bracket as her dad, as Danny Manelli.

Her past came tumbling back. Her father leaving her mother. Being broke after being accustomed to being wealthy. Getting kicked out of their apartment. The lack of stability.

And the man responsible was walking down the same street she'd be using every day.

Had it been a mistake to take this job?

No!

There was no way to get beyond her stupid past but to

move forward, to be courageous, to enter this world and put all that behind her. Particularly given that this job provided the stability and security she hadn't had since she was twelve.

She took a breath, knowing acknowledgment was the first step to shattering the hold her past had over her. "It's okay. I just saw someone I knew."

He peered up the street and then down again. "Someone you knew?"

Face it. Look the past in the eye and steal its power.

"Actually, it was my dad."

He frowned. "Your *dad*?" He glanced around again. "I didn't hear anyone say hello. You didn't stop—"

She batted a hand. The best way to regain control was to minimize what had happened. Think of it as unimportant. A blip. "It's nothing." She turned the stroller toward Danny's building. "He... Well, I'm sure he didn't recognize me. He hasn't seen me since I was twelve. He took my brother and left me and my mom."

Danny stared at her, so confused he sputtered, "He left your mom, and you haven't seen him since?"

"Yes," Marnie said, as if she were giving a report in a boardroom. Calm. In control. "I found his condo and tried to visit when I was fourteen. I wanted to let him know my mom was fine and that we should...you know...visit or something, but he wouldn't see me. Wouldn't let me see my brother either. He had a maid tell me to leave." She gazed around, as if seeing the whole street with a different perspective. "He must have moved again...to Park Avenue. I know he wouldn't walk more than a block for the paper."

Sympathy washed through Danny. "I'm sorry."

She shrugged. "Don't be. Lots of time has gone by. I'm accustomed to it now." She smiled brightly. Too brightly. "It's no biggie."

"It would have been a biggie to me."

"It was. In the beginning." She bit her lip, then her demeanor brightened again. "But, you know, life goes on."

"Still, a father who didn't want to see you? That's awful." He sniffed. "Look at what I'm saying. I literally found out a few months ago that I had a biological father. I went through a phase where I was almost incapacitated by the realization that, no matter how much he was edging into my life now, he hadn't wanted me when I was born. Or he wouldn't have had my biological mother give me up for adoption." He sniffed again. "He kept saying he'd wanted me. That he'd hidden my two sisters and me for our safety. But…" He shrugged. "Actions speak louder than words."

"My dad's a selfish, self-centered perfectionist."

"That's my dad too." He shook his head. "I don't want to be like him."

She smiled. "Good plan."

She rolled the stroller up to the penthouse's building, but Danny stopped her.

She gave him a confused look.

"We're going to the bakery for bagels, remember?"

"That's right." She shook her head, embarrassed that she'd forgotten, then she winced. "I was kind of hoping for a Danish."

He laughed. "Whatever you want."

They ambled into the nearby bakery, and she examined the pastries as if she were choosing a diamond. He almost told her to pick two, but something stopped him. If her dad lived on Park Avenue, he had to be wealthy. Yet, here she was, a nanny, because her father had left her and her mother.

Their lives were flipped.

She'd started off the child of a wealthy man and had become lower middle class. He'd started off the child of a lower middle-class blue-collar couple and was suddenly wealthy.

And he was complaining?

Guilt surged through him, but an unexpected suspicion

tiptoed in on its heels. Was it odd that she'd admitted something so personal to someone she barely knew? As a lawyer, he was accustomed to people telling him their troubles. But he wasn't her lawyer. He was her boss.

Jace, as administrator of the Hinton security team, and his two half sisters who were living his nightmare had warned him that now that he was heir to one of the world's biggest fortunes, people would scam him. Work to get close to him, tell him sad stories and hope he opened the purse strings.

The thought was so shocking he shook his head to clear it. Marnie was a good person. He could feel it in his bones. And her life had been hard. She wouldn't lie about that.

Watching her so carefully choose a simple Danish confirmed that. Having had to scrape for money, he knew pride when he saw it. The fierce need to never overstep boundaries. Never exploit a kindness for fear of looking greedy.

He wouldn't buy her two Danish. She wouldn't eat the second one. He would buy the one she selected. And not make her feel uncomfortable.

They returned to the penthouse. Wiggles raced inside, and Danny had to wrestle the exuberant pup to remove his leash. "I think it's time to talk about obedience school."

"I have a whole list saved on my laptop. I can print it out for you or send it to your phone."

"Send it to my phone."

"Okay." Marnie sat Rex in the highchair and gave him a sippy cup of milk before she headed for the one-cup coffeemaker. "Do you want coffee with your bagel?"

"Yes. But I'll get it. You're not a maid, remember?"

She smiled sheepishly. "No. But there's no reason we can't be friends. We are living together. We'll be in each other's hair a lot. Might as well work together."

His suspicions about her crept up on him again. But he squelched them. They were living together. Being kind just made sense. Particularly since she was the first person in months with whom he felt comfortable talking. Maybe because her life was as messed up as his?

"I don't mind making coffee for my friend."

He forced the suspicion away. "Okay. A cup of regular, please."

Wiggles barked. Danny walked to the counter. "I give him a treat when we get back from our walk."

He pulled a biscuit from a cookie jar in the corner. The dog grabbed it and raced away.

Marnie's eyes widened. "Good thing I didn't look in there. I might have thought they were cookies and eaten one."

Danny laughed, back to feeling good about hiring her. Not just because she was a great nanny, but because she deserved a break. After a few minutes of making coffee and finding cream, they sat at the counter, her with her Danish. Him with a bagel slathered in thick cream cheese.

She took a bite, squeezed her eyes shut and groaned. "Oh man! This is *sooo* good."

"Best bakery in the area," he replied, but he watched her. The clicks of rightness he kept getting with her had probably been his subconscious picking up on the similarities in their lives.

"We seem to have a lot in common."

She peeked over at him. "Oh yeah? Like what?"

He ignored the lightning bolt of attraction that shot through him when their gazes connected. Not only was it a cliché to have a thing for the nanny, but it seemed like she needed a friend as much as he did.

"We both understand being lower middle class."

She glanced around his penthouse. "Looks like you've moved up in the world."

"But I won't forget my roots. I don't want to."

"I get that. I didn't really want to forget my dad, either, but he made his choices."

"And my biological dad made his."

She pulled a small bite off her Danish. "You're the first person I've told about my dad."

He could have drowned in her soft green eyes and almost did drown in the sense of rightness that filled him. Not just that he could tell her almost anything, but more.

More?

Now that the attraction had coupled with a real connection, what he felt for her grew and edged in the direction of something with relationship potential. But he didn't want to be a cliché. And he sure as hell didn't intend to drag her into something she didn't want.

And *he* didn't want.

Did he?

No. A woman with whom he'd had a one-night stand had had his child and not told him. His parents had hidden the fact that he was adopted. His biological dad kept saying he loved all his kids, but he'd lived decades without making contact with any of them.

The problem wasn't that Marnie was his employee. It was trust. Right now, Danny's trust issues had trust issues. That's why he kept getting weird suspicions about her. He couldn't look at a situation normally. He couldn't look at a person without wondering what they were hiding.

She was a good person with a hard life just trying to make a living, and his thoughts had jumped to a very bad place over her telling him a simple truth about her life.

So, no. Even considering a relationship right now was out of the question. No matter how beautiful she was or how soft she looked or how happy he was when she was around—

He jumped off his stool. What the hell was he thinking! He had to stop letting his thoughts go crazy when she was around. "It's time for me and Rex to video call my mom and dad."

"The ones from upstate?"

Her question was normal. Easily spoken. Like a conversation between employer and nanny. She hadn't noticed him mooning over her. This had to be the end of thinking things like wanting more. He didn't want more. He had enough on his plate with a child to raise, a new dad and co-workers who didn't know how to deal with him now that he was superrich.

He strolled over to Rex in the highchair. "Yes. Video calling is a good way to stay in touch."

The smile she gave him sent goose bumps shivering down his arms. Which was nuts. He barely knew her. Plus, he had a million reasons his reactions were wrong. That's why he was taking Rex and leaving her to herself. The woman had had enough trouble in her life. She didn't need her boss developing a crush on her.

He took Rex out of the highchair and headed for his room, confusion making him shake his head. The problem was what he felt for her wasn't a crush. It was a connection. If it was a crush or a simple sexual attraction, he could squelch either one of those. The connection filled him with longing for something important, something real.

But he wasn't in a place for any of this. After everything that had happened to him, he might never trust again. If Marnie was as good a person as he thought, she deserved better.

CHAPTER FIVE

HE KEPT HIMSELF and Rex busy for the rest of the morning, letting Marnie continue to settle in. She helped with Rex's lunch, then they took the little boy to the nursery for his nap. Danny stepped back so Marnie could change him. It wasn't that he didn't want to do diaper duty. He was still monitoring Rex's reactions to her. She might seem perfect, but they were in a probationary period. He couldn't forget that. He had to get his head in the game.

The little boy giggled as she chatted with him while removing one diaper and putting on another. Danny's heart lifted. Diaper change complete, she picked up Rex and cuddled him. Danny's son returned her cuddle, snuggling against her neck and shoulder. She and his son were a good match. And *that's* what mattered.

Not some nebulous feeling that kept nudging him to want things with her that weren't appropriate.

His phone rang. Glad for the distraction, he pulled it from his pocket and groaned when he saw the name on the screen. "I have to take this."

"That's fine. I'll put him down for his nap."

Danny said, "Great. Thanks."

Closing the door behind him, he stepped into the hall feeling better. He had no idea why he felt a connection with her except that both of their lives had been weird. He'd never had a nanny before, so sure—maybe he'd let himself go overboard with the chitchat. But he could end that. She was too good with his son for him to ruin it because his thoughts veered off in the wrong direction.

And just in case those crazy suspicions that tiptoed into his brain were valid, not giving in to his attraction would protect him.

He finished his call. When he found her in the kitchen, sitting at the center island, reading Alisha's notes, he said, "I've never employed a nanny before, so I'm not sure how this works. Do we eat lunch together?"

She glanced up and smiled. "Sometimes, I guess. If we have things to discuss." As he walked into the kitchen area, she said, "In my other assignments, most days I'd grab a sandwich and take it to my room to study. But I got my degree in May."

"Shirley mentioned that you'd just graduated."

"It took a boatload of years, because I couldn't afford to take a full course load most semesters. Anyway, that's over. Now I move on to phase two of my career path."

"Phase two?" He looked at her. "I did say I hoped this situation would turn permanent, right?"

She batted a hand. "I won't be leaving you. My plan is to start my own nanny service, but that's at least a decade down the road. Maybe two." She bit her lower lip. "Honestly, the money you're paying will go a long way to help me reach my dream."

After tossing a loaf of bread to the counter, he opened the refrigerator door saying, "Ham or turkey?"

"I should say turkey, but I'm in the mood for ham. Mustard too, if you've got it."

"I have everything." He brought the deli meats to the island, feeling better. They were alone and holding a normal conversation. No weird attraction. No noticing odd things about her. No suspicions.

"Tell me about the business you want to start."

"It's going to be a lot like Shirley's, but I plan to cater to people who want their kids to get a certain experience. I'm starting to map out ways to get music and art into kids' daily routines."

"That's right. You did mention something about that."

"As Rex gets older, he'll be exposed to a lot of it."

"That's great!" He handed her the plate holding the sandwich he'd made for her. "You think you need to work for me a decade or so to save sufficient cash to get started?"

She nodded.

"Why don't you borrow some money, or better yet, look for investors?"

She rolled her eyes. "Seriously? You know someone who wants to invest in a nanny service?"

"You'd be surprised what people will invest in."

"No one I know."

He slid the plate containing his sandwich to the other side of the island, walked around it and sat on the stool beside her. "Who do you know?"

"That's just it. No one."

"Hey, you now work for a fairly well-connected guy. I won't exactly put out feelers but if someone mentions looking for an investment, I can give your name."

Her face flushed. "That's kind of you, but I think I need the years I'll be spending with your son to hone my idea."

He could see he'd embarrassed her and remembered how she'd been dumbstruck when she'd seen her dad and even how she'd eagerly chosen her Danish. He backed off. He might have confessed his entire messed up life to her, but he only knew bits and pieces of hers.

For a second that struck him as odd. Lopsided. For as much as it had confused him when she'd told him about her dad, she knew a lot more about him than he knew about her. He fought not to shake his head over his craziness. He got suspicious when she told him about herself, and now he was worried that she knew more about him than he knew about her?

He shrugged off those concerns. He had to stop imagining things that weren't there. "Okay."

"Thanks."

"But just for the heck of it, start looking at the people around you. You could even make note of who comes and goes in *my* life. You never know when a good investor will pop up."

"I will." She picked up the plate holding her sandwich. "I think I'll go to my room. Maybe call my mom."

She didn't look angry or embarrassed, so he forced himself to interpret her retreat as simply a desire to touch base with her mom.

He said, "Sure," but as she walked down the hall, he called, "Research business plans. That'd be a great way to see what you need to have to entice investors."

She called back, "I'm not ready for that yet."

But there was a laugh in her voice. He really didn't want her to quit the job he'd only given her the day before, but finding investors sometimes took years. Plus, having something impersonal to talk about worked to keep things simple between them, like two friends conversing. If nothing else, thinking of her as a friend was a good idea.

A normal way to treat her.

Neutral.

He didn't want his Hinton Heir suspicions to cause him to lose a very good nanny, a woman who deserved a good job, a woman who was clearly working hard to make a better life for herself.

After Rex finished his nap, they gave him a snack and played with him for a few hours before feeding him dinner, playing again and then getting him ready for bed. Once he was in his crib with the monitor on and the sound machine spreading the soft patter of rain through the room, Danny watched TV in the great room and Marnie retreated to her suite.

Sunday went by in pretty much the same way. Monday, he left her alone with Rex while he went to work. Twice, he video called to check on them. Both times he felt like an idiot. Rex giggled and clung to her. He even kissed her cheek once.

The first week went by in a gloriously simple fashion. No drama. No more spilled milk. Suspicions gone, he made easy conversation with Marnie over dinner that he had delivered. There was no trauma at bedtime. There were no visits from Mark, who was busy planning his wedding with his fiancée, Penny, Charlotte's mother. And, finally comfortable, Rex slept through the night.

Marnie took the following Sunday off to visit her mother, sleeping at her mom's apartment and was back—cheerful and happy—on Monday morning at a quarter to eight.

His work life improved. As if the excitement of discovering their coworker was a billionaire had lost its luster, lawyers, investigators, secretaries, assistants and paralegals all returned to treating him like just another lawyer.

The next Saturday, Danny woke feeling fantastic. Through the monitor by his bed, he heard the happy sounds of Marnie dressing Rex for the day and Rex's giggles. Peace and joy filled him, and he bounced out of bed, heading for the shower.

His world was back in order, and he got to spend the entire day with his two favorite people in the world, his son and his son's nanny.

He didn't let himself dwell on the comment that had raced through his brain as he slid into jeans and a T-shirt and ambled into the kitchen, where Marnie fed Rex. He'd settled his attraction by acknowledging she was gorgeous and easy to talk to and shifting his attention to being her friend. She needed help. He was in a position where he could help. That was their connection.

Walking into the kitchen area, he said, "Hey! How is everybody today?"

He bent and kissed Rex's forehead, and the little boy said, "Dad!"

Nothing rivaled the fierce love that surged at the sound of his son calling him Dad. And nothing could ruin this day. Danny wouldn't let it.

The doorman arrived, mail in hand. Danny offered him a cup of coffee, but he refused it, saying good morning to Marnie and retreating to the elevator.

"He seems like a very nice guy."

"He is," Danny said, making himself a cup of coffee. "He's like you. He has a business that he's organizing. It's kind of a cross between doormen and security guards." He rifled through the mail. "I put him in touch with my half-sister Charlotte's fiancé. They're working on something together now."

She laughed. "Is that what rich people do? Look for business opportunities in every person they meet?"

"So far, I haven't been the one to invest." He paused, pondering that, realizing that he'd never offered her money. He'd squelched his suspicions about her worming her way into his life to get part of the Hinton fortune, so that could only mean he'd taken her caution that she wasn't ready to heart. A very *normal* thing to do. His instincts about her seemed to finally be back on track.

"It's more like I remember myself when I was scrambling to find my place. I identify with people trying to make a move, so I notice things, connect things, put people together."

"That's very nice of you."

He flipped through the mail. "Not really." He wasn't nice. This was him as he normally was. No more freaky suspicions or overwhelming attractions. Just him, living his life.

He got to a fancy envelope, something made of high-quality paper, clearly an invitation. His old address had been scratched out and his new address written over it.

He opened the envelope and discovered an invitation to a gallery event, featuring the work of Sally McMillen. "This is tonight."

She glanced over. "So?"

"It needs an RSVP and I missed the date. I guess I could still go if I called the coordinator and explained my invitation had been sent to the wrong address, so my RSVP is late."

"You guess you could go? It sounds like so much fun!" She laughed. "It's not like you have to worry about a baby-sitter."

He peered over at her. "Or maybe I do. This is exactly the kind of thing you should go to, to meet potential inves-tors. It's sponsored by the McCallan family."

She sucked in a breath. "I've heard of them."

"Everybody's heard of them. And anybody who is any-body will be there."

She put her hand on her chest. "And you think *I* should go?"

"Sure? Not to ask for investment money, but just to min-gle. Let me introduce you around."

Her face scrunched. "As your nanny?"

"You are starting a nanny business."

"In ten years…"

"Whenever. If you go to one or two of these kinds of things a year, eventually the big players will start remem-bering your name. Then when you need money, their pock-etbooks will already be loosened."

She snorted. "You're nuts."

"I'm serious. We don't have to stay forever. Just a couple minutes. An hour tops." He frowned. "Is it so horrible to be seen in public with me?"

She said, "No," but she said it too quickly and there was a squeak in her voice. Warmth fluttered through her and she had to hold back a groan. It was not horrible to be seen in public with him. The idea was too appealing.

"Come on. You need a break and it won't hurt to schmooze the players. Plus, my sister Charlotte loves to babysit. She called yesterday to say I should fire you be-cause she hasn't gotten to babysit Rex since I hired you."

She laughed. His half-sisters had visited during Marnie's first week of employment, and while Leni was sweet and kind, Charlotte was a hoot. Plus, she'd comfortably settled into being Rex's nanny, and her life had become wonderful. She didn't want to ruin that by saying or doing something wrong. Especially at a fancy gallery opening.

"Please… This way I don't have to go alone."

She heard a note of something in his voice that reminded her of her first days of working for him. He'd been lost and befuddled but determined to be a good dad. Every day he got a little smarter in his ability to care for Rex. Every day he seemed happier. It might not be her job to keep her boss happy, but the human being in her related to feeling a beat out of step with the rest of the world and wishing for a friend.

"Okay." Her decision had nothing to do with thinking he was adorable. He was a fabulous employer and a good person, and considering how much he tried to help her, she kind of owed him. She didn't have anything to wear, but she had some money saved.

"I'll need a few hours this afternoon to get a dress."

He slid his cell phone from his pocket. "I'll call Charlotte."

She bought a simple black dress, something she could wear again and again, something that would help her blend in. A subway ride took her to her mom's apartment, where she borrowed a string of pearls with teardrop earrings—a set her dad had bought as an anniversary gift. One of the few things her mom hadn't sold for rent money before she finally got child support from Marnie's dad.

The reminder of her dad abandoning her mom filled her with trepidation, but she ignored it. Danny, adopted by middle class parents, was nothing like her father. Plus, this wasn't a date. It was an employer helping his employee.

And the people she would meet? She would see them as investors. She wouldn't fear them. She refused to fear them.

But what if she saw Roger Martin?

Her heart stuttered. Despite running into her dad, two

weeks of happily living on Park Avenue, taking Rex and Wiggles for walks, and going to the bakery had shown her that Manhattan might be a small world, but she hadn't seen Roger in it. She'd become settled. Almost confident. She didn't want to lose that over the fear of seeing someone who could have moved out of the city. Hell, he could have moved to Europe. She couldn't be afraid of what *might* happen.

Charlotte arrived around seven to give Rex a chance to get accustomed to her, and Marnie went to her room to dress. Ready by eight and knowing they needed to leave soon to get to the gallery, she walked into the open area, snapping closed the clasp of her black clutch bag after stashing her ID and cell phone.

She glanced up to see Charlotte's lips curve into an odd smile and Danny's mouth fall open.

"Wow."

"You can say that again," Charlotte sing-songed. "You look amazing."

She twirled around once. "It's remarkable what a bubble bath and a new hairdo can do."

Danny quietly said, "You didn't cut your hair while you were back there, did you?"

She blinked. Dramatic and sexy in his dark tux, Danny stared at her. She wanted to stare right back. Some men were born to wear a tux, and he was one of them. Women would probably drool over him.

"No. It's an updo." She ventured a little farther into the living space. "I just swirled it around and pinned it up."

Charlotte said, "Well, you look very sophisticated."

Her eyes stole over to Danny again. She knew it would appear that she was hoping for his approval. But she wasn't. He had such presence and sex appeal with his black hair, dark eyes and tux that she couldn't stop staring at him. "That's the look I was going for."

Danny glanced at his watch. "We better get a move on or we'll arrive so late they'll think I decided not to come."

Something warm and fuzzy trembled through her. Forget what the press said. *She* was going out with the sexiest man alive.

Going out?

Not hardly. He was taking her to help her. She had to remember that.

Holding Rex, Charlotte walked with them to the elevator. "Have fun, you two." She picked up Rex's hand to wave it for him. "Say bye to Daddy and Marnie."

Marnie kissed his cheek. "Bye, sweetie."

Danny kissed his cheek. "Bye, big guy."

Charlotte's eyebrows rose. Marnie frowned. The weird feeling rippled through her again. They sounded like parents saying goodbye to their son. She took a breath, reminding herself to keep her wits about her.

The elevator door closed, and they headed down.

Staring straight ahead, Danny said, "You do look amazing."

Unwanted pleasure poured through her, and she had to work not to groan. What was wrong with her? It would be so wrong for her to get a crush on her boss.

Oh, who was she kidding? She already did have a crush on him. She was simply wise enough not to act on it. Not only did she have an odd past—a secret—but Danny was rich, smart and funny. He could have his pick of women, and someone like her would not be at the top of his list. She wouldn't humiliate herself by taking anything he said as romantic.

"Thanks. I'm not one of those women who typically worries about appearances, but I didn't want to stand out."

"Oh, you'll still stand out."

The pleasure turned to a hiccup in her chest. It was impossible to miss the approval in his voice.

She chose to believe it was his way of saying she wouldn't embarrass him in front of his friends and glanced down at her dress. "In a black dress and pearls? Half the women there will be in a black dress."

The elevator door opened. "You'll still stand out." He peeked down at her. "You're stunning."

Happiness rose again, breath stealing and fierce. Their gazes locked. His dark eyes glowed. The attraction she'd been fighting wasn't one-sided.

She swallowed hard. Even as her happiness turned to radiant joy, her stomach plummeted. She couldn't have him. If she ever fell in love, it would be with a normal guy, someone whose life wouldn't be affected by her kind of secret. But there was a more immediate issue. How the hell would she be able to work for this guy for *years* if they were attracted to each other?

She had to defuse this.

CHAPTER SIX

DANNY DIRECTED HER out of the elevator into the lobby, wrestling a case of desire so strong he reached up and loosened his collar.

He shouldn't have told her she was stunning. No. The stunning part was fine. It was the eye contact that had nearly done him in.

With her auburn hair pulled off her face, her eyes were a sharp, alluring green that almost made him stutter... If he'd been able to speak. But he'd held the contact so long, he could tell he'd unsettled her.

She frowned. "Was I that bad before? I know ponytails and yoga pants are comfortable, but I guess I looked like a slob."

He laughed and strode out of the building into the beautiful summer night, not only maintaining a discreet distance between them but mimicking her light tone. "No. You didn't look bad. You just look different tonight. You're going to be a big hit."

"I thought we were keeping this low-key?"

"That was the plan until you—" he motioned toward her dress "—got all fancied up."

She sniffed. "I'm telling you, there are going to be thirty women dressed exactly like this."

There weren't thirty. But there were enough women in black dresses that Danny had to admit defeat. Which made her laugh. Proving they'd succeeded in overcoming the awkward stare after he'd told her she looked stunning.

The gallery had been decorated with white lights and beach decor—wood that looked like it had washed up on a shore, pictures of the sun rising over the Atlantic, beach balls and seashells scattered around—but still it somehow looked posh and dripping with money.

She glanced around. "This is so beautiful."

He could relate. Six months ago, if someone had brought him here, he'd have reacted the same way. But right now, he couldn't seem to take his eyes off her. He told himself that was because she was clearly enjoying herself. So it was okay to notice the sparkle in her eyes.

"The woman who owns this gallery is known for her displays."

"Wow. It's amazing how the paintings match the displays."

She laughed again, but the farther they walked into the gallery, the more her chest tightened. Her father had always been drawn to the glamorous life. He could be here.

But a quick sweep of the area didn't find him.

Or Roger. Or Roger's dad or mom.

Her shoulders loosened. Danny grabbed two flutes of champagne from the bar. "To your introduction to the world of investors."

She drew in a long breath. With the fear of running into someone from her past eliminated, she relaxed and took the glass he handed her and clinked it with his.

Everything was so elegant. Men in tuxes. Women in cocktail dresses. And for once she fit.

Of course, it didn't hurt that she was on the arm of the final Hinton heir.

No. Danny Manelli being a Hinton heir was irrelevant. He was without a doubt the best-looking guy in the room.

Out with her.

She felt all shivery and blamed it on the champagne, but she knew it was the night—with him.

He put his hand on the small of her back, directed her to another room of paintings, and she closed her eyes and savored. Wishes flurried through her brain like snowflakes on Christmas Eve. She wished she belonged here. That her dad hadn't deserted her but had brought her up in this world. She wished Danny would look at her again the way he had on the way to the limo. She wished she was free enough to turn and slide her arm beneath his, to walk nonchalantly from painting to painting, enjoying them. Enjoying *him*.

The last wish suddenly didn't seem so far out of line. No one from her past was in the gallery. She'd seen her dad once, on the street, on his typical Saturday morning jaunt to get a paper. She might not be free, but maybe she wasn't as ensnared as she believed.

Danny turned suddenly and they were face-to-face, so close that every cell in her body blossomed. Oh Lord. What would it be like to be allowed to flirt with him, to lure him to kiss her—

He pointed beyond her. "If we really want to make this a good trip for you, I need to introduce you to some people."

He stepped around her, easily heading toward a group closer to the door.

"Come on."

And just like that her moment was broken. She drew a long breath. That was probably a good thing.

Wasn't it?

She worked for him. She had a complicated past. Plus, she had her eye on a good future.

But, oh, what would it be like to be Cinderella, to catch the Prince's eye and have one glorious evening—

Smoke and mirrors. That's what. She needed this job. Needed to start her own company to make enough money to change her life. She did not need a romance.

Danny introduced her to the McCallan clan, Jake and his wife, Avery, Seth and his wife, Harper, and Sabrina and her husband, Trent.

"Marnie is nanny for my son, Rex," Danny said casually. "She's thinking of starting her own nanny service in a few years."

Marnie picked up the cue. "It will be a little bit more of a boutique service. Maybe a service that doesn't actually nanny as much as provide a few afternoons a week of specialty services like art and music appreciation."

Beautiful blonde Sabrina McCallan Sigmund sighed. "So, our nanny could get an afternoon or two a week off?"

"Yes."

Sabrina's dark-haired, dark-eyed husband, Trent, said, "Interesting."

But Jake's gorgeous red-haired wife, Avery, laughed. "Our nanny would kiss your feet for coming up with something that would give her time off."

Marnie chuckled, and the conversation turned to the paintings around them and eventually all the McCallans drifted away.

Walking through the exhibit, admiring the paintings and displays, Danny introduced Marnie to a few other donors, older couples who didn't have kids and weren't quite as attuned to her idea as the McCallans. Still, Marnie's face shone. Her smile couldn't have been any wider. Starting a business clearly meant a lot to her.

The feeling returned. The click of rightness between them that reminded him of how well their lives meshed. She was smart and beautiful, everything he wanted in a woman. The perfection of it started a tingling in his chest. Every time he realized how well they fit, he took the leap from friends to more. And with it came the desire to hold her hand, to lean in close and laugh with her, to steal a kiss—

He fought to ignore it. "I told you there was no reason to be afraid."

She raised her eyes until their gazes connected. His chest tightened even more. Desire swam through his blood.

"These were just introductions. Everybody was being kind."

He wished he could kiss her. Wished he could tell her she was the most beautiful woman in the room.

He swallowed. "Speaking from experience, I can tell you that anyone with a child and a career isn't being kind about appreciating childcare."

"I suppose."

They'd looked at every picture. Had their fair share of champagne. Chitchatted with everyone he knew. And there was nothing else to see, no one else to meet...

But he didn't want the night to end. She looked glamorous and happy. It didn't seem right to whisk her home. He wanted to take her to dinner. To walk down Park Avenue on this warm night with the bright moon. To hold her hand and enjoy the city.

Wrong thoughts. Wrong wishes.

He shoved his hands in his pockets. "I guess it's time to go."

She set her champagne glass on the tray of a passing waiter. "Yeah. I'm feeling a little bit like Cinderella, and my coach is about to turn into a pumpkin."

The words to ask her to dinner sprang to his tongue. He bit them back and led her to the door. "Did you just call my limo a pumpkin?"

She laughed, but she glanced behind her longingly.

The urge to continue the night rippled through him.

Just twenty more minutes.

But he couldn't do that. He'd said they'd stay an hour. They'd stayed two. He hadn't mentioned dinner in his original invitation. He couldn't add it now—not when everything in him was warm from champagne and buzzed from the first fun outing he'd had since he'd discovered he'd been adopted. The emotions flowing through him were razor-sharp, as sexual as they were romantic, and probably wrong. The woman was his nanny. Not a date. His *nanny*. Someone he was helping.

The driver opened the limo door and they slid inside.

The ride to his building didn't take long, and they exited quietly, walked through the lobby without a word and rode the elevator in silence.

Charlotte and Jace were waiting for them. Marnie hadn't met Charlotte's fiancé. Danny introduced Jace, who had thick dark hair and a build like a tank, then he offered him and Charlotte a drink, but both refused.

Charlotte snickered. "Jace has a big meeting in the morning with a rock star. They're the only ones able to get him out of bed on a Sunday. Even though he grouses about guarding them."

"They pay top dollar," Jace grumbled, but his ears turned red as he pressed the button for the elevator. It opened and then they were gone.

Danny and Marnie stood staring at the doors, alone in the suddenly silent space.

She pivoted to face him and said, "Good night. I had a great time. Thank you."

And everything inside Danny froze, except his brain, which spun out of control.

She *sounded like* a date, thanking him.

He *felt like* a guy who'd just had a great night with a woman he more than liked.

He *did* more than like her. Everything about her appealed to him. She loved his son, fit in his world and was so pretty his heart sat up and begged for him to kiss her.

Her eyes flickered and he suspected it was with the same recognition he felt. Forget the fact that she was his nanny. Something more was happening between them.

The need to kiss her expanded into a fireball in his chest. He could imagine the feel of her soft lips, the smoothness of her cheek—

Seconds ticked off like hours. A debate raged in his brain—

Then the puppy raced up the hall, his nails clicking on the

hardwood. Fat and eager for love, he slammed into Danny's ankles, bounced off and rolled ten feet back.

Marnie burst out laughing. "Oh, Wiggles," she said, walking over to pick him up. He licked her face a million times. "You have to get control of those paws."

She handed him to Danny. "I think he wants to go out."

Danny held her gaze, not quite able to shift gears from imagining the feel of her skin, the taste of her lips, to taking his dog out for a walk.

She smiled softly. "You might want to get a move on before he does something neither one of us will like."

That brought him back to reality. He had a child, a dog, more money than he needed and a weird father. Getting romantic with his nanny would only be trouble.

But, oh, he wanted to.

CHAPTER SEVEN

MARNIE WOKE THE next morning at five, the alarm on her phone sending soothing music to her until her eyes opened and she shut it off.

She always got up early, showered and dressed for the day before Rex woke at six. This morning, after that heart-stopping moment with Danny by the elevator, she'd stayed in bed a few seconds, the memory of it tiptoeing through her brain, not so much as pictures but as feelings, a shower of tingles as time spun out between them. Breathless anticipation. Fierce need, the likes of which she'd never felt.

Her common sense had told her to look away...walk away. But the fanciful part of herself that she'd believed to be long dead pleaded with her to stay. To wait. To see if he would kiss her.

She thought of her secret and shook her head. What difference did her secret make? If he'd kissed her, it would have been once and only because the night had been so romantic. It wasn't like they'd start something.

And even if they did? No one had been overly interested in him the night before. The press in attendance had flocked around the McCallans, sponsors of the event. The artist, Sally McMillen, never came to her showings. So the sponsors got the spotlight.

She and Danny Manelli had just been two attendees.

She hadn't seen her dad. Or Roger. Or his parents.

Another piece of her fear drifted away. And maybe it was time? Her bad past was a decade behind her. Something inside her yearned for a normal life. A life where she could be herself. Be loved—

Finally loved.

Which was exactly what had gotten her into trouble the

first time. The life she'd had with her mom in the apartment in Brooklyn had been spare and sometimes lonely. She'd just wanted to belong again—

And that had ended disastrously.

She rolled out of bed, showered, dressed and walked into the kitchen to get things ready for Rex, but suddenly the sound of his crying made its way from his room, up the hall, to the kitchen area.

She dropped his sippy cup to the center island and raced to his room. Turning on the light, she said, "Hey, buddy. What's wrong? How come you're up early?"

He all but leaped into her arms when she reached for him. She squeezed him tight before laying him on the changing table. Still, he sobbed. She took care of his diaper, leaving his pajamas on. In case he spilled some breakfast, these were already dirty, and his daytime clothes would be safe.

She pulled him from the table into her arms again. "It's okay."

"Why is he crying?"

She turned at the sound of Danny's voice and her heart tumbled. Whiskers covered his chin and cheeks. His hair was sexily mussed. Pajama pants hung on his lean hips. He wasn't wearing a shirt, showing off a perfect chest. The kind of chest a woman could lay her head on while she listened to the slow beat of his heart.

"I'm not sure." Her words came out breathless, and she hoped Danny thought she was whispering. "Go back to bed. I'll take him to the kitchen for breakfast. Maybe he's just hungry."

"I'll help." He reached for Rex. As he leaned in to take him, their gazes met and all the air whooshed out of her lungs. Her mind went back to those few minutes in front of the elevator the night before. A sense of unfinished business skimmed her nerve endings.

His dark eyes flashed. Rex flung himself into his father's arms.

He caught him just in time. "Hey, buddy. What's the matter?"

He only cried louder and harder, but he snuggled against his father's shoulder.

Danny headed for the kitchen. "How about some milk?"

Marnie raced to the kitchen before them, grabbed the sippy cup and filled it, then handed it to Danny. He gave it to Rex, who tossed it on the floor. When the cap popped off, milk flew everywhere.

"I think this kid likes seeing milk on the floor."

Marnie laughed with relief at the joke. "If he won't take milk, there's something wrong. I'm guessing he's getting a tooth. Let me feel along his gums."

As soon as she ran her finger along his gums, Rex settled. She felt the bumps of a molar. "Yep. It's a tooth."

Rex sniffed.

Danny snuggled his son. "What do we do?"

"First, let's see if eating something will help him. Sometimes chewing numbs the gums. If not, we can use some over-the-counter pain reliever."

Danny squeezed his eyes shut. "His mother told me about this. I forgot."

"Did she by any chance send over some pain reliever?"

"Yes."

"Then we're good. We'll feed him, maybe take him to the park for a walk to distract him, and just play with him hard-core to keep his mind off things."

Danny sighed. "Okay. Seems like a plan."

She took the toddler from his arms. "You go change out of your wet clothes and get the pain reliever. I'll see if I can get him to eat a banana or some oatmeal. We don't want to give him meds on an empty stomach."

"Okay. Good. I'll be right back."

Rex ate the banana and some oatmeal, while Marnie cleaned up the milk mess. They gave him a dose of the pain reliever and Marnie changed him into a T-shirt and

board shorts with little tennis shoes for their trip to take
Wiggles outside.

They walked through the park with Rex happily settled
in his stroller. After an hour, with neither Rex nor Wiggles
looking eager to return to the penthouse, they found a park
bench. Watching everything around him, Rex chewed on
a soft plastic toy.

"Is that good for him?"

"Yes. It works the gums and as I mentioned before, sometimes chewing numbs them. Don't worry. I made sure it
was clean."

He caught her gaze. "I wasn't worried. You know what
you're doing."

"Thanks."

She looked away from his mesmerizing eyes. He wanted
to say something. It was all right there in his dark orbs.
Even as part of her waited breathlessly, she hoped that he
wouldn't. Everything was happening so fast. And he was
her *boss*. She had plans for her life. Not to mention that a
longing like this had derailed her once before, resulting in
a secret that always rode in the back of her brain.

"I had a good time last night."

She glanced to the right, away from him, long enough to
squeeze her eyes shut for a few seconds before she looked
back at him. "I did too."

"I almost kissed you at the elevator."

"I know."

"I want you to know I won't." He pulled in a breath. "I
need you too much. And I don't want to be a cliché."

She laughed. "Cliché?"

"You know…guy who falls for the young good-looking
nanny."

She couldn't remember the last time someone had called
her good-looking. Her mom had told her she looked nice
before she went out. Even Danny had called her stunning

the night before. But this was different. His praise was all encompassing, not a passing compliment.

"What about me? Nanny who falls for her good-looking boss. We'd both be clichés."

"Maybe the problem is that we're both good-looking?"

She laughed and playfully tapped his upper arm. "Stop."

"No. I'm serious. I almost hired an older woman. Not that she wasn't attractive. But she didn't make me want to kiss her."

She gaped at him. "I am not having this conversation!"

"Hey, this isn't just about you and Mary Poppins."

"Mary Poppins?"

"She sort of reminded me of Mary Poppins. But this isn't just about you and her. You said I was good-looking."

"You're ridiculous."

"No. What I am is happy. Ever since you came to help me with Rex, I've felt it. And I worry that what I think is attraction might actually be relief."

Her brain stalled. "What?"

"Relief. You know… I'm so glad to have one part of my life settling that I might be attaching the wrong meaning to it. I have a crazy dad, parents who didn't tell me I was adopted, and a woman who didn't tell me she was pregnant. My trust issues have trust issues. I don't have time or space for a relationship. Yet this feeling comes naturally. So, I figure it has to be relief."

She peered over at him. "Oh." She thought for a second. "I'm also making really good money with you. Better than I ever had. You're helping me reach phase two of my career. There's a bit of relief on my part too."

"Add that we're good-looking to all these feelings of relief and we might be imagining something that's not there."

Disappointment tried to spike. She wouldn't let it. It was ridiculous to long for something that wasn't right. "Yeah."

"See? I think I hit the nail on the head. And you didn't want to talk about this," he scoffed. "If we hadn't, we'd have hung around worrying about something we don't need to worry about."

Like a past that might surface. A dad who didn't want her. A mom who was always a drink away from destroying her life.

Looking at it objectively like that, she realized she'd spent her life mired in fear. "I do have a history of that."

"Well, now that you're working for me, we're going to stop it."

She grinned. "I feel like that might be happening. You know... I love Rex. I'm comfortable in your house. No one seems to think I'm out of place on your street, at the bakery, walking Wiggles. It's all—" she laughed "—a relief."

"So, we agree? We're good for each other in so many ways that it feels romantic but it's not."

"That has to be it. We're both too smart to do something stupid."

"We can go back and eat lunch like normal people."

"We did skip breakfast."

"Another reason to stop at the bakery. And this time get two Danish."

She laughed. "What?"

"We're friends now. There's no reason for pretense. If you want two Danish, get two Danish. If you want a bagel, get a bagel. Let's be ourselves."

The idea of being herself sent another wave of relief rippling through her.

She'd been in hiding for ten years. Not letting herself be or do much of anything. Now, suddenly she was a twenty-six-year-old woman. The past seemed far away. Especially with no one having had reason to dredge it up for a decade. Her dad didn't matter. Her mom had been sober for fourteen years, thanks to Alcoholics Anonymous.

Had she really worried for nothing all these years?

She rose from the bench. The colors of the sky seemed

brighter. Rex laughed at Wiggles, who whipped over to lick his cheek.

"Since we're being ourselves, I'll admit I'm starving. Let's go now."

Danny rose too. "Bakery it is."

The weekend passed quickly. Talking about their feelings seemed to work for Marnie. She was light, happy. Rex made it to Monday despite his sore gums. But at breakfast, Danny felt odd. All day Sunday, he'd reminded himself that his happiness around Marnie was relief. But at a certain point he had to admit that wasn't true. He liked her and he'd basically warned her off.

He should have kissed her Saturday night.

If she'd quit, he could have asked her for a date.

If she hadn't quit, they'd have figured something out.

But he'd taken the high road. And now look where he was. Watching the woman who filled his heart with joy play mother to his child. He might have only known her a few weeks, but they fit.

And he'd blown it.

It didn't help that he spent Monday in court and returned home exhausted and grumpy. Rex spilled his juice. Wiggles peed on the floor. Marnie handled it all like the pro she was.

She retired to her room after putting Rex to bed. Danny walked to the family room, a large room in the back with a big screen TV and enough toys and games to entertain fifty people.

He tuned the television to a baseball game, racked the balls on the pool table and grabbed a cue stick from the holder.

He shot two games, groaning at the ineptitude of his favorite baseball team and trying to unwind.

"Hey."

His gaze shot up when Marnie entered the room. "I'm

sorry if I was too loud. I forgot I'm on your side of the penthouse."

She meandered a bit closer. "It's okay. I couldn't hear you, but..." She bit her lower lip, a habit he'd observed she indulged when she was nervous. "Well, at dinner I noticed you were stressed."

He straightened, searched for his next shot, then leaned over to take it. "That's a natural result of spending a day in court. You have two sides who both believe they're right." He slid the stick between his fingers and smacked the cue ball into three other balls with a resounding crack. "I handle mostly estates so the only times I enter a courtroom are when relatives are fighting over money."

He hit the cue ball again. The red ball flew into a pocket. He drew a satisfied breath. "Fighting families are the worst."

"I'll bet." She plopped down on the sofa, tucking one leg under her butt and laying one arm along the back pillows. It was sweet that she wanted to talk him out of his stress, but she had no idea that the more he saw her, the more he wanted her, and right now she was playing with fire.

"But, honestly, I don't have much family. My mom was an orphan. My dad single-minded. We didn't host relatives for Thanksgiving. Our guests were his clients."

He longed to talk about his day, hear about her life. But wasn't that part of the problem? The connection they were making lured him in to want more.

He took another shot. "That sounds lovely."

"It wasn't." She paused a beat. "What about you?"

He looked up. Her eyes were warm, her gaze friendly. If he didn't answer, she'd know something was wrong.

"Before I met Leni and Charlotte, I didn't have any brothers and sisters. My parents were never chosen by another birth mother. I did have oodles of cousins though."

She came to attention. "Really? What's that like?"

A memory of a week at the lake popped into his head,

and—amazingly—he laughed. "Chaotic. There was only one girl cousin and we terrorized her."

"You didn't!"

"Hey, we were boys in the woods. If we found a snake, it wasn't our fault that we wanted to show it off."

She laughed.

Finished with his game, he should have gone to his room. Instead, with his muscles loosening and the stress of the day slipping away, he motioned to the table. Just like always, being with her did something to him. Something he liked. Something he needed.

"Do you play?"

She looked at her fingernails. "A bit."

"Don't tell me you're a ringer."

She pushed off the sofa. "No. But I have my days."

She chose a stick and he let her break. She ended up with the striped balls and had four put away before he got his first turn.

Focused, he worked to get three in the pockets. Then she bent across the table to shoot and her yoga pants outlined her butt.

He took a quick breath and blew it out slowly.

She only sank one ball before she lost her turn. As he studied the table, she said, "What else happens in court?"

She had a good idea keeping the conversation neutral, but it didn't work when she used that breathless voice.

"Lawyers try to trip up witnesses from the opposing side." He took a shot, missed and wasn't the slightest surprised.

She leaned across the table again. He looked at the ceiling. "Your job is essentially tripping people up?"

"No. My job is looking for loopholes, mistakes in thinking, and law, precedents, that support my position."

"You're a trickster."

"No!" He thought of his dad and fought the urge to ball his hands into fists. "I'm the one who uncovers tricksters."

"Much more interesting."

The breathless voice was back. Most of the balls were in the pocket. Both would shoot for the eight. He suddenly wished he could stand back and just watch her. Her movements were easy, fluid. Her proficiency at the game a total turn-on.

She tried for the eight, missed. He ambled to her side of the table as she walked to his. They met at a corner that she'd taken too sharply and suddenly they were in front of each other, almost brushing, both breathing funny.

They'd had the talk about how they weren't going to pursue anything romantic, but after a day in court with his nerves strung tight, his defenses worn down... He couldn't for the life of him remember why he'd agreed to that—

No. He couldn't remember why he'd *suggested* that.

Familiar feelings rumbled through him. Primal. Quiet. Resurrecting an instinct so deep it merged body and soul.

He was suddenly the man he'd been before he'd met his dad and discovered he had a child. For thirty seconds, he was just a guy with needs. A hunger for the pretty girl in front of him.

"I thought we weren't going to do this."

His voice came out rough as he said, "I can't for the life of me remember why."

"Neither one of us wants to be a cliché."

"If that's our only reason, it's not a good one."

CHAPTER EIGHT

MARNIE'S HEART POUNDED, making her chest tight enough she worried it would burst. They were so close she swore she could hear his heart beating. Everything had been good over the weekend, then he'd come home tired and out of sorts and something inside her had yearned to make him feel better.

She whispered, "You're sure it's not a good one?"

His head began to lower. "Very."

When their lips met, a symphony of longing sang through her blood. Almost powerful enough to drown out her fears, it filled her heart, wove through her soul. Their connection was strong, but their attraction was stronger. She didn't know how to fight it. Even when she reminded herself that he lived in a different world, part of her scoffed that he was a simple billionaire. Not one of the guys who attracted attention. And any private time she got with him would be worth it.

He deepened the kiss, his tongue delving into the recesses of her mouth. The longing intensified, whooshing through her, stealing her breath. Thoughts of where this was going, what they were doing should have terrified her. Instead, they stoked the flames of the fire.

He pulled away unexpectedly. She blinked up at him. Something wild and wonderful shivered between them. For a breath, she considered springing to her tiptoes and getting them back to kissing…but something serious had settled in his eyes.

"I think we both know where this was going and we both need to think about it some more."

Drowsy, confused, she stepped back. After a second for his words to sink in, to remind her of consequences and ramifications, she said, "Yeah."

He ran his hand through his hair. "I'm going to my room now."

"Me too."

As if he couldn't take his eyes off her, he started backing toward the door. "See you in the morning."

She nodded.

He left, and she stared at the door, her arousal subsiding, her needs mixing and mingling then breaking apart when she added her past and everything didn't exactly mesh. Not only was he sexy and amazing, but he was a good person. Genuinely good. And she should be thankful he'd been levelheaded.

Even thoughts of his control sent warmth cascading through her. He could have taken advantage of her. She'd had that happen too many times to count, when the hole in her life left by her missing father had caused her to go looking for love all the wrong ways. His respect for her filled her eyes with tears and her soul with yearning.

For something she couldn't have. Because she'd made a mistake. And that mistake followed her.

The next morning, she continued her routine of showering and getting things ready for Rex before he woke at six. She changed him, put him in his highchair and was fixing his breakfast when Danny walked into the kitchen for his coffee.

Her breath filled with something so light and bemusing it fluttered in her chest. Trying not to look like a smitten fool, she monitored her smile, kept it a reasonable lift of her lips, not a beaming grin. "Good morning."

He bypassed the coffeepot, walked over and put his forearm around her waist, pulling her to him. His lips met hers quickly, hotly, and her limbs turned to jelly.

He broke the kiss but didn't release her. Staring into her eyes, he said, "Good morning."

Her mind went blank. No matter how wrong, something inside her desperately wanted this.

"Everything happened so fast last night and escalated before either one of us was ready. So, I thought we'd introduce…you know…'it' into our routine. So it isn't shocking and overpowering."

Which made perfect sense. Maybe if she had a chance to get accustomed to the idea of something between them, it wouldn't seem at odds with her life. At odds with her past. A past that had been buried for ten long years.

After a few seconds she said, "That's a heck of a way to start the day."

He laughed and walked to the coffeemaker. "And that's what I like about you. Right there. You are so wonderfully honest."

His words like a punch in the gut, her good feelings shattered like glass. She wasn't honest. She hadn't told him her secret—

"Or maybe it's not that you're honest. It's more like you're yourself."

That she had been. She was absolutely herself. He'd let her be herself. In fact, he'd encouraged it.

"Court again today," he said, leaning against the counter, looking sexy and sophisticated in his white shirt and black trousers, as his cup of coffee brewed. "I'm leaving early to get some time in the office to prepare."

"For the fighting family?"

"Yes. I got to thinking last night that if I was as good of a lawyer as I think I am, I should be able to find a way to settle this. Today. Before another long, frustrating day in front of a judge."

He hadn't been thinking about their kiss?

She'd spent hours tossing and turning.

But maybe that was better? Prioritizing was a good thing. And too much passion too soon might ruin everything. Which was what he'd been trying to say after he'd kissed her.

Oh heavens.

He was right again. He was always right. Doing the correct thing. While she was crazy, floundering, picking apart every move, everything he'd said. And why? Because she didn't want to get burned again?

Even if what they started didn't pan out, he wouldn't burn her. He wouldn't embarrass her. He wouldn't take pictures of her while she was sleeping—

A chill raced down her spine. None of that had entered her mind with Roger. That's why she overanalyzed now. She carefully considered every man she dated before even the idea of sleeping with them came into the situation.

But with Danny all her rules were going out the window. Trust had been swift, easy.

Did she have any idea what she was doing with him?

What she might be doing to herself?

He left without taking Wiggles for a walk, which was fine. Maybe even good. Fresh air and sunshine might clear her head.

Dressing Rex in denim shorts, a T-shirt and his fancy tennis shoes, she told Wiggles not to panic. They would be going out soon.

With Rex ready and in the small umbrella stroller, easier for her when she was alone with the puppy and the baby, she fastened Wiggles's leash, then they piled into the elevator.

In the lobby, the doorman said, "Good morning."

She returned his greeting and soon they were out on the sidewalk.

The second she stepped into the sun, she felt better. With Wiggles's leash attached to the arm of the stroller, she put on her big sunglasses—a gift she'd bought herself while shopping for her art gala dress—and headed toward the nearest park.

Rex grinned happily. Wiggles trotted along. And all things returned to normal. Her nerves stabilized. What she felt for Danny wasn't pressing or confusing. It sat above her brain like a happy little rainbow.

She found a bench in the park, turned Rex's stroller to face her so they could chitchat and loosened Wiggles's leash to let him roam a bit.

"This is nice."

Rex said, "Nice."

"Oh, I see you're catching on to some new words."

"Words."

She laughed. "You're adorable."

He grinned.

She took a breath and leaned back. The warm sun beat down on her, soothing her soul. The night before, Danny had said they both needed time to think this through. Not while in crazy panic mode, but the way Danny seemed to analyze things. Slowly. Deliberately.

She went back to the beginning. From the way she'd thought he was gorgeous when she'd met him to the way she'd gone to the game room the night before. Nervous, tense, he'd needed to relax. She knew she could help him.

She *wanted* to help him.

There were genuine feelings there. Not just attraction, but emotion. She couldn't deny it.

Danny was obviously wealthier than her typical employers, who were usually two-income executive parents, working to get rich, not already rich. Yet, he was a normal guy. Probably because he'd been raised middle-class.

Score one for him.

But score one for her too. She'd adjusted to his lifestyle rather easily. She'd slid into his world as if she was made to be there.

And maybe she was?

They were a normal girl and guy finding love on Park Avenue.

Her fears melting like butter in the morning sun and the wonder of actually being able to have these kinds of emotions, she giggled. Rex grinned at her.

And that was another thing. She and Rex had become

fast friends. He snuggled her and took to her as if he'd liked her immediately.

Second score for her. If she and Danny started something, there'd be no worry about Rex liking her.

Of course, if their romance failed, Rex would lose her.

Drat. That took away one of their points.

Wiggles pulled on the leash, yanking the stroller and Marnie bounced up. If the direction of the leash was correct, the crazy dog had gotten himself caught in a bush. She grabbed the stroller handles and headed toward the bush. Pushing the stroller around it, she said, "Hey, you crazy dog—"

She stopped dead. On the bench across the walking path was her dad. He looked older than he had the day she'd gotten the glimpse of him as he walked by her and Danny. Older and thin. As if he'd been ill. He also wore a sweater on a hot end-of-July morning.

Wiggles barked and he glanced up, over the rim of reading glasses. He set his newspaper on the bench beside him and speared her with a look. "Oh, for heaven's sake."

Marnie's lungs froze. Her tongue numbed. She could only stare as he glared at her.

From out of nowhere, a young guy in a T-shirt and jeans reached into the bush, untangled the leash, then pulled Wiggles out and handed him to her.

"Here you go, ma'am."

She might have stumbled over the word *ma'am*, but her frozen tongue wouldn't work. The guy walked away, and she stared at her father.

With a heavy sigh, he folded his newspaper and rose from the bench. "If you can't manage both a kid and a dog, you shouldn't come to the park."

Memories from when she'd lived with him cascaded in her brain. Being yelled at. Being criticized. Both reasons her mom drank. Every time her parents went out, somehow her mom had screwed things up. Said the wrong thing to someone important. Danced too much or not enough. Her dad would return home disappointed. Her mother had walked to the bar. Her mom might have been an alcoholic, but her dad had driven her over the edge. Even at twelve Marnie had known that.

Staring at his grouchy face, it seemed he hadn't changed. If he had even an ounce of compassion, she'd never seen it.

Newspaper under his arm, he stormed off.

She licked her suddenly dry lips. The second time in fourteen years that he'd seen her, and he'd scolded her.

Why was she surprised?

Why did she care!

CHAPTER NINE

DANNY CAME HOME to an energetic puppy, a happy little boy and an extremely quiet nanny.

Damn. The kiss that morning might have been over-the-top. But he hadn't been able to help himself. He was the kind of guy who went after what he wanted, and he wanted her.

He'd thought his plan to casually introduce romance was a good one. Clearly, though, he'd pushed a bit too hard. He would draw back. Give her space. After all, he wasn't in any position to rush things. The slower they took this, the more chance she'd learn to trust him.

"Hi." He headed back to his bedroom. "Give me two minutes to change and I'll call to have dinner delivered."

"I actually made something for dinner."

He stopped halfway to the master. "You did?"

She shrugged. "Just veal cutlets."

He ventured a few steps back. "*Just* veal cutlets."

"Yeah."

"Okay."

Her usually bright green eyes were dull. Her voice one shade above somber.

Something was really bothering her, and the only new thing in their world was him kissing her. Still, he wasn't sorry. If she was, all she had to do was say so. She hadn't ever been shy about telling him anything.

But dinner was quiet. She picked at her food.

And damn it, he wanted her to like him.

He thought about it as he loaded the dishwasher. Maybe ten hours away from him had her thinking too much? Yes, he'd told her they needed to think this through, but he felt like defense counsel when they didn't get an opportunity for rebuttal.

They needed to talk. He might not have been able to get her to open up yet, but he could, if they spent a little time together.

"Hey, how about a movie tonight?"

"A movie?"

"I'm subscribed to enough services that we're sure to find something you'll like."

Her face perked up. "That would be nice."

Okay. Good. She wasn't averse to spending time with him. But something was wrong.

"And I swear. No kissing this time."

She laughed, then met his gaze. "I liked the kiss."

"I *loved* the kiss. But if you want to go with *like*, that's fine. I'll wear you down."

She laughed again.

That was more like it.

They watched the movie as two friends, no kiss this time, and the next morning, she was herself again. The only thing that had changed between them was that they'd spent two hours together watching a movie and he *hadn't* kissed her.

He all but decided to totally back off, but by Friday morning her good humor had completely returned.

Saturday morning, she suggested a couple of hours in the park and another stop at the bakery.

"Sounds great!"

Thrilled that she was happy again, he helped her pack up Wiggles and Rex. But when she turned right out of their building rather than left, he put a hand on her arm.

"Park's that way."

She nodded. "I know. There's another park just up the street, though."

"It's not *just* up the street. It's blocks up the street. By the time we stroll Rex that far, Wiggles's bladder will have exploded." He shifted his voice from shocked to cajoling. "Come on. I worked all week. I need bench time in the sun."

He turned the stroller to go in their usual direction and

though she sort of smiled in agreement, he noticed her stiffen. When they got to the bench, she sat cautiously.

After setting the brake on Rex's stroller, he lowered himself beside her with a satisfied, "Ah... What a week."

She tucked a strand of her long hair behind her ear. "Yeah."

He might have spent three days in court, but he'd also kissed her. They'd played pool, watched a movie. Yet her, "Yeah," was cautious.

"I mean, I love being a lawyer, helping other people unravel problems, but fighting families get to me."

She shifted on the bench. He knew her parents were divorced and almost cursed himself for the dumb remark.

"Though, I'm beginning to think all families are crazy."

She sniffed. He felt a little better and decided maybe he shouldn't talk. Up until kissing her, their relationship had developed naturally. Then he'd kissed her and become an idiot.

So, no. No more forced discussions. From here on out conversations would develop naturally.

An older gentleman in a sweater walked by. He didn't say anything, but Danny could swear he heard the man growl.

Marnie froze for a few seconds before she caught Wiggles's leash and rose. "You know what? I'm tired. Could we go back?" Her gaze moved toward the guy, then jerked back again.

Danny glanced from her to the old man, who had taken a seat on the bench behind the bush, and this time he froze. He recognized him. At least, he thought he did.

He whispered, "Is that your dad?"

She wouldn't look at him. "He saw Wiggles get caught in the bush the other day." She paused, sucked in a breath. "He didn't know who I was."

"Is that why he growled as he walked by?"

She shrugged. "He told me if I couldn't handle both a kid and a dog, I shouldn't come to the park."

Danny's eyes widened in disbelief at the man's rudeness. "He *said* that?"

"Let's just go."

"No. Even if he wasn't your dad, this is a public park." Without a thought, he charged across the path. "Did you yell at my nanny the last time she was here?"

He didn't look up from his newspaper.

"Hey, I'm talking to you." He shoved the paper down a bit so he could see the old man's face. "This is a public park and my nanny is one of the best. She put herself through university and plans to start her own agency. She didn't deserve your criticism. I'm not exactly sure why you thought you had the right to yell at her, but you didn't."

He turned and stormed back to the stroller, the dog and wide-eyed Marnie. He caught her arm with one hand and the stroller with the other, glad Wiggles's leash was tied to the handle and pushed them out of the park.

When they reached the sidewalk, he let go of her, and they headed up the street as if nothing had happened.

"I'm sorry if I overstepped."

She didn't say anything, just looked at him, absolute shock written all over her face.

"I don't usually have a temper."

"That was hardly a temper. It was…a rebuttal."

He laughed, and they walked the rest of the way to his building in complete silence. He might have laughed, but after a few seconds, he realized her voice had been somber, nowhere near happy. He expected her resignation when they stepped off the elevator. Instead, she took Rex back to the nursery. When she came out, she walked to him, slid her hand around his neck, brought his face to hers and kissed him.

Her mouth met his chastely but she'd surprised him so much that instinct took over, and he opened his lips, letting the two of them fall naturally into the emotion that both pleased and bedeviled him. Sensations washed over him. Need. Hunger.

And a link that reached into his soul and filled it with something indescribable. He didn't have an idea in hell what was happening to him. He just knew he liked it.

She pulled away from the long, slow, erotic kiss. "Do you know how long I've wanted to say something like that to him?"

"Why haven't you?"

"In my head, I'm still twelve."

"Well, now he knows you're not twelve anymore. That you've gotten a degree and intend to start a company."

She laughed, ran her hand through her hair. "That was surreal."

It was for him too. Not standing up for her to her dad. But feeling things so intensely they caused him to act before he thought. "Want to go back and yell at him again?"

Her laugh deepened, filled with relief and joy. "No. I'm good." She took a quick breath. "I'm really good." She looked around as if seeing his condo for the first time.

"You're sure you're okay?"

"I think I need to go see my mom."

His breath puffed out on a sigh, but he caught it. She didn't want to talk to him about what had happened that morning. She wanted to talk to her mom. "What?"

"I haven't taken any time off in a while. At least no time out of the house." She shrugged. "I think she needs to know I've seen my dad."

He ran his hand along the back of his neck. "Yeah. Okay. I get that."

She nodded and ran back to her room. In seconds, she reappeared. Still in the yoga pants and T-shirt, what he considered her nanny attire, but holding her purse with one hand as she slid her big sunglasses on with the other.

"See you."

He said, "Yeah. See you," and watched her leave. But the strangest feeling passed through him. All the wicked suspicions that had overwhelmed him the first time she'd seen her dad in the park and told him—even though they didn't know each other.

Part of him understood that Marnie would want to talk to her mom about seeing her dad. But once again, it suddenly all seemed incredibly coincidental.

Could she have really "accidentally" gotten a job close to where her dad lived?

And was it really an accident that she kept running into him?

He shook his head. *Was he crazy?* He and Marnie were like two peas in a pod—

They meshed. Like she was made for him—

Why did that suddenly strike him as odd, too?

Why did it sound an alarm bell?

The memory of Marnie telling him she'd seen her dad the first time came back like a scene from a movie.

She'd been so open about it. Up-front. But had she needed to tell him? At that point they'd only known each other a day—

Then she'd seen her dad again that week and today on their walk. Rather coincidental.

Sure, weeks had gone by. And, yes, her wealthy father could live on Park Avenue. But what if she'd known? What if she'd wanted to edge her way into her dad's life? What better way than to work near where he lived?

And what better thing than to have a smitten employer approach him, tell him things, pave the way, so she didn't have to?

Then she thanks him with a kiss and races off to report to her mom? Maybe to make plans of some sort to extort money—

He dropped his head to his hands.

Damn.

Had he just been conned?

Or had being Mark Hinton's son officially made him crazy?

As crazy as his father, who always said money ruined trust?

Always.

CHAPTER TEN

"OF COURSE, YOU'RE SUSPICIOUS." Danny's sister Leni sat on the paisley chair across from the sofa where Danny sat. "You're a newly rich guy who didn't merely discover he was adopted. Your biological dad also may or may not have faked his death after poking into your life enough to discover you had a son, who you are now raising alone. In a few months, you went from a middle-class single guy to a wealthy dad. And a very eligible bachelor."

Danny sat back. Leni had called him right after Marnie left, said she had cookies for Rex and was in the lobby.

Befuddled, he'd let her up. Still, he'd forced himself to behave normally through making coffee, happily taking one of the cookies she'd brought for him and Rex and even making initial chitchat.

But when she'd asked about Marnie, he couldn't quite fake it. He'd shaken his head, as his fears had spilled out of his mouth. "I'd been suspicious that first walk in the park when she casually told me—a virtual stranger—that she'd seen her dad—the dad who abandoned her and her mom. So why the hell hadn't I listened to myself?" He squeezed his eyes shut, then popped them open again. "I think I've snapped."

"Or…" Petite Leni with her long brown hair and big eyes filled with wisdom, leaned forward on the paisley chair. "You could give yourself the benefit of the doubt. A lot of things that happened with Marnie do seem coincidental."

"I thought we were soul mates or something because we'd been able to talk so easily, when the whole time she might have been setting me up."

"So what if she'd found her dad before she'd gotten the job with you? So what if she's taking this opportunity to meet him or get to know him? Does that really impact how she cares for Rex?"

He combed his hand through his hair. "Not so far. She's a great nanny. Rex loves her."

"And you have no proof that she tricked you?"

"Just suspicions."

"Charlotte and I both went through something like this. When you first find out you're not who you think you are, you question everything that's happened in your life. Plus, Mark made you attorney for his estate, as if you'd earned it, then you discovered he's your biological dad and *he* was setting you up." She shook her head and laughed. "I'd worry about you if you weren't overly suspicious."

He snorted. "Yeah. That's a valid point."

"You're probably right on track with where Charlotte and I were when we discovered we were Hinton heirs." The sound of Rex crying came through the monitor. "Let's go get the baby. We'll eat cookies and play. Forget all this."

"We'll spoil his dinner."

"Okay, we'll give him one cookie and play." She rose from the chair. "What time is your nanny coming back?"

"She didn't say."

And maybe that was his real worry. That she *wasn't* coming back—that their wonderful, explosive kiss had been a goodbye kiss. She'd seen her dad. The old man knew she'd gotten her degree and had plans for her future. Now she could move on.

Maybe even make a call or two to the people he'd introduced her to at Sally McMillen's showing.

He sucked in a breath. He couldn't figure out if he was the world's biggest chump or the most suspicious guy on the planet.

But he did know getting involved with a woman he barely knew, someone he *employed* had been reckless.

"You're a Hinton heir," Leni continued as they walked the hall to Rex's room. "As attorney for the estate, you warned me and Charlotte to watch ourselves. That people would befriend us because of the money. Friends would behave oddly. There's a weird satisfaction in getting to return your warning. Watch yourself."

He nodded, but sadness gripped him. It took a second or two of thinking, but he realized why Leni's warning made him sad. Marnie was the nicest, sweetest woman he'd ever met. He was the one with the problem. A crazy biological father. A bunch of doubts and suspicions. The weirdness of finding out he wasn't who he thought he was—

How could he blame Marnie, be suspicious of her, when he was the one with all the issues?

Marnie raced up the stairs to her mom's apartment and used her key to let herself in. "Mom?"

"In here." Her mother appeared at her bedroom door. Tall and willowy with auburn hair sprinkled with gray and wearing jeans and a loose purple top, Judy Olsen said, "What's up?"

"Come into the living room." Furnished with a yellow floral sofa and chair her mom had purchased secondhand, the combination living room/family room was as far away from Danny Manelli's sleek, sophisticated main room as it could get. Windows were covered with yellow drapes and blinds—also out-of-date. But everything was clean and light, pretty and airy, like her mom.

Judy took a seat on the sofa, beside her knitting. Marnie fell into the chair. "I saw Dad."

Her mom blinked. "Oh?"

"He must live near my employer's penthouse, because I've seen him a few times at the park where I take Rex and Wiggles."

One eyebrow rose. "Wiggles?"

"Not the important part of the story, Mom."

"I know, but frankly I'd rather not hear about your dad." She closed her eyes, took a breath and popped them open again. "But I promised myself that if you wanted to have a relationship with him, I wouldn't stop you."

Marnie shook her head. "He seems exactly as he was when he left. Miserable."

"I always blamed myself for that. You know…having a drunk for a wife embarrassed and humiliated him, so he was grouchy."

"Well, I think you can forgive yourself and move on. Living on Park Avenue with you being in no way involved in his life, he's still a… I won't say the word in polite conversation."

Her mom laughed.

"The first time I saw him, he didn't notice me. The second time, Wiggles was caught in a bush, and he scolded me, saying if I couldn't handle a kid and a dog I shouldn't go to the park."

"He didn't help you?"

"No. Some guy strolling by pulled Wiggles out. All Dad did was criticize."

"Hmmm. Sounds like him."

"Then this morning, my employer was with me and I had to tell him the story and he stormed over and told Dad never to harass his nanny again…or something."

Judy laughed.

"But that's not the best part. Danny told Dad I was smart and had graduated university and was planning on starting my own company and didn't deserve his comments."

"Wow."

"It was like… I don't know? Getting the chance to show him who I was, that his leaving hadn't ruined me. All without the nasty business of fallout. He doesn't care about some nanny in the park…but I got my say."

"It probably did feel good."

"It felt like closure, and I have Danny Manelli to thank."

Her mom's eyes narrowed, and she studied Marnie's face. "You told your new boss a heck of a lot about yourself."

She shrugged. "He's easy to talk to." And kiss. And in general, be around. But her mom didn't need to know that.

"What else did you tell him?"

Marnie sat back. "You mean, did I tell him about Roger Martin?"

She didn't even try to hide it. "Yes."

"No. Because it wasn't relevant. I told Danny about Dad because I hadn't wanted to go to that side of the park...the side where I'd seen Dad before. I ended up having to explain."

"I'm still not sure how telling your dad about your successes crept into defending you."

Marnie quietly said, "It made sense at the time."

"Oh, sweetie, don't be angry. I'm just concerned. In a few weeks, you've all but told your boss your entire life story."

"We live together, eat together, care for his son together—"

"And you're getting close?"

She took a breath, praying for patience. "It's hard not to."

Judy ran her hands down her face. "Your dad showed you that there are some men who will take what they want and when things don't go their way, they bolt. They don't talk. They don't try to fix things. They simply move on. That's what privileged men do. Roger Martin, richest kid in your school, took advantage of you. I'm not saying your Danny Manelli is like that. I'm saying be careful."

Relief fluttered through Marnie. "I'm always careful."

Maybe too careful.

The words popped into her brain unbidden. But there was a bitter truth to them. She'd been nothing but careful since high school. Since the pictures. Since the two-year rebellion that had landed her in bed with a predator.

Wasn't it time to forgive herself?

Wasn't it time to step out and have a real life instead of sporadic dates with guys so safe they hadn't made a ripple of reaction in her life?

Her mom huffed out a sigh. "Look at me. Projecting my own insecurities on you."

"You have good reason."

"We both have good reason." She shook her head. "I guess maybe what I'm saying is think this through. The man is your boss. And you might be taking things out of context—"

"I'm being smart. Nothing's really happened." She fought the urge to squeeze her eyes shut. Danny's kiss a few nights ago had been fraught with hunger. Her kiss that very afternoon had been the answer to it.

She wasn't being smart or careful or wise or even prudent.

Her mom was right. She was charging forward on instinct. A need she hadn't felt in years. Which meant she might not know how to control it.

She rose from the chair. "We should make tea and play rummy."

Her mom also stood. "Are you staying!"

"I could. But I probably shouldn't. I have Rex on a great schedule. I'd like to keep that going."

"Okay. We'll play one game or two, then you can get back."

That was the thing she liked best about her mom. She could worry and give warnings, but she trusted Marnie to make good choices and do the right thing.

After two games of rummy, Marnie took public transportation back to Danny's, reminding herself of all the reasons her mom was right. But when she stepped off the elevator and saw Danny coming up the hall from having put Rex to bed, a towel over his shoulder, his shirt askew, his hair a mess, she pressed her lips together.

Everything she felt for him rose and bloomed. She couldn't even look at him without her heart thundering.

What she felt for him was right. If she shoved away her

fears and only examined his behavior, he was the best man she'd ever known.

And she wanted him. Wanted everything.

She didn't want to be afraid anymore.

Danny saw Marnie step off the elevator and stopped dead in his tracks. Their eyes met and she started walking toward him. She was the most naturally beautiful woman he'd ever met. Good with his son. Good with him. Good *for* him.

Maybe Leni had been right? Maybe his suspicions were only his fear of making a mistake, holding him back when he longed to go forward. Alisha hadn't been honest with him. His parents hadn't been honest with him. Mark had made him look like an idiot, giving him the job as attorney for his estate then faking his death.

No wonder he feared. But there was no reason to doubt himself, his instincts. Everything that made him suspicious had resulted from the behavior of someone else.

Not him...

Not his choices.

Not his decisions.

And when he looked at Marnie, all his concerns melted away. He was himself again. Because she was honest. Kind. Wonderful.

He took a step, then another, then another, and before he really understood what was going on, they were running to each other. They met in a blistering kiss. Arousal poured through him like the hard rains of a hurricane. Mindless, ravenous, he reached for her top as she plucked his shirt out of his pants.

Two seconds before they would have been naked, common sense hit. "Not here." He barely raised his lips above hers. "There are too many people the doorman is authorized to give the elevator code to." He walked backward toward his room, kicked open the door and led her to the bed.

They fell to the mattress and he rolled her once so that

he was on top and could kiss her with all his pent-up need. Their tongues dueled. She rippled her fingers over his naked chest and his muscles hardened.

The kiss turned rough, desperate. He maneuvered them until she was on top and he could run his hands along her torso, her hips, her breasts. Her sharp intake of breath had him pulling her down, giving his tongue access to her soft flesh.

Frenzied need drove him. There would be time to be gentle, patient, later. Once the hunger was assuaged. Limbs tangled. Desire spiked, compelled. Their bodies moved in unison until they finally joined.

A sense of rightness nearly overwhelmed him. The word *mine* whispered through his soul. The notion that he'd spent his entire life looking for her urged him on until completion took them both. Then his breath stilled. His body calmed. His mind quieted until only one thought remained.

He hoped he hadn't made a mistake.

He rose up, caught her gaze—

She smiled. He smiled. His confusion flitted away. Looking at her, being with her, everything in his world righted.

CHAPTER ELEVEN

MARNIE COULDN'T TAKE her eyes off him. Her first sexual experience had been tainted by the pictures. Her subsequent experiences had been tame, careful. Making love with Danny had been explosive and powerful. Not just sexually, but emotionally. Everything they felt had been right there, in everything they'd done. Every move. Every taste. Every breath of longing.

Her eyes locked with his, she whispered, "That was amazing."

"Totally." His answering whisper, filled with the same awe, made her smile.

He rolled to his back, his arms around her waist so he could pull her with him, and she cuddled into his side. She wanted to lay her head on his chest, but despite her boldness while they were making love, she couldn't quite bring herself to do it. She settled for letting her hands drift along the hard muscles, ease through the dark hair, luxuriate in the feel of the firm skin beneath her fingertips.

Nothing had ever felt so right. So perfect, but also so normal. As if this was where she was meant to be.

The thought should have scared her. Instead it filled her with wonderment. She hadn't trusted anybody like this in decades.

"We should go out sometime."

Danny's out-of-the-blue comment made her laugh and sit up so she could see his face. "What?"

"We should go out."

She held back a laugh. "Like on a date?"

"It is customary for people who like each other to do that."

She swirled her index finger along his chest. "We did go out…once."

"So now we'll go out again. Maybe dinner."

"Charlotte likes to babysit."

He snickered. "No kidding. I have no idea what's gotten into her. You know, she used to run the operations division of a development company." He shook his head. "Money makes people do crazy things."

"Or maybe it makes them do the things they've wanted all along but just never realized."

He sniffed.

"What have you always wanted to do?"

He met her gaze. "Exactly what I'm doing now."

Pleasure rippled through her. She couldn't tell if he meant being a lawyer or lying here with her, but her heart had taken it that he wanted to be with her.

"I'm serious. Is there nothing you want? Nothing you'd change?"

He took a long breath. "There is one thing that was perfect but got screwed up when Mark announced I was his third kid."

"What's that?"

"I have no idea how to fix things with my adoptive parents. I moved to New York City to find a great job. Not just a good job, a great one." His hand drifted up her side from hip to waist and back down again to settle on the curve. "Once I landed at Waters, Waters and Montgomery, Mark began bringing work to them until they had pretty much taken over all his legal matters."

"What's that have to do with your parents?"

He shook his head. "It's just another piece of distance between us. Another way Mark edged in, taking their place."

Pride shimmied through her and an emotion so deep and fierce she couldn't name it. The way he trusted her with the facts of his life all but cemented their feelings for each other. The way he wanted her advice made her long to be wise enough to help him.

Finally, she said, "Leni was adopted. How did she reconcile that?"

"She and Nick live in her small town in Kansas. Mark is the visitor into her life. Her parents are still her parents. Mark is the guest."

"So maybe you need to think of a way to do that too?"

His eyebrows angled together. "Bring my parents here?"

"Or get a house near them."

"I'd have to commute to work."

She laughed. "Oh, silly man. Don't you know rich guys have weekend homes? Houses in the country?"

He frowned. "That's true."

"And wouldn't you love giving Rex and Wiggles time in the small town you grew up in?"

He laughed. "Yes."

"So the answer is easy."

He rose up, put his hands on her shoulders and maneuvered her down to the pillow again. "Nope. I think the truth is you're brilliant."

Her lips lifted into a smile. "I have been told I'm smart."

He laughed, then kissed her. The simple meeting of their mouths morphing into the scorching need that always ignited between them.

But the sound of the elevator door opening rippled down the hall. Danny had kicked open the master bedroom door and hadn't closed it. Anybody stepping out would have an unobstructed view of the corridor, into his room.

He lifted his head, stifling a groan over being interrupted when he least wanted to be.

The list of people authorized to get that day's code raced through his brain. He jumped off the bed and into his pants. "This could only be one of about seven people." He smiled at her. "Let's hope it's Arnie, the doorman."

She pushed herself up onto her elbows. "I'm guessing that's best-case scenario?"

Yanking a T-shirt over his head, he said, "Yeah. You stay. I'll be right back." Then, unable to help himself, he bent across the bed and brushed a quick kiss across her mouth.

Everything inside him wanted to slam closed the bedroom door and crawl back into bed with her. But one or two of the people who knew the code would have come looking for him. Jace for sure. Charlotte a definite maybe. And Mark—

"Hey, Danny?"

Damn! It was Mark!

Even as he thought that, his father, Mark Hinton and Penny Fillion, his fiancée, peeked down the hall.

He hoped he didn't look like the jumbled mess that he felt.

"Hey…"

He ambled up the corridor, picking up his discarded shirt and rolling it into a ball that he tossed into the guest bathroom, trying to look calm and composed and not like he'd just had desperate sex with a woman he might be falling in love with.

Oh, Mark would love that. He'd give him a sermon on responsibility. Or maybe safe sex—

Oh God! Acting like a real father after thirty years of nothing?

That was the thing about Mark that really rattled him.

"What do you want, Mark?" If his voice came out gruff and angry, so be it. The simple high of having made love to the most beautiful woman he knew evaporated. "You can't just pop into my house."

Even as he said that, he heard a door close behind him. He turned, saw Marnie, fully dressed, walking up the hall. She said, "Rex is asleep." Then seeing Mark and Penny, she smiled. "Hello."

"Marnie, this is my biological father and his fiancée,

Penny Fillion." He motioned to tall, slender Mark with white hair now growing on his formerly bald head and short, sweet Penny, who had long yellow hair and bright blue eyes. "Mark, Penny, this is Rex's nanny, Marnie."

To her credit, Marnie casually reached out and shook hands with them both.

"I was just telling Mark that he shouldn't just barge in."

"I'm sorry," Mark said, turning to Marnie. "I apologize if you just got the baby to sleep, but I needed to talk to my son."

The easy way *my son* spilled from Mark's lips sent a crackle of annoyance up Danny's spine. He'd known this man was his father less than three months. Yet Mark behaved as if he'd been around for softball games and soccer practice.

Much kinder than Danny, Marnie smiled. "That's okay."

"Good. Glad I'm not interrupting anything."

Danny's last nerve frayed. "What do you want?"

"Well, I'd hoped to see Rex. But if your nanny put him to bed, I can wait until tomorrow." Mark turned to Marnie. "Isn't that baby adorable?" His brown eyes glowed. "And smart. And I'm not just saying that because he's my grandson. The kid is special. Wonderful." He motioned to Penny. "We're hoping Rex will be ring bearer at our wedding. We're getting married in September."

"In Paris," Penny said dreamily.

Marnie hugged Penny. "That's wonderful."

Mark's smile warmed. "We're here because we decided Danny should be our best man."

Danny's head about exploded. Trying to give his dad the benefit of the doubt, he told himself Mark had simply chosen his words poorly. But... Seriously? He'd *decided* Danny should be his best man? He didn't ask?

Mark glanced over at him. "Will you be our best man?"

Danny's anger deflated a bit. All right. He'd asked. "I

don't know, Mark. Everything's different now that I have custody of Rex."

Mark grinned. "That's the beauty of you and Rex both being in the wedding. With you as best man and Rex as ring bearer, you'll be in the same place at the same time."

Danny gaped at him. "He's *two*. I'm not sure he can walk down the aisle on his own yet. Unless you have a flower girl who's willing to hold his hand and drag him to the altar, Rex being ring bearer might not be a good idea."

"Okay. I get that."

Guilt flooded Danny. Mark might be a tornado, but when Danny least expected it, he'd pull back, clearly demonstrating he was trying to get along.

"I'm not saying no. We just have to see what he can do and what he can't."

"I get that too." Mark smiled ruefully. "We're happy to wait for your answer about being best man." Then he turned to Penny. "Ready for cheesecake at Junior's?"

She laughed and looped her arm through his. "That means we eat salads tomorrow."

They headed for the elevator. "You're no fun."

"I'm tons of fun. I simply won't let you eat a totally unhealthy diet."

Marnie wistfully watched them leave, and Danny remembered what they'd been doing before they'd been interrupted. They'd been in the middle of something life changing when Mark had simply walked in.

All the books he'd been reading on raising children said that a person couldn't reward inappropriate behavior. His dad might not be a child, but Danny couldn't let him go on thinking it was okay for him to interrupt him.

"Mark," he called right before the pair entered the elevator.

Mark turned. "Yeah."

"I'm serious about coming up to the penthouse without letting me know. You need to respect my time and call before dropping in. Otherwise, I'll have Jace change the locks and instruct the doorman that you're *never* to be let up."

Danny's words came out harsher than he'd intended, but Mark laughed. "You should come work for Hinton, then I could see you at the office."

And wouldn't that be peachy? Him, working for a man he wasn't even sure he liked. Having him pop into his office when he was knee-deep in reading a contract. "I love my current job. I don't want another."

Mark batted a hand. "You'll come around."

Marnie watched as Mark and Penny stepped in the plush car that would take them back to the lobby. But it wasn't empty. The guy from the park, the one who'd rescued Wiggles from the bush, stood along the back wall, dressed in a suit with a wire coming out of his ear.

Pretty Penny waved goodbye. Mark saluted. Danny sighed. The elevator doors closed, and the car headed down.

"Who was the guy in the elevator?"

Danny faced Marnie. "What guy?"

"Blue suit, white shirt? Receiver in his ear—" Everything came together in her brain. "Like a bodyguard."

"Oh, you mean Bruce! That *is* a bodyguard. He's one of about twenty guys who discreetly follow us around."

"He's the guy who pulled Wiggles from the bush."

Danny shrugged and headed for the kitchen. "It must have been his day to guard Rex."

Gobsmacked, she fell into one of the paisley chairs. "Guard Rex? There's someone been guarding Rex the whole time I've worked for you and you didn't tell me?"

He pulled the fixings for a sandwich out of the refrigerator. "Of course, I told you."

"No! You didn't! Dear God, Danny, I would have remembered something like that."

"Marnie, when I interviewed you, I said something about how my life was different. I know I mentioned bodyguards."

"You dropped it into the conversation. You didn't explain that I'd actually have one. You didn't tell me to look for one or how to deal with one."

"Because there's nothing for you to do. They are in the background, discreet. They're not supposed to be a part of your world. They're only watching."

Disbelief trembled through her. "For weeks I've had someone following me around?" It might not have been as bad as a boyfriend taking naked pictures, but it felt like an intrusion, a betrayal, that she hadn't been told.

"No. If you'd taken the limo to your mom's, you would have had someone following you around. Or shopping the other Saturday. The bodyguard is the driver. When you have the baby outside for a walk, *Rex* has someone following *him*." He took a breath. "My dad is a couple billion away from being a trillionaire. His grandson could easily be snatched for ransom."

She shook her head, confusion hardening her voice. "It still feels like a betrayal. If I look at this the right way, I could think you were spying on me."

He dropped his sandwich to the island. "How can you think that?"

"How do I know you're not getting a report every night?"

"Of what?"

"Of what I did that day."

"They never come into the penthouse unless I ask them to. Most are drivers. When they aren't taking Rex somewhere or following Rex on a walk, they sit in the car, watching the building. They know who comes and goes. Know the postmen."

She stared at him. "That sounds a hell of a lot like a prison."

He combed his fingers through his hair. It had taken him weeks to get accustomed to all this, to find his footing, to accept it. And with a few words, she threatened to undermine it.

"It's all in how you look at it. I do exactly as I want. They are the ones who scramble to keep up with me."

Her eyebrows rose.

"I'm not sure what your beef is. You should be glad Rex is being protected. You are his nanny. His caregiver."

She rose. "Yeah. I guess that's true. As Rex's *nanny* I don't have rights. I don't have a say in the big picture." She cleared her throat. "I don't know what got into me thinking I was more."

She turned and headed down the hall to her room, and Danny groaned. "Marnie…wait! I'm sorry. It's like we're arguing two different things."

She stopped. Faced him. "Oh, don't worry. I won't be like one of your families fighting over an estate. I won't dig in my heels and try to get something I don't deserve. I *know* I have no rights."

With that, she turned and walked back to her room. Part of Danny ached to follow her. But it was getting Rex that had made him see the necessity of high security and bodyguards—

Though bodyguards really weren't the issue. It was that he hadn't told her. Meeting her dad in the park, he realized she had trust issues and why. And she was justifiably angry tonight. He'd thought he'd told her about the bodyguards and assumed she'd know that included Rex. But he didn't want to argue and end up making concessions he shouldn't make because of what had happened in his bedroom.

He thought about making love. How passionate and happy they were. How all that perfection had disappeared because she had issues too. His trust issues might be fresher, but hers had had time to fester.

He sank to the sofa and put his forehead in his hands, refusing to panic. Tomorrow they'd both be in a better frame of mind. A little sleep and some distance would put it all into focus and they could talk like normal people.

But tonight, he wouldn't have the pleasure of holding her until they both fell asleep. They wouldn't make love again, slowly. He wouldn't get to leisurely explore her curves or sink into her soft skin.

He shook his head, forced his brain to stop. He'd thought he and Leni had talked out his suspicions, but the thing he hadn't mentioned was his feelings for Marnie. Too fast. Too deep. Too much.

Maybe it was good they were stepping back?

CHAPTER TWELVE

MARNIE HAD REX in the highchair when Danny came into the kitchen the next morning. Their gazes met and she quickly looked away. She knew he didn't understand why she'd gotten so angry the night before.

He walked to the coffeemaker. "Good morning."

"Good morning."

He busied himself with closing a pod in the holder and putting a cup under the drip. "If you go out today, a bodyguard will be watching Rex."

She shook her head. "I know. I'm sorry. I thought about it last night and realized a kid with a near trillionaire for a granddad would need security."

"But that really wasn't the issue, was it? It was trust. I thought you understood what I meant when I talked about bodyguards in your interview, and you didn't fully get it. So you felt like I'd kept something from you."

"I'm not sure what I felt."

"Marnie, your dad is a louse. Not to mention that you probably had some bad times when you were a kid, before your mom went to A.A."

She licked her lips.

"I get it."

"You shouldn't have to get it. I'm a professional. Our… personal stuff is making me act differently than I normally would."

"I get that too."

She dragged in a breath. Every second of what they'd done the day before played through her brain. The wonderful pleasure. The closeness she'd never had. Her realization that she couldn't have it. She couldn't drag him into her craziness. Not when he had his own things to deal with.

"Please, stop being so understanding. I'm a mess. Not someone a smart man has a relationship with."

His eyes softened. "Marnie…"

"Stop. Really. This is why I don't date a lot. I'm not crazy. I just had some things happen to me that make me so paranoid that I react oddly about normal things. Get suspicious over things I shouldn't."

He sniffed a laughed. "I just had this same conversation with my sister Leni yesterday while you were gone. She'd made cookies for Rex, and I ended up telling her that I had worried that you'd only wanted to work for me to get access to your dad."

Surprise poured through her. She didn't know why she'd thought he'd fallen into their relationship without thinking. The fact that he hadn't made her feel the tiniest bit better.

"No. I'm not exactly a fan of my dad. Seeing him threw me." She laughed unexpectedly. "Had I known I had a bodyguard I might have confronted him myself, sooner."

"Good. See? We're at the stage where we can laugh about the bodyguard."

She rolled her eyes. When she'd woken that morning, she'd been so sure they'd made a mistake. Now, calmer, she didn't know what to think.

"My point, though, is that I've got some unusual stuff in my life too. I love my parents with every fiber of my being, but the fact that they never told me I was adopted broke trust."

"I can see how that would happen."

"Then my biological dad storms into my life because he's found out I have a child."

"How'd he do that?"

"A private investigator apparently took note of new people in my life and occasionally checked on them. He found Rex, did some math and confronted Alisha."

"Wow."

"In one big swoop, I discovered I was adopted, had a

child and had a dad who'd literally been spying on me my whole life."

"Makes a bodyguard look insignificant."

"Yes, it does." He added cream to his coffee and walked it to the center island. "Still, that doesn't make what happened to you insignificant."

She sniffed. She loved that he was so understanding, but he didn't know her real pain. She hadn't told him her secret.

Her past came back in a wave of memories. She wanted to tell him. Longed to tell him. But the humiliation of it froze the words in her throat.

"Marnie?"

Her gaze jumped to his.

"Come on. We're both coming clean. Our circumstance is unique. If we really want to have something, we can't have secrets."

She squeezed her eyes shut. "We can't have something."

"Because of a little misstep about a bodyguard?"

She shook her head. "I was bullied at school. I erased my social media profiles, changed schools, took my mother's maiden name and in a weird kind of way, disappeared. If you search me, it's like the beginning part of my life didn't exist."

His mouth dropped open and he snapped it shut, thinking for a few seconds before he said, "You must have been bullied pretty badly."

"I was." She took a breath, surprised at the sense of a weight being lifted off her shoulders. "Actually, it's sort of a relief to tell you. Now I don't have to look like an idiot walking away from something good. Something I want."

His eyes darkened. "Why does being bullied at school make you feel you have to walk away?"

"I was bullied because my mother called the police on a jock who'd taken pictures of me after…we…" She closed her eyes, sucked in a breath. "My first years in high school, I was kind of a tease. The boys had this bet going about who'd get my virginity. I didn't know anything about it. I fell for the jock, and after we'd done it, he took pictures as proof. He showed them around to the boys at school, then offered them for sale."

"Oh my God." Danny looked so shocked that she almost felt sorry for him.

"When I found out, I raced home and told my mom. She called the police, who came to the school. They made him delete the pictures from his phone." She stopped, caught his gaze. "But I don't really know that they were destroyed. He could have them somewhere, like an old thumb drive." She sucked in a breath. "I can't date you. I shouldn't even be seen in public with you. Someday somebody's going to get interested or curious and a good reporter will do a thorough search and piece it all together. Then it'll come out— my association with someone so newsworthy will make it a headline instead of an article buried in the newspaper. And I'll go through it all again. The humiliation. The feeling that I'm worthless. Nothing. Just someone to be abused."

He held her gaze for a few minutes. His sympathy for her right there in his dark orbs. She hated it. All she'd ever wanted was to be normal and it seemed life couldn't let her have that.

He set his coffee on the island. "Let me look up the law, see if there's anything we can do... Times have changed, Marnie. And the statute might not have run out."

She put her hand on his forearm, her heart in her throat. The memories of the episode that had destroyed her life riffled through her brain. Humiliation rose and cut deep. Typical fears for her future raced through her.

"Oh my God. Don't you see? That's what I *don't* want. I don't want one of the richest men in the world going after him. The press would have a field day. And I'd be front and center in every newspaper in the country." She sucked in a breath. "I just want to be left alone. And maybe someday start a little company and live a quiet life."

* * *

She caught his gaze, her eyes filled with a misery that some-how held a glimmer of hope, and Danny's heart shattered. All these weeks he'd been feeling sorry for himself for dis-covering his parents weren't his biological parents and his actual dad was an eccentric billionaire. While Marnie had real troubles. Real problems. A real ache from her past that could explode into her present.

He wanted to kick himself for being so selfish. So self-absorbed.

He reached for her hand. "How does a person come back from something like that?" He wanted to say, "How does a *kid* come back from something like that," because she couldn't have been more than a teenager when it happened, but he thought better of it.

She shrugged. "My mom was pretty smart. My father owns one of the biggest real estate companies in New York State. He left her and ultimately had us evicted from our condo because only his name was on the deed. He has so many friends in high places that she got virtually no child support for me until she found a lawyer willing to dig really deep into his finances. She can hold her own."

"Smart woman."

She sniffed a laugh, pulled her hand from Danny's and rose. "Yeah. She learned some hard lessons." She headed back down the hall again. "I'll go pack and call Shirley. It's Sunday, but she can still have someone here in a couple of hours. I'll stay until the new nanny arrives."

His heart stopped. Something strong and angry rose in him. He might be part of a family that needed protecting, but he couldn't deny this woman a job she so clearly de-served. "You don't have to leave."

She stopped and returned to the kitchen. "Have you ever thought of what your future brother-in-law would do if he heard my story? You say your dad's biggest worry is of one of you being kidnapped... What about extortion? Roger hasn't been a blip on the radar of my life for a decade. But what if there's a picture of us in the paper when we're walking Wiggles? What if he comes out of the woodwork? If Jace finds out about my past, that's what he's going to consider. Extortion. If Roger comes after me, asking for money, your father's estate wouldn't have to do a thing. Once they fired me, they'd be free. I'm the one who'd be picking up those pieces."

She shook her head. "I'd sort of thought of all of this as I was packing to work here. On the train, I'd decided not to take the job. But then I got out of the elevator, and Rex was crying, milk was everywhere…and you were so nice." Tears filled her eyes. "I just wanted to help you."

"You are helping, Marnie. Your secret's stayed a secret for ten years. It may never come up again."

She wavered. He saw it in her eyes, and something compelled him to persuade her. Maybe he wanted to return everything life had taken away from her. Maybe he simply couldn't stand to see her so hurt, so empty, when she deserved the world.

"Stay." He reached out and squeezed her hand. "Rex loves you. I need you. You could leave now, but what if you stay and nothing happens?"

She worried her bottom lip.

"Stay."

She raised her eyes until their gazes caught. "If I stay, there can't be anything between us. Seeing the bodyguard, realizing just how rich and different you are, it hit me in a wave that anything between you and me would be a nightmare. You have to promise there will be nothing between us."

He thought of everything that had happened the day before. Thought of confronting her dad. Marnie kissing him. The suspicions that had rolled over him like a freight train. His chat with Leni and how in the end, no matter that he'd had suspicions, he hadn't been able to resist Marnie.

He said, "I promise," but something inside him told him it was a lie. He'd never felt the things he felt for her. Sometimes they drew him along before he had a chance to really think them through.

Still, after everything she'd endured in her very young life, he couldn't be the one to put her through anything more.

Especially not for something as trivial as a romance...

The thought died in his brain. What he felt for her, with her, wasn't trivial.

And maybe that was the problem.

For the next week, every day when Danny went to work, the temptation to search the name of the guy who had ruined Marnie's life nearly overwhelmed him, but he didn't even open his browser. He reminded himself that Marnie didn't want her secrets unburied. The irony of it rolled through him as he turned to look out the wall of glass behind his desk.

The man whose life had been undone by secrets had fallen for a woman whose secret could destroy her.

Which led him to realize that maybe the real issue wasn't that there were pictures potentially out there, but her fear of them.

He returned home that night tired, worn down, but the second he saw her, sitting in front of the highchair feeding Rex, his spirit rose.

"Hey! Hi, everybody." He walked from the elevator to the island, where he set his briefcase. He reached for the spoon to give Rex his next bite and Marnie melted back, away from him. He told himself it was to let him have special time with Rex and turned his attention to his son.

"So how was your day?"

Rex giggled and said, "Good."

"Today's bodyguard, Paul, took him for a nice, long walk."

His chest tightened. "Did you not want to go?"

"No." She busied herself at the sink. "I just thought I'd eliminate the middleman. Let Rex go out and the bodyguard have total control."

"You don't have to do that."

"I know."

"You don't want to go outside?"

She hesitated. "I'm fine inside."

Where no one could see her. Especially not with his child.

His little boy finished eating and Danny unstrapped him from the highchair and pulled him into his arms.

Marnie raced over. "Don't forget his juice. He didn't drink a lot today, so I'm encouraging fluids."

He turned to take the cup from her. Their hands brushed and a million sensations roared through him. Enough that his breath caught.

Their eyes met and she blinked, but not before he saw the shimmer of longing that she banked.

"I should probably go to my room. Let you have some playtime before he goes to bed."

His soul shattered into a million pieces. He wanted to hold her, to make it better. To take her to his bed and love her until nothing else mattered. But her walls were solid, and he understood why.

Still, they were on the top floor of an exclusive building. With a doorman and bodyguards and no one to see…

"Why not play with us?"

She smiled slightly. "Because he needs time alone with you. Not just with me."

"You love playing with us. Rex loves when we all play together—"

"True, but it's been a long day. I'll just go get a shower."

Disappointment gripped him. His pride bruised. He stepped back. "Yeah. Sure."

He left the kitchen and took Rex to the nursery, where he entertained his son so long that he got him ready for bed.

Marnie tiptoed in. "You didn't have to do that. I would have helped."

"It's okay." He'd fought off the injury to his pride with cold, hard facts. He knew he didn't understand anything she felt. He'd tried to imagine the horrible betrayal she'd gone through, but how could he get the full impact of something like that? He couldn't. He thought about what she'd said about extortion and what Jace would say if he knew, and he honestly didn't have any answers. Particularly when he remembered the revelation of Mark's secrets had ruined his life. Changed it so much he would never be the same again.

That's what outing Marnie's secrets would do to her.

No matter how much it hurt him, confused him, filled him with longing that morphed into anger sometimes, he thought of her.

He said, "Good night," and retreated to his room, walking to the window.

He could buy anything he saw. Fancy cars. Fancy meals. Fancy clothes. Even a whole damned building. But the one thing he really wanted he couldn't have.

Anger lit in his soul. A fight between the part of him that understood that she had to be careful and the part of him that wanted her to let go.

Test the waters. See if there really was a reason to be worried.

But it only took asking her to go for a walk with him and Rex on Saturday morning for him to see the genuine fear in her eyes.

It made him crazy and his heart ached for her, but he also missed her. He hated that he was the cause of her withdrawal, then he'd think about how happy they'd been. Even before their feelings for each other had pulled them into something she didn't want, they'd been happy.

He'd been even more contented than he'd been before he'd discovered he was the son of an eccentric billionaire. It was as if being with her made everything in his life unimportant, except her and Rex. Those were his priorities and his joy. And he knew he'd been changing her feelings, her life too.

They'd both fallen into something wonderful, and now it was gone.

Monday morning, his phone office phone buzzed, and he hit the button to answer. "Yes."

"It's Monty. Your sister Charlotte and her fiancé are on their way up."

Normally, a visit from Charlotte and Jace would have been a welcome announcement. He loved Charlotte. Quick-witted and smart, she always made him laugh. But she had Jace with her. And, after Marnie's story, anytime anyone mentioned Jace, Danny stiffened.

What if Jace had investigated her?

What if Jace had uncovered her secret?

Was he here to tell Danny he had to fire her? After all, the Hinton family didn't take chances. Jace axed anything that could potentially lead to trouble.

The elevator door opened. Charlotte strode out. Wearing dress slacks and a silky tank top and blazer, she looked like she'd been born to money. In his black suit and tie, Jace was clearly her match.

As Danny rose, she walked to the desk and planted a big kiss on his cheek.

"You're in a good mood."

Jace said, "We have news."

Danny's heart stumbled at the possibilities. But would Charlotte be so chipper if Jace had uncovered Marnie's secret and they were here to force him to fire her?

No. She wouldn't.

They couldn't know.

He motioned for them to take the seats in front of his desk.

"What's up?"

"I'm pregnant!" Charlotte said without preamble, clearly so happy she was ready to burst.

Jace shook his head. "She's nuts about it."

"Are you kidding? A little Jace!" Her face glowed. "What could be cuter than that?"

Danny laughed and rose, coming around the desk to shake Jace's hand and hug Charlotte. "Congratulations!"

"That's not the best news," Charlotte said. "We're getting married next week—in *Scotland*!"

"Next week?"

"In *Scotland!*"

He laughed. "Yeah. I got that part."

"Why aren't you jumping for joy?"

He shook his head. "Now that I'm a dad, there are logistics to think about."

Charlotte blinked. "You are bringing Rex, right?"

"Of course."

Jace gave him a funny look. "And you have a nanny."

"Right."

"See?" Charlotte pointed her finger at him. "That right there. That's what lawyers do. Make a big deal out of things that don't need to be a big deal."

His head tilted. "What?"

"Danny, when we thought Mark was dead, you made a production number out of everything that had to do with his estate. You did three DNA samples on me and Leni and sent them to three different labs. You kept Leni locked away in a hotel room and tried to stifle me, but I'm not so easily corralled."

Jace nodded. "It's true."

"And now you're making a production number out of going to Scotland when we have private jets and can stay anywhere we want. For once just relax. We're going to Scotland…for a *wedding*. Because Jace and I are going to have a *baby*." She glanced at Jace. "Our own little bundle of joy. Don't pick it apart. Don't ask yourself if you're being too happy. Just come with us to Scotland, dance a bit, drink as much as you want and let go."

He stared at her.

She chuckled and rose from her seat. "I know the concept of relaxing eludes you. But try it—for me." She patted her stomach. "For us." She glanced at Jace again. "For all of us. Maybe it's time we stopped second-guessing things about our new lives and were happy. Stop picking until we find the dark cloud that we can hide under."

Danny blinked, watching them leave. They'd said goodbye, but he'd been preoccupied with what Charlotte had said.

Did he really pick everything apart until he found the dark cloud?

And was that what Marnie was doing. So afraid of being hurt, she kept her dark cloud front and center?

Let it guide her life?

Let it *ruin* her life?

CHAPTER THIRTEEN

Marnie had just finished giving Rex a bath after feeding him spaghetti for dinner, when Danny arrived home. He dropped his briefcase on the center island and took Rex from her arms, then kissed his forehead.

"I ordered Chinese for dinner. It should be here any minute."

She backed away. Several days had gone by with her keeping her distance. She had finally adjusted, and she didn't want anything to happen to bring back the sadness that had threatened to suffocate her when they'd stopped talking.

For at least six of the first seven days, she'd ached the whole way to her bones. Not because she liked him, but because he liked her. Just as she was. They could talk about anything. They understood each other... And making love? She'd never experienced that kind of fire, tempered by the sweetness of the emotion they felt for each other.

Thinking about it now filled her chest with such longing her breath hitched and her voice stuttered when she said, "That's okay. I can make a sandwich."

"You can't live on sandwiches. Besides, we have something to talk about."

Her gaze leaped to his. "We do?"

Before she could jump to myriad conclusions that would have paralyzed her, he said, "Yes. Charlotte and Jace are getting married."

Relief made her weak, but happiness for Charlotte and Jace superseded that. "Well, of course, they are. They're engaged."

He slid Rex into his highchair, buckled him in. "No.

I don't mean they're getting married in general. I mean they're getting married next week. In Scotland."

Her mouth dropped open. "Oh my gosh! That's so cool."

"She's pregnant, thrilled and running on adrenaline."

She laughed, picturing already-energetic Charlotte running on adrenaline. "I'm so happy for her!"

The elevator pinged and the doorman stepped out carrying two bags. "Your food is here."

Danny took it from him. "Thanks."

He winked at Marnie and was gone.

Forgetting she was supposed to keep her distance, she said, "The doormen love you, even though I've never seen you tip even one of them."

Danny brought the Chinese to the center island. "Every month my father gives each of them a couple thousand dollars to take care of tips." He rooted through a bag and brought out a container with a metal handle. "I raised it another thousand."

A laugh bubbled up, even though she didn't want it to. But this was what always happened when they spent time together. They laughed. They talked. They connected.

She took two plates out of the cabinet and brought them to the table. They couldn't help it. They clicked. But maybe instead of fighting it, she should redirect it, temper it. They couldn't very well go on not talking. Discussing something as neutral as him tipping the doormen was a safe way to ease them into a normal nanny/employer relationship. Maybe if they could talk without getting personal, she'd get her bearings and the yearning in her heart would go away.

"You stacked the deck."

"Not really." He pulled out a container of egg rolls. "I just wanted to distinguish myself from my father. This isn't really my penthouse. I'm only using it." He paused, seemed to think about something, then said, "From what I know of the family holdings, no one actually owns anything. It's all owned by a Hinton shell company. We simply have access to anything we want. Anytime we want."

One of Marnie's eyebrows rose. To a person who'd rented her entire life, owning a home was a dream. The American Dream. She couldn't wrap her head around having access to everything and owning nothing—

"That's weird."

He caught her gaze, clearly surprised she'd continued the conversation. "It takes a while to get used to."

She filled a plate and walked around to the stools, sitting on the first one, determined to get them back to solid ground by talking about something so neutral it didn't matter.

"You can go anywhere you want, anytime you want?"

"We have access to planes. Big planes. Small planes. Jets." He finished filling his dish and sat beside her. "Mark owns two islands."

She gaped at him. "Are you kidding?"

"And something like twenty-six houses, including condos in Barcelona and Paris."

"He has a condo in Paris?"

"It's probably more like a penthouse." He took a breath. "There are boats, Jet Skis, houses in places like Aspen. There's a ranch in Canada and one in Texas. And he's mentioned buying one in Montana."

"Wow."

They fell silent as they both dug into their food, and Rex amused himself with a small bear. Her father and Roger Martin's father were paupers compared to Mark Hinton.

"The point is, we can use anything he owns anytime we want."

"What if somebody else is already there?"

"Leni's Nick employs three people who do nothing but track the properties, insure them, maintain them. They have a schedule."

She shook her head. "It boggles the mind."

"You should be me, Leni or Charlotte, three only children, raised in solidly middle-class families. Charlotte, I think, adjusted the best because she had a sense of humor about it. Leni adjusted because she's kind. Generous. Sweet. She wants the world to get along. She walks the walk."

Marnie glanced over at him. "And what about you?"

He shrugged. "Are you sure you want to hear this? We'd sort of made a pact not to be friends."

"Making a pact doesn't mean I stopped liking you, being interested in your life. I'm trying to get us to a normal place where we can talk as boss and employee and not be miserable all the time."

"I don't want you to be uncomfortable. But I haven't stopped liking you either. You were the balance that I needed. Someone to care for Rex who was easy to talk to."

And she'd loved that. Loved that he needed her as much as liked her. With him, she'd felt as if she'd found a place, a home. Not four walls and a bed, but a niche that warmed her, gave her a sense of self and independence she'd never had before. Particularly since he'd needed her and enjoyed her company as much as she'd needed a home, a space to be herself.

He shrugged. "Telling me I'm not allowed to like you is equivalent to telling the sun not to rise."

She knew exactly what he meant. Her feelings were too easy, too genuine. She'd had to retreat to her room every night for the past few days to keep them from overwhelming her. Even now, just talking to him, had warmed her heart.

"So, to get back to the point… We're going to Scotland with you as Rex's nanny."

Gobsmacked, she pressed her hand to her chest "*I'm* going to Scotland?"

"Rex is invited to every party and celebration, but he still has a bedtime, needs to be fed on a schedule…"

"*I'm going to Scotland?*"

He laughed. "Your enthusiasm reminds me of Charlotte's."

"I don't care if I'm seeing the country with Rex on my

hip, I still get to see Scotland!" She bounced from her stool.
"I need to buy a few things."

His head tilted. "Like what?"

"I'm not running around Scotland in yoga pants and
T-shirts. Actually, I'll need to Google the weather to make
sure we pack appropriately for Rex too." She tapped a finger
on her lips. "So many things to do." She glanced at Danny.
"What day is this wedding?"

"Next Friday. But we're leaving Tuesday."

"Okay. Four days is good. Plenty of time to get everything together."

With that, she raced back to her room, and Danny watched
her go. Her delight at going to Scotland filled him with a
pleasure that swelled his chest. It was almost as if her joy
gave him permission to be excited. Charlotte wanted everyone to stop trying to figure things out and just be happy?
Well, that's what Marnie did for him. She grounded him.
Maybe because they were raised in a similar way. But whatever the reason, he was so glad he could take her to Scotland, show her the country, enjoy the week of Charlotte's
wedding celebration.

He cleaned up their dishes and put away the leftover
food, talking to Rex. "What about you? Do you want to
see Scotland?"

He giggled.

But a reality he'd thought he understood hit him hard,
harder than it ever had. His two-year-old son was about to
become a world traveler. In a few years, he'd attend the finest private schools. Go to any university he wanted, anywhere in the world.

"You'll grow up so different than how I did."

Being wealthy had wiped out any financial worry Danny
might ever have, but what no one realized was it added an
even bigger worry.

How did one lead a normal life with access to anything

and everything they wanted? Harder still, how could he possibly raise Rex to be a normal kid when his life would be anything but normal?

The kitchen cleared, he took Rex back to the nursery, read him two stories and put him to bed. When he came out, Marnie was nowhere around. But that didn't surprise him. She had worked to level them off, re-create a normal employer/employee relationship. And now she'd retreat before they took it too far.

He respected that. But his big penthouse was empty and lonely once Rex was in bed. It hadn't been before Marnie came. It had been a normal home to him. Then she'd entered his world and made everything fun. He wouldn't lie to himself and pretend it wasn't her loss that made him lonely. He wanted her. *Her.*

But she hated all the trappings of his new life. And he accepted that.

He went to the family room to play pool, hoping to entice her out of her suite for another game.

But she stayed in her room. Probably looking up the weather in Scotland. He almost knocked on her door to join her to share the fun of the preliminary research before a trip across the Atlantic. But he knew her fears.

And having her eat with him, albeit in a limited way, was better than nothing… Wasn't it?

CHAPTER FOURTEEN

As they approached Scotland, Marnie pointed at the little islands in front of the mainland, then the mountains and green fields separated by trees.

"See, Rex? Isn't it beautiful?"

He said, "Yeth," but squirmed in her arms.

"Come on," Danny said, gesturing for Marnie to hand him over. "Let me get him in his car seat and buckled in. We'll be landing soon."

Marnie helped secure Rex, then took the seat beside him. "Just in case," she said, but Danny shook his head.

"He's fine."

"You never know."

He sat across from them in a little conversation grouping that was both convenient and cozy. The plane landed and she hopped up to get Rex out of his seat.

"I know you're excited, but the door won't open for five or ten minutes. There are checks the pilots have to make."

She said, "That's okay."

Danny took Rex from her. "Look over there," he said, leaning down beside the window, pointing beyond the private airstrip to the countryside. "Uncle Jace's family lives out there."

Rex grinned.

Marnie slid the strap of her duffel bag up her arm. "It was gorgeous from the air."

"Charlotte said it's the most beautiful place she's ever seen. She called it enchanted. I can't wait to see it."

She frowned. "You've never been to Scotland?"

He pointed at his chest. "Middle class, remember?"

"Yeah."

They spent the short trip to the MacDonald compound

pointing out scenery to Rex. He really didn't understand, but Danny enjoyed it. A sense of contentment blanketed him. He wasn't working. He wasn't at home with someone whose company he enjoyed, having her ignore him. They were in Scotland, about to celebrate his sister's wedding and Marnie was being herself.

"What are you smiling at?"

"I'm think I'm tapping into what Charlotte feels. I'm happy for her."

"I am too. She and Jace are a great couple and she obviously wants kids."

"That she does."

The limo pulled into the compound into a sea of limos.

"Wow. So, this is what it looks like when the rich get together." She shook her head. "This is going to be a logistical nightmare for Jace's people."

He wondered if she realized how well she knew his family, how she fit. "His upper echelon staff is top-notch. They'll have this area cleared in minutes."

They exited the limo, leaving luggage duties to the driver and the staff Jace had on hand. The huge stone house welcomed them. A carriage house beside it was both quaint and homey. Trees dotted the property. Enough to provide shade and beauty, but not so many that there was no lawn. Green grass flourished between gardens filled with colorful flowers.

The wide-plank front door actually had a crest and a little plaid.

"Look at that," Marnie said, reverently tracing the brass crest. "It must be fun to be Scottish."

Having been given instructions to enter without knocking, they walked into the high-ceilinged foyer. The sound of conversation and laughter filled the air.

Carrying Rex, Danny headed to the kitchen. "We're here!"

Charlotte pushed away from the counter and raced over

to give him and Marnie a hug before she kissed Rex's cheek and stole him from his father. "Here's my little love."

Mark was by her side in seconds. "You see him all the time. I've been in Paris buried in wedding details. I hold him first."

They sounded so much like a normal family that a wave of belonging washed over Danny. His adoptive parents rose from the table and walked over too. His mom hugged him. His dad shook his hand, then did a shoulder bump.

"Do we have to take a number to get to hold our own grandson?"

Danny laughed. "I didn't know you guys were coming."

"Of course, they were coming," Charlotte said, sounded affronted. "We have the biggest, weirdest family on the planet, but we are all family."

The truth of that trickled through him. No one wanted him to desert his adoptive parents. He was the one who was having trouble adjusting.

He thought of Marnie's plan for him to get a house in his hometown and he smiled.

Leni's adoptive dad toasted. "To family." A short, stocky construction worker, he'd gone through a surgery and was now project manager on Leni's vision to totally modernize and refurbish her town. Her pretty brunette mom sat beside him.

At the counter, Leni poured champagne as Nick passed it around. Nick's mom and dad were the first to take glasses from the tray.

"Nice to see you, Danny."

"Nice to see you too, Mr. Kourakis."

"Who's your friend?"

Danny winced. "Sorry. This is Marnie Olsen. She's Rex's nanny."

Marnie smiled sweetly, shyly. "Hi, everybody."

"It's lovely to have you here," Nick's mom said. The Kourakis family had had their share of troubles too. An automobile accident killed their younger son. Nick had been driving. His grief had been intense and protracted. There were times Danny had wondered if he'd ever be the same... Then Nick had met Leni.

He glanced at Marnie. Her pink cheeks. Her bright green eyes.

His chest tightened the way it always did when he looked at her in an unguarded moment. But Nick was suddenly in front of him with the tray of champagne. Charlotte made a joke about not being able to toast at her own wedding celebration because she couldn't drink alcohol while pregnant. Her mom, Penny, beamed with pride. Jace looked rough and rugged in jeans and a plaid shirt. Danny's adoptive parents, Terry and Gene Manelli, laughed with Jace's mom and dad.

And Danny got a picture of the rest of his life. Especially when his mom picked up a plate of hors d'oeuvres and offered one to Marnie, who happily popped the stuffed mushroom into her mouth.

Danny shook his head. "You're going to ruin your dinner. You're *all* going to ruin your dinner."

Someone threw a stuffed mushroom at him. "Who invited this party pooper?"

"I did." Charlotte walked over and slid her arm beneath Danny's. "We're all so crazy. We need a stuffed shirt to keep us in line."

Everybody laughed, but Danny frowned.

He wasn't a stuffed shirt.

Was he?

Was that part of what Charlotte had meant when she'd told him that he worked to find the dark cloud in everything?

Rex began to fuss, and Marnie edged her way through the crowd in the country kitchen to find him. The toddler fell into her arms, rubbing his eyes.

"Nap time. He snoozed on the plane, but his body knows that every day at two he goes to his crib. It might be evening here, but it's two at home." She smiled at Jace's mom. "Is there someone who can show us to the room he and Danny will be using?"

Jace came out of the crowd. "Actually, you're not in the house. You're in the suite above the carriage house. There's a room for you and one for Danny large enough to put the crib in. It's the biggest, quietest space we have to make sure Rex isn't disturbed." He winced. "Unfortunately, you have to share a bathroom."

Danny said, "That's fine."

But Marnie's heart skipped a beat. She'd never been in a house packed with so many people before, all of whom thought they were funny. In fairness, most were. Still, her overriding impression was of three unique families, blending into one big family with Mark Hinton as patriarch.

She tried to imagine her dad doing something like this, and when she couldn't she suddenly liked Mark Hinton. What he'd done to bring his family together, including adoptive parents and in-laws was remarkable.

Jace's dad walked to the kitchen door with her, having said he'd show her to the carriage house, but Danny unexpectedly joined them.

"I'm fine. I can get Rex to sleep. You go. Enjoy your family."

He gave her a strange look. Something she hadn't ever seen from him. She thought that he might not want to be with his family, but as they walked out the door he said, "I'll be back in ten minutes."

The enthusiasm in his voice told her he meant it.

Jace's dad, a big lumberjack of a guy, happily chatted as they walked along a stone path to the carriage house. Inside the spotless garage that housed two cars, one sensible sedan and another that looked like a race car, he led them up a set of steps and into a sitting room with a small kitchenette in the back.

"It's lovely," Marnie said, knowing from the expression on his face that he awaited approval.

An open door on the right led to a bedroom, as did an open door on the left. Their luggage had been neatly piled in the sitting room at the center of it all.

"Bathroom's back there." Jace's dad pointed to a closed door, equidistant from each of the bedrooms. "If you need anything, just tell me or my wife. We have anything you might have forgotten." He pointed at the bedroom to the right. "Crib's in that room."

His laugh was big and jolly as they thanked him, and he headed back to the party in the main house.

She glanced around. "This place is fabulous."

Danny frowned as he took off his suit coat, then his tie. "The suite?"

"No. The whole place. I'll bet they own acres and acres of that green grass out there."

"No, doubt," Danny agreed. "Here." He reached for Rex. "Let me get him settled."

For once she didn't argue. She grabbed her luggage and headed for the bedroom on the left. Tossing her biggest case on the bed, she glanced at the pretty blue bedspread and the lace curtains. Old-fashioned, but so comfortable and cozy, like stepping back in time.

She wondered what it would be like to have a family history. To have customs and traditions—and a crest and plaid. But before she could think it through, Danny appeared at her door.

"Everything okay?"

"Everything's great."

He strolled into the bedroom. "Rex went out before his head hit the blanket."

"Travel makes some kids antsy and others sleepy." She slipped to the right, away from him, because it seemed so natural, so normal that he'd be in her room. And it shouldn't.

"Rex must be one of the kids that travel makes sleepy."

She nodded. "You go on back to your family. I'll sit here while he sleeps. That way I'll be only a few feet away if he stirs."

He nodded and headed for the sitting room door to leave, but as his hand reached the knob, he stopped, looked over at her.

"What?"

"I don't know. Everything just feels different here."

"Charlotte said it's enchanted."

He sniffed a laugh. "Yeah, she always says that as if there are fairies who grant wishes."

"So maybe you should wish not to be the family stuffed shirt? Maybe a passing fairy will hear, snatch your wish from the air and grant it?"

He laughed. "Really? You think I'm a stuffed shirt too?"

"I think you are practical and pragmatic, and I think the world needs that."

He shook his head. "Practical and pragmatic?"

"You think things through. You don't jump on band-wagons."

He groaned. "I *am* a stuffed shirt."

She laughed. "Go have fun with your family."

"I'll go but when I get there, I'm telling jokes and break-ing out the good whiskey. I'm *not* a stuffed shirt."

Danny left the suite, bounded down the stairs and outside. Clean air filled his lungs, along with that sense that Char-lotte talked about. He wouldn't call it magic. He would call it serenity.

He entered the kitchen to the sounds of laughter. He didn't have to ask about the good whiskey; apparently Jace's dad liked that a lot better than champagne. Some of the guests had drifted outside to enjoy the pleasantly warm evening. Some had retired to their rooms. Toddlers weren't the only ones who got tired from a long flight.

He took two fingers of whiskey and splintered off from

the small bundle of people still chatting in the kitchen. He found a chair and settled in to enjoy the scent of the pond, the trees, the gardens all around.

"Mind if I sit?"

He glanced up at Mark. He wasn't Danny's favorite person in the world, but he refused to be considered the wet blanket anymore. If he had to talk to Mark, so be it. "No. Sure." He motioned to the other chair. "Sit."

"Penny's been riding my back about giving you a penthouse to live in, then keeping the elevator codes and showing up when I want to."

"She's not wrong."

He winced. "So, I'm apologizing and also promising it will never happen again."

Mark's unexpected apology and promise surprised Danny so much, he looked over again. "Thank you."

Mark shifted on his chair. "Okay. Now to the real reason I'm out here." He took a breath. "You haven't adjusted."

"Adjusted?"

"To being my son. To being wealthy. To any of it."

"I'm working on it." He chuckled. "I didn't get up and walk away when you sat down."

"Yeah, that's progress. But the girls adjusted so much faster. Within six weeks, Leni found a purpose. It took Charlotte more like eight, but once she realized she could be, have or do anything she wanted, she decided to use her construction expertise to help Leni and her free time to love Jace. It was simple for them both."

"You didn't humiliate Charlotte and Leni by making them attorney for your estate then faking your death."

"You're still mad about that? Because I didn't fake my death."

"Yeah. Yeah," Danny said, rolling his eyes.

"I didn't."

"Either way, you did make me attorney for your estate

when I'm your *son*. Do you have any idea what an idiot that made me look like?"

"I do now. But back when I was setting it all up, I just saw it as a good way for you to get an understanding of my…*our*…holdings. To see everything with neutral eyes."

Danny sighed. "Whatever."

"Look, hiding you guys could be considered a mistake by some people but not by me. I had enemies and I had money. You were all targets."

Danny peered over. "And we're not now?"

"I've retired. Made friends with my enemies, and I have the best protection under the sun in Jace's group. It's why I couldn't leave Rex out there unprotected. When I learned about him, I knew other people could too. I had to get him under the umbrella. That was reason enough for me to come clean about everything."

"By faking your death."

"You've got to let that go, Sergeant Pepper."

"Sergeant Pepper?"

"Yeah, the guy with the Lonely Hearts Club Band."

Danny snorted.

"You're moping about something."

"Haven't you heard? I'm pragmatic and practical."

Mark laughed. "All I heard was stuffed shirt. And that was a joke. Who called you pragmatic?"

"Marnie. She was trying to make me feel better about the stuffed shirt teasing. She made me feel worse."

"Ah."

"What's that supposed to mean?"

Mark rose from his chair. "The biggest mistake of my life wasn't not being a part of the lives of my children. It was leaving the love of my life. I thought about Penny every day. Sometimes I out-and-out mourned the loss of what we could have had." He swirled the whiskey in his glass, then peered down at Danny. "Don't do that. Don't walk away from the woman you want. Do whatever it takes to keep her."

He strolled away without giving Danny a chance to argue, so all his wonderful retorts died on his lips.

With a growl of annoyance that Mark just couldn't seem to stop butting into his business, he started to lift himself out of his chair, but his parents came over. His mom sat. His dad looked around as if he'd finally found himself in heaven.

As much as he wanted to dislike Mark Hinton, seeing the happiness on his parents' faces, he couldn't.

Mark really was giving all of them things they never could have earned on their own. He was unselfish. He was easygoing. And to make as much money as he had, Mark also had to be smart.

Oh, who was he kidding? Everybody knew Mark Hinton was brilliant. Probably one of the smartest men of his generation.

And he'd told Danny to do whatever it would take to keep the woman he loved.

The thought whispered through his brain.

Tiptoed into his soul.

Did he love her?

If he did, did he want to be like Mark, alone and pining for the woman he loved, but couldn't have because his wealth separated them?

CHAPTER FIFTEEN

JACE AND CHARLOTTE's outdoor wedding surpassed Marnie's expectations. The air shimmered with the enchantment Charlotte believed hung over the MacDonald compound. A beautiful bride in a long-sleeved lace gown that slid along her tall, slim frame, she gazed lovingly at her groom, who wore a kilt. Marnie could have sworn she swooned.

Then she looked from Jace to his brother Oliver, the best man, and to Danny, also a member of the wedding party.

No one was more handsome than Danny Manelli in a tux. With his hair neat and tidy, his bow tie tight and his white shirt crisp beneath his black suit coat, he was perfection.

His eyes moved and suddenly his gaze snagged hers. She sat on one of the white folding chairs facing the flower-covered arch where Jace and Charlotte said their vows, holding Rex. Wearing a little navy blue suit, he looked cute as a bug. And Marnie had to say she didn't look so bad herself in a simple pink dress.

Her head tilted. Was that why Danny kept staring at her? Why he couldn't seem to break eye contact as his sister promised to love and cherish her new husband? Because she looked nice? Because she was mothering his child…

Or was there something more in that look?

A shiver wove through her, reminding her of the connection she'd always felt to him. It was almost as if he was trying to tell her something.

The ceremony ended. Congratulations and toasts to the bride and groom went on for an hour, as everyone at the small, private wedding felt entitled to say their piece.

Filet mignon and salmon cooked to perfection were served under a huge white tent. There were more toasts, dancing and cake.

Close to eight, Rex's bedtime, he fussed. It amazed Marnie how quickly he'd adjusted to the time change. He'd slept through the night and got up at six as he always did, but on Scottish time. Then he napped at two that afternoon and now he was tired at his regular bedtime. Surprised, but not one to go looking for trouble, she searched the crowd for Danny. Without making a ripple in the celebration, she motioned to him that she was taking the baby to their suite to check his diaper and give him a cookie.

He nodded.

In the room, she changed him into pajamas, found a cookie—or rather a biscuit, as Jace's mom called them—in the stash in the diaper bag and led him to the sitting room. He ate his cookie, laughed and played a bit, but she could see he was worn out. Two minutes after she put him in the crib, he was asleep.

Tired herself, she glanced at the TV in the sitting room but headed to her bedroom to get her pajamas and toiletries. Her hair piled on top of her head in a loose bun, she soaked in the tub for at least twenty minutes.

Feeling refreshed, she dressed in her pajamas, put her wet towel in the hamper, gathered her things and stepped into the main room, just as the suite door opened and Danny walked inside.

Seeing her, he immediately spun around. "I'm sorry."

She laughed. "Danny, I'm in very covering pajamas. You probably saw scantier clothes on the street last week."

"I know, but it's you."

Her heart skipped a beat. He'd said it as if she were special, unique. Her feelings for him rose and tightened her chest.

"I respect you."

She swallowed hard, as new emotions swamped her. He'd said that before, but tonight she realized that though she'd never voiced it, she'd been angling for respect since the day her dad left, when she couldn't abandon her unconscious mom, and her dad had called her a traitor.

"Thank you." His words filled her with something that made her stand taller, even as her nerves settled. "But it's fine. Really. I was planning on watching some television." She headed for her room. "So, give me a minute to dress." She stopped suddenly and squeezed her eyes shut. He hadn't returned looking for her. Stupid that she would think that.

She turned to see he was already heading for Rex's room. "You're here to check on Rex."

"Yes…and no." He peered over his shoulder. "I'm really tired. I could use an hour of television to unwind and then about fourteen hours of sleep."

She understood what he meant. His family was wonderful. But they were also noisy and sometimes overwhelming. She couldn't ship him out there again just because she wanted to see what was on Scottish television.

"I don't mind having company while I watch TV."

He turned a little more. "I'd be very happy for the company."

Her lips lifted slightly. "Okay. You check on Rex. I'll put on yoga pants and a T-shirt and we'll be set."

He nodded and she went to her bedroom and changed out of her pajamas and into her usual nanny attire of yoga pants and a T-shirt. She looked at her hair and winced. If she fixed it, it might look like she'd done it for him.

If she didn't, it remained a mess.

So maybe better a mess than sending the wrong message? She liked him. She'd always liked him. But there could be nothing between them.

She left her hair in the sloppy bun and joined him in the sitting room.

In the back, making popcorn, his tux exchanged for a T-shirt and sweats, he turned and smiled. "What do you think we'll find on TV?"

She shrugged and plopped on the sofa. "Hard to say. Are you sure you don't want to be at the reception?"

"It's winding down. I told my parents I needed to check on Rex, and I got a kiss on the cheek and an 'I'll see you in the morning,' then they went back to dancing."

He brought the popcorn to the sofa and she sighed. "Dancing. That looked like so much fun."

He gaped at her. "You should have said something! We could have danced."

She scrunched her face. "Not really."

"Marnie, there's literally no one here who cares who I am. Who *you* are. I think we should enjoy that."

She took a handful of popcorn, glancing around. The room was silent save for the muffled sounds of music and laughter coming from the MacDonald's backyard. He was correct. There was no one here but family.

"It's a wonder there's been no press here."

"Part of it was Jace's maneuvering. The other part though is that people in Scotland have known this family for generations. They don't think of them as wealthy. They think of them as neighbors."

She listened to the sound of the music from the wedding reception, interspersed with bursts of laughter. "You couldn't do this in New York City."

"Precisely. Which is why I think we should go somewhere tomorrow."

"Take Rex to see the countryside?"

"No. Take *you* to see a bit of the country. We won't have all day or anything, but I'm sure I can talk my parents into watching Rex for a few hours." He caught her gaze. "Enough time maybe for lunch in the village a few miles down the road."

She said nothing.

"Come on. No one will care, and I want so badly to do this." He took her hand. "Every time I look at you, there's this thing that builds in my chest. A longing. I would show you the world, if I could. But I can't. And I respect your wishes on that. But this is one time we can skirt the rules, be ourselves, and I want it."

Looking at their joined hands, feelings swamped Marnie. Memories of going to the art gallery, their first kiss, his standing up for her to her dad, her thank-you kiss and making love. Now they were sitting here like two normal people and the emotion running through her was hotter, deeper, than the things she felt in the high points of their relationship. The connection that wove them together filled her with such yearning her heart almost burst.

She wanted it too.

"Only if your parents don't mind watching Rex."

He slid his arm along her shoulder and nestled her against him as he leaned back on the sofa. "There are four or five couples who'd be happy to keep him."

She leaned into him, taking a handful of popcorn and reveling in the simplicity of the moment. "I suppose."

"So, don't overthink it."

"I won't."

Suddenly, in the quiet, secluded room, the past didn't matter. She sank deeper against him, breathed in his scent. Refusing to let her brain race back to the memories that always haunted her, she closed her eyes and simply enjoyed being with him.

Everything felt different in the car on the way into town. Last night, after a chaste kiss good-night, Danny had gone to his room, knowing this was what he wanted. A little time with her. Not necessarily to persuade her that they could have something together, but if the opportunity came up, he wasn't going to let it pass unused.

He'd thrown on jeans and a T-shirt with tennis shoes, working to look as completely unlike a wealthy person as he could. After breakfast with the family, he'd also gotten permission to use the sedate sedan in the carriage house.

As he and Marnie zipped along the country road, looking at rolling hills with mountain backdrops, where he was and what he was doing finally hit him.

It might not have been a normal date, but it was a date.

Marnie also wore jeans, but she'd topped hers with a pretty pink shirt that brought out the red in her hair, which she'd left down. Thick tresses flowed around her shoulders and to her back.

Delicious feelings tumbled through him. Simple longings that mixed heart and soul and made him tongue-tied, unsure. If he could, he'd catch her hand and keep her with him forever. But she had doubts—about him, his life. About her past. Most of the time, he didn't even know how to address those, let alone assure her that none of it mattered. Because in Manhattan it did. He wouldn't lie to her and pretend it didn't.

Still, he had a few glorious hours. To be himself and let her be herself. Simple American tourists.

Who liked each other—

"You looked really nice yesterday in that pink dress."

"I better. I paid enough for it that I'll be wearing it to the next six weddings I go to."

He laughed. Naturally. Easily. Not just because he'd been middle-class enough to understand stretching a dollar, but because he could. No one knew him here. No one knew her. That's how he'd enticed her into spending a day with him.

They could literally do anything they wanted.

"I think we should look at today as an adventure."

She laughed. "Seriously? Unless you've found a hoard of Vikings to fight, I think it's going to be a normal morning."

"Hey, I'm trying to make this work." As soon as the words were out of his mouth, he knew he'd made a poor choice.

Her gaze shot to his. "I don't want you to have to *make* it work."

"Actually, that's our problem. We've never had to make

it work. When we're together, alone, not thinking about who I am or who you are, it does work. That's been our trouble from the start. It worked so well we forgot about boundaries."

She fought not to close her eyes and remember the night they'd made love. Because he was correct. Everything they did felt right. Every time she looked at him, she had the sense that he was hers. Hers to love. Hers to laugh with. Hers.

But that was a pipe dream. Her subconscious longing for something it couldn't have. It made her curse fate at the same time she questioned her sanity. She knew better than to fall for someone so far out of her league—

"You're overthinking."

She ran her hands down her arms, warding off the cold that suddenly filled her. "I guess I was."

"If we do that, we won't enjoy the day and I want to enjoy the day. To be myself again if only for four hours."

His words hit her in the heart. All these weeks of worrying about herself, she'd forgotten what Mark had stolen from Danny. A normal life. A chance to climb the ladder of success to earn and deserve his achievements. The possibility of meeting someone on a street or in a coffee shop, falling in love without worry of motives or their past.

She sucked in a breath. She, of all people, should want him to have this little space of time to be himself, not Mark Hinton's son, not one of the Hinton heirs. "You're right. Let's enjoy the day."

They stepped out of the car into a space so quaint and wonderful it seemed they'd walked into a fairy tale. A small, old village, it still boasted cobblestone streets that looked to be as old as time. Shops could have been gingerbread cookies, iced with colors that made roofs, doors and windows with curtains.

"Wow! It's so beautiful."

Danny sucked in some air. "And quiet."

He wanted the quiet. She knew he did. But he needed more. In the same way that she longed for the ability to make a real human connection, to love someone without fear, he needed some time without worry. No stress. Only simple happiness.

She could give him that. Easily. As naturally as breathing.

The idea simultaneously thrilled and scared her. If she let her guard down, she knew what would happen—

But wasn't that what she wanted too?

The first time they'd made love had been rushed by overwhelming need. What would it be like if they took these few hours of privacy and did what they really wanted to do?

Bliss.

Memories.

No. More of a touchstone for her. The kind of memory she could point to and say *that's* what it's like when I'm free. When no one cares. Not even me.

The thought of having that memory wove through her. Not a temptation, but a necessity. Something to hold on to.

She definitely wanted this.

Sliding her arm beneath his, she cuddled close, hoping to warm his blood, to make him feel the need that tiptoed inside him and sent nudges to touch her, to kiss her, to just follow through on whatever he wanted.

"Let's go shopping."

Expecting him to say something romantic, she blinked, then peered at him. "What?"

"If nothing else, let's get souvenirs."

Her eyes narrowed. That was about as far from the afternoon she thought they both wanted as he could get. "You mean like get T-shirts?" She frowned. "My mom might want one."

He nodded. "I think my assistant would too."

She said, "Okay," and Danny let her lead them down

the street. They eased in and out of the local shops. First buying T-shirts, then Marnie buying crazy things. Knitted scarves. Rain boots. Things that made him laugh. But when they came to a shop dedicated to menswear and she zeroed in on the kilts, she decided she'd found the way to give him a more direct clue that everything had changed.

CHAPTER SIXTEEN

Danny frowned as she pointed at the row of kilts. "You should have worn one yesterday. Jace and his brother did."

"I'm not Scottish."

She ignored him, sliding kilts along the rack until she found one that resembled the plaid of Jace's family. "You should try it on."

"Are you kidding?"

"You'd need a white shirt…" She rummaged some more. "And this sash."

He gaped at her. "No!"

Her voice dipped and she leaned in closer. "I think you'd look incredibly sexy."

His heart fell to his stomach. She'd never flirted with him before, always been too careful. "If you don't stop that, I'm going to kiss you right here."

Her eyes lit with mischief. "Well, for once, you're allowed, correct?"

She was right. No one noticed them. No one knew or cared who they were.

He moved in swiftly, didn't give himself time to think, just let his lips meet hers, linger sweetly for a second, then go in for what he really wanted. The desire. The heat. The arousal that raced through his blood and set his nerve endings on fire.

Remembering they were in public, he pulled back, bumped his forehead to hers with a laugh. "Why'd you do that?"

"To push us to where we really wanted to be. We have one day." She shook her head. "No. We have a couple of hours. I don't want to waste them being polite. I just want a taste of what it would be like if we didn't have to care."

His inner self suggested he take her to a hotel, to ravage her, to give them both what they really wanted. But there were no hotels in the small town. Instead, they made the twenty-minute drive back to the carriage house and pulled inside the garage.

"What are we doing?"

"Jace and Charlotte left for their honeymoon today. All the parents went with them to see them off. My parents told me about it when they agreed to watch Rex. They said they needed the car seat so he could go too."

She licked her lips. "We're staying here?"

He opened his car door, stepped out. "Yes," he said as she got out of her side before he could open her door for her. "But there's a lock on the suite door and one on each of our bedrooms."

She finally got it. "Ah…"

They made short order of the steps, and once inside the cozy suite he locked the door. Before she could say anything, he pulled her to him and kissed her, long and deep, looking inside himself for that place of slow-build passion. There'd be no rushing this time.

He let his hands roam her back, ease her closer to him. He knew they didn't have all day, but they had hours. Hours to themselves. Something they'd never had. And he intended to enjoy it.

He slipped her pretty pink shirt over her head and tossed it to the sofa. She reached for his shirt, but he was faster.

She smiled. "I thought we had a few hours?"

He winced. "We do."

"So, what do you say we put on some nice music, maybe go to your room and talk—"

He hauled her to him and kissed her greedily. She laughed, but she was with him all the way. He walked backward to his room, kicked the door closed, locked it and fell with her to the bed.

He tried to slow them down twice, but there always

seemed to be a ticking clock. Still, when she was warm and naked beneath him, everything decelerated to a crawl and he let himself savor. He took in her face, her sparkling eyes, the curve of her mouth and let them imprint themselves on his brain.

The fact that he felt the need to create a memory sent a shaft of sadness through him. He forced it aside, running his hands down her torso, luxuriating in the feel of her hands on him.

The sense of time standing still filled him. The feeling of eternity. The essence of forever. He relished it. Let it waft through him like a warm summer breeze before the need rose swift and sharp and they tumbled on the bed, each fighting for supremacy. He won, pinned her hands to the pillow and joined them. But the attitude of forever trembled through him again. For as much as he liked her sweetness, he also loved her sense of whimsy, balanced by her seriousness about Rex, about schedules, about them. She was small and soft and, oh, so warm. Sensual. Subtly daring. Fun. Interesting.

Longing filled him at the same time that they reached the peak. The word *mine* roared through him, along with a contentment so fierce he believed he could reach out and touch it. He could be anyone with her. A sharp lawyer. A single dad. Even a crazy billionaire's son. Being with her made him realize Mark, his job, even how he and his adoptive parents mended their relationship were all secondary to having her in his life.

He thought all those thoughts and feelings would disappear when they were cuddled together, drowsy, ready for a nap even though they'd probably have to get up soon and dress for when Rex returned.

But none of it disappeared. The feeling of completion, of accepting who he was and wanting her to be part of it wouldn't go away.

He told himself it was wrong.

He told himself he was going to be disappointed.

But he couldn't stop the happiness or the surety that he could make this work. Then he kissed her, and she laughed and the sense that this would last forever overwhelmed him to the point that he forgot how quickly time was passing and that his parents would be home with his son.

He took them to the place of passion and need quickly, easily and completely. They both rode the wave, longer this time, so that the end was deep and fierce. Stronger than any he'd ever felt. Sending the word *mine* through him again, and again, and again.

He barely had enough time to get his breathing under control when his phone rang. He gave himself a second to simmer down, closing his eyes, before the phone rang again.

Rolling to the side, he picked up the phone, saw it was his dad and answered. "Everything okay?"

"Yeah. You know, since Rex is fine, the group decided we'd get lunch."

"The group?"

"Everybody just piled into a couple of limos to see Jace and Charlotte off at the airport. The MacDonalds mentioned a place up the road, a B and B that serves lunch and dinner and we thought we'd all go there."

"Rex will be tired at two."

"We should be back by three."

Danny smiled at Marnie. "Good enough."

He disconnected the call, glanced at the clock and rolled over to kiss Marnie. "We have two hours."

She laughed. "Want to go back to town and get lunch?"

"Maybe." He flopped down on his pillow, enjoying the feeling of her skin skimming his as she settled beside him. "But first I just want to do nothing for a few minutes."

She levered herself on her elbow, so she could look into his eyes. Her hair fell across her shoulder. Her beauty took his breath away. The ease of their connection, the easy contentment, always amazed him.

"When was the last time you took a vacation?"

He snorted. "You sound like Mark."

She ran her hand along his chest, sending soothing chills down his spine. "Which isn't such a bad thing from my point of view."

He gaped at her. "Really?"

"Yeah. I mean, I definitely get that he's out there. And I absolutely understand how what he did embarrassed you. But I see him pulling your family together."

His eyebrows rose.

"I'm serious. He's included everyone. He doesn't act like he's supreme, almighty biological dad who doesn't want the adoptive parents around. He wants everyone around. He wants everyone to be whole and happy."

He remembered the joy on his parents' faces the day before. "My mom and dad would have never visited Scotland had it not been for Mark."

"And I'll bet they will be going to Paris next month for the wedding."

"They are."

"Sometimes when I look at your family, I see a puzzle. There are five hundred scattered pieces and you guys are the ones who have to figure out where they fit. Mark brought you all together. He's giving you every opportunity to simply enjoy it. But you guys are the ones who have to make the picture."

He thought about that for a second. It was exactly what Mark had done. And it was exactly what he, Charlotte and Leni had to do. Make the picture.

A sense of wonder tiptoed through him. Not just the rightness, but the perfection of Marnie. How she understood him. He'd never met anyone he wanted as much. Never had this feeling of a partnership before.

He caught Marnie's shoulder and brought her down for a kiss. "When did you get so smart?"

She laughed. "I have always been smart. I just don't get the opportunity to use my smarts very often."

Because of her past. Because she hid. She was an excellent nanny, but she could be so much more. She knew it...

And it hurt her.

For the first time, he saw that in her eyes.

And he cursed it. Without Mark's money, he wouldn't have thought twice about dating her. No one would have cared about her past. But now they had to. He wouldn't care if a reporter did a huge write-up about it, but she did, and he would swim the deepest sea, fight the biggest battles to protect her.

Even if it meant staying away, when he wanted everything.

The thought filled him with indescribable loss. Emptiness so deep, his soul blackened as if lost in a storm.

But there was no shelter. For the second time in his life, he had no idea what to do. He'd been gobsmacked when he'd discovered Mark Hinton was his dad, and he'd floundered. Now he wanted Marnie but there was no open door. No way to make it work.

And the loss felt like one from which he'd never recover.

The truth of the thought brought him up short. Forced a decision he never thought he'd make. He couldn't let this be a loss.

He'd fight for this.

They flew home the next day, and Marnie had never been so depressed to see Manhattan. They settled Rex in the limo that awaited them at the private airstrip, silently drove to Danny's building and got out as quiet as two church mice.

Danny carried Rex to the elevator. Marnie followed behind, her head down, her thoughts going a million miles a second. What had felt like home when they left now felt cold and empty. Scotland had been full of people and fun.

Green grass. Big blue sky. Wide-open spaces with no media. People she could talk to without worry. Fun dinners.

And love. Danny hadn't said the words, but she'd felt it in his touch. They'd slept together in her bed that night. Not for sex, though that had happened naturally, but to be close. Gloriously close. Connected. Secure.

To return to a building with a doorman and bodyguards and millions of people with a phone was a potential disaster. No matter how beautiful the penthouse, it was a prison.

The driver carried up their luggage. Instructing him to leave the luggage by the elevator with a wave of her hand, Marnie told him they would take care of separating it and getting it to the appropriate rooms.

When he was gone, Danny laughed. "Do you see how easily you just gave orders to your bodyguard?"

She walked over and into his waiting arms. "I thought he was Rex's bodyguard?"

"Doesn't matter whose bodyguard he is. You just gave him orders." He dropped a quick kiss on her lips. "But in a way that's good because I wasn't sure you'd be happy if I told him to take your bags to my room too."

She pulled back. "Seriously?"

"You don't want to sleep with me?"

She wanted to *everything* with him. She simply wasn't sure how long it would last. And every time she thought that, her chest hollowed out. Her breaths hurt. Still, that was a worry for another day, wasn't it?

She peeked up, met his eyes and smiled. "You know I do."

He kissed her and she returned his kiss, but the sound of Rex pounding on his highchair tray reverberated through the open space. They broke apart and she walked into the kitchen.

"Did Daddy forget to give you juice?"

Danny walked in behind her, slid his arms around her waist and pulled her back against him. "You know with the time difference he's going to be ready for bed soon and sleep all day."

She turned in his arms. "I'll handle it. I'll let him sleep long enough this morning that he's got some energy, then give him his usual nap this afternoon and, voilà, he'll be ready for bed at eight."

He laughed and he kissed her. "You're such an optimist."

"No. I'm just really good at what I do."

"Okay, then I'm going to change and head to the office."

She nodded. "We'll be fine."

Danny's smile said he knew that. Because they had bodyguards and security protocols in place.

And maybe she was being ridiculous?

They could be anyone they wanted behind the closed doors of his penthouse, and that's what she should focus on. That happiness. That joy. And not worry about the future.

CHAPTER SEVENTEEN

DANNY WAITED TWO weeks for Jace to return from his honeymoon with Charlotte. He walked into the spare, but adequate workspace Jace maintained as a home base for his staff and was immediately ushered back to Jace's private office. Decorated with modern furniture in coral, aqua and beige, the place was almost beachy. Until Danny sat on one of the chairs.

"These are the most uncomfortable seats in the world."

Jace laughed. "I know. It keeps visitors' stays to a minimum." He leaned back in his obviously comfortable desk chair. "What can I do for you? You said it was urgent. Something happen with Rex?"

"I'd like you to investigate Marnie."

He came to attention. "Why? What did she do?"

"It's not something she did. It's what she told me."

"Something from her past?"

"Yes."

"High school?"

"Yes."

Jace leaned back again. "We already know."

"You do?"

"Of course, we do. You don't think I'm going to let someone near Mark's grandson without knowing every little detail of her life, do you?"

He squeezed his eyes shut. "I was hoping you wouldn't be able to find that."

"It was an easy leap, Danny. Her name seems to appear out of nowhere when she turns sixteen and enrolls in high school. But she had records from another high school. We quickly realized she'd begun using her mother's maiden name. We found her mom's married name...realized her dad was Eddie Gouse. Followed that name and, voilà, there she was."

"So you know what happened to her?"

"Yes." Jace sat forward again, put his arms on his desk and said, "Danny, she's a good person. No trouble. But from what I've read, women who go through that kind of harassment can end up with post-traumatic stress disorder. Her mother got her out of the situation very quickly, but who knows the impact of being violated that way."

"She worries."

"That the pictures will come forward?"

"That it will ruin her life." Danny pulled in a long breath. "And your team being able to dig up her past so easily doesn't help."

"Maybe just don't tell her that we know."

"I was going to use you not being able to find anything as a way to convince her that she shouldn't worry."

One of Jace's eyebrows rose. "Worry about dating you?"

Danny rose. "And other things."

Jace stood too. "Danny, she's a really, really nice woman. But if she can't face this, she's not the one for you."

Not the one for him? He wanted her. Wanted everything they had in secret. Casual happiness. An easy, loving relationship. He could not let her get away. He had to find a way to make this work.

"She's faced it once. She shouldn't have to face it again."

"Yeah, but she's never been under the kind of media scrutiny she'd get as your girlfriend."

"So, it's my fault?"

"Actually, if you're going to place blame, put it on the ill-mannered teenage boy who took the pictures. Or Mark for making you a celebrity of a sort."

Danny fell to his seat again. "I've just started to make my peace with Mark. But I don't want this position anymore. I don't want to be an heir. I don't want to be a Hinton."

"You can't go backward." Jace sat too. "That was Charlotte's big plan. She'd renounce the estate and return to being a vice president at her development company. But that's not how it works. The press would be even more interested in someone who refused billions of dollars."

"We could move to Scotland."

Jace laughed. "And they'd find you. They'll always find you if you're part of a delicious story. Frankly, you're less interesting as someone who accepts he's an heir and takes the money."

"Except for Marnie."

"Except for Marnie."

Danny drew a long breath. "I hate everything you just said."

Jace put his hand on his chest. "Hey, I don't make the rules. I just know them and know how to work with them. I can tell you exactly what's going to happen here. If the press gets suspicious, somebody's going to start poking, the way they did when Leni first got here. All it takes is one person to find one thread. To go to the high school in the school district for her mom's apartment, the one she's rented for over fifteen years, realize Marnie *Olsen* just appears one day—but with transcripts from another school that doesn't have a Marnie Olsen—which means she used another name, figure out who her dad is, look under Marnie Gouse and, voilà. Once a smart reporter or investigator gets her name…she's out."

Defeated, Danny rose.

Jace leaned back again. "Want my advice? Put the story out yourself. Control the narrative."

"She shouldn't have to face this again."

"But she does. That's life. And the only way to get ahead of it is to put the story out yourselves."

When Danny stepped off the elevator of the penthouse, his eyes met Marnie's and she knew something was wrong. Not only was it midafternoon, and he normally didn't get home before six-thirty or seven, but also his usually bright eyes were dull. Listless.

She walked over and kissed him. "What's up?"

He stepped back, away from her and the first level of panic hit. "I could use a drink." He strode to the wall bar tucked behind the piano. "You want a drink?"

She ambled over to him. "I'm on the clock."

"One drink won't hurt."

"Okay, now you're scaring me. What happened?"

He set his empty glass on the bar. "I talked to Jace today."

"Oh, that's right! He and Charlotte are home from their honeymoon."

"It wasn't a cheery visit. I asked him to investigate you."

Mouth open, she fell to the teal-colored sofa. "Oh."

"I wanted to see how difficult it would be for someone to uncover your past."

That was actually a smart, positive step. "Okay."

He closed his eyes and let his head fall back. "He knows. He's always known."

A weird sensation bubbled through her. Her past and her present met. And not kindly. It left the room cold, the conversation awkward. "Well, that didn't take long."

"I don't know how long it took. He said he couldn't trust the care of Mark's first grandchild to someone unless he knew everything about her."

"And he let me stay?"

"That's a point in your favor. He didn't let you stay because he likes you—though he does. He let you work for me because you aren't the bad guy. You were the victim."

Everything he'd said was good. Which meant there was more. "But—"

"But he believes there's trouble on the horizon if the press finds out."

Relief rippled through her. "Of course, there is. But the press isn't going to find out."

"Jace thinks they are. Maybe not today or tomorrow but eventually and you'll have to face this."

Her blood froze. "Face this?"

"He believes the only way around this is for you to come out in the open with it."

"That's ridiculous. I'm your nanny. How silly will it look for me to call a press conference or give an interview?"

His eyes met hers from across the room. "Not silly at all if we wanted to come out in the open about our dating."

Her frozen blood stopped flowing. "No."

"Marnie, just listen. I'm trying to figure this out." He walked over, sat beside her. "I want this so bad I can taste it. We're good together naturally, easily. You know as well as I do that what we have doesn't come along every day."

She squeezed her eyes shut. That had always been her touchstone—that what they had didn't come along every day. That's why she savored it, wrote in a journal, pressed certain memories into her heart. She wanted to have all of this to remember.

Danny rose unexpectedly. "We don't have to make a decision today. And no matter what we choose, Jace will be with us every step of the way."

Marnie's breath returned. Her lungs filled with air. Her world righted. "Okay."

He walked into the kitchen as if totally back to normal. "Paris is next week. Is there anything I need to do to help you get ready?"

She rose from the sofa. "No. I have everything under control."

"Only staying a weekend makes a big difference."

"Yeah."

He reached for his phone. "What do we want for dinner?"

She shrugged. "I don't care."

"I'd love a steak." He pursed his lips. "But I don't want it delivered. Too bad we can't go out."

His words sent a shaft of fear into her heart as the reality of their situation hit her. He would eventually tire of having to tiptoe around her life. And she wouldn't blame him.

He brightened suddenly. "I know! Let's get Italian."

"I love spaghetti."

"Me too."

And just like that her fears disappeared again. But the sense that she'd witnessed the beginning of the end of their relationship lodged in her brain. Not because Danny was a demanding guy or even impatient. Because there was no future. People had relationships in secret because there was no way to come out into the light. And Danny and Rex deserved light. Light and love and laughter that they didn't have to hide.

They arranged to have dinner delivered at seven, so Rex could help Marnie eat her spaghetti. When Rex went to bed a little after eight, Marnie shoved her fears away. If this was all the time she got, she refused to waste a minute fretting about the future.

They slept together, made passionate love, but for Marnie there was a ticking clock. An end. A vibrant, attractive, interesting man like Danny wouldn't live a lie, have a secret.

In fact, the one thing they'd both forgotten was that Mark Hinton's lie, his multiplicity of secrets, had already ruined Danny's well-planned life. It was no wonder he was trying to get them out from under her past. Once he realized that what they were doing was no better than what Mark had done, he'd be gone.

Or he'd ask her to go.

He wouldn't be able to live a lie.

Wouldn't live under the shadow of secrets.

CHAPTER EIGHTEEN

EVERY DAY BECAME SPECIAL, important to Marnie. She cuddled Rex a little more, loved Danny a little harder and didn't make weekend visits to her mom's anymore. Judy didn't mind. Having loved taking care of Wiggles while Marnie and Danny were in Scotland, she'd gotten herself a dog. A big, mixed-breed variety, Charlie walked her mom, instead of the other way around. In a fragile sort of way, everyone seemed to be happy, moving on with their lives.

As the little jet Danny had been assigned flew into Paris, she could see the Eiffel Tower, and an unexpected peace filled her lungs with air. Out of the country, where no one really cared about the Hinton family, the trip would be glorious.

With no property large enough of his own to use as a family headquarters, Mark had booked two floors of a luxury hotel. As in Scotland, Marnie and Danny were assigned a suite with Rex's crib in Danny's room.

She entered the sitting room with a gasp. "Wow." Drapes were open, revealing a view of Paris that stole her breath. Bowls of white roses sat on every table. Plush rugs covered hardwood floors. White sofas sat across from each other, with white club chairs beside the table in front of the window.

Danny looked around. "There is no denying that being rich has its perks."

She laughed, taking Rex from Danny's arms, so she could get him ready for his nap. "What's on today's agenda?"

"Nothing. There's not even a rehearsal dinner. Mark said the ceremony will be simple. As his best man, I'll stand beside him with the ring. Charlotte will be her mom's maid of honor, and Leni will do a reading."

"We can do anything we want tonight?"

"Yep. Sightsee. Have a nice dinner out. Take a walk along the Seine."

"I'm getting Rex on France's time. What's going to seem like afternoon to us will be his bedtime."

"That's okay. I've arranged for my parents to watch him tonight."

"You have?"

"Don't worry. They figured things out long ago. Most of the family has." He caught her gaze. "Are you okay with that?"

Everyone had always treated her more as a friend than an employee. "Yes. I mean... I suppose we do have a certain glow."

He laughed, then caught her up for a quick kiss.

His parents arrived at eight o'clock Paris time, actually one o'clock in the afternoon, New York time. She gave them the instruction to let Rex sleep but Danny's dad all but shoved them out the door. "Go! Have fun! We got here two days early. We got most of our sightseeing in. Rex is in good hands."

Walking down the hall, Marnie said, "Coming a few days early was smart."

"My dad has been with his employer a long time. He has oodles of vacation time. I don't."

The elevator came and they stepped inside. "You could if you went to work for Hinton, Inc."

He groaned. "That's not going to happen."

"Okay, then don't be jealous of your dad's many vacation days."

Danny laughed and shook his head. "Let's just focus on our own stuff. Like the house that's in escrow down the street from theirs. There's absolutely no furniture and I sold my condo furnished. So that's a big job that'll be waiting for us after we close."

She sighed. "That's a lotta house to furnish."

"We can hire a decorator."

They stepped out into the warm Paris night. The scent of pastries drifted around her. The streets were crowded with tourists and residents of the world's most romantic city.

"Hiring a decorator seems cold. Impersonal."

"I'm glad you said that because my mom asked if she could help get the place organized."

"I think that's a great idea."

He took her hand, turned her to the right, and they began walking up the street. "You do?"

"Sure. That house is all about cementing your adoptive parents' place in your life. She's your mom. Moms usually like a part in things like this."

"Then it's settled?"

"Yes." And she felt good about that. She felt good in general. The night was perfect. Not a cloud in the sky. She was with a man she adored. His parents seemed to like her. "Where are we going?"

"Restaurant's just a few blocks up the street. I thought you'd like to walk."

"I would." She glanced around. No one was looking at them oddly. No one was really looking at them at all. "Where's the bodyguard?"

"Outside the hotel, watching Rex."

"Good idea."

He slid his arm across her shoulders and nestled her close. "The best idea. There's nothing like being in the most romantic city in the world with the woman you love."

It took a second for the words to sink in but when they did, she stopped dead. "You love me?"

"You don't love me?"

Their gazes met. Her past tried to overshadow her, but she was in Paris. The man she loved had just told her he loved her. *In Paris.* She refused to let her past ruin this moment.

Warm fuzzies filled her. Dreams that she didn't even realize she had came into focus. Her eyes filled with tears. "Yes. I do."

He caught her by the waist and hauled her to him, kissing her deeply. She remembered every second of the kiss, the habit of memorizing every detail so engrained that it happened automatically. She cataloged the feeling of his lips, the way their bodies met, the warmth in her soul—

And a little voice whispered, *You don't have to give this up.*

She didn't want to. It cut her to the core to think of moving on to protect her secret.

So, don't think of it. Test the waters of believing this is your future.

Even the thought was scary, but they broke the kiss, their gazes staying connected, and she felt what her soul was trying to tell her. This was it. Danny was the man she was supposed to spend the rest of her life with.

The question was… How?

No answer came, but throughout the night she noticed that no one paid them any mind. Danny's last name, the name on his credit and bank cards was Manelli. Not Hinton. When he paid for dinner or pastries at the little café just a few blocks down from the restaurant, his name aroused no curiosity. As they strolled along the Seine, passersby smiled politely but no one knew who they were… Who *he* was.

Like Scotland, no one knew who he was. No one cared who he was.

A plan began to form. A simple one. Danny wasn't ready to leave his job at Waters, Waters and Montgomery yet. But he would be one day. The whole world had opened up for him, and someday—with no restrictions to bind him—he'd realize he could be, have or do anything he wanted, the way Leni and Charlotte had.

And when he was ready, she would suggest that they move to France or Spain or get a vineyard in Italy.

Suddenly, their future opened up to her. The life she wanted. The life she could have.

And she knew moving was the answer.

Mark and Penny's wedding was held at the Musée Rodin. Penny looked spectacular in a short white dress with a skirt of tulle ruffles and a short veil. Mark was resplendent in his tux. The wedding party posed for pictures around the manicured grounds, inside the museum, with Rodin's sculptures sometimes, sometimes without.

Danny did not give a flying fig that the pictures took forever, the wedding planner was like a drill sergeant or that Rex was cranky. The night before, Marnie had been different.

His.

Totally his. No hesitation. No fear.

He could feel it in her touch. He could sense it in the way she fell into a deep, peaceful sleep.

So he'd made a plan. He'd decided to talk to Jace again when they returned to New York. They'd find a sympathetic reporter, someone who would know how to tell Marnie's story correctly, and they would come out.

Just the thought filled him with relief. Dancing under the stars, they'd laughed more than usual. She hadn't held back or hidden her feelings for him around his ever-growing family. Charlotte had beamed as if she were the matchmaker who'd set them up. Leni had smiled knowingly, reminding them that the family was meeting in Mannington, Kansas on Christmas Eve and she expected them to be there.

It was the best night of his life.

When Rex couldn't stay awake even a moment longer, his parents volunteered to take him back to Danny and Marnie's suite. They loved the elaborate, elegant wedding, but they loved Rex more.

Danny and Marnie stayed, dancing until the band quit. Then they took a limo to the hotel.

This time, when they stepped out of the car, she saw a gaggle of guys huddled together beside the door, smoking.

Odd for such a high-class hotel.

When Danny turned from helping her exit the limo, a rumble went through the group. They spoke French so the only word she understood was Danny.

At the sound of his name, Danny caught her elbow and hurried her inside the hotel. Out of the corner of her eyes, she saw their driver, Danny's bodyguard, walk up to the entrance and stand in front of the door. As if guarding it.

Of course, he was guarding it. That was his job.

When the elevator doors closed behind them, she said, "What was that?"

"I'm guessing someone recognized me."

Fear raised gooseflesh along her arms. "Recognized you or was waiting for you?"

He took a breath. "My entire family is here. For all we know they were waiting for Charlotte. She's the pregnant one. The interesting one."

The elevator doors opened. "But they knew who you were."

He motioned for her to walk down the hall. "I'm going to say that they didn't know who I was. They took a guess and got lucky."

Which was why they hadn't raced to follow him inside. Her fear subsided. They hadn't known for sure he was Charlotte's brother.

Relief sighed through her as they entered their suite and though she didn't forget what had happened, she put it to the back of her mind. But when they returned to Manhattan and exited the limo in front of their building, there was no guesswork among the reporters.

"Danny! Danny! Mr. Manelli!"

Marnie unbuckled Rex from the car seat and pressed him to her as she raced to the door.

"How was the wedding!"

"Is Mark happy?"

"Do you like your new stepmother?"

They entered the building to the sound of questions. None of the reporters was foolish enough to follow them, but Jace's men closed in on the door, standing in front of it.

As the elevator door shut behind them, Marnie turned to Danny and just gaped at him.

He sighed. Staring ahead, at the elevator door, he said, "The wedding might have been a secret, but Mark released a statement that he'd gotten married before he and Penny left for their honeymoon." He ran his hand along the back of his neck. "The reporters were just curious."

He peered at her. "And not about you. They barely saw you. They were curious about Mark and Penny."

The elevator door opened, and she stepped inside the penthouse. Realizing she was still clutching Rex, she loosened her hold but a thought hit her. She was holding him like a mother, not like a nanny.

Reporters weren't going to assume she was the nanny. They'd think she was Rex's mom—

Or Rex's stepmom—

At the very least Danny's girlfriend.

Her heart sped up. Her fears washed over her like a bucket of cold water.

Danny took Rex. "This doesn't have to be a big deal."

"It *is* a big deal."

"But it doesn't have to be." Carrying Rex, he led Marnie to the sofa, then sat beside her. "I talked to Jace for a minute at the wedding. I told him that I realized the wisdom of the advice he'd given me the day I went to his office to talk about you. I told him I agreed with him. That I totally understood that we needed to get ahead of your secret with an interview. He said he knows a hungry reporter who'd do just about anything to get the story."

Her heart stopped. "You talked to Jace? Again?"

"After you said you loved me, it all came together." He

shook his head. "Marnie, you have to know we can't go on living like this."

"I thought we'd move to France…or Belgium or Spain or an island in the Pacific."

"My work is here. My life is here."

She licked her suddenly dry lips. "Danny, you're not going to stay at Waters, Waters and Montgomery. Even if you don't want to work for the family, you can be anything you want. Work anywhere you want."

"No! I won't give up my job. That's the only solid piece of me I kept from my old life."

"That and your parents—"

"Who aren't really my parents. My relationship with them is back to being good, but it will never return to what it was. I'm different now. My profession—*that choice* is the only part of me that's me." He leaned back on the sofa, taking Rex with him. "I never put all that into words before, but it's true. I didn't wake up one day and say I wanted to be a lawyer. I worked to figure it out. I busted my butt in law school to be the best. It is like an anchor now—who I am."

"And my secret is who I am." Her words came out soft, discouraged. Because this was their real problem. As much as it felt like they meshed, their lives didn't.

He caught her hand. "Your secret might be part of your past, but it isn't who you are."

"Isn't it? It guided my career choice, caused me to change schools, kept me in the background no matter how much I wanted to leap forward."

"And now all that's going to end. With one succinct conversation with a sympathetic reporter."

She closed her eyes as the feeling of finality squeezed her chest. "It doesn't matter if the reporter is the most sympathetic person in the world. There are a million reporters and bloggers and podcast people who will jump on the bandwagon, speculate, call me names…"

"You can't go on living a lie."

"I don't live a lie. I have a secret."

"But if you told that secret, it would lose its power over you."

She shook her head, imagining being mobbed on the street, seeing her own picture in tabloids, not even being able to buy a pastry without someone looking down his nose at her because no matter how clear she would be about what happened, people would embellish. It would be like high school all over again but a million times worse. And this time she wasn't the only one who'd be hurt...

"No. No! I can't do this."

Rex fussed, crawling up on Danny's shoulder. "Let me put him down and we'll talk about this."

"No." She rose as he rose. "To me there is nothing to talk about."

"Not even the fact that you love me, and I love you?"

She looked him in the eye. This time she didn't want to remember what she saw there. Pain. Confusion. And maybe a little anger. She didn't blame him. She was angry too. But when she saw herself talking to reporters, getting questions shouted at her about the night she lost her virginity or why there'd been a bet on who would get her virginity, her skin crawled. She remembered the bullies. The kids who'd thought it all nothing but a game and ruined her life. Reporters would consider it their jobs to get the truth—no matter how ugly. No matter how much it was none of anyone's business.

She took a breath, fought back the torrent of images, found the strength to speak without tears.

"I always knew it was going to end. I just didn't think it would be this soon."

He caught her hand. "Give me a minute to put Rex down for a nap. I'll be right back. We can make a plan."

She smiled slightly but didn't nod her head or verbally agree. She had enough trouble in her life. She didn't need to add lying to it. When he returned, he would want to discuss outing her and she just couldn't do it.

She'd be sixteen again. Alone. Vulnerable. So fragile she'd shiver every time she stepped out her front door. While vultures picked at her bones. Not caring if they shattered her.

As soon as Danny reached the nursery, she headed for her room, quickly packed her meager belongings and was gone.

Her phone rang a hundred times that night. Danny left at least ten text messages. She deleted them all without reading them.

He was better off without her.

In fact, his life would be good without her.

The truth of that shattered her.

CHAPTER NINETEEN

MARNIE WOKE THE next morning to the sound of traffic. She opened her eyes, saw her old bedroom at her mom's apartment with the window raised to combat the late September heat.

Tears filled her eyes. Her empty soul billowed in the breeze left when everything she wanted had been yanked away. Her heart and mind were like a ghost town.

She sat up, positioned herself to rise, but she couldn't. *This* was the moment she'd spent her life fearing. The time when her past would rise up, albeit privately, and cost her her future.

She hadn't yet saved enough money to start her business. She'd lost the man she loved. The child she loved.

There was nothing to look forward to. Nothing to hope for.

These walls and temporary nanny jobs were her future. Nothing more.

The noise of the apartment door opening rent the air.

She squeezed her eyes shut.

And she was back to living with her mom.

Her door suddenly slammed open and her mom's monster dog raced in, jumped on her bed and knocked her down. Judy flew in behind him.

"Charlie! Sit!"

The dog just looked at her.

"I'm telling you. Obedience school did not work."

Marnie gave Charlie a quick pet before she nudged him off her bed. "He just needs more lessons."

"We don't have the money."

"You can have the money I saved." She lay down in the bed, a solid ball of misery. She didn't have enough to start her business, and probably wouldn't get another job with an inflated salary like the one Danny offered. There'd be no nanny business for her. "It doesn't matter anymore."

"Oh, it's pity party time."

She sat up, gaping at her mother. "Look at the pot calling the kettle black."

"I told you rich men were trouble. I warned you. But no. You had to go to Scotland with the guy, then Paris! You got a taste of all the money and things and then you thought you were in love."

"I didn't think it, Mom."

"Sure. Sure. You fell solidly in love in three months... with a guy so far out of your league you probably didn't even really have anything in common. Sure. I buy that."

Disgusted that her mom had it all wrong, she toyed with a loose string on her worn bedspread. "Don't worry. It's not like I thought it would last. I knew it wouldn't, so I saved most of my salary."

Judy eyebrows rose. "Really? Most of your salary?"

Marnie laid back on her pillow. "I had an exit plan."

"I thought I had an exit plan with your dad too—"

Her disgust returned, rising up so unexpectedly Marnie didn't have time to combat it. "Mom, this is totally different! You and Dad were married. I worked for Danny."

And I love him.

Thinking that made it hurt to breathe. She'd barely said it to him. Realizing that now only hurt worse.

"I have enough of a past that I knew I had to be smart. I didn't let my thoughts go any further than that. You taught me that. Taught me not to dream."

Judy's face fell, as if Marnie had slapped her. "Oh, Marnie!" She pressed her fingertips to her forehead. "No. I never told you not to dream. I was warning you to be careful."

"Well, I was," she said, unexpected anger pouring through her. Her parents' marriage had been a mess. Her mom herself had been a mess for decades before she finally pulled herself together. And right now, Marnie didn't want anybody preaching at her. She'd finally, finally found what she wanted, a man she could spend the rest of her life with—and she couldn't have him.

She didn't need anyone reminding her that she'd lost something she'd never really had. She'd lived the last ten years with the knowledge that most good things would slip through her fingers.

"I am always careful, Mom." She fought the tears that wanted to form in her eyes. She refused to give in to the misery of it. She'd long ago accepted her fate.

Judy shook her head. "Okay. I'm seeing something here that I don't like."

Marnie cursed her mom's therapist for always phrasing things as if she were in a session.

"I never told you not to dream."

"You never told me I could dream either, Mom."

"It's not the same thing."

"Of course, it is!" Regret rattled through her. "And you can tell your therapist I said that. Because, you know what? Splitting hairs the way we always do, looking for the path of least resistance was great, but it caused me to stagnate."

"I don't think you stagnated! I see lots of progress in your life. You got your degree. You had a great job. Hell, you said yourself you have a plan."

But she didn't really have a life. She had a plan. Always a plan. Never a real sense that she was living. Only existing. Never the feelings she'd had in Scotland or Paris, where everything was simple and beautiful. Never the glorious freedom of being with the man she wanted more than her next breath of air.

The agony of his loss broke her, but when it did, something wild and bold poured from the cracked shell of her soul. In the same way that fear had always paralyzed her, this thing—this *courage* rising out of the ashes of loss—seemed to give her life and energy.

Charlie tried to leap on her bed again. Judy cried, "Charlie, no!" She grabbed his leash from the floor with a heavy sigh. "I'll take him to the kitchen, get him a snack so you can get up and get dressed."

Her mom left with Charlie, closing the door behind her, and Marnie squeezed her eyes shut. Without Danny, *this* was the rest of her life.

The courage that had puffed out of her soul whispered through her again. She hated this life. Always had. But she suddenly wondered if her mom did. Judy had always blamed being shoved into high society for ruining her marriage, and Marnie had simply thought that was an excuse for her drinking.

But what if she *had* hated high society life?

What if she'd feared being in the spotlight so much that she shrank from it with alcohol? She'd cleaned up rather easily once she'd been out of Eddie Gouse's life. And had stayed sober as long as she was hidden—

And what if that's what she'd taught Marnie?

That she'd only be safe if she was hidden?

Marnie pressed shaking fingers to her forehead. What if she'd handled her entire life, the big high school mess, all wrong by hiding from it?

Danny wasn't surprised when Mary Poppins, real name Mary Grant, had shown up at his apartment the night before. She made short order of getting Rex to bed, liked the list of rules and hints Alisha had provided and got herself set up in the room that had been Marnie's—

He squeezed his eyes shut. Even thinking her name hurt his chest.

He couldn't believe she'd left without telling him, then wondered why that had surprised him. Revealing her secret would be painful, awful and oh, so public. Why would he be surprised that she'd run rather than even discuss it? He'd called a hundred times. She hadn't answered once.

He forced himself to go to work, settled in his seat behind the big desk and told himself that having the weight of Marnie's troubles lifted was a good thing, but he knew it wasn't true. He might be able to replace her as a nanny, but he'd never connected with another human being the way he had with her.

The things he'd told her the night before about her life being a lie rumbled through his brain like thunder, and he took a long, slow breath. She didn't really lie. She hid. But in a way, wasn't that the same thing? When a person hid, technically, they were putting on a show, pretending, lying about everything.

The thought froze his brain. He didn't want to believe she didn't love him. If she lied about that, something inside him would die.

He knew it.

He didn't feel like quite the idiot he believed himself to be when Mark Hinton announced he was his biological dad and all the progress he'd made at his job, all the promotions, all the accolades were actually the partners of his firm sucking up to their biggest client. Still, thinking through Marnie's life, he felt sorrier for her than he did for his own loss.

What they had had together was amazing, and the loss bruised his soul, but her loss was worse. She'd never had a normal life. A normal *anything*.

His heart broke for her, but just as quickly he forced himself to think about work. Think about documents. Do something good for one of his clients.

The pages swam before his eyes. Not from tears, from exhaustion. He hadn't slept the night before, torn between going after her and staying right where he was. If he went after her, persuaded her to tell her story to a reporter, it wouldn't be her choice, her idea. He'd always wonder if he'd forced her hand. If things got bad, he'd be the culprit who'd convinced her to do something she hadn't wanted to do.

The choice had to be hers, and when she'd left his penthouse, she'd made it.

And now he was tired. Tired. Hurt. Gutted.

He picked up his phone and called Nick. "Hey, Dude."

Nick snorted. "Danny? Did you just call me *dude*?"

He laughed. "I'm exhausted today."

"You must be if you let loose with a *dude*."

He took a breath. "Look. I was thinking I'd like to get away with Rex. I want to go somewhere quiet and serene. I need a break."

Nick chuckled. "Yep. I knew this was coming. At some point you all fall apart. There's no shame in this, Danny. Finding out Mark is your dad was hard enough. Finding out you were adopted, your job was a setup—those hurt. Add back-to-back weddings in Europe and, yeah, you need a break." He paused. "Let's see. There are mountain cabins, a little cooler now that it's the first week in October or there are island retreats. Still hot. But quieter because kids are back in school and summer vacations have officially ended."

"Heat and sun sound good."

"My recommendation? The house in the Florida Keys. There are Jet Skis and fishing boats. We even have a captain on retainer... Let me look. Yep. There's a guy to drive the boat so you can drink beer and fish."

"I think I'd like that."

"Okay, then, give me two hours to get a jet ready."

"That's about how much time I'll need to get Rex and his nanny packed—if she'll go."

He laughed. "Marnie enjoyed Scotland and Paris as much as we all did."

Danny's breath caught as he realized no one knew Marnie was gone.

Nick casually said, "How long are you staying?"

With thoughts of Marnie still washing through him, living without her, having the park, the bakery, even his home remind him of her, Danny stayed silent another second. When he spoke, it was quietly. "Not sure. Maybe forever."

His heart officially broke as he said those words. But he was so tired. So awfully tired of the circus his life had become since Mark had entered his world. Clinging to his job hadn't helped. So he'd leave his job. Take his child. Go off the grid.

And never think of Marnie Olsen again.

Marnie's next assignment was nannying the twins of a very sedate banker and his pediatrician wife. She had a moment of pride when Dr. Sponsky told her she was doing everything right. That she was the first nanny Shirley had sent her who didn't need coaching.

So, she was good. On target. The pay wasn't as high as working for a Hinton heir—which was how she referred to Danny, so she didn't have to think his name and have pain swallow her for days. And though she was in the same neighborhood, she'd heard he'd moved. Gone to the Florida Keys. Charlotte hadn't been able to let Marnie go onto her next assignment without an explanation, so she'd called and that had been awkward.

But here she was, the first of December, eight weeks after the great loss, in the park where she'd walked Wiggles, now pushing a stroller with twin girls. Two cute-as-a-button sweethearts.

She rolled the double stroller up to her usual bench, turned it so she could talk to her darling girls and sat.

"So, good day today, right?"

Nine-month-olds, they could only babble. But she loved it. Sheila was a little more expressive than Sandra. She knew a few words. Nothing like Rex—

She stopped the painful thought. Rex had become like her own child. If she let herself think of losing him, she'd splinter again. And she couldn't do that. Not again. Not anymore.

She tucked a blanket around Sandra. The day wasn't freezing, but there was a chill in the air.

And she did not think about the Hinton heirs. Ever.

She leaned back, enjoyed the sun that poked through the clouds, enjoyed the final leaves that had fallen from the trees, dancing around her in the breeze, and started counting the months it would take to save enough to have first and last months' rent on a tiny place she'd found. Knowing how much her mom's opinions had impacted her, Marnie couldn't live with her anymore. She hadn't said anything. Didn't want to hurt her mom, but she had to get out on her own. Be herself. Figure out who she really was.

The apartment might be taken by the time she had the necessary cash, but the landlord had said he had another one opening up first of the year. Renter was a deadbeat. Couldn't pay the monthly allotment.

She stopped the rush of sympathy for the girl. Marnie was poor too. And she got weekends off. She needed a place—away from her mother. Though, truth be told, now that she had Charlie, Judy Olsen was a lot less negative. She actually went out. Had friends—

"I see you're back."

Damn it! Her father.

He hadn't been here any of the other times she'd brought the twins to the park. Why now?

He snorted. "Twins this time? You switch jobs like I switch underwear."

She gaped at the stupid old coot. "Then you must not change your underwear very often."

He laughed, plopped down on the bench and opened his newspaper.

Of all the unfair things that had happened to her in her life, having him for a father was the one thing she didn't have to let hover over her head. It was what it was and he shouldn't be allowed to spook her.

"You know what, old man?" She called across the space

that separated them, causing both of the twins to look up at her. "You shouldn't laugh at me so much. You're partially responsible for who I am."

He lowered the paper. Scowled at her. "How do you figure that?"

She bounced off the bench. "Because you're my dad. You left *me* when you left my mother. You refused to see me when I came to try to make a connection. You had a maid tell me to leave. And this is who I became. So, get off your high horse. You're partially responsible for me."

He stared at her. "Marnie?"

She stood tall, defiant. "Yes."

He set the paper on the bench and rose as if bemused. "Oh my God."

She grabbed the stroller handles. "Yeah, amazing, right? I knew you probably lived around here somewhere. I just never realized we'd run into each other so damned often."

"Only a few times." He studied her. "I don't know what to say."

"You don't have to say anything. I wouldn't have told you who I was if you hadn't annoyed me so much. I don't want you in my life. Don't want anything from you. Except a peaceful visit to the park."

She set the stroller in the direction of the Sponskys' condo. "So, if you see me here, don't come in. And if I see you got here first, I won't come in."

She left him standing openmouthed in front of his bench.

But as she strolled her babies back to their home, she couldn't help remembering the shocked expression on his face. He'd been numb.

A chuckle rose.

It didn't just feel good to stand up to him. It felt good to tell him who she was—

His daughter.

The enormity of admitting that almost paralyzed her, and she stopped pushing the stroller. She was a child who'd been abandoned by a wealthy man, who'd gotten confused in her teen years, looked for love all the wrong ways—

And had been victimized.

She'd been victimized.

She wasn't the criminal here. She wasn't the one who should be hiding—

Her breath stuttered.

Danny was right.

He was always right.

Her eyes filled with tears, but she laughed through them. It had taken her weeks to realize he'd had the plan—she had to come clean. But that could only happen after she'd faced her first demon. Her dad.

Now that that was done, she wanted it all to be over.

All.

Of.

It.

She wanted her life back.

She pulled her phone out of her pocket. Hit a speed dial number.

"This is Marnie Gouse Olsen. I'd like to speak with Jace, please."

CHAPTER TWENTY

MARNIE WALKED THROUGH the lobby of the Trusik Building, home of Lancaster Media, her head high, adrenaline pumping through her. Jace followed her. Not discreetly as he normally did, but beside her like a friend, not a bodyguard.

They took an elevator to the appropriate floor, spoke to a receptionist and were guided to a small space that looked like someone's living room. A young, hip producer attached a mic to her collar, then walked away.

Two minutes later, Angelica Cabala ambled over. Tall and slender, with long red hair, she read some note cards.

When she reached Marnie, she extended her hand to shake Marnie's. "Ready?"

"Actually, the sooner we start the better."

"Great." Angelica nodded once. She straightened in her chair, then faced a camera. "And we're back," she said, as if they were just returning from a commercial break, when they were actually taping this segment to air the next morning.

"Today, we have a special guest. This is the woman who used to be the nanny for Danny Manelli's son, Rex. As anybody who's turned on the news lately or read a newspaper knows, Danny is missing Hinton heir number three."

"Welcome, Marnie."

The camera panned to Marnie. Her chest froze. Her stomach fell. But she thought about Danny. How much he'd been through for her and how she'd run—even though she'd promised herself she'd never run again.

She sucked in a breath. "Thank you."

Angelica opened her delicate hands with fingernails adorned with green nail polish that matched her dress. "Let's get right to it. You called me and told me that you and Danny had a more personal relationship than employer and employee and that you had a story to tell."

Jace had told her that admitting the personal relationship was the quickest, best way to get a reporter to sit up and beg for her story. And he'd been right. Angelica had invited her to come to the studio immediately.

"So, I'll ask the question that's on everyone's lips… Seriously? A nanny falling for her boss? Isn't that a bit of a cliché?"

Danny had told her that. It was his first defense against their attraction. The memory of the day in the park lifted her lips into a goofy smile. Everything she felt for him when they were together tumbled through her.

"Actually, we both acknowledged that right off the bat. We did not want to be a cliché."

"Yet, here you are."

"We may be a cliché to you, but we aren't to each other. You know Danny's world had been turned upside down. The lives of all three of Mark's kids were upended."

Angelica's perfect eyebrows rose. "You call realizing you're filthy rich upended?"

"Leni, Danny and Charlotte all had life plans. Leni had parents she loved. Danny didn't even know he'd been adopted."

That reminder sent sadness rippling through her. He'd been going through so much and she'd hurt him. She hadn't said goodbye. Too afraid he'd talk her into something that she wasn't ready for.

She raised her head, straightened her spine. "It's like winning the lottery. Everybody thinks it's wonderful. Everybody sees the good side. But there's another side."

"So poor little rich kid?"

Anger sputtered through Marnie. "No. And you know that." She glanced around. "You didn't just one day get dropped into this studio."

Looking affronted, Angelica said, "I worked my way up."

"And had years to adjust."

"Well, yes."

"The Hinton heirs didn't. From day one of their discovery, they've been followed. They've been in the news. If they didn't have such good protection, I'm sure people would have gone through their garbage."

Folding her hands on her lap, Angelica leaned forward. "And what about you?"

"I was the nanny mostly for young, upwardly mobile executives. I'd never worked for someone so wealthy." She looked into the camera. "And I made mistakes."

Angelica's smile grew predatory. "Mistakes?"

"You said yourself a nanny and an employer getting involved is a cliché."

Angelica said nothing.

Marnie swallowed. It was now or never. Do or die. She couldn't handle that she'd hurt Danny. Couldn't handle another day of being afraid.

"I changed my name, ran from my past. Because of a predator."

Angelica's eyebrows rose to her hairline. But again, she said nothing, giving Marnie the chance to say something explosive.

Marnie took a breath. "Someone took pictures of me in a compromising position." She shook her head. "No. He took nude photos. When my mom called the authorities, I was the one villainized, harassed, bullied. I wasn't running from the person who took the pictures. He was told to delete them, and I believe he did. In ten years, there's been no evidence that he didn't. What I ran from was bullying."

Angelica blinked. Looking speechless. She didn't know what Angelica had been expecting, but clearly this wasn't it.

"I won't run anymore. And I won't hide. If the pictures show up because I'm involved with one of the richest men in the world…so be it. That's life." She glanced at Jace. "A good friend told me that I'm undoubtedly not the only person this has happened to and maybe I needed to set an example for how to handle it."

Angelica's face scrunched. "So, you're facing it head-on?"

Marnie nodded. "Yes. All of it. The fear. The running. The secrets."

"That's admirable." She set her now-useless note cards on the table. "That's powerful."

"Not powerful. It's real."

"Yes. It is. And you're right. It's probably a story shared by hundreds, if not thousands of other women. Do you see yourself as a crusader, a leader who will help other women?"

She shrugged. "Everybody has to handle this in their own way. I simply got tired of hiding, of being afraid. Maybe I'll inspire someone else to come forward, but really most women don't have to. They just have to give themselves permission to stop being afraid."

"Again. Powerful words." Angelica leaned forward, squeezed Marnie's hand. "Marnie, thank you for being here."

"Thank you for letting me tell my story."

"We're out of time, but I'd love to have you back to hear about your life with Danny Manelli. Hear about the world of the Hintons."

Marnie laughed. Her secret wasn't a secret anymore. The weight that had been lifted was incomprehensible. The most delicious thought trickled through her. *She was free.*

"Thank you, but no." She wasn't really in the Hinton world anymore. She'd hurt Danny. Exposed the Hinton family to public humiliation and embarrassment…and more press. As if the media needed a reason to hound them.

Angelica waited another few seconds, maybe hoping Marnie would say more. But she didn't. This time, though, she wasn't keeping a secret. She was being discreet. The difference between the two was sanity.

When the director said, "Cut," Marnie reached for her mic. Angelica breached the distance between them. "I mean it. Anytime you want to talk, I'm here."

Marnie said, "I'll think about it." Then she walked up to Jace, who accompanied her out of the studio, then out of the building.

Even before Jace's limo dropped her off at her mom's apartment, Shirley called. She'd been fired by the Sponskys. No one wanted a celebrity as a nanny. Shirley knew this notoriety would fade away in a week or two, but the Sponskys didn't.

She'd lost yet another thing—a good job.

And lots of parents might not want to hire her.

The step that was supposed to fix her life had actually broken it even more. The relief of not having a secret ebbed into reality. Everybody knew her. She was a broke, famous nobody.

Two weeks later, with no jobs coming her way, she got the news from Shirley that there was a long list of employers who didn't want her.

She nodded, though tears filled her eyes. She crawled into bed that night with her mother tucking her in.

"I'm telling you. This too shall pass."

"Another saying from your therapist?"

"Nope. That one's in the good book."

Marnie shook her head. "I'm fine."

"Sure. Sure. We're always fine."

"You know that money I've been saving to get my own apartment?"

Her mother's eyebrow rose. "Not really, but go on…"

"I think I might have to move to another city." She'd thought of that the night she'd officially become Rex's nanny. It had made sense then. It made more sense now.

Her mom pressed her lips together, then whispered, "Yeah. You might." She rose from the bed. "Good night, Marnie."

She could hear in Judy's voce that she regretted the way things had turned out. She caught her mother's hand. "It's not your fault."

"Thanks, but some of it is."

"How about if we just say it is what it is and go forward from here?"

Judy smiled. "I'd like that."

"Me too." She'd lost her dad, lost her job, lost Danny and Rex. She didn't want to lose her mom too. Now, that they were both aware of the mistakes, they could heal together.

After a restless night, Marnie woke the next morning to pounding on the front door. She waited a few seconds for her mother to get it. When she didn't, Marnie called, "Ma! Get the door."

The pounding increased, and no sound came from the main room of the apartment. With a groan, she threw off the covers, slid her shabby robe over her pajamas and marched to the door.

Stupid salesmen!

She yanked open the door and there stood Danny Manelli.

"Hey."

She gaped at him. Her heart sped up to a million beats a second causing her pulse to race and her thoughts to scramble. "Hey."

"Can I come in?"

She looked back at the poverty she called home, remembering that she'd made a firm choice not to run, not to hide from who she was. She and her mom barely had enough money to pay the rent. But that was her life. Her truth. She wasn't running anymore.

"Sure." She motioned for him to enter. "Come in."

He looked fabulous in his camel-colored overcoat. His hair dotted with snow. His black leather gloves in his hands instead of on them. "Rex misses you."

She smiled as she thought of the toddler who'd loved her.

The little boy who was so easy to love in return. Blinking tears from her eyes, she said, "I miss him too." She walked to the coffeemaker. "Can I get you something to drink?"

"No. What I have to say will only take a minute."

So, he was here to say his piece. Maybe yell at her for leaving so abruptly. An arrow plunged into her heart. Now that she was down, it seemed everyone wanted to kick her. She was surprised her father hadn't called. He knew who she was. It would be a simple thing for him to track her down. After all, he had resources.

"I saw the interview."

"I thought you were in Florida." *And wouldn't see.*

"I was. But my sisters saw it, and I called the station and they sent me a video."

She winced. "I should have thought that through. Jace had said that dropping hints about our relationship would get me the interview. The chance to come clean publicly, so I wouldn't have a secret anymore. It was a bad time for me." She combed her fingers through her hair. "A mess. I didn't think it through. I'm sorry."

"You sort of hinted that your feelings for me weren't gone."

"Hinted?"

"You don't have a poker face, Marnie." He laughed. "Your expression said a lot more than your words. But you started the interview talking about us."

Her gaze jumped to his. *No more lying. No more hiding.* "Yeah."

"So, telling me you love me in Paris… That was true?"

"Yes."

"And leaving without a word, not answering my calls that night… What was that?"

"I thought I was protecting you. From me. My past. My mess."

"It's what Jace thinks."

She squeezed her eyes shut. "You talked to Jace?"

"Yes. He's squarely on your side in this."

She laughed sadly. "He's a good guy. I'd have never gotten through this without him."

"And Charlotte would have shaken him silly if you hadn't gotten through it."

Charlotte. She pictured her round and pregnant. Leni cheerful. Mark and Penny newlyweds. She missed them all.

"I guess you're going back to Florida?"

He looked at her. "It's no fun without you."

Her heart stumbled. Her lips trembled as a million wishes pounded in her brain. But she wasn't the kind of woman who got wishes. Wasn't the kind who put herself out on a limb.

"I also don't think I can ever go back to Scotland again. I'd see you everywhere. That wouldn't be any fun either."

She pressed her lips together, blinked to stop the tears from spilling from her eyes.

"Unless you went with me."

She laughed. "Might as well. Nobody else wants to hire me."

"Oh, I don't want to hire you either."

Her head snapped up. "You don't?"

"It's what got us into trouble the first time."

"Yeah."

"I'd really like to marry you."

This time, when her heart stumbled it was with hope. The words tried to sink in and almost couldn't. She'd hurt him, hurt herself. She was a mess.

"No answer?"

She passed a hand through her hair. "My life is in shambles. Not something you should be getting involved with. Don't say things you don't mean."

He faced her. "I mean it. Watching you on that video." He shook his head. "That was the bravest thing I've ever seen."

"You think so?"

"Yeah. And crazy as this is going to sound, I liked that you didn't do it for me. You did it for yourself."

She swallowed hard.

He opened his arms. "Come here. I love you."

She raced over, threw herself against him. "I love you too. I think I always did. But it was so much."

"Too much," he agreed before he kissed her.

They broke apart slowly and stared into each other's eyes. "I actually do live in Key West now."

"Charlotte told me."

He laughed. "She does like being the link that keeps us all together." He kissed her again.

"What about Waters, Waters and Montgomery?"

"I didn't really want to work for them as much as I simply wanted to practice my craft. Believe it or not, there's a market for good lawyers in the Keys. But I don't have to deal with crazy, fighting families. I write wills, help with property transfers, write a lot of agreements for the businessmen who want the same thing I do—peace and quiet and the ability to fish when I want to."

She laughed.

"I love it there. Would you care if we lived there?"

She laughed. "Sun and warm weather all year round... And you and Rex? I'd love living there too."

"And maybe we can get married in Paris?"

"I liked Scotland. You think the MacDonalds would let us use the compound?"

"I think they're family, and they'd be happy to have us."

"So, it's settled. Another wedding in Scotland."

"Another wedding in Scotland." He peeked at her. "Next summer?"

She stood on her tiptoes to brush her lips across his. "Next summer." She grinned. "Get a kilt."

He threw his head back and laughed. The sound echoed through the small apartment and followed them to the limo and the airstrip where his private jet awaited.

When they were in the air, Marnie sank into the plush seat and closed her eyes.

This was the rest of her life. And it would be a good one.

No more fears.

No more worries.

No more secrets.

EPILOGUE

DESPITE THE HEAVY snow falling on Mannington, Kansas, on Christmas Eve night, the Hinton family's smallest jet made a safe landing at the private airstrip. Marnie bundled up Rex for the walk from the airplane's steps to the limo Jace had waiting, as Danny grabbed the handle for Wiggles's carrier.

He groaned. "We've got to buy him diet dog food."

"Don't be silly. He's a Lab. He's growing."

They stepped out into the big, fat, fluffy flakes that fell around them, creating a winter wonderland.

"I can see why Leni doesn't want to leave here."

Marnie looked around in awe. "Yeah. But this cold white stuff will get old in a week or two. I like the ocean. The sun."

When they reached the limo, Danny opened the door for her. It was one of the compromises they had found. They needed to be able to do simple, normal things for themselves and each other.

Before Marnie slid Rex into the car seat, she removed his big coat, fastening him into the seat wearing only his hoodie. Danny had already gotten the sermon on how big coats can leave the harness too loose. So, he said nothing, just followed her into the car when Rex was secure.

"Nervous?"

"About seeing your entire family again?" She laughed. Wearing a black wool coat with her auburn hair tucked under a thick white knit cap and a matching scarf wrapped around her neck, she looked like she was prepared for frozen tundra, not a snowstorm in Middle America. "I did an interview that caused every person in Manhattan to know who I was. I've handled worse than the six sets of parents at your sister's house."

He took her hand, kissed the knuckles. "You've been very brave."

She laughed. "Stop teasing."

He couldn't help it. He loved hearing her laugh. There'd been something about her from the very first second he'd met her. Something that had drawn him. On the deepest level, he'd known he'd fight heaven and earth to keep her, and in some ways he had.

The limo driver took them to the door of the huge house Nick and Leni had built. Danny pulled the hood of Rex's sweatshirt up to cover his head and raced inside, Marnie on his heels.

They stepped into the high-ceilinged foyer, open to almost the entire first floor amid a cry of "Merry Christmas!"

Removing Rex's hood, Danny said, "Merry Christmas!" as his family poured over to hug Marnie first, then him. As always, someone took Wiggles's crate to let him loose and someone scooped his son away from him. This time it was Penny.

"He's so cute!"

"You're going to have your own cute grandchild in a few months."

A round, pregnant Charlotte grinned. Jace shook his head, laughing.

Penny glanced at Danny. "Technically, Rex is my grandson too... Step-grandson." She winced. "Good gravy, we have a lot of family."

A laugh erupted from the group. Leni's adoptive parents, Danny's adoptive parents, Leni and Nick, Nick's parents, Charlotte and Jace, Mark and Penny—

And Danny and Marnie. It had almost taken a miracle to get them together.

As if reading Danny's mind, Mark slipped away from his new wife, over to Danny. "Thank you for coming, son."

For the first time, having Mark call him son didn't send blistering anger crackling along Danny's nerve endings.

He glanced at Marnie, who'd removed her coat and walked into the kitchen area. She took one of Leni's cookies, bit into it, and her face filled with bliss. Going through what she had, had shown Danny the realities of what Mark had been facing every time he'd brought a child into this world and made him see the validity of Mark's fears.

But Marnie had also taught him to count his blessings, see the good before the bad. Not care so much about how or why and simply enjoy the life with which he'd been blessed—

He'd go through it all again, because she'd been worth it.

And this reunion, the huge family created by parents, adoptive parents, kids and of course Penny and Mark, might be the payoff Mark had always lived for. A time when he could be with his kids, have the family he'd longed for, finally be a real dad.

"You don't think I'd miss Nick and Leni's Christmas Eve party, do you—" he glanced around, then caught Mark's gaze "—Dad?"

Mark's eyes filled with tears. "That's the best Christmas gift I ever got."

Danny clasped his shoulder and maneuvered him in the direction of the kitchen area, where everyone had gathered around a baked ham, homemade rolls and so many cookies Danny was sure no one could count them. A huge Christmas tree decorated with white lights and red bows sat by the fireplace in the adjoining family room, and Christmas carols played softly in the background.

"Oh, so you don't want the watch I bought you?"

Mark sniffed. "I think I have forty of them."

Danny threw his head back and laughed. All animosity, all confusion, wiped away.

As Penny ambled to the big center island with the promise of a cookie to Rex, with Leni and Nick taking drink requests while Jace talked on his phone handling a teeny-tiny problem with a rock star who wanted Tiffany's opened because he forgot to get his mom a gift, Danny joined Marnie by the platter of cookies.

He slid his arm along her shoulders. "Welcome to the rest of your life."

She cuddled against him. "It's going to be an adventure, remember?"

He laughed. "Yes. It is."

* * * * *

LAWFULLY UNWED

ALLISON LEIGH

For Amanda and Chad
with all of my love.

Chapter One

"Delicious cake, Nell."

"It's going to be a great year, Nell."

"Don't look a day older, Nell."

With a smile that felt wooden on her face, Nell Brewster returned hugs as the well-wishers departed The Wet Bar one after another.

Fortunately, there weren't as many people at the pub as Nell's best friend, Rosalind, had expected. She was the one who'd insisted on the party for Nell. Her reasoning was that Friday afternoon on a holiday weekend would be perfect. Prime time for their crowd to escape their offices for a little more R&R before the long weekend. The July

Fourth holiday—on the coming Monday—meant no court proceedings until Tuesday.

"It's not every day a girl turns thirty-six," Ros had said on a laugh not even a month ago when she'd emailed the invitations.

Thank God for that, is what Nell had thought. At the time, she'd been thinking only about becoming another year older and feeling like she was spinning the same wheels she'd been spinning for years.

Now, as far as birthdays went, she couldn't have imagined a worse one. If she could have skipped the celebration altogether, she would have.

Ros had—a fact that had earned more than a few comments.

Instead of telling the truth behind her absence, Nell had just let everyone assume that her friend was stuck on a case. Anyone who knew Ros knew that she wasn't the type who would have escaped for an early holiday celebration if she still had work to do. She was too devoted to her career.

And why not? Rosalind Pastore was the heir apparent at her father's law firm. She'd just been made a partner. Working was a reasonable excuse for her absence that afternoon, and a far more preferable one than the truth.

That was going to come out soon enough.

The legal community in Cheyenne—in the

entire state of Wyoming for that matter—was a tight one.

Nell suffered through a final hug from Scott Muelhaupt—the newest associate at Pastore Legal—as he wished her a happy birthday for what felt like the tenth time. He hugged her longer than necessary, but she supposed he figured he had a right to, given the fact that they'd been casually dating for several weeks now.

"Sure I can't take you out somewhere for dinner?" He smiled hopefully. He was a nice-looking guy. Decent. He smelled clean and he even took his mother out for dinner every Sunday afternoon.

He just didn't make any real bells ring for Nell, much less any cymbals crash.

She wondered if he'd be as interested in her once word got out that she'd quit her job at Pastore Legal. Or if he, like Ros—with whom she'd been friends forever—would decide it was time to cut all ties. If he—again like Ros—would land on the other side of the line that had been drawn in the sand between Nell and Martin Pastore.

Martin. The founder of Pastore Legal. Champion of the people.

As long as the "people" weren't an associate named Nell Brewster.

Quit or be fired.

Those had been her choices. She'd figured that

out quickly enough even though she hadn't been so quick to see everything else.

She hated knowing how oblivious she'd been. Hated knowing that she'd been such an easy pawn. Really, *really* hated facing the fact that for so long she'd put her trust where it didn't belong.

At thirty-six, she was no smarter than she'd been at twenty-six. Or sixteen, for that matter.

"I'm sure." She slid off the seat where she'd been tensely perched as those who *had* stopped by for birthday cake and adult beverages said their goodbyes, and kept the tall metal-backed stool between them. Casually dating a work associate was fine and dandy. Until it wasn't. "Thanks, though."

Scott shrugged, ever good-natured. "Next time."

She kept her wooden smile in place as she waved toward the slab of cake that remained on the long table. "Take some cake. There's plenty."

It was sized for the crowd Ros had initially expected. The crowd that hadn't panned out.

At another time, the two of them would have laughed about it, just figuring that left more cake and wine for them. Neither of which was ever a bad thing.

But it wasn't another time.

Still, what was a copious amount of leftover cake when the rest of Nell's life had landed in such an unexpected mess?

No job.

No best friend.

She stifled a sigh, then nearly jumped out of her skin when a tall man brushed against her as he took the barstool next to hers and greeted the bartender by name.

She automatically shifted aside with a murmured apology, but pressed her lips together when she realized who the man was.

Well, this was just the icing on the cake, wasn't it? Proof that she really *was* oblivious.

One portion of her pathetic mind heard the newcomer order a drink while the rest of her bristled with fresh awareness.

It was always that way when it came to Archer Templeton.

Bristling nerves. Bristling irritation. Bristling…whatever.

The last time she'd seen him had been almost a month ago, in a small courtroom several hours away from Cheyenne.

Now, before she could even ask what he was doing here, Archer turned to her, the squat glass Cheri the bartender had given him clasped in his long, square-tipped fingers and said, "Happy birthday, Cornelia." His lips were curved slightly as he lifted the glass in a toast.

Even though she knew better, she couldn't help feeling a secret thrill at the notion that he was there at The Wet Bar because of *her*. Her pulse quickened, and she felt a vague but inevitable cymbal crash. And it annoyed the daylights out of her. "Why are *you* here?"

The faint lines arrowing out from his vivid green eyes deepened with obvious amusement. "Ah, Nell." He waved his whiskey glass slightly in the direction of the table and the leftover cake. "Is it too hard to believe I'm here to wish an old friend a happy birthday?"

She steeled herself against the charm that he'd no doubt been radiating since birth. He'd certainly had it ever since they met half her lifetime ago. But it was dangerous to be sucked into that charm. She'd had too many of her own court cases decimated because of Archer's charm, which made it so easy to forget how fiercely brilliant he was.

"Yes." She narrowed her eyes at him. "You've heard, haven't you." It wasn't a question. "*That's* why you're here."

His tawny eyebrows rose a fraction. "Heard what? That you and Muelhaupt are a thing?" he goaded, his eyes glinting. "You always did go for the mousy type. What's he in charge of again at Pastore Legal? Keeping the flowers fresh in the conference room?"

Her jaw tightened. Scott was a very competent tax lawyer and she knew the more she defended him to Archer, the more he'd make of it. And Archer never had anything good to say about her law firm and particularly the man who'd founded it. "Go away, Archer."

He smiled and a dimple flashed in his lean cheek. "Is that any way to treat an old friend?"

She dragged her eyes away from the dimple and the cheek. Not without noticing it was smooth. Freshly shaven. Which meant he had probably been in court that day. Otherwise, he would have sported the unshaven look.

She'd seen him both ways so many times over the years and it was a toss-up which was more appealing.

And now, because of him, she felt too warm in her suit jacket. And she'd rather chew glass than let it show. "Just because we've known each other for years doesn't mean we're old friends." Her voice was flat. "You're just Ros's brother." Stepbrother, technically.

Was it her imagination or had his smoothly charming smile become a fraction less smooth? He lifted his hand and tucked an escaped curl behind her ear. "Your understanding is as faulty as your allegiance to Martin Pastore," he drawled, with the usual anti-Pastore edge in his voice.

Then his hand dropped away and he lifted his glass again in salute.

Only the salute wasn't for her any more than the relaxed smile that crossed his face was. The aim was off entirely. Instead, both were directed toward a smashingly attractive blonde who was crossing toward Archer, a brilliant smile on her beautiful face.

Her name was Taylor Potts. *Judge* Taylor Potts.

Nell hid a grimace as the judge offered her cheek for Archer to kiss when he stood to greet her. She settled her palm on his chest with the familiarity of a lover. "Sorry I'm late," she practically purred. "Got caught up on a new ethics case. Hope I was worth the wait."

Nell practically choked. She slid back onto the barstool she'd nearly abandoned just minutes ago and caught the bartender's eye as she turned her back on the couple. "I'll take that champagne now," she said, trying with all of her might to tune out Archer and his judge.

Of course he hadn't come to The Wet Bar because of Nell.

The bartender held up the bottle that she hadn't wanted earlier. The bottle that had been a gift from Ros.

She nodded and waved her hand in invitation to pour a glass. "That's the one, Cheri. Open up that puppy," she said with false brightness.

After all. It's not every day a girl turns thirty-six.

"You sure I can't talk you into coming with me?" Taylor angled her lovely head as she smiled up at Archer.

It had been several hours since they'd shared a drink at The Wet Bar. After they'd left, they'd had dinner at the most expensive restaurant in Cheyenne. There was nothing fast about the service at Clever Bacie's and Archer would have preferred a steak dinner to the Asian fusion cuisine, but it was Taylor's favorite place and the food was good.

He'd always enjoyed her company. She was smart. Funny. Attractive. And had been as disinterested in serious ties as he'd been.

Until lately.

He was thirty-nine years old. He recognized the signs.

"Sorry," he said, and he actually was. Because he'd miss their easy, no-ties relationship. "I've got to be in Braden early in the morning." It was the truth. His hometown was several hours away.

Even when she made a face, she did it beautifully. "Well, a rain check, then."

He smiled noncommittally and opened her car door for her. "Drive careful."

He heard her faint sigh, though the smile on her face didn't fade as she sank into the driver's seat of her luxury sedan. "Will I hear from you next week?"

"If I'm in town." He leaned down and brushed a kiss over her cheek.

"Gage Stanton needing you again in Colorado?"

"Gage isn't the only one I do business with in Denver," Archer reminded her, though it was true the real estate developer had paid the lion's share of Archer's billable hours over the last few years. Most recently because of a hotly contested property on Rambling Mountain near Weaver, also several hours north of Cheyenne. Braden and Weaver, situated about thirty miles apart, were both small towns. But together, they managed to meet the needs of the residents in their region and if Gage's plan to develop a resort came to pass, it would change the tourism landscape altogether for both communities. "I *do* have a practice in Denver."

"And a few others spread across Wyoming," she said wryly. "I don't remember you being so ambitious back in our law school days."

He chuckled. "I don't remember you aspiring to be a judge, either."

She shrugged. "What can I say? Legal aid is satisfying but it's hard to pay the bills on that sort of wage." She pushed a button and her car started, the window rolled down, her seat automatically adjusted and a soft voice began reciting her schedule for the day.

"Particularly bills that come with cars like this." He closed her door for her and backed away.

Her smile widened and with a light wave, she drove away.

He blew out a breath and started walking down the street to where his truck was parked outside The Wet Bar. When he reached it, though, he didn't get in.

Instead, he stood there on the sidewalk, dithering like some damn fool.

"Be smart, Arch," he muttered aloud, not caring that he earned a startled glance from an older couple walking past. Nell hadn't appreciated his making an appearance for her birthday earlier. If she were still inside—and that was a pretty large *if*—she wouldn't feel any differently now.

He was supposed to be in Braden early in the morning. Not because of the Rambling Mountain deal—that was currently on pause, tangled in the red tape that Gage Stanton was paying him to untangle—but because his sister Greer expected all hands to be on deck for her son Finn's first birthday party.

Archer hadn't been home in nearly a month. He didn't have a problem helping out even though he knew there were plenty of other able-bodied and willing helpers Greer could count on.

He pivoted on his heel and pulled out his keys to unlock the truck.

He'd known Nell in law school, too. She and Ros had been just starting out when he and Taylor had been finishing. He'd known Nell even before that, though, thanks to her friendship with Ros.

She'd accompanied his stepsister to Braden one summer during one of Ros's forced visits with her mother.

Nell, whose mother had recently died, had seemed to enjoy the time more than Ros had. His stepsister hadn't been there because she wanted to be. She'd been there only because she had to be. Ordinarily, Ros lived with her dad, Martin, in Cheyenne and wanted nothing to do with her mother or the family that Meredith had made with Archer's dad in Braden.

Be smart, Arch.

He pocketed the keys, turned back around and crossed the sidewalk in long strides. He doubted Nell would still be there. Once he confirmed that, he'd go back to his place, grab his bag and drive on out to Braden tonight. There was always somewhere to sleep at his folks' place, even though it might be on the couch if they were on grandparent duty watching one of his sisters' kids.

And if, by chance, she *were* still inside—

He entered the pub, which was a lot more crowded now than it had been hours earlier. A lot more raucous, too, with classic Stones on the jukebox vying to be heard over voices and laughter.

But there was no sign of Nell; he couldn't make out her tightly knotted dark hair or boxy gray suit among the crowd. The table where the cake and gift bags had been was now covered in beer bottles and surrounded by several good ol' boys obviously out for a good time as they shouted encouragement to a trio of ladies dancing for all they were worth in one corner.

That wasn't disappointment he felt.

Nope.

Just relief.

Keys in hand once more, he turned to go, waiting as a gaggle of kids who barely looked old enough to drive, much less drink, shuffled inside. While he stood there, a peal of high-pitched laughter rose above the jukebox and he glanced over his shoulder toward the source just in time to see a couple of the good ol' boys helping the dancing ladies up onto the bar top.

Last time Archer remembered anyone dancing on a bar top, he'd been in college. Smiling ruefully because he suddenly felt like he'd gotten old, he reached for the door before it swung closed after the kids entered. Another edgy laugh rose above the general din and he glanced over at the dancers again.

And stood stock-still.

The loud voices and the louder music dimmed.

The swinging door knocked into his shoulder.

"Dude, mind if we—" The kid wanting to get past him broke off, his Adam's apple bobbing when Archer's attention slid from the woman dancing on the bar to him. "Sorry," he muttered and turned the other direction.

Archer didn't pay him any mind and entered the fray, pushing his way through the people crowded inside the pub, aiming for the bar. Maybe it was the fact that he stood several inches above six feet. Maybe it was the frown he could feel on his face. Whatever it was, people moved aside and he reached the bar in a matter of seconds.

He reached up and grabbed Nell's wrist. "What the hell are you doing?" His voice was swallowed by the hoots and hollers that were rising in scale by the second, thanks to the gyrations of the women on the bar. One of them had even yanked off her T-shirt and was dancing in just her bra and a short denim skirt.

Fortunately, Nell wasn't that far gone. Yeah, the shapeless jacket of her suit was nowhere to be seen, but at least her silky sleeveless blouse was still where it belonged.

Was it any wonder he hadn't noticed her at first?

No jacket. No shoes. Her hair let out of that godforsaken knot she always sported and springing down beyond her shoulders.

She shook off his hand with an annoyed glare. "Go away!" She twirled again and the hem of her plain skirt slapped him in the face.

"Thatagirl," someone hooted when the second

woman tore off her shirt and swung it around her head.

Archer caught Cheri's eye. "It's just a matter of time before the cops come," he said loudly, leaning toward her so she could hear.

The bartender shrugged helplessly. "Won't be the first time," she shouted back.

Archer grimaced. He tried to catch Nell's hand again, but she wasn't having any of that. Her cheeks were flushed, her dark eyes wild.

He leaned toward Cheri again. "How much has she had?"

"I didn't think it was enough for that." She turned away to stick another glass under the taps.

Archer followed Nell as she danced her way along the bar. "Where's Ros?"

He knew that Nell heard him because her eyes skated over his before she spun away again.

Only this time her bare foot slipped on a wet spot and she started to fall.

His heart shot up into his throat and he barely caught her before she toppled over the edge. He grunted when her elbow caught him on the nose and he muttered an apology to the stunned woman he nearly unseated when he caught Nell.

Nell, who wasn't showing the least bit of gratitude that he'd prevented her from tumbling head over heels right onto the floor of The Wet Bar with what seemed like half the town's population looking on.

"Leggoame," she slurred, pushing ineffectually at his hands.

"You're drunk." He set her on her feet but grabbed her arms when her knees failed to do their job and she swayed wildly.

"Amnot." Her head lolled against his arm when he slid it behind her back. She looked up at him, but her eyes—dark as chocolate drops—were unfocused. Her dark hair was a riot of curls clinging to her cheeks and the long column of her neck. "Jushavinfun." Her eyes rolled slightly but she jerked herself upright. "Issmybirthday," she announced as if it were news.

"Where's Ros?" he asked again.

Nell's forehead wrinkled. Her lips pinched together. Those chocolate-drop eyes suddenly gleamed wetly. "Snothere."

"I can see that." He renewed his grip around her shoulders and looked toward Cheri again. "Jacket? Purse?"

The bartender jerked her chin. "Behind here. Just give me a sec."

"Why *isn't* she here? You two never miss celebrating each other's birthdays."

"Haddafight."

Surprise jerked at him. He knew *he* had plenty of fights with his stepsister—they hadn't been able to agree on the time of day from the moment his father had married her mother.

Nell was sniffing hard as if she was trying not to cry.

"About what?"

Her lips moved and he almost thought she was going to tell him. But the days of her confiding in him were long gone, and instead, annoyance suddenly crossed her face again. She pushed against him. "Lemmego. I can stand."

It was easy to evade her puny efforts. "Sure you can. I'll let you go as soon as I pour you into a cab to go home."

The tears came back and she looked even more miserable. Which was saying something.

"Toldyou. Haddafight. Can't." She shook her head.

As far as Archer could tell, that just made her sway even more dizzily. He caught her around the waist, trying not to remember the last time he'd held her so closely. That had also been a long time ago. Too long ago to still be so vivid in his mind. She was thinner now. Not a lot, because she'd always been slender. But—

"Here's her stuff." Cheri interrupted his thoughts, pushing a bundle of dull gray fabric and an oversize purse into his other arm. "No idea about her shoes."

"Thasmapurse," Nell observed.

Cheri gave Archer a dry look. "Better get moving," she warned, cocking her head to one side. "Think I hear the siren."

Archer wasn't particularly concerned about the police. But he knew Nell would regret getting caught up in the fray once she was sober. Her fall from the bar hadn't stopped the other two women from dancing, and a dozen people had begun pounding their fists on the bar in tempo with the drums.

He decided her missing shoes weren't worth the time it would take to find them and he hitched her up once more around the waist as he headed toward the door. It wasn't all that easy when she seemed determined to go the other way, but he prevailed, finally pushing through the doorway and getting her out onto the sidewalk, where the police siren was close enough to be deafening. Blue-and-red lights danced over the vehicles parked at the curb.

Including his own truck.

The sound of the siren at least seemed to quell Nell's efforts to escape and she didn't fight him when Archer lifted her up into the truck. "If you don't want to go back to the condo, where *do* you want to go?" He braced himself to hear Muelhaupt's name, but she didn't say anything.

She just shook her head again, looking sad and pale and pathetic.

He didn't need Nell Brewster tugging at his heartstrings. *Those* days were supposed to be long gone, too.

"Fine," he muttered, and yanked the seat belt around her, clicking it into place. There was no point in calling his stepsister on Nell's behalf. Ros always took her sweet-ass time returning his calls. Which was one of the reasons why he generally went with the in-person route with her, despite the fact that it annoyed her no end. "Hotel it is."

Nell didn't react. Her eyes were closed.

When he closed the door, she leaned heavily against it, and her cheek smashed inelegantly against the window.

If he weren't so concerned, he would have been amused. Would have considered snapping a shot of her on his cell phone just for the pleasure of tormenting her with the image some day off in the future.

But Nell had never been one to tie one on.

She'd always been too uptight for that.

He quickly rounded the truck and sketched a wave at the police officers who were now leaving their vehicle and heading quickly toward The Wet Bar.

"Hey, Arch." The senior partner—a woman named Donna Rhodes—greeted him with a resigned look. "You coming from in there?"

"Yeah. Probably over occupancy, but nobody's naked and nobody's fighting."

"Yet." That came from the younger partner—a guy named Marcus Welby. He was so young that Archer couldn't help but wonder if his parents were aware they'd named him after an iconic television character from decades past. "Place is dull as ditchwater on weekdays but come the weekends?"

The two officers entered the bar as a second patrol car pulled up with its lights also flashing.

Archer didn't hang around to see what would happen next. He got in the truck and left the scene before it had a chance to actually become a scene.

When he was a couple of blocks away where the sirens weren't as loud, he pulled over again at the side of the road and nudged Nell's shoulder with his fingertips. "Hey. You conscious over there?"

Her answer was a resounding snore.

He sat back and exhaled. "Well, hell, Arch. Now what are you going to do?"

Chapter Two

Her mouth tasted like a rabbit had taken up residence inside, and maybe even decided to die there, too. Her eyes felt gritty—too gritty to dare trying to open. Her dry lips matched the dire condition inside her mouth. And her head…oh, the pain in her head was something to behold.

Nell groaned, grimaced and gingerly rolled onto her side. At least the pillow was smooth and wonderfully cool against her cheek as she hugged it close and tried to block out all of the wholly unpleasant sensations involved with waking.

For a brief moment she had a vague thought she

might have the flu. But memory surfaced quickly enough. She didn't have a virus. She wasn't sick.

She was paying the price for drowning her miseries the night before in a veritable vat of alcohol.

She snuggled her face deeper into the cool, squishy pillow, seeking comfort and escape from the hideous hangover.

How long had it been since she'd suffered even a fraction of this misery? Five years? Ten? There'd been a lot of cocktails at Ros's thirty-fifth birthday the year before, but—

Ros.

Nell rolled onto her back and sighed, though it came out more like a groan. She and Ros just needed to clear the air. They'd been friends for so long that Nell couldn't imagine her life without Ros in it. She was the only "family" that Nell even had. Her and Martin.

Her head pounded anew at the thought. He'd been a father figure to her, whether he'd ever intended to be or not. He had certainly been her mentor when it came to the law. If it hadn't been for him, she'd have never even gotten into law school. Instead, she'd probably still be working at a used-book store.

She gingerly rubbed her aching forehead, knuckled her eyes, then after a quick, bracing breath, shoved back the covers and swung her bare feet off the bed.

Instead of feeling the warmth of soft sculptured carpet under her toes, though, she encountered a solid surface. A cold, smooth, solid surface.

Her eyes flew open despite the grittiness and she squinted against the light streaming through the mullioned windows next to the bed.

Her bedroom had carpeted floors. And it definitely did not have mullioned windows.

Horror was congealing inside her stomach and she breathed carefully, very afraid that she was going to be sick.

Where was she?

There wasn't one single thing about the bedroom that was familiar. Not the floor—a deep brown wood, she saw through her slitted eyes—or the navy blue sheets and pillowcases on the bed. The nightstand next to the wide, wide bed—hers was the same full-size thing she'd owned since college—was also wood. Good, solid, maybe even an antique. It didn't quite match the massive dresser across the room from the bed, but it coordinated well. Nothing sat on the top of the nightstand except an angular Tiffany-style lamp.

Her stomach roiling, she cautiously slid from the bed, tugging the hem of her silky tank into place. She was still wearing her blouse from last night, as well as her skirt. Surely that was a good sign.

It was bad enough to wake up in a place she

didn't recognize. But at least she wasn't naked to boot. *That* would bring on a whole new height of alarm.

And she already felt like she was perched on the platform of a high dive.

She took a cautious step on the wood floor, freezing in place when it emitted a soft creak.

She listened intently for a sound in response from beyond the closed bedroom door, but couldn't hear a thing. Maybe because her head was already filled with the sound of her heart. It was pounding so hard it seemed to reverberate through her chest as well as her aching head.

She realized she was holding her breath when she started to feel dizzy, and she exhaled shakily, which also sounded excessively loud. She took another step. This one was unaccompanied by a creaking floorboard. Then another. And another until she reached the dresser and the silver-framed photo next to a jumble of coins and a half-empty pack of chewing gum.

Her hand was shaking as she carefully reached for the photo to angle it so she could see what it was, but despite all the care she took, she still managed to fumble with the frame and it slid into the change, knocking several pennies and quarters off the side of the dresser. She swore under her breath, hearing the ping as the coins hit the floor and bounced and rolled. She grabbed the picture with both hands, holding it down on the dresser as if the thing were in danger of taking flight.

Considering her clumsiness, maybe it was.

Still, there was no noise from beyond the bedroom door. Feeling weak with relief, alarm and outright disgust with herself, she rested her elbows on the dresser and sucked in unsteady breaths as she studied the photo. It was an old one. She was making that judgment based on the style of clothing the pretty blonde woman wore. She was holding a baby who could have been a boy or a girl—the yellow blanket it was wrapped in gave no clue.

Nell propped her aching head in her hand and closed her eyes again.

Should she just straighten her spine and leave the room to find out where on earth she was? Or should she snoop some more and gird herself with more knowledge before she opened the door?

Snooping was sort of in her nature.

She was a lawyer, after all.

Her fingers toyed with the pull on the dresser drawer. She tugged lightly and the drawer slid open an inch. Another inch. All she gained was a glimpse of white before she heard a thump outside the door that had her hastily closing the drawer.

She whirled so that her back was to the dresser, hiding her shaking hands behind her, and watched the door while her heart hammered and her stomach skittered around uneasily.

She flinched as though she'd been struck when there was a soft knock on the door. One, two, three of them in a quick little row.

Knock-knock-knock.

She chewed the inside of her lip, her breath building and building against the dam inside her chest.

"Nell?" The voice as well as the knock was still soft.

It was also distinctively male.

She clenched her teeth and frowned. The voice was male. Scott's? She was embarrassed even more that she couldn't tell for sure. She'd never been to his place, but if this *was* his home, maybe she wouldn't have to feel quite so annoyed with herself.

They were dating. More or less. She hadn't slept with him, though he'd made it plain he was interested.

Her gaze slid guiltily to the bed. The bedding was tumbled. The pillows askew.

Had she slept with him? The state of the bed didn't give any clue at all.

She rubbed her forehead. Scott had left the bar the night before, though. She didn't remember him returning. But then again, she didn't remember a lot of—

"Nell?" The deep voice and the knock were a little louder this time. "You awake yet?"

Scott's voice wasn't that deep. Was it?

She shook her head, wishing this was a really bad and really realistic dream. She could feel the ridges of the well-preserved wood beneath her feet, for goodness' sake!

She stared at the door handle, her mind dancing fatalistically among the nonsensical thoughts, when the voice caused a spark.

A sudden, quick, awful spark of familiarity.

"No." She shook her head. "No, absolutely *no.*"

But the doorknob was turning, and she watched it as though the worst sort of slow-motion nightmare she had ever endured was unfolding. Then the door swung open to reveal the owner of the voice.

His green eyes were brilliant and showed no signs whatsoever of his having tied one on the night before. And when he spotted her standing there all frozen with her backside pressed against the drawer she'd peeked into, he arched one of his tawny eyebrows slightly. "Well, well, well, Cornelia," Archer drawled. "You *are* awake."

"You!" Accusation flooded her voice.

His other eyebrow rose, too. "What'd I do?"

She knew her mouth was gaping like a water-starved fish's. "What *didn't* you do?"

He shrugged, which only drew her attention

to the breadth of his shoulders beneath the plain white undershirt he was wearing.

He padded barefoot into the room and set the breakfast tray he was holding on top of the dresser. "I'm sure you'll tell me in several dozen more paragraphs than necessary." He lifted one of the plain brown mugs from the tray and extended it toward her. "Assume you still like it light and sweet?"

She dragged her eyes up from the slouchy navy-colored pajama pants hanging precariously on his very male hips. "What?"

"Coffee." He pushed the mug into her numb hand and wrapped her fingers around it. "Don't drop the mug. It's one of the last ones I have of hers."

She was having a hard time putting two coherent thoughts together. Not only had he brought coffee, but there was also a stack of golden toast sitting on a paper plate and a jar of jam with a knife sticking out of it.

Cymbals were crashing, and not necessarily inside her head. The only thing she knew for sure was that whatever was going on here, it was his fault. Knowing it was an uncharitable thought—he *had* made toast, after all—didn't stop her from having it. "Hers?"

"My mother." He tapped the photo frame before putting a finger beneath her hand to nudge it—

and the mug—upward toward her lips. "Drink. You'll feel better."

She actually took a sip of the coffee, which had exactly the right amount of cream and sugar, before she determinedly set the mug back on the tray. Considering everything, it was a minor miracle she didn't spill it or drop it. "What have you done? Why am I here?"

He leaned leisurely against the doorjamb and cradled his mug in his wide palm. "I'm wounded." He sounded mildly amused. The corners of his sinfully shaped lips curved upward. "You don't remember? And here I've landed myself in the doghouse with my sister for choosing you over my nephew's birthday."

"No I do *not* remember." She shoved her tangled hair away from her eyes, the better to glare at him. "Obviously." She drew out the word with what Ros—a diehard *Harry Potter* fan—had long ago termed Nell's best Snape-ishness.

His green eyes seemed to gain an extra sparkle as they traveled from the mop that her hair must resemble, down over her wrinkled silk tank and even more wrinkled skirt, to her toes that were actually clenching against the wood floor.

Her cheeks felt hot. Naturally, she needed a pedicure in the worst way, too. She hadn't made her last standing appointment with Renée because of a filing Martin had—

It all came tumbling down on her again, managing to supplant even the worry over what had occurred here last night.

Martin's betrayal.

The argument with Ros.

Her recent change from being among the gainfully employed.

The weight of it all slammed down on her shoulders, making her slump.

Every muscle and joint and hair follicle aching, she sank down on the edge of the bed, then just as hurriedly pushed off it again.

The bed belonged to Archer Templeton. She had no idea at all how she'd come to be sleeping in it, whether she was still fully clothed or not. She knew the man from old, and he was cleverer than the devil himself.

She snatched a piece of his gum from the dresser, peeled off the foil and shoved it into her mouth to banish the deceased Mr. Cottontail. Then she steeled herself to brush past him to leave the room. Not that she knew where she was headed, but anywhere was better than the bedroom.

As soon as she was in the hall, she spotted the staircase and aimed straight for it. She pounded down the steps as though Archer was at her heels, even though he wasn't. She felt breathless and even more nauseated when she reached the bottom. The living room was straight ahead. The kitchen to the right. She turned left and fortunately found the powder room.

She slammed the door, locked it and spent several minutes hanging over the sink while cold water ran over her wrists until she felt a little better.

Oh, her head still felt as heavy as a bowling ball with loose rocks clanging around inside, but at least she didn't think she'd vomit on her poorly maintained pedicure.

She wrapped the gum in a square of tissue paper and tossed it in the small gold trash can in the corner next to the vintage pedestal sink that—knowing Archer—was probably an original. He was the most annoying person she'd ever met, but he'd always had impeccable taste. No reproductions—no matter how excellent—for him.

She cupped water in her hands and rinsed her mouth, then splashed more water over her face. When she straightened again, her reflection in the oval mirror over the sink was genuinely frightening but at least her eyes didn't look as bleary as she felt. She raked her fingers through her hair, spreading the dampness beyond her hairline, and longed for a clip or hair tie, but—like everything else in her life at the moment—no luck.

She adjusted her skirt so the vent was once more in the back where it belonged and tucked in her blouse. Barefoot and jacketless or not, she couldn't very well hibernate in Archer's elegant little powder room.

She straightened her shoulders and left the room.

He had come downstairs and was now sprawled in a leather chair, without a care in the world, coffee mug still cupped in his wide palm.

His smooth jawline of the night before was now shadowed in a golden-brown stubble and his thick, gilded hair tumbled over his forehead.

He was the most annoying man she knew and the most attractive. Still.

Didn't it just figure?

With no small amount of relief, she spotted her oversize purse sitting on a table in the foyer and pounced on it. "Shoes?"

"God only knows."

Her stomach churned all over again. Not because of a lost pair of shoes. But because losing them at all was just more evidence of behavior she couldn't recall.

Her fingers were shaking as she pulled her cell phone from her purse where it was tucked in its usual pocket. The battery was nearly dead and she had a couple of dozen notifications for new messages. She ignored them as she sent a request for a rideshare. Without looking at Archer again, she went out the front door.

He had a wooden garden bench sitting on the

porch beneath the wide mullioned windows of the living room. She perched on the edge of it while she dug in her purse for her sunglasses.

They afforded her clanging head with a small bit of ease when she put them on.

Her knuckles were white around her phone as she watched the progress of her rideshare on the screen, praying for all she was worth that the car would arrive before Archer decided to come out and torment her some more.

He had the ability to do that simply by breathing the same air as her. It wouldn't have been so problematic, except that he was perfectly aware of the effect he had.

At least he had been back in the day.

Still, it remained a good reason to avoid him.

The clock on her phone told her it was almost noon. She had no sense of how long she'd slept, except that it hadn't been long enough.

She lifted her sunglasses enough to rub her eyes, and then consulted her phone app again. The ride was around the corner.

She breathed a little easier now that it was almost here, because she was certain she could feel Archer's eyes drilling into her through the window. She just hoped he didn't come out onto the porch. She pushed off the bench, dragging the strap of her purse over her shoulder, and walked barefoot down the shallow brick steps. She crossed the neat patch of summer-green grass and wondered if Archer actually mowed it himself.

And wondering *that* annoyed her, too.

She marched a little more briskly from the grass to the sidewalk and toward the corner where a little hybrid vehicle had just come into view. She waved her arm, flagging it down, and peered into the window, making certain the driver matched the one on her app. She did, so Nell opened the back door, tossed her purse inside and folded herself in after it.

"Morning." The driver was a gray-haired woman with a cheerful chirpy voice. She read off Nell's home address. "That's where we're heading, yeah?"

Nell closed her eyes and pressed her head against the seat back. "Yes. Thanks," she added a little belatedly once the car lurched into motion. It felt odd the way the vehicle moved along so silently without the noise and feel of a typical gas engine. "How does this thing run in the winter?"

The driver gave another chirp of laughter. "Going to have to wait until this winter to see. I just bought her." She tapped her hand against the steering wheel. "She's a good girl, though. Hasn't failed me yet." She slowed and turned the corner again. "Get a lot of looks from other people, though. Not quite the usual sight yet here in Cheyenne."

"Or the rest of Wyoming," Nell surmised.

The driver laughed again. "Of course, ride-sharing is still pretty new to most folks around here, too." Her cheerful tone was soothing. "Even though it really isn't. I've been doing it nearly five years now."

"Guess you must like it."

"Sure. I can work as much or as little as I want. And the money's better than you might think. I earn more doing this than I did even after twenty-five years in mortgage banking. And retirement is too boring for me." She laughed. "For now, anyway. I like filling my time. What do you do?"

"I'm a lawyer." Nell rubbed a finger against the throbbing in her forehead.

"Mind if I ask where? Person never knows when they might find themselves in need of one."

Nell's lips twisted. "I'm evaluating things at the moment."

"Ah." The driver nodded sagely. "Well, if you need a little financial boost during the evaluation period, I can recommend my company. Decisions sometimes come easier when you let your mind focus on something entirely different. Driving is like that."

"Hmm." Nell owned a nice enough car. She and the bank, anyway. If she needed to, she could squire people around from one address to another. At least until she got settled again in a new law firm. Cheyenne wasn't the largest city around, but Pastore Legal wasn't the only game in town.

She didn't have any idea how long that might take. She'd been working for Martin since she'd passed the bar. She had plenty of friends from other firms—mostly professional acquaintances if she were strictly honest—and she imagined that she'd be able to use that network to get some meetings sooner rather than later.

She hoped.

She wasn't a penniless college student anymore. She had savings. But between her student loans, her car and the rent on the condo she shared with Ros, that nest egg would quickly be consumed. "I'll keep it in mind," she told the driver. "Thanks."

The driver let her off shortly after and quickly drove away in her silent car, already on the way to her next fare.

Nell straightened her shoulders, blew out a deep breath and headed up the steps. She unlocked the door and went inside, automatically pushing the door closed firmly to make sure it latched, and listened.

The absolute silence told her that Ros wasn't there, and Nell's shoulders relaxed again.

She picked up the mail that was scattered on the floor from where it had been pushed through the mail slot in the door and left it and her purse on the narrow acrylic table behind the couch. The presence of the mail on the floor told her that Ros hadn't come home the night before, either.

It wasn't the first time. Unlike Nell, Ros *was* sleeping with the guy she'd been seeing for the past year. But none of the messages on Nell's phone was from her roommate, and Ros always let Nell know if she was staying out.

At least she had until their argument the afternoon before.

She scrubbed her hands down her face and carried her phone with her upstairs to her spacious room.

When she and Ros had rented the condo a few years earlier, they'd both been giddy with delight because one of the previous owners had combined two units into one, making for much larger digs. Both bedrooms were set up like master suites, with their own bathrooms. They shared a study that was lined with legal tomes on one side and the books that Nell's mother had collected while she'd been alive on the other. Both of them spent far more time in that room than they ever did in the gourmet kitchen that the unit also possessed.

The only time the kitchen was ever used for its intended purpose beyond rudimentary sandwiches or coffee was when Ros's boyfriend, Jonathan, was there to cook.

The only drawback was the lack of central air-conditioning, but A/C was needed only during the worst of summer anyway. More often than not, they spent their days at the well-cooled office and at night, window fans sufficed.

Because of the size, the rent was high, but between the two of them, they'd deemed it worth the financial stretch.

Now, Nell flipped on the shower to get it hot and plugged in her phone to charge the battery while she listened to all of the messages that had piled up overnight.

The first few were birthday wishes. But the tone of the messages began to change quickly enough from celebration to shock. Commiseration.

None of them, however, was from Ros.

Nell debated sending her a text, but set aside her phone instead. She brushed her teeth—twice—then showered until the hot water started to run cold.

Then, wrapped in a towel, she checked her phone again. Another half-dozen messages had arrived. Word was definitely getting around that she was out at Pastore Legal.

It was too depressing to respond to any of them so she turned off her phone altogether. Her head still pounded, but she felt somewhat more human. Mopping at her dripping hair with another towel, she went back downstairs and into the kitchen.

Coffee was the next order of business. And maybe some food. She had time on her hands now. She could buy a cookbook. Learn to make something besides a grilled cheese sandwich.

Her gaze fell on the plastic-wrapped loaf of bread.

He'd fixed her toast.

She snatched open the cupboard door to grab a coffee pod and shoved it into place, jabbing viciously at the button to start the brewer.

Had Archer heard the news yet?

She could just imagine what he'd have to say if he had.

"Should have taken me up on my offer," she muttered aloud as the coffee burbled out of the spout and into her bright yellow mug with *Lawyers have feelings too* printed on one side, *Allegedly* printed on the other. "Then you'd be partners in a multioffice firm instead of out on your behind."

She shook the thought out of her head. Nearly finished with law school, she'd believed it would be disastrous going into practice with Archer Templeton. Her allegiance had been to Martin Pastore. Becoming a junior associate there was her dream come true.

The coffee had barely stopped dripping when she yanked it out from beneath the spout. She followed the splash of cream she added with a chaser of sugar—the real stuff—and finally took a sip. It scorched her tongue, but in seconds she could feel the blessed caffeine hitting her system.

She aligned the loaf of bread neatly next to the side of the stainless steel refrigerator and carried her coffee out of the kitchen just in time to hear the rattle of the door lock.

Ros was home.

Nell's stomach churned. She tightened the knotted towel and perched on the narrow arm of the white leather couch.

A moment later, the door swung inward and Rosalind, who looked only slightly better than Nell felt, entered.

Her eyes skated over Nell. "You're here."

"I live here," she said quietly. "My leaving your father's firm doesn't change that."

Ros's lips thinned. She elbowed the door closed and tossed her keys into the stylized bowl sitting on the table next to Nell's purse. "Maybe it should."

Nell's breath left her in a puff. "*Ros*, come on."

"Why? You accused my father of collusion!" Rosalind spread her arms. "The very idea is so ridiculous it's pathetic."

Nell's fingers tightened around her coffee mug. "And as little as a week ago, I'd have agreed with you," she said quietly. "But I saw the records with my own eyes. While he was supposed to be acting on behalf of the court in a probate matter up in Weaver, he was taking money to influence the outcome of the case!" A whole lot of money, as it turned out.

"Well, the outcome *wasn't* influenced," Ros said flatly. "Instead of dying intestate like everyone thought, Otis Lambert *did* leave a will and when it came to light that was that. He left everything but his ranch on that mountain he owned to the state of Wyoming and instructed the ranch itself to be sold off. End of story."

"That doesn't erase what your father tried to do before the will was discovered! He was taking bribes, Ros!"

Her roommate's expression was set. "We're not going to agree about this, Nell. My father would never behave unethically. His reputation is impeccable."

Nell's hands were shaking. She set aside her coffee cup. "I didn't want to believe it, either. There's no way I'm mistaken." She was also badly afraid this instance hadn't been Martin's only transgression, despite his impeccable reputation. He'd been too blasé when she confronted him.

"He showed me the bank account, Nell. It's your name that is on it. Not his."

Nell swallowed hard. She was a lawyer. She knew better than to sign anything she hadn't read. But the amount of paperwork that flowed through

Martin's office was staggering. And she'd trusted him. A note left here or there for her to initial, to sign… She hadn't thought a thing about it. "He put it there."

Ros's expression turned pitying. "If this is about me making partner and you not—"

Nell stood. "This isn't about becoming a partner! For God's sake, Ros, you're my oldest friend. You're like a sister to me."

"And my father was like a father to you. Only he wasn't. You had your own, except he ran out on you when you were sixteen. And *my* father took you in!" Ros raked her fingers through her hair. It was just as dark as Nell's but where Nell's was uncontrollably curly, Ros's was thick and enviably straight. "*My* father who got you into law school. *My* father who hired you even though your grades were mediocre."

Nell's jaw tightened. Her grades might have been mediocre. But that didn't mean she wasn't good at her job now. She just hadn't been good enough, or she would have recognized what Martin had been up to earlier than she had. She would have never initialed this or signed that.

And Rosalind could talk until she was blue in the face about Martin's paternal devotion, but it had always come at a cost. He'd never been the loving father type. If Ros wanted his affection, she'd had to earn it by being a perfect reflection of him.

"You should be thanking him that he's not reporting the situation." Ros was shaking with her anger. "He's still showing loyalty to you and that certainly wouldn't be the case if he *hadn't* been like a father to you." She looked at the diamond watch around her wrist. "I think it's time you move out," she said abruptly.

"What? Right this minute?"

"Obviously not," she snapped and dropped her arm. "I've been thinking about this for a while."

That stung. "Since when?"

Her friend avoided her eyes. "Since a while now," Ros said defensively. "We're not college kids. We're too old to want or need a roommate. It's, well, it's embarrassing frankly."

That *really* stung. "And if I don't want to move? The lease is in both of our names."

"Then I'll move." Ros crossed her arms. "Jonathan and I have been talking about taking things to the next level. He wants a family and—"

Nell's eyebrows climbed into her hairline. "Do *you*? With Jonathan? Two months ago, you told me he was good in the kitchen, but outside of it, not so much!"

Ros looked annoyed at the reminder. "Even if you hadn't done what you did—"

"What *I* did?" Nell's voice rose even more.

"Rosalind Pastore, when have you *ever* known me to lie about something?"

Ros plowed onward. "It still would be time for us to start acting like the grown women that we are. I'm a partner at Pastore Legal now. I should—"

Nell lifted her hand, steeling herself. "Don't. I don't even want to hear it. Your father wants me out at the firm. You want me out of here. You always said you wanted to be like him, and you've succeeded. Congratulations." Her voice went a little hoarse and she picked up her coffee, struggling for composure. "Soon as I can arrange it, I'll be out of your hair, too."

Ros's eyes finally flickered, showing at least some semblance of emotion. "This didn't have to get this ugly, Nell."

She locked her knees. She felt like she'd been betrayed by everything she'd held dear for the last twenty years. She stared straight into her friend's eyes. Because she knew in her heart that she hadn't done one single thing wrong. Except put her faith where it didn't belong. "Didn't it?"

Ros was the first to look away. Then without another word, she ran quickly up the stairs. A moment later, Nell heard the slam of a bedroom door.

She sank down on the couch arm again, and covered her eyes with a shaking hand.

"You all right?"

Startled, she slipped right off the narrow edge of slick white leather to land ignominiously on the floor, hot coffee splashing everywhere. She grabbed the towel that had also slipped, barely keeping it above her breasts and below her butt, and stared at the door, which was slightly ajar.

Right at Archer's damned face peeking through the crack.

Chapter Three

Her cheeks burning more than her coffee-drenched thighs, Nell quickly righted herself so that she was on her knees. "Haven't you done enough? What are you doing here?"

He pushed the door open farther and stepped into the house. "I could hear your voices out on the street." He picked up the coffee mug, as it had continued rolling across the black-tiled floor right toward his feet.

"That doesn't give you permission to barge in."

He held out his hand. "Need help?"

"Not from you." With one hand keeping the bottom of the towel tucked against her thighs and the other keeping the top of it tucked against her chest, she managed to get to her feet. While she had only a length of coffee-splattered white terry cloth protecting her dignity, since earlier this morning, Archer had changed from the undershirt and navy pajama pants into blue jeans and a black pullover.

"And it wasn't closed, by the way."

She couldn't even argue the point with him, because the door often failed to latch the first time around. "If you're here to see your sister, she's upstairs."

He snorted and set the mug on the sofa table. "Stepsister. And no. I'm not."

"Then have you come here to gloat?"

"Because you've left Pastore Legal?"

She didn't understand why it disturbed her so much that he, more so than anyone else who'd been leaving her messages, knew about it. But it did.

"Nothing to gloat about," he said calmly, completely ignoring her stony silence. "I figure you're showing more sense than you have in the last ten, fifteen years." He angled his head, his gaze roving over her. "Did you burn your legs?"

She had, but what was the point of confirming it? "If I ask you to please, *please* leave, will you?"

His lips twitched. Her life felt like it was in the

toilet, but the man's infernal green eyes still had the nerve to sparkle. "What do you think?"

She let out an impatient sound and turned to make her own run up the stairs. Ros's bedroom door was tellingly shut as she passed it heading for her room on the opposite side of the hall.

She shut her door and went into her bathroom again, wetting a fresh cloth to wipe away the coffee on her legs. The skin was red and tender when she blotted it dry. Rather than dress in jeans, she pulled on a calf-length T-shirt dress that she usually wore only to sleep in.

As her hair was drying, it had begun twisting into its usual corkscrew curls and now she yanked it up and into a careless knot. Her reflection in the mirror looked a little feverish, but there wasn't anything she could do about it, so she went back downstairs.

Archer was sprawled on the unforgivingly hard, straight-backed couch as comfortably as he'd been sprawled on the overstuffed chair in his own home.

The coffee had also been wiped up from the floor, though there was a small wet spot on the edge of the area rug. It could have been a lot worse. The rug was as white as the couch.

"Just sit down, Nell," he said calmly when she hovered there at the base of the stairs. "And tell me what happened with Pastore."

Her hand tightened over the newel post. "After you tell *me* what happened last night." Her cheeks felt as feverish as they'd looked in her mirror.

"You mean after you were finished dancing on the bar?"

She winced. "I had hoped that was just a bad dream."

"Look at the bright side. At least you still had on your shirt when the cops showed."

She released the post and slunk over to the opposite end of the couch. The side chair that matched it was piled with law books that she kept meaning to take to the office. "Guess it's good I've already parted ways with Martin. If he heard about that, I'd have been in a different heap of trouble."

"Why *did* you part ways?"

She pressed her tongue against her teeth, studying his unfairly handsome face. "I didn't make partner." It was the truth; just not the truth he'd requested. "I thought it was time for a change."

His eyes narrowed, but after a moment, he shrugged slightly. "Okay. So now what? Have a plan?"

"I have a lot of contacts," she managed. "I'm sure I'll find a new firm without too much trouble."

"You can always work for me."

She couldn't stop the choked sound that rose

in her throat. "I know you don't mean that." And when he'd made the proposition of working together all those years ago, it had been a *with* situation, not a *for*.

He shrugged again. "It would sure piss off Ros, though. Which is par for the course. I'm already in the doghouse with one of my other sisters. Why not make it two."

She pressed her lips together and silence fell between them. She crossed her ankles, then uncrossed them. He showed no sign of leaving. And he still hadn't answered her question about what had occurred the night before.

She toyed with her ragged thumbnail and changed tack. "What doghouse with which sister?" Not including Rosalind, he had four, three of whom were identical triplets.

"Greer. Her youngest, Finn, turns one today. She and her husband, Ryder, are having a big party."

She gave him a sharp look. "Then why are you here?" He'd always put his family first. He was even loyal to Ros in a way. Despite the strained relationship Ros had with her mother, who lived several hours away in Braden, Archer made a point of personally delivering messages and the gifts that Meredith kept sending for birthdays and Christmases and every other little reason she could think of. Ros said he did it to annoy her. Nell had never been so sure. She would have loved to have a mother still around to send her messages and silly little gifts.

"I'll get over to Braden soon enough for cake," he told her.

Which reminded her of her own birthday cake from the day before. Birthday cake and champagne. Way too much champagne.

She folded her fingers together. "Why was I in your bed? We didn't, uh—"

"Play doctor like we used to?"

She gaped. "We never played doctor," she said in a fierce whisper.

He leaned across the cushion separating them. That faint, annoying smile played across his lips. He drew his finger slowly along her cheek, then tapped it once, lightly, against her lower lip.

Her skin burned and she found it very hard to breathe.

He leaned a few inches closer and his deep voice seemed to drop another octave into a whisper of his own. "Then how do we know what each other's bits and pieces look like?"

Every cell in her body lurched. "We agreed not to *ever* talk about that," she managed after a moment.

His smile widened slightly. "Times change. We didn't do anything wrong. As I recall, it was quite…right."

One night. One night during her last month of law school when she'd succumbed to his appeal.

Nell had never told anyone.

Not even Ros.

And it had taken her years before she'd managed to file the experience away in the dusty past where it belonged. While he had just continued onward, changing one woman on his arm for the next with routine ease.

The amazing thing was he'd never seemed to leave anyone with hard feelings.

Except her.

But admitting that then or now was anathema.

She stiffened her resolve. "You still haven't answered the question, either."

His lashes dropped slightly. He sat back, stretching out his long legs, and smiled his unreadable smile. "You were in my guest room," he finally said.

Relief swept through her. "Thank God."

He raised an eyebrow. "Don't need to sound so relieved there, Cornelia."

"Heaven forbid someone bruise your considerable ego." She pushed to her feet and stepped over his legs. "Your nephew's birthday party is waiting." She opened the door with a pointed flourish.

He exhaled as if she were the one trying his patience, and stood. He walked over to the door. "If you need me, you know how to reach me."

Her hand tightened around the doorknob. "I won't need you."

The amused tilt of his lips twisted slightly. "I know."

Then he stepped past her and strode down the walkway toward the fancy pickup truck parked at the curb.

She was still standing in the doorway watching when he drove away.

No. She wouldn't need him.

She wouldn't need anyone.

It was a lesson she'd learned when she'd been sixteen. And every time she'd forgotten it since then, all she'd earned was pain.

"I'm sorry, Nell." The director of the legal aid agency smiled apologetically. "I appreciate your offer, but we just don't have space for you."

Nell kept her own smile in place with an effort. It had been nearly six weeks since she'd left Pastore Legal. She'd put in her name at every firm in Cheyenne—whether they had openings or not. But now, to have her services—her *volunteer* services no less—turned down was the last straw.

"Sally." She met the director's eyes. "We've known each other for years. We have lunch at least once a month. Since when have you ever turned down a capable volunteer?"

Sally looked pained. She looked beyond Nell's

shoulder toward the open office area beyond. Then she folded her hands together and leaned forward over her untidy metal desk, her voice lowering confidentially. "I can't afford to get on the wrong side of Martin Pastore, Nell. You know how much pro bono his firm does for us."

Nell's fists curled. "What's he been saying?"

Sally lifted her shoulders, looking helpless. "Nothing actionable. But there are rumors about, well, I'm sorry, but about your overall competency. Things falling through the cracks that other people have had to cover for. Little things that add up to larger problems."

Nell's nerves tightened. After two weeks of failing to gain so much as a single interview, she'd begun wondering if Martin was manipulating things behind the scenes. She'd told herself she was being paranoid. But then a third week passed. And a fourth.

Ros had already managed to break the lease on their condo and move out. She'd been staying with Jonathan for weeks now. Which had left Nell on the hook for that month's rent on the oversize condo. She'd put in notice that she'd be vacating it in eleven days, even though she hadn't secured a replacement just yet. There were places she could rent. Just not ones that wanted an unemployed lawyer whose name was apparently mud.

"You know me better than that, Sally."

"I do, but… *Ros* made partner at Pastore."

"She's Martin's daughter," Nell reminded her stiffly.

"So did Scott Muelhaupt." Sally looked genuinely baffled. "He's new with the firm. You'd been there for years." She shook her head again. "I'm sorry. I wish I could do more for you, Nell. You know I like you, but—"

"But your agency likes Martin's firm more," Nell finished bluntly.

"Needs Martin's firm more," Sally corrected.

Nell exhaled. She stood. "I appreciate the honesty, Sally." At this point it was more than she'd received from anyone else.

"I'm sure things will work out in time." Sally followed her through the desks crowded into the office area toward the front door. "Once there's more distance from your departure from Pastore Legal."

Time was the one thing Nell didn't really have. Not that she intended to share that information with Sally Youngblood.

Once outside, she crossed to her car in the pitted parking lot and tossed her briefcase onto the passenger seat. Her back seat was filled with packing boxes. Same as her trunk. She'd rented a small storage unit and had been methodically transferring things there from the condo. These were the things she couldn't bear to part with—

like all of her mother's books—but that she didn't need for day-to-day living.

Even though she was loathe to part with any more cash than she had to, she needed coffee, particularly after that depressing meeting with Sally Youngblood. She drove to the coffeehouse on the corner of the next block where she paid for an exorbitant but delicious coffee before she proceeded to the storage facility.

Once she got there and parked, she couldn't find any of the carts that were supposed to always be available but weren't, so she carried the heavy boxes of books one after another to the unit. She'd chosen one on the second floor because it was cheaper. Unfortunately, the elevator was as readily available as the elusive carts and she always ended up having to use the stairs.

She figured it made up a little for the fact that she'd canceled her gym membership in order to save that monthly fee, too.

With her back seat and trunk empty once more, Nell sat in her car with the windows open because of the heat of the day and finished her coffee.

She'd lived in Cheyenne all her life and had never seriously contemplated relocating elsewhere. But how could she stay in Cheyenne and make a living considering the long reach of Martin Pastore?

She needed either a new location or a new

profession. Cheyenne was only a few hours from Denver. The city was huge compared with Cheyenne. But the rents were proportionately higher, as well. She was trying to make ends meet, not move those ends even further apart.

Which was the lesser evil?

No closer to an answer, she drove back to the condo. She couldn't even think of it as "home" anymore. Not with more than half of the furnishings gone after Ros had taken them. Not with Ros herself gone.

Despite everything, Nell couldn't help feeling the sharp, painful edge of her absence.

They'd been friends since elementary school. When Nell's mother had died when she'd been fourteen, Ros had cried with her. When Nell's father had run out on her just two years later, Ros had talked Martin into letting her live with them.

Nell's stomach churned. Stress had been taking its toll. Adding coffee on top of it had probably not been the wisest decision in the world.

Vowing to drink more water and less coffee, she went inside. She left the front door open as well as the windows in the kitchen in the back to encourage a cross breeze through the unit. The month of August was never very pleasant, but was even less so without central air-conditioning.

She made herself a tall glass of ice water, then went upstairs to the study.

It was nearly empty now, save the built-in desk where Nell's laptop sat looking forlorn, and one last shelf with a smattering of books. They were all first-edition children's books penned by her mother.

Julia Brewster had owned a bookstore. It had been small. Not hugely successful. And the first books she'd placed on her shelves had been the twelve books she'd written about a curious penguin named Monty. In fact, the first title had been just that. *Monty the Curious Penguin.*

Nell could still remember the vaguely dusty smell of the books as well as her horror when her father had sold the store and most of its contents lock, stock and barrel only months after her mother died.

Nell had spent years tracking down the Monty books. She had recovered them all except one. The tenth. *Monty Meets Mary.* In the eleventh book, Monty and Mary get married. And in the last book of the series, they have twin baby penguins.

Nell trailed her fingers along the colorful dust jackets, pausing between volumes nine and eleven. The books had been mildly successful for the two years when they'd been published thirty years ago. But there had been only the one printing and the publisher had gone out of business when Nell was still a teenager.

She'd finally had to give up on ever finding a copy of *Monty Meets Mary*.

Shaking off her melancholy, she placed the books in an empty box that she'd picked up at the grocery store. It smelled vaguely of the apples that it had originally contained, but that was better than bananas. And Nell had no room to be picky. With the books packed, she tucked in a few winter sweaters that she didn't figure she'd need in the next month, and carried the box downstairs.

She was just in time to meet the mail carrier, who seemed consternated over Nell's open door— it meant he couldn't push the postal items through the mail slot. She leafed through the small stack he'd finally put in her hands. Circulars and bills.

Sighing, she tossed them onto the side chair. It was the only piece of furniture left in the living room after Ros had taken her stuff.

Until the room was nearly empty, Nell hadn't put much thought into the fact that her roommate had chosen and paid for nearly everything on the first floor of the condo. Ros had liked a particular style and could afford to get what she'd wanted and Nell had never had a reason to argue with her.

She didn't even own a television. Not that she really needed one. A person could get all the news they wanted on their phones these days and Nell had always been more of a reader than a viewer.

With a legal pad and a pencil in hand, she took

her glass of water and went out the back door to sit on the step. She drew a line down the center of the page. She wrote *Stay* at the top on one side of the line and *Go* on the other.

Then she began to enumerate every point she could think of on each side of the decision.

Unfortunately, the exercise didn't garner any information she hadn't already thought of. She tossed the yellow pad of paper onto the cement step beside her and propped her elbows on her knees.

"You look like you're still fourteen years old."

She jerked, turned around and looked up to see Archer standing on the threshold of the back door. Apparently he'd just waltzed right through the apartment, meaning he'd been in her condo twice now in the span of six weeks. It was a record. And she was far less shocked to see him than she ought to have been.

"What are you doing here?"

He held up a package wrapped with brown craft paper and twine. "A care package from Meredith for Ros. But considering the lack of furniture in there, I'm assuming she's moved. Naturally, she wouldn't bother informing us about it. So I don't know where to take it."

"Could take it to her office," she pointed out waspishly.

"Yes, but then I'll have to breathe the same air

as her father, and I've already suffered that experience more than once this year. You know, anyone and their mother's brother could walk in through your open front door."

"Anyone *did*."

He leaned over and picked up her glass of water, then sat down on the step beside her.

She gave him a frowning look. "Seriously. What do you *want*?"

A hint of annoyance clouded his perpetually amused expression. "Seriously, maybe I don't *want* anything. That so hard to believe?"

"You are one of the busiest attorneys in the state." And how he managed it with only a few employees based in Denver totally escaped her. "You probably bill by the half second."

His lips twitched. "Every other minute."

She rolled her eyes, then reached past him. "Give me the pad."

He handed it to her.

She flipped to the next page and quickly wrote out Ros's new address. Then she tore off the page and extended it toward him. "She's living with Jonathan these days."

Archer glanced at the address, then folded it into a square that he pushed in his back pocket. His shoulder brushed against her when he did so and she tried hard not to react.

"How's the job hunting?"

She shrugged and was glad that her Stay/Go list was flipped over and away from his too-observant eyes. "Haven't found the right fit just yet."

He sipped her water as if he had every right to do so. "What really happened between you and Pastore?"

"I told you."

"You said you didn't make partner. That doesn't explain why he's been dropping little nuggets here and there about your professional fitness."

Her face burned. "Maybe I'm not fit." She hadn't yet reported Martin's actions on the Lambert estate to the bar association, and it should have been the first thing she did. But Ros had been right about one thing. Lambert's wishes with regard to his estate had been ultimately fulfilled regardless of the money Martin had accepted to manipulate the probate.

"Don't be stupid." For the first time, Archer looked and sounded impatient. "You're a good lawyer. Better than Pastore deserved, for damn sure."

Her eyes suddenly burned and she quickly looked away before he could see.

He shifted again, broad shoulder once more pushing against her while he reached into his pocket, this time extracting something. He held it out to her.

"What's that?" Though it was perfectly obvious what it was: an ivory-colored business card containing a single telephone number and nothing else.

"That's my grandmother's number. Vivian Archer Templeton. She lives in Weaver."

Nell eyed him, not sure where he was going with this. Weaver was as far away as his hometown of Braden. And both municipalities put together were still smaller than a quarter of Cheyenne. "So?"

He nudged the card toward her again. "She's looking for someone to head up her latest pet project."

"I don't need your pity any more than I needed your so-called offer to work for you."

He let out a short laugh. "Trust me. You wouldn't have gotten it working for me and you definitely won't get it working for Vivian. She's rich and eccentric. Which makes her a force that can only be understood through experience. My cousin Delia would attest to that. She's Vivian's personal assistant when she's not off gallivanting around doing something else like she is right now."

Nell still didn't take the card but she couldn't keep herself from being curious. "What's the project?"

"She wants to get a new public library built in

Weaver. Raising money, finding the property, getting it through the red tape. All of it."

She'd been there numerous times because of the Lambert estate. It had never even crossed her mind to think it would be a great place to live. "I'd have to go to Weaver."

He gave her a look. "And that's a negative? What've you got going here that's better?"

"I'd have to find a place to live there, too."

"Vivian's got a big house. If she takes a shine to you, she's got space for you to stay right there. And if that's too close for comfort for you, you can use the guesthouse out at my place," he added, sounding casual. "I'm never there and you can feed my cat."

"You don't have a cat." Then she frowned at him. "Do you?"

His lips twitched. "What do you think?"

She exhaled and rolled her eyes again.

"Look, I don't care where you live. I'm just saying there are options for you."

She wasn't really going to consider it, was she? She slowly slid the card from his fingers, carefully avoiding touching him. "I'll think about it."

"Don't think too long. Vivian's not a young woman. She needs help on the project sooner rather than later. If you don't step up, someone else will. If you were working for her, it'd give you time to regroup. Figure out what it is you really want to do."

"I'm a lawyer. That's what I really want to do." She narrowed her eyes at him. "What's that look for?"

He spread his hands innocently. "What look? You going to call her or not?"

"I said I'll think about it."

"Right." He suddenly stretched out his legs and stood, then picked up the twine-wrapped package. "Let me know if you need me."

"I won't need you," she replied by rote.

"I know." He lightly knuckled her head as if she were a little kid, then went into the kitchen. She could hear him whistling softly as he left.

Nell picked up the yellow pad and looked at her Stay/Go list.

On the Go side, she penciled in one word.

Archer.

Then she sighed faintly and tossed aside the pad.

Chapter Four

Vivian Templeton turned out to be a diminutive woman well into her eighties. She had perfectly coiffed silver hair and diamond rings on every finger, and lived in a mansion—an honest-to-goodness mansion—located on the edge of Weaver.

Thanks to all of the work that Nell had done on the Lambert estate and the Rambling Mountain matter, she was fairly well versed with the Weaver demographics. In a region populated by more cows than people, as a general rule, mansions weren't the norm. As often as not, a person's barn was bigger than their abode.

She'd been hard-pressed not to stand there with her mouth hanging open when she'd arrived for the meeting that she'd arranged with Archer's grandmother. She'd been met at the door by a bald guy wearing an ivory ascot and formal black suit who'd introduced himself as Montrose before leading her through to a two-story atrium.

Vivian's office was on the second floor. It had windows that overlooked the rear of her property and Rambling Mountain loomed violet and gray in the distance.

Nell had never stepped foot on the mountain— it had been privately owned land until Otis Lambert died. She wondered if Archer had.

She pushed the thought of him out of her mind and focused harder on the petite woman across from her.

"The biggest challenge," Vivian was saying now, "is the town council. One of the members in particular who is unreasonably opposed to anything I try to accomplish in this town." Her lips thinned. "But not even people like Squire Clay can stop progress when it's warranted, and a library properly sized and outfitted for a growing community is certainly warranted." She looked over the top edge of her reading glasses at Nell. "Do you read, my dear?"

Feeling bemused, Nell nodded. "My mother owned a small bookstore, actually."

"A businesswoman." Vivian nodded approvingly. "Has she given it up?"

Nell shook her head. "She died when I was fourteen. My father sold the business shortly after."

That earned another look over the edge of the glasses. "I'm sorry."

Nell assumed Vivian was sorry about her mother versus the business, but she wasn't entirely certain. "Thank you," she said, which seemed to cover her bases either way.

Vivian was giving Nell a close look as she toyed with the heavy strands of pearls hanging around her fragile-looking neck. Her demeanor told Nell she was already moving on. "Archer speaks highly of you."

She was grateful that her cheeks didn't get too hot. "I'm not sure why," she admitted. "More often than not we've been on opposing sides in the courtroom."

"Respecting a worthy opponent is as valuable as respecting one's close associates." Vivian took off her glasses and dropped them atop the résumé that Nell had brought with her. A résumé that Vivian had completely ignored. "I'm afraid the position doesn't pay as much as you must be used to getting."

She proceeded to name a figure that Nell had

a hard time not choking over. Not because it was so low. But because it was so high.

Whatever Vivian Templeton was used to paying her lawyers, it bore no resemblance to what Martin had paid his associates.

"If that's acceptable—" Vivian's expression was confident, and at that high a salary, why wouldn't it be? "—when would you be able to start?"

Nell hid the relief bubbling inside her and glanced at her résumé. "Any time, really," she said calmly. "Once you've had an opportunity to review my references—"

Vivian waved a dismissive hand and sunlight caught in the diamonds on her fingers, dancing across the mild look of distaste on her face. "My grandson is the only reference I need," she assured. "I trust his judgment."

If the woman knew, or cared, about the rumors Martin had been circulating regarding Nell, she didn't show it.

Vivian folded her hands together. "So, that leaves the metaphorical ball in your court, dear. Would you like the position? I can't promise you a nine-to-five—frankly the thought of that makes me shudder. Dreary, don't you think?" She didn't wait for a response. "But I can promise you an interesting variety of tasks. If you like to be busy—"

"I do," Nell said quickly.

Vivian looked pleased. "Excellent. Is next Monday agreeable?"

It was already Thursday. That would leave Nell with a very busy few days before Monday, but she nodded with more confidence than she felt. "Perfectly agreeable." She'd been preparing to move out of the condo anyway. What difference did it make if she did it over this weekend or the next?

"Will you need assistance getting settled here in Weaver?"

Nell prided herself on her independence, and the last several weeks had already given her a blow in that arena. The last thing she wanted was for her new employer to think she couldn't handle such basic matters. "I have it covered, thank you." She didn't, but she would.

Again, Vivian smiled as if pleased. "When Archer called me this morning, he told me again just how eminently capable you are. He mentioned you've known one another since law school. As many lawyers as I've needed in my life, perhaps I should have gone to law school myself. Would have saved a fortune in retainer fees. Obviously you weren't Archer's type, but you were good friends with Meredith's daughter, Rosalind, is that correct?"

Were. Vivian couldn't know how correct she really was. But Nell highly doubted that Archer would have bothered sharing the details of her fractured friendship with his stepsister. "Ros recently moved in with her boyfriend, but up until then, we'd been roommates since school." The facts were accurate, despite the real cause behind Ros's actions. And Nell wasn't touching Vivian's blunt comment about not being Archer's type. "Your grandson was in his last year when she and I were in our first."

"I've met Rosalind," Vivian said. "Takes after my son's wife in looks. Quite beautiful. I never trusted beautiful female attorneys." She looked at Nell and nodded with satisfaction. "Welcome aboard."

Nell managed not to wince. Vivian obviously didn't consider *her* a beautiful female attorney.

Her new employer stood and tugged lightly at the three-quarter-length sleeves of her nubby pink suit. Nell didn't have a lot of personal experience with high-end designer clothes, but she was willing to bet that the suit carried a very fancy label.

She'd learned enough about Vivian Archer Templeton to know that she hailed from Pennsylvania and that most of her money came from her first husband—Archer's grandfather—who'd been in the steel industry. The several husbands who'd followed had only added to her wealth.

As a result, Nell doubted that Vivian had ever had to worry about retainer fees stretching her beyond her means.

She stood too and stuck out her hand. "I appreciate your confidence. I'm looking forward to proving it isn't misplaced."

Considering her overall air of delicacy, Vivian's handshake was surprisingly firm. Then she led the way out of the office, lightly clasping the filigreed balustrade that overlooked the rest of the atrium below. She went as far as the curving staircase where Montrose was waiting, as if he had some magical sixth sense that the meeting between Vivian and Nell had concluded.

"Montrose will see you out," Vivian told Nell. "He can give you the tour on Monday when you arrive. He also can answer any questions you might have before then. One of my granddaughters has been acting as my personal assistant, but she's away right now. So my man is delighted to fill in for Delia." Vivian smiled at Montrose, and Nell was certain that she saw a hint of deviltry in her eyes.

The same kind of deviltry that often lurked in Archer's eyes.

As for Montrose, he was clearly *not* delighted to be doing any such thing but he managed to exude both boredom and superiority.

Under other circumstances, Nell would have been hard-pressed not to giggle. She felt a little as if she'd landed in some alternate universe.

Instead, she kept her composure firmly in place

and followed Montrose's sedate descent down the fancy, curving staircase. It had a twin staircase on the other side of the room. Both led up to the second-floor landing that circled the entire space. "Are you in charge of the plants, Mr. Montrose? I've never seen anything so incredible."

The windows looked out on the wilds of Wyoming, but inside, a person would think they'd landed in a rain forest. The atrium was filled with exotic plants.

Just one more reason why it all felt a bit unreal.

"It is just *Montrose*," he was saying with the faintest of sneers. "And I'm Mrs. Templeton's *chef*."

For a moment she wished Ros could have heard him. He made Nell's Snape-ishness sound tame. "I certainly don't need to take you away from your usual duties. I'm sure I can find my way out if—"

He cut a glance her way that effectively silenced her, and she followed him down the rest of the stairs and through a few doors that disappeared seamlessly into the wall as they swung shut behind them.

Eventually, he reached the massive door through which she'd entered the mansion and held it open for her, bowing his head as she passed through. "I suppose you'll be moving into one of the guest rooms." His tone didn't change but it was clear as day that he didn't welcome the idea.

She was no more inclined to discuss her housing needs with him than she had been with his boss. "Not that I'm aware of," she said with her own measure of coolness. "It's not something that has been discussed."

"It will be. Since she's come to Wyoming, Mrs. Templeton has developed the habit of taking in strays."

"I'm not a stray," Nell said evenly. "I'll see you Monday morning, Montrose. Have a pleasant afternoon." Before he could say anything else, she turned and briskly crossed the courtyard paved in herringbone bricks to where she'd parked her car. Her nerves were jangling as she got behind the wheel and drove away from the mansion.

But she didn't give in to them until she was well away from the mansion.

Then she pulled off the side of the highway, put the car in Park and lowered her forehead to her steering wheel, hauling in several long, deep breaths. She had a job. She'd have money coming in again.

And even though the position with Mrs. Templeton was temporary, it would give Nell some needed breathing space until she could situate herself more permanently.

Regroup. Figure out what it really is you want to do.

Archer's words circled around inside her head

but then a livestock semi roared past, making her car rock slightly, and she sat up again. She blew out a cleansing breath.

"You're moving to Weaver," she said aloud. She absolutely was not going to entertain the notion of living at Vivian Templeton's mansion if that option even arose. And although Archer had tossed out the suggestion that she use his guesthouse, she couldn't imagine that he'd been serious.

She'd find a place to rent that didn't involve him.

She waited until the narrow highway was clear again, then pulled out and finished the short drive into the town proper. Because of her previous times there, she was already somewhat familiar with Weaver. She knew that the newer part of town was on the far side, toward Braden, which was the next closest town—some thirty miles away. She was now driving through the more historical center of town. The speed limit was cut in half as the highway turned into the main drag.

She drove past a picturesque park with a white gazebo in the middle of it, then the courthouse where she'd spent many hours sitting next to Martin Pastore as he administrated the Lambert estate on behalf of the state. And all that time she'd been oblivious to his under-the-table dealings.

She let out a frustrated grunt directed solely at herself. "Move *on*, Cornelia," she muttered as she slowed even further for a pickup truck reversing out of a slanted parking space into the street.

When the truck was finished, it drove ahead of her and she impetuously angled her car into the spot it had just vacated. When her front wheels bumped the curb slightly, she parked, grabbed her briefcase and climbed from the car. She automatically locked it, then crossed the sidewalk and entered the restaurant on the other side.

It was crowded. Lunch rush, Nell thought, and instead of joining the group of people standing to one side against the wall who were obviously waiting for tables, she crossed to the counter where one stool remained unoccupied near the cash register.

The older gentleman sitting on the stool next to it glanced at her when she set her briefcase on the floor.

"Mind if I sit here?" She touched her fingertips to the red vinyl-covered seat.

"Only if you mind sitting next to me," he said with a drawl. He had iron-gray hair, and the lines on his face could mean he was anywhere from sixty to eighty. His blue eyes were strikingly pale, sharp and clear, and held a glint of humor.

She smiled in return and slipped out of her suit jacket. She folded it and laid it over the top of her briefcase. "Busy place." She slid onto the round stool.

The man smiled. The humorous glint in his eye seemed to take on a new dimension. "That it is. Take it you haven't been to Ruby's before." His gaze flicked to her briefcase sitting on the floor between their seats.

She shook her head.

"You're in for a treat, then. Specials are there." He nodded toward the chalkboard on the wall. "I'm partial to the meat loaf sandwich." He glanced at the very young, dark-haired waitress who approached and set an insulated coffeepot in front of him. "Thank you, darlin'."

The woman had a friendly smile and a pencil stuck in her untidy ponytail. "Sounds like Squire's been telling you about the menu," she said, nodding at Nell in greeting.

Nell couldn't help her small start of surprise at the name. She figured he was likely the same Squire whom Vivian had mentioned. It wasn't exactly a common name.

"I'm Tina." The waitress was sliding a plastic-coated menu on the counter toward Nell. "Can I get you something to drink? Water? Soda pop?"

The man next to her—Squire—was loosening the lid on the urn filled with fragrant coffee.

She started to order coffee, too, but hesitated when she saw him pour his coffee into a nearly flat saucer rather than the cup itself. Then with the saucer balanced on his fingertips, he sipped from the edge.

She realized she was staring and looked quickly toward Tina. "Coffee," she finished, "with cream and sugar, please." None of the other diners seated at the counter seemed to even notice Squire's unorthodox use of his drinkware.

Tina set a cup and saucer on the counter, turned the cup upright and filled it from another pot of coffee that she pulled from the warmer on the giant machine behind the counter. With her free hand, she set a small pitcher containing real cream on the counter, then added a tall glass sugar dispenser with a metal cap. "Specials are on the board," she said, reiterating what Nell's counter mate had already pointed out. "We're out of cherry pie, though."

"Order up!" A grizzled man's face briefly appeared in the pass-through window to the kitchen. A thick white plate full of food clattered slightly when he set it on the stainless steel ledge. Then his face disappeared from view again.

Tina turned away from Nell and grabbed the plate. "Thanks, Bubba," she called through the pass-through before delivering it to a patron at the far end of the counter. On her way back, she scooped up a check and a wad of cash and coins.

There was music playing—presumably from the shining jukebox standing in one corner. It wasn't loud enough to rise above the clatter of dishes and voices, though. Half the occupants of the diner were men; nearly all possessed hat marks in their hair from the cowboy hats and ball caps that sat on tables or the ledges on the backs of booths. Three women still wore their cowboy hats and one had a mass of dreads piled to a spectacular height atop her head.

The cash register pinged softly as Tina deposited the money, then she turned to Nell once again and pulled her pencil from her ponytail. "What can I get you?"

The slab of meat loaf between thick slices of bread on Squire's plate did look appetizing, but the scent of grilling burgers reigned supreme for Nell. Even though she hadn't really looked at the menu and it wasn't listed on the chalkboard, Nell ordered a cheeseburger and fries.

"You bet." Tina turned away again and stuck the order she'd written on the revolving rack in the pass-through. She turned back again with almost balletic grace and looked at the man next to Nell. "Squire, anything else I can get for you? Slice of chocolate pie?"

The man shook his head. "Think I'll pass, darlin'. All these weeks o' this fine food and my shirts are getting tight." He patted the front of his faded blue chambray shirt.

Nell glanced at him. His stomach looked flatter than her own. Regardless of his age, he also looked fitter than her, too. "You eat here often, then?"

"Every day since I've worked here," Tina answered before Squire could. She set a napkin and flatware in place for Nell. "Nearly four months now." She winked at Squire. "My boyfriend's completely jealous, too, of my lunchtime date."

Squire chuckled, though the sound of it seemed a little forced to Nell.

Another waitress—this one older than Tina— stopped at the cash register and stuck a check on the spindle. She gave Squire a stern look that was belied by the smile on her face. "You promised you'd stop flirting with my servers, Squire. What am I going to do with you?"

"As much as I love you, Tabby girl, I'm too old to change my ways now. That grandson of mine you married should have told you that by now."

Tabby's eyes sparkled. When she rounded the counter again, she dropped a fond kiss on Squire's tanned, weathered cheek, greeted another customer by name as he entered, and headed off.

Nell didn't know if Tabby managed or owned the restaurant, but given the comment about her servers, she figured it was one or the other. It dawned on her, then, that the look in Squire's eyes earlier had been pride.

Vivian wore a similar expression whenever she spoke of Archer.

Nell looked at her counter mate. "Something tells me you know a lot about this town." She extended her hand. If this man actually was Vivian's roadblock on the town council, she might as well get off on a good footing with him while she had a chance to. "I'm Nell Brewster. I'm moving here from Cheyenne."

His eyes crinkled as he returned the handshake. "Squire Clay," he offered, thus confirming Nell's assumption. "And you've made a fine choice. I'll take Weaver any day over Cheyenne." He slanted a look toward her briefcase. "Not many folks carry one of those around these parts."

She lifted her shoulder. "Professional habit, I'm afraid," she admitted wryly. "Lawyer by trade."

His eyes narrowed slightly as he studied her face. "You coming on with Tom Hook? Heard he was looking for someone."

"No." She didn't even know who Tom Hook was. "Not planning to officially practice here." Not yet, at any rate. She unfolded the large paper napkin over her lap as Tina set a basket heaped with glistening golden fries and a plate with her cheeseburger and fixings in front of her. "Thanks, Tina."

"Ketchup and mustard?"

"Just the mustard." She took the bottle when it

quickly appeared and squirted out a dollop on her burger. She arranged the lettuce and sliced tomato on top of that, fit the bun in place and decided she was never going to be able to get her mouth around the thing. She picked up her knife. "I have the feeling that you know everything about this town, Mr. Clay," she told Squire as she cut her burger in half. "Can you give me the skinny on where I should begin looking for a place to rent? I don't have the luxury of a lot of time."

"Make it Squire, child," he said immediately. "Lot of apartments out by Shop-World. If that's your cup of tea."

"Whatever is affordable and safe is my cup of tea right now," she admitted wryly. She took a bite of the hamburger and nearly groaned in pleasure.

"Ain't a thing Bubba Bumble can't cook," Squire said with a knowing nod.

She dabbed her napkin at her chin and sent a chaser of French fry after the burger. It was salty. Perfectly crisp on the outside. Tender and airily light on the inside. "Oh…my," she said once she swallowed. She eyed the man next to her. "No wonder you come here every day."

He chuckled but the humor in his eyes seemed dimmed. "Things become a habit when you never expect it." He looked over his shoulder. "Tabby," he called out, "you have any vacancies at your triplex?"

The waitress, delivering a tray of food to a table of three women and six children, paused. "Not right now." When the delay in service earned her a cacophony of whiny complaints, she quickly turned her attention back to her customers and began doling out the baskets of food to the children. "Check the bulletin board," she suggested. "People tack up all sorts of notices."

Squire glanced at Nell again. "By the door. You passed it on your way in." He dropped his napkin atop his unfinished sandwich. "Most of the people who come in here are locals. You won't go wrong with anything posted here." He dropped some cash on the counter and stood. He was taller than Nell expected. "But if you have a question 'bout anything, come back here for lunch again tomorrow. I'll be here." He gave her a faint wink and then strode toward the door, offering a few comments to other patrons as he departed.

Nell turned her attention back to her meal and watched as Tina cleared away Squire's plate. The only thing he'd finished was the coffee. "He's really here every day?"

"Seven days a week," Tina confirmed. She filled another insulated carafe and left it for Nell. "You doing all right?"

"Yes, thanks." Since it didn't seem as though anyone was in a rush to claim Squire's vacated seat, she moved her jacket to it and flipped open the top of her briefcase. It was an old-fashioned sort of thing but it was sturdy enough to cart around the mountain of legal files and briefs that she no longer needed to tote around. She pulled out her cell phone and flipped the case closed again and then caught Tina's attention. "Don't clear this away. I'll be right back."

The busy waitress nodded and Nell went over to the front door and quickly scanned the bulletin board that was no longer blocked by waiting patrons. There were only two for-rent notices, though. She snapped photos of both, then turned back to return to the counter, but the sight of the tall blond man striding along the sidewalk outside the windows stopped her.

She had the silliest desire to duck and hide, but it was almost as if Archer knew it, because his head turned and his eyes met hers. A moment later, he'd reached the door and was pushing through it.

His eyes were devilish. "As I live and breathe. It's Cornelia Brewster."

She gave him a look and returned to the counter and her meal. He slid onto the seat that Squire had vacated. There was just as much space between the two seats as there had been before, but now it felt like it had been cut in half.

She angled her shoulder as far away as she

could to keep it from brushing against him. "I'll never believe it's a coincidence that you're here."

"Why not? The world revolves on coincidences."

"You've talked with your grandmother."

"Nope. I was, however, meeting with a client over at the jailhouse. And anyone who knows anything knows that when you're in Weaver and you have a chance to eat at Ruby's, you don't pass it up." Looking as if he had frequently not passed it up, he reached right over the counter and retrieved a clean mug from the rack stored below. Then he filled it from the coffeepot that Tina had left for Nell.

She thought about protesting, but concentrated instead on the excellent food. And she couldn't really complain since he topped off her own cup at the same time.

"Unless you're checking out other opportunities of employment here," he said after he tightened the lid on the urn again, "I'll assume that *you* have talked with her."

"Yes." She almost didn't want to tell him, because he'd probably just crow about it. But then again, if it weren't for him, she'd have never met with Vivian in the first place. Which meant he had more of a right to crow than she did to feel churlish. "I start on Monday."

He didn't look surprised at all. His arm brushed

hers as he lifted his coffee mug in a toast. "Congratulations."

She managed a smile and shoved two French fries in her mouth because she felt oddly shaky all of a sudden.

"Need help moving?"

More fries went into her mouth as she shook her head emphatically.

"And you wouldn't admit it if you did."

She wasn't going to deny it. She toyed with her coffee cup. "Thank you for putting in a good word for me," she finally said once her mouth was French fry–free. "I owe you."

His shoulder bumped hers, this time quite deliberately. "Almost kills you to say that, doesn't it."

She wasn't going to deny that, either.

He knew it, too, judging by the soft laugh he gave.

He waved at the second half of her cheeseburger. "You going to eat that?"

"Yes." She covered it protectively with her hand. "So don't think you're going to have it." That's what he'd always done back in law school, too. Finished whatever food was left alone for a moment. He'd always been ravenous and she'd never quite understood where he put it, since there had never been an ounce of extra weight on his broad-shouldered frame.

"Just making sure you are," he said blithely. "You're very thin."

It wasn't a compliment.

Tina returned. "Hi, Archer." She leaned her hip against the counter and smiled in a way that made Nell wonder just how serious the girl and the supposedly jealous boyfriend actually were. "What can I get for you?"

"Just the coffee."

"You sure?" Tina's cheeks turned a rosy pink despite her bold tone. "I've got a lot more to offer."

His chuckle was just the right amount of rueful not to cause offense. "One vice at a time, doll."

Tina sighed loudly and dramatically. "One of these days you're going to realize what you're missing."

He lifted his coffee cup. "No doubt."

She laughed and went off again to serve her other customers.

"She's way too young for you," Nell muttered from the side of her mouth.

"Calm your outraged sensibilities."

"I'm not outraged," she retorted. "But I imagine Judge Potts might have something to say about your flirtations."

"I doubt that, too." He folded his arms on the counter and leaned on them as he watched her. "I'm glad things are working out with Vivian."

"You could have warned me about her house, you know. It's a little more than just *big*."

"Ten bedrooms at last count. She's made some noises lately about adding another wing."

Nell nearly choked on her coffee. "For what?"

"Who knows?" His green eyes stayed focused on her face in a way that felt intensely intimate. "Vivian knows her own mind. I've seen what she can do with her money for others. I say if she wants to build another wing for herself, it's her business."

"Maybe it's a wing for Montrose."

Archer laughed outright. "He's a trip, isn't he?"

Nell couldn't keep from smiling, too. "That's one word for it."

"He's devoted to Vivian, though. And she to him, I'd have to say."

Nell lifted her eyebrows. "Are they—"

"God no," he said immediately, grimacing at the thought. "That's an idea that makes me want to wash out my brain. I take it she hasn't mentioned 'dear Arthur—'" he air-quoted the words "—to you, yet?"

She shook her head.

"He was her final husband and according to her, the most decent man to ever exist. And he was the greatest love of her life. Most of those good things she's done with her money since she's transplanted herself here have been because of the late, dear Arthur."

"How long ago did he die?"

"Quite a few years now. None of us ever met him. But he's a presence in Vivian's life regardless of how long he's been gone. She's still trying to live up to his standard."

"I don't know if that's romantic or sad."

Archer shifted and his arm brushed hers again.

Then she realized he'd pulled out his wallet and the cash he extracted and set on the counter was far too much for just a coffee.

She bristled. "I can afford to buy my own lunch."

"Actually, it's for the cat food."

"What?"

"The cat." He pushed the stack of bills closer to her. "Food," he repeated as if she were thick.

"We're back to that again?"

"He doesn't have a name. But he keeps coming around to eat and I'm going to be gone for the next several weeks on a case. Wouldn't want him to starve."

She didn't touch the money. "Why is it up to me to get him fed? You spend a lot of time in Cheyenne and Denver. More time than here, probably. What do you do then? Surely you have someone else who—"

"You just said it yourself. You owe me. And I

know you like cats because you told me so a long time ago."

She remembered the conversation very clearly. Because it had been the same day she'd ended up in his bed.

Not a guest room bed, either.

She shifted, trying to squelch the memory of bells ringing. Cymbals crashing. "My last experience taking care of a cat was more than twenty years ago." The cat she'd told him about. The one who had been her mother's. The one who'd disappeared after she died.

Only later, after her father had sold the bookstore, did Nell suspect the cat's exit had been his doing, too.

"It's not complicated," Archer said drily, completely ignoring her discouraging tone. "You pour some kibble in the bowl and the cat comes around and eats it."

"Don't you live out toward Braden?" She distinctly remembered Ros mentioning it once. She'd been highly annoyed because she'd needed to see him about something and it had necessitated the long drive.

"Yep." He tipped the coffeepot over his mug again, getting the very last few drops.

"I am *not* going to use your guesthouse," she warned adamantly. "If that's what you've got brewing in your mind." There was absolutely no logic to that offer, if he'd even been serious about it in the first place. She wouldn't be beholden to him, and he knew it.

"It's going to be a pain driving out there just to feed a cat, but that's up to you." He honestly sounded as if he didn't care.

She exhaled, impatient with herself for even allowing herself to get sucked into this. "There's really a cat?"

He gave her an innocent look that she didn't buy for a second. "Would I lie?"

Chapter Five

Nell eyed the empty pet food bowl.

She'd filled it with dry cat food the afternoon before, set it on top of the stone pillar where Archer had told her to set it, and now it was empty.

She looked at the pillar. It was about a foot across and at least six feet high. Taller than she was. Not so tall that a cat wouldn't be able to get up to it, though.

It was part of a gate marking the entrance to Archer's property. Archer said he never bothered to close the gate. He didn't keep any livestock on his ten acres of land. He just liked having the space around the house.

The house that Nell had chosen not to drive to. She didn't need to see it up close.

It was bad enough to know that the land where it was located was positively majestic in a stark sort of way. Scrubby brush grew in pale grayish-green shoots and sprigs of wildflowers clung around the bases of the boulders that dotted the relatively flat landscape.

It looked like a home for dinosaurs and snakes. Not for a stray cat.

Did birds eat cat food?

It seemed like a more plausible reason for the empty bowl.

Still feeling like she was playing in some silly game with Archer, she poured more food into the metal bowl and returned it to the top of the pillar.

It was her second day of working for Archer's grandmother. And her second day of driving nearly twenty miles out of town to feed his cat that may or may not actually exist.

She was an idiot. That's what she was.

She twisted the top of the cat food bag closed and returned it to the back seat of her car, then got behind the wheel and drove to Weaver. Twenty miles in a metropolitan area wasn't much of a big deal. Twenty miles on the very winding road running between Weaver and Braden, on the other hand, took a long time.

When she reached the Cozy Night motel, where

she'd been renting a room since Sunday night, it was nearly dark.

Inside the room, though, the lamp worked just fine. She dropped her purse on the nightstand between the two beds—one which was covered entirely with suitcases containing all of the clothes that she hadn't left in the storage unit in Cheyenne—and kicked off her shoes. It was warm and stuffy in the room after being closed up all day and after she changed out of her suit into a pair of shorts and a T-shirt, she opened the door again to let the air circulate.

It would cool off soon enough and she preferred fresh air rather than the rattling noise and forced chill provided by the air-conditioning unit that was located beneath the room's only window.

The Cozy Night wasn't fancy. But it was clean and it was affordable, even if she ended up having to stay there for a month. Which was how things were looking when it came to finding an actual rental.

The two listings on the board at Ruby's Diner hadn't panned out. Both had already been rented when she called. There were two apartment complexes on the other side of town, but they were both nearly full. The units available were either too large—and astonishingly, too expensive—or they weren't coming available until next month.

Nell still didn't believe she'd have difficulty

finding a place to live. Not in Weaver. But if she had to, she could continue staying at the Cozy Night for a while. It wasn't perfect. With only a dorm-sized refrigerator and a hot plate, it wasn't exactly equipped with kitchen facilities.

But then again, she hadn't exactly cooked back in Cheyenne, either.

She extracted a bottle of juice from the refrigerator and carried it with her outside the room.

There was an old-fashioned metal chair that had obviously been painted over a number of times—it was currently a not-unattractive shade of salmon—sitting outside the door of each room. Twenty-two chairs, stretching from one wing to the other. Depending on a person's viewpoint, it looked either stylishly retro, or completely out of date.

She sat in her chair with her legs outstretched and debated whether she could satisfy herself with a can of soup heated on the hot plate or if she needed to go farther afield. But having spent more than an hour driving back and forth to feed a possibly nonexistent cat with no name, going out again held little appeal.

"Can of soup it is," she murmured to herself.

But later.

For now, she relaxed in her chair—the metal bounced slightly if she shifted, sort of like a rocker—and sipped her juice.

The motel was situated on top of a small rise on the road before it dipped down again toward what she'd termed "Old Weaver."

"New Weaver" was the Shop-World region. Cee-Vid was located in New Weaver. It was a large gaming company owned by one of Weaver's longtime residents, Tristan Clay. She'd learned that from Vivian's nemesis, Squire, who had indeed been sitting on that same stool in Ruby's Diner that very afternoon. Tristan was Squire's youngest son. He'd also told her about his other four sons, who all lived in the area, too.

She'd run into the diner to grab a quick sandwich between errands for Vivian and he'd waved her over, patting the seat beside him.

There was something decidedly engaging about the old man, even though he was one of the roadblocks in the way of Vivian's library project. Something engaging but also something that struck Nell as a little sad. Maybe the fact that he talked about all of those sons, but still spent every afternoon having lunch in a diner?

But what could a person learn about another person over a half hour? Considering her debacle with Martin, she was having a hard time trusting her own sense of judgment.

From her salmon-colored perch, Nell watched lights begin to flicker. There were a lot more clustered together on the New Weaver side. The population of residents on that side of town was denser. Younger. They were the employees at Cee-Vid. At Shop-World. At the dozens of other small businesses that inevitably cropped up in everyday towns to support the growing needs of those citizens as they settled. Got married. Bought houses and had babies.

An old, rusting car turned into the motel parking lot. Its headlights washed over Nell before it came to a stop in front of the unit next to hers. Even before the engine cut out, the back doors opened and three ginger-haired kids tumbled out.

They spotted her and waved, but their steps didn't really slow as they raced around the car toward the small, fenced swimming pool that the Cozy Night offered its guests.

George, Blake and Vince.

She'd met the boys on Sunday when their mom, Gardner, who was obviously an avid country music fan, had ordered them to help their new "neighbor" carry her suitcases in from her car.

Gardner and her boys had been living at the Cozy Night for most of the summer now. Which was one of the reasons why Nell figured she could hack it for a while there, too, if it came to that.

"Need any help?" she called to the young mother as she opened her trunk.

Gardner shook her head. "I don't have much, Nell. Thanks, though." She ducked momentarily below the opened trunk, then straightened and slammed it shut. When she rounded the vehicle, she was carrying a single paper bag bulging with groceries. In addition to the dorm-sized fridge, Gardner's unit next door possessed a double-sided hot plate and a microwave. "How'd your day go?" she asked as she unlocked the door of the unit next to Nell's.

"Good. Yours?" Gardner was a hairdresser by trade but was currently making her motel rent by working at an ice cream shop in New Weaver.

The other woman hadn't explained more than that when they'd met on Sunday. And Nell hadn't explained any more about her own situation.

"Not bad," Gardner said as she pushed open the door to her room. "This heat has a lot of people in the mood for ice cream, so that's the good thing. I'll be out in a second. Want a cold drink?"

Nell lifted her juice. "I'm fine. Thanks."

The other woman disappeared and emerged a few minutes later. She'd exchanged her "Udder Huddle" T-shirt and jeans for a plain blue one-piece swimsuit. She had a striped towel draped around her neck, but instead of following her boys to the pool, she threw herself down into her own salmon-colored chair and popped the top on a can of soda.

From the pool area, they could hear the whoops and splashes from the boys.

Gardner exhaled and stretched out her legs far enough that she could prop the toe of her sandal on the bumper of the car, right next to the worn-looking Ohio license plate. "Good thing they were wearing their swimsuits under their jeans today." She sent Nell a humorous look. "I hope they remembered to leave them on when they were tearing off their clothes before jumping in. At one place we stayed earlier this summer, they didn't." Her lips twitched. "Needless to say, we were quickly asked to move along."

Nell chuckled. Aside from being noisy, she thought the boys seemed pretty well-behaved.

"You should put on a suit and head over there with us," Gardner encouraged. "I bought hot dogs. Thought I'd toss them on that grill that's next to the pool. The boys'll be starving despite the food they get at their summer camp."

Nell's stomach rumbled right on cue. "I don't have a swimsuit."

Gardner looked vaguely scandalized. "That doesn't matter," she said quickly. "I saw Mrs. Goldberg—over there from number eleven?" She pointed with her soda can toward the other wing of the motel. "She was in the pool last week wearing a pair of bright green leggings and a matching long-sleeved T-shirt." She grinned. "She looked like an amphibian with white hair, but what the heck."

Nell laughed. It was hard to resist Gardner's contagious smile. "Maybe."

An outraged yell sounded from the pool area, followed by a squeal and a whole lot of splashing. Gardner stood. "Sounds like refereeing is required." She adjusted her towel over her shoulder and jogged off, her sandals flapping noisily. A few moments later, her raised voice joined those of her sons. "George, how many times have I told you not to pick on Vince?"

Nell let the noise wash over her.

She was thirty-six now. She had no prospects for a relationship, much less one with daddy potential.

But if she didn't start thinking about these things now, when would she?

When it was too late altogether?

Nell and Ros had both gotten birth control implants in their arms several years ago. But even Ros—who was more committed to her career than anyone—was evidently thinking about having a baby. Was she hearing the tick-tock of a biological clock that before neither she nor Nell had believed actually existed?

Was Nell hearing her own clock?

The yelling over at the pool increased in volume and intensity. Nell heard Gardner shout, "Out. Right this minute. All of you!"

Two minutes later, the sopping-wet lot of them

were trooping back across the parking lot. Gardner's beach towel was soaking, too. "Rain check on the hot dogs," she said before she ordered her boys to march their rear ends into the room. The door slammed shut after them, not entirely cutting off their noisy arguments.

Nell looked out over the lights of Weaver again.

Maybe her clock wasn't ticking as loudly as she feared.

The lights lining Main Street had almost all come on now. She followed the glimmering line from New Weaver to old. Then she continued down the line as it dimmed again and disappeared with only an occasional headlight to mark the road's whereabouts. Farther still was where Vivian's mansion was located. And beyond that, the shadowy peaks of Rambling Mountain, where a man named Otis Lambert had lived in a ramshackle cabin on a barely functioning ranch for a considerably long life.

Nell had never met Otis. Everything she knew about the apparently miserly old man she'd learned after his death.

Regardless of what had happened with her career, she was glad that the old man's will had surfaced. Glad that his wishes to donate most of his mountain—either to the state of Wyoming if they'd have it or the town of Weaver if not— would have a chance to be honored. The part of the mountain not being donated, the cattle ranch called the Rambling Rad, had been sold to a Colorado developer—Gage Stanton, with whom Archer had worked for years now. The money from the sale of the Rambling Rad went to the man who'd run the ranch and cared for Otis in his last few years of life. Jed Dalloway had continued taking care of the Rad after Otis died and while the probate had been in Martin's hands, she'd had a few occasions to meet the man. She'd been impressed with his integrity.

Unlike the "long-lost" relative of Otis's who'd surfaced after his death.

If it had been left to Martin's manipulations, the smarmy Louis Snead would have inherited the entire mountain including the ranch, and he would have sold it all off by now to a mining company for his own quick, huge profit.

Even though that hadn't come to pass, Nell still felt guilty by association. She finished her juice and squeezed the thin plastic bottle between her fingers. It crinkled loudly, which helped drown out the sound of the boys still arguing from inside the room next door.

The light fixture above her door gave a few fizzy snaps, then blinked to life.

What she needed to do was worry less about what Martin had been up to and worry more about formulating a plan to get Vivian's library completed.

She took the empty juice bottle inside the room and tossed it in the trash, then pulled her yellow legal pad out of the briefcase that had been sitting in the room untouched since she'd unpacked it three nights ago.

She carried it back to the chair outside because the yelling still going on next door was less noticeable there, and clicked her pen as she studied the Stay/Go list that she still hadn't torn off and thrown away.

She tapped the end of her pen against the pad. On the Go side, she wrote in Vivian's name.

The list was purely pointless, of course.

Nell had already made the move from Cheyenne. Aside from the boxes left in a second-floor storage unit, there was nothing there for her anymore.

She hoped the day that she felt convinced she'd done the right thing would come sooner rather than later.

Sighing a little, she flipped to a clean page and wrote down all of the arguments she could think of supporting the new library. There were very few reasons not to support it. Most had to do with local taxes and finding either an existing building that was suitable or a parcel of land on which to build one.

To Nell's mind, raising the necessary funds seemed the least of the hurdles. For one, Vivian had already raised nearly half of the estimated cost. If she hadn't realized the importance of a buy-in from the entire community, she would have already personally donated the rest of the needed capital.

When she became really frustrated with the project's progress, Nell knew it took considerable self-control on Vivian's part not to simply throw more money on the table with the expectation that it would flatten any hurdles standing in her way.

And while that was often true in some places, it wasn't necessarily true right here in this small town.

She heard her cell phone ring and only then noticed that the argument next door had finally ceased. She pushed out of her seat again and went inside to grab her phone. She glanced at the name on the display before she answered. "Good evening, Vivian," she greeted.

Her new boss didn't mince words. "Do you have a cocktail dress? Or just a closetful of those shapeless suits you're always wearing?"

Nell winced. She couldn't help sliding a look toward the bar where she'd hung three of her work suits. She turned her back on them and returned to her salmon-colored chair. "Why do I need a cocktail dress?"

"I've decided to have a little soiree on Friday evening for the town council members. It'll be here at the house, of course."

Nell grimaced. Bugs had begun buzzing around the light above her head. She swiped at a moth that flew past her face. "Are you certain that's wise, Vivian?" Nell was certain it was not, but she also wasn't sure her boss of two days was ready for such bluntness to begin going both ways.

"Why wouldn't it be wise?"

The moth flew past Nell's face again and she waved her hand at it, grimacing when her wrist made contact with the chalky body.

She gave up the fight against nature and went inside the room again. She didn't close the door, but she did turn off the lamp so as not to draw the beasties inside. "Because of the optics," she told Vivian as she wet a washcloth and wiped off her wrist. "Even though the library seems like an effort that the entire community would support, the council members need to be objective. Or at least give the appearance of remaining objective. If they don't, they'll be out of their positions when the next vote occurs in September."

"I ran a few years ago," Vivian said. "I nearly won, too."

Nell was glad Vivian couldn't see her smile over the obvious consternation in her boss's tone. "You didn't want to try again?"

"I decided there were better ways to accomplish what I want than by sitting on a dreary committee. But had I won, I would have kept Squire Clay from doing so. He still holds the seat he won against me. You can relax, though, because I'm not intending to bribe any of the council members."

Nell was glad Vivian couldn't see her wince.

"And you still haven't answered my question. Cocktail dress. Yes or no?"

"No," she admitted. "I don't have a cocktail dress."

"Get one. There's no time to call one of my designers but you can visit Classic Charms."

Designers? Nell shook her head a little as the thought lodged in her brain.

"It's on Main Street not far from the sheriff's office," Vivian continued. "An odd little shop, but I've found what it carries at the very least to be of good quality. Montrose can give you the exact address."

Montrose, whose attitude darkened toward Nell with every task that Vivian put on his plate. As if Nell were the one at fault.

"I know where it's located." She was still a little distracted by the fact that Vivian had *designers*. "I drove by it twice today." There had been an eclectic collection of furniture in the storefront window. Learning they had clothes was something of a surprise.

"Tell them to establish an account with your name on it and send the bill to me. Come in tomorrow after you've taken care of that. I won't need you in the morning for anything else."

Before Nell had a chance to respond, Vivian ended the call.

Nell looked at her screen, not entirely sure she hadn't simply lost the connection.

When the phone vibrated again a moment later, she decided she'd been right. "Sorry I lost you."

"You've never lost me, Cornelia," a deep voice said.

Nell's phone slid from her suddenly nerveless fingers, landing on the bed. She eyed the screen that bore a number that was *not* Vivian Templeton's, but instead belonged to the woman's grandson.

"I thought you were Vivian," she told Archer when she'd picked up the phone again. She flipped on the lamp because talking to Archer while sitting in the dark just didn't seem like a thing she ought to do. "What do you want?"

"Still haven't learned the art of pleasant chit-chat, have you?"

A moth dared to enter the room and she swatted the air around it with her legal pad, encouraging it to reconsider. "Archer," she said warningly.

"How's it going with the cat?"

The moth flew up to the ceiling and landed there, upside down.

She really hated moths.

"The food is getting eaten by something," she allowed. "But I'm still not convinced it's being eaten by your mysterious cat." She kicked off her tennis shoes and climbed up onto the mattress. It was overly soft and dipped deeply wherever she placed her feet, which meant it was an exercise in balance just to keep from tipping over.

"Tired of driving out there yet?"

She steadied herself with her fingertips against the wall above the fake-wood slab of a headboard and stretched higher with the pad of paper. But the moth was still out of reach. "I'm not tired of anything except your harping about it." She went up on her toes to try again but missed when the moth flitted a couple of inches farther away.

Nell's precarious stance wobbled. Her shoulder hit the wall and her breath rushed out of her lungs.

She was pretty sure the moth was taunting her.

"What the hell are you doing?"

"Nothing." When the phone refused to stay tucked between her shoulder and ear, she hit the speaker button and tossed the phone down onto the bed. "I have a moth in my room."

"At Vivian's?"

"Just because you talked about all the rooms

she has doesn't mean I'm automatically using one of them." She gingerly adjusted her stance on the mattress and tossed her notepad toward the moth. She didn't really want to smash it and leave moth bits clinging to the ceiling. That was as unappealing as having a living one clinging to the ceiling. She just wanted it to decide to go elsewhere.

The pages fluttered and the notepad plummeted downward, knocking into the lampshade and sending it askew. The moth's wings didn't move an inch. The chalky thing remained right where it was.

"You found an apartment already? That was fast."

She gave the moth a baleful look.

The jouncing of the mattress had sent her phone skittering off the side and onto the outdated shag carpet. She hopped off the bed. "I'm at the Cozy Night," she said a little breathlessly. She moved the phone to the nightstand, ignoring the blue oath her announcement earned.

"Does my grandmother know that?"

Nell wrinkled her nose at the phone as if he were able to see her. "I haven't hidden it if that's what you're implying."

He swore again, sounding genuinely irritated. "I'm not implying anything. The Cozy Night's a dive."

Annoyance bubbled inside her, too. "Just because it's not up to *your* lofty standards doesn't mean there is a single thing wrong with it. It's clean, affordable and—"

"—and riddled with moths."

She glared up at the grayish body clinging to the ceiling. "*One* moth," she argued, "and they throw themselves against lights in even the finest places." She yanked her hair out of her eyes, feeling like she wanted to yank it out of her skull. "And how is it that I get drawn into *the* most ridiculous debates with you?"

"Because you're lucky?"

"Is there anything else you wanted, Archer? Besides my assurance that I'm feeding your invisible cat, that is."

"If you only—" He broke off with a sound that she didn't have a hope of interpreting. "No," he finally said. "There's nothing else."

She picked up the phone, moistened her lips. "Then good night, Archer." Before she could second-guess herself, she brushed her finger over the screen, ending the call.

And told herself she imagined hearing "for now" in the moment before the phone disconnected.

Chapter Six

"Everything good in Weaver?"

They were sitting in Gage Stanton's Denver office and Archer looked over at his friend. He was sitting behind his desk, feet propped on the edge as he continued making notes on the Rambling Mountain material that he and Archer had been reviewing all that day.

"No." He pocketed his phone and plucked a slice of pizza from the box that Gage's secretary had delivered earlier before she'd left for the day. "But it's good enough."

He didn't like the idea of Nell staying at that

cheap motel but he didn't know how on earth he'd be able to change the situation.

Irritated with himself as much as with her, he sank his teeth into the pizza and tore off the tip. The slice was cold. Colder now than the bottle of beer he'd been nursing for the last hour.

Gage dropped his feet to the floor. He scrubbed his hand down his face and tossed aside his pen. "Why did I think it was a good idea to develop a guest ranch on Rambling Mountain?"

"Because you're a sucker for a pretty face?"

Gage grunted. "Sucker for a good employee who has defected on me, more like." He reached for his own slice of cold pizza. "April quit working for me more than a month ago, remember? She's busy with Jed now planning their wedding. She dumped all that money into this guest ranch business and can't think about anything else except orange blossoms and wedding dresses."

Archer figured that was somewhat of an exaggeration.

He knew the wedding planning was well in the works, all right. He'd gotten the invitation from April Reed a few weeks ago with her handwritten note saying that she fully expected him to be there to help her and Jed celebrate.

Or else.

Typical April. If it weren't for her, Gage would have scrapped his interest in the mountain that

Otis Lambert had owned and moved on by now. And Archer, who'd been on retainer with Stanton Development for years now, would be focusing on something else that wasn't a constant reminder of Nell Brewster.

When the ailing Otis Lambert had contacted Gage earlier that year, the developer had immediately started envisioning one of his trademark luxury resorts on Rambling Mountain—which had always been privately owned land. But once Otis died, ostensibly intestate, Gage had determined that the development wasn't worth the cost—not after he'd learned there was a mining company prepared to outbid him.

But April—who'd been sent to Weaver by Gage in hopes of getting a jump on the deal—had instead fallen hard for Otis's right-hand man, Jed Dalloway.

Then Otis died and it looked as though a distant relative of his would inherit it all. Gage had determined then that the development wasn't worth the cost—not after he'd learned about the mining company's interest.

April, though, had other ideas. Jed had worked Lambert's mountain ranch, and once his boss's will had actually been found, it was clear that Lambert had wanted the proceeds from the sale of the Rambling Rad to go to Jed. Otis also—despite a lifetime of hoarding the rest of his mountain—had bequeathed everything except the ranch to the state of Wyoming for the purpose of establishing a state park.

Rather than see the man she'd fallen for lose the home that had come to mean so much to him, April convinced Gage to reconsider his interest in the mountain ranch. Instead of razing it all and starting fresh—which had been his initial idea—she talked her boss into saving it. She'd even kicked in her own trust fund to sweeten the deal and ensure that he succeeded.

Now, instead of a luxury resort, Gage was looking down the barrel of a guest ranch plan for a property that clung to the side of the Wyoming mountain. And a guest ranch was something he'd be the first to admit he knew nothing about. Jed and April were set to live on the ranch, with Jed running the operations the same way he had when Otis was alive, but adding in the element of guests.

It was the type of nightmare that hazard insurance agents salivated over.

The ranch sale still hadn't made it through all the red tape, and the state's powers that be still hadn't decided whether they could—or even wanted to—establish a new state park with the rest of the land. If that answer turned out to be a polite "no thank you," then the responsibility for the mountain would be tossed squarely into the lap of the town of Weaver.

Either way, Otis's intention was that his pristine land become available for public use. And people *would* come to Rambling Mountain. It was a sportsman's paradise just waiting to happen. Whether they stayed at the planned guest ranch to play at herding cattle and God only knew what, or crowded into dive motels like the Cozy Night in Weaver, they would come.

It was simply a matter of time.

But until then, Gage was keeping Archer busy navigating through all the moving parts, hedging against the worst-case scenarios while laying groundwork for the best-case one.

Generally, Archer appreciated a challenge. But his mind kept drifting away from the business at hand to Nell.

He didn't exactly blame her for it, but he wasn't thrilled by the distraction.

Until Lambert's will was discovered, she'd been assisting the attorney assigned to administer the estate. She'd also unexpectedly been the one to give Archer the heads-up that Winemeier Mining was working with Louis Snead, who would have inherited the land if not for that will being found, literally at the eleventh hour. Snead, whose only interest in his dearly departed relative was the mountain, would have signed off on a sale to the mining company while the ink was still drying on the court's decision. If that had happened, the mountain would have been sliced and diced until none of its natural resources remained.

Archer still was surprised by Nell's actions. Not that she'd been breaking any rules. There'd been no confidentiality breach. But all the same, she'd approached him. And usually, she avoided him even more than his stepsister did. She had ever since he'd made the mistake of making more out of their furtive friendship than she had.

"I need something stronger than a warm beer," he muttered, more to himself than the other man.

"Amen to that." Gage immediately shoved away from his desk and stretched as he stood. "The lounge or my place?"

"The lounge," Archer said immediately. It was three floors down from Gage's high-rise office. Closer than his penthouse that was five floors up.

It helped that the man owned Stanton Tower from the ground floor to the top.

They took the elevator down to the restaurant, which in reality was one of the best in the city. And—not surprisingly—also owned by Gage Stanton.

Gage greeted the hostess as they passed her on the way to the private club where one needed an official invitation to enter. There were a few patrons sprinkled around the tables. Nobody gave them any attention as they walked through to the open-air patio hugging the corner of the building.

They'd barely sat down when an attractive woman in a svelte black dress appeared. She set a tray on the low table between them. "Shall I bring your usual, Mr. Stanton?" She directed the question to Gage, but her eyes slid over Archer.

"As soon as possible, Theresa. Thanks."

Theresa immediately glided away and Gage reached for one of the fancy little appetizers on the tray she'd left. He popped it in his mouth and pulled out a pack of cigarettes. He extracted one and rolled it between his fingers as if he were savoring the feel of it.

Archer had yet to see his old friend actually light up one of the cigarettes he always carried. "You're not that worried about the guest ranch, are you? We can bring in an expert to consult. I've already been looking into some of the more successful outfits out there. There's a place called Angel River near the Wyoming-Montana border that's been winning awards for years with rates just as high or higher than some of your resorts. Pretty swell setup. Definitely not all sleeping on straw beds and shoveling manure. And if you can talk Jed and April into adding a smaller winter resort at the summit as well—" He spread his hands, wordlessly.

"I know I'm not going to lose money with you

watching out for things," Gage said a little drily. Then he rubbed his forehead like there was a pain there. "Noah's in rehab again."

Understanding hit. Noah was Gage's younger brother and he'd been in and out of treatment for years. "Thought he'd been doing pretty well."

"So did I." Gage held up the cigarette and eyed it expressionlessly for a moment before slipping it back inside the pack that he pocketed once more. He rubbed his forehead again. "I don't know what to do about him," he admitted.

"Maybe don't do anything," Archer suggested bluntly. "He's a grown man."

"He's a spoiled kid in a grown man's body," Gage corrected wearily. "All he has ever cared about is himself." He fell silent while Theresa delivered their drinks. When she disappeared again, he looked at Archer. "Thought you and Theresa weren't seeing each other anymore."

"We aren't." He sipped the scotch and it hit the back of his throat with welcome warmth.

"She's sure giving you the looks."

"Is she?" Archer hadn't really noticed. He sank deeper into the thick cushions of his chair. Gage never did anything halfway. Everything he surrounded himself with was first-rate.

He was also one of the hardest-working fools Archer had ever known.

Gage had been raised by a single mom who'd

worked for a pharmaceutical magnate. If he'd ever known his father, he'd never said. He'd earned every bit of success he had, whereas his little half brother, Noah, had never had to work for a single thing thanks to being the only child of that pharmaceutical magnate.

Money. It could bring out the best in people. So often, though, it brought out the worst.

Archer looked up at the inky sky. Thought about Nell. About the night he'd brought her home from The Wet Bar.

The only reason he'd put her in the guest room bed was because she'd been drunk enough to climb into *his* bed, first.

It would have been way too easy to take advantage of that situation.

If he were honest with himself, he very nearly had.

Only the ringing of his phone had brought him to his senses. He'd dragged Nell's arms from around his neck. Somehow managed to button her back into her clothes and literally dumped her into the guest room. The only reason she'd stayed there was because she'd finally, mercifully passed out.

When—*if*—he was going to go down that rabbit hole with Nell again, he wanted her fully aware that she'd chosen to go down it with him, too.

"My grandmother's having a party on Friday," he told Gage abruptly. Before Archer had phoned

Nell, Vivian had called him specifically to let him know she expected him to be there regardless of how much rearranging of his schedule it might entail.

It wasn't the first time it had dawned on him that he was surrounded by a lot of strong-willed women with expectations where he was concerned.

"It's for that library project of hers," he went on, "but if the mountain ends up under Weaver control—and my hunch is that it's leaning that way—it'd be an opportunity for you to start making some connections with the locals."

Gage was shaking his head. "That's what I've got you for."

It wasn't the first time Gage had avoided going to Weaver. Archer knew it couldn't be because of Gage's ex-wife, Jane, who lived there. Gage had staked Jane in her purchase of a local bar and grill and admitted more than once that they were far happier with each other's company as exes than they'd ever been during the few years they'd been married more than a decade earlier.

"I already know the power players in Weaver," Archer countered. "That's not the point. They're going to want to know *you*. Know who they'll be inviting into their world. Once all the dust is settled about the mountain, what you do on it is going to change things for that town, and they all know it. Tourism is a whole new ball of wax for that area."

"Then I'll do the meetings I need to do." Gage's lips twisted a little. "But what I don't need to do is crash your grandmother's party. I've already donated money to her library deal."

"Afraid she'll ask you for more?"

Gage's expression finally lightened. "Now you've got it."

Theresa returned and leaned close to Gage, murmuring in his ear. He didn't react, but when she was gone again, he slammed back the rest of his drink and stood. "Ever think about finding an island where the only things to worry about are which hammock makes for the most comfortable nap?"

Archer shook his head. "Nope." Still, he was the man's attorney. If there was a problem that needed his expertise, it was his responsibility to handle it. "Anything I can help with?"

"Just business," Gage dismissed. "Stay and enjoy yourself," he said before he strode away.

"I plan to," Archer murmured. He popped three of the little fancy crackers into his mouth and pulled out his phone. It wasn't often he voluntarily called his stepsister. She was definitely a strong-willed woman, but when it came to Archer, Rosalind's only expectation was that he stay out of her way.

But he had enough scotch warming his belly to blunt the edge.

Amazingly, she answered on the fourth ring. "Archer." Her voice was cool. "I'm in the middle of something, so this better be important."

"What's going on between you and Nell?"

He could hear the very loud irritation in her silence. "I have nothing to say to you about that," she finally said, in what he considered an alarmingly polite way. She usually told him to do the physically impossible before she'd hang up on him.

Which meant there *was* something more going on than a simple parting of the ways. "She's living in a third-rate motel in Weaver, Ros. You saying you don't care about that?"

"I don't care about that," she echoed flatly. "So you can go f—"

"Now, now, now," he cut her off. "Don't say anything you might really mean." He poked through the delicacies displayed on the tray. "You know every time we speak, I have to remind myself that you carry Meredith's genes in you, because the older we get, the only ones you show are the ones you got from your dad."

"What do you want me to say, Archer?" She actually sounded pained. "There's nothing I can do to help her. Nell chose her side."

"And I'm asking you why! Why are there sides

when you've been friends for better than twenty years? I know Martin's at the root of whatever it is." Ros, ironically enough, was a stickler for fairness. At least where people beyond her own family were concerned. She wouldn't stoop to spreading rumors and innuendo about an enemy, much less Nell. Whereas those tactics were exactly what Martin would do, even to his own family.

The fact that Meredith hadn't been able to keep custody of Ros when she'd managed to escape him was proof of that.

His stepsister's silence turned stony. It was all too easy to picture the face that went along with it.

He exhaled wearily. "I'm not your enemy, kiddo. No more so now than when we were young." When he was being raised with his sisters by her mom and his dad—a boisterous, secure and happy family—and she was stuck alone with Martin. Even then, he'd known she was envious, just as he'd known she'd blamed Meredith for that situation more than she'd ever blamed her father. Such was the effectiveness of Martin Pastore's manipulations. "You can talk to me if you've got a probl—"

"Goodbye, Archer," she cut him off, and hung up on him.

Theresa chose that moment to sit down on the arm of his chair and trail her fingertip along his forearm. "You're looking a little lonely sitting out here, Archer."

He slowly looked up from the swirling screen-saver that had appeared on his phone to her face. "Then I'd better do something about that." He finished off his drink and gave her a pat on the arm as if he were her uncle before standing and making his own exit.

He kept his own apartment in the city not far from Gage's building. After he'd retrieved his files from Gage's office, he stopped at his place and grabbed a few more files that he added to the box he kept in his truck. He left a message for Jennifer, who ran his office with far more skill than he'd ever shown, and was on the highway thirty minutes after leaving Theresa.

It was well after midnight when he reached Braden. He considered driving through to Weaver and the Cozy Night. But if he went to Nell now and forcibly removed her from that particular hole-in-the-wall, she'd think he was just as crazy as he felt.

It was the only reason why he turned off the highway when he reached the narrow road that led to his house. He drove between the stone pillars of the gate he never closed and soon after, he was home, walking through the darkened rooms until he reached his bedroom.

He tossed himself down on the bed still fully

dressed and closed his eyes, happy to fall into familiar dreams where Nell never pushed him away.

The cat food bowl was empty again.

Nell propped her hands on her hips and looked around, but all she saw were the same things that she'd seen the day before. Only this time, she was seeing it through the beams of her car headlights.

Vivian had kept her busy that afternoon. And that evening.

Which meant that the scrubby brush now looked more gray than green. The boulders were nothing more than black shadows and the wildflowers were only an occasional flash of yellow if the breeze sent them swaying at the right angle to catch her headlights.

All cats were nocturnal, weren't they?

"Here kitty, kitty, kitty," she called softly, feeling a little foolish. Any stray who was out here coming around to eat food off the top of a stone pillar was probably not the kind of feline that'd come at a call.

She peered beyond the beams of light, but saw nothing more than before.

She tipped the cat food bag from her back seat over the bowl. It wasn't a very large bag and she would need to buy more soon because it was going to be empty in a couple of days. With the bowl full again, she stood on her toes to return it to its usual spot.

When she went back down on her heels, she glanced around again, then went stock-still at a tall shape in the distance out of range of the headlights.

No cat stood that tall.

Her heart shot up into her throat and she felt entirely incapable of movement while every monster movie she'd ever seen whizzed through her mind.

She was the worst sort of monster movie victim. The kind whom she and Ros had always yelled at at the movies for showing their stupidity so clearly. For not turning and at least *trying* to escape.

The shape grew larger and she felt sweat crawl down her spine. The thick paper of the cat food bag crinkled loudly when her fingers tightened on it. The bag wasn't much of a weapon, but if she threw it at the beast—it obviously couldn't be a monster movie one, but who knew what sort of animals besides stray kitties came out after dark?—maybe it would be warning enough to send it off in another direction.

She bounced on the toes of her low-heeled pumps, hearing her heart pound inside her head, and when the shape gained yet a little more substance, she balled up the bag as tightly as she could and launched it wildly in the air. Then she raced back to her car, practically diving head-first inside it.

She yanked the door closed and shoved the car into Reverse, backing away from the pillars in preparation of turning around. Whatever was out there—mountain lion or worse—was welcome to the kibble.

Nell would buy another bag and make sure she didn't come out here again except when it was still light.

She shifted out of Reverse and started to turn the car, but the shape was barreling toward her and when it crossed her headlights, she realized that it wasn't an animal at all.

It was Archer.

She shoved the car into Park and launched out of the car, barreling right back toward him. She reached the pillars at the same time that he did, and shoved her hands against the solid plane of his chest.

The fact that he was laughing infuriated her even more.

"You're supposed to be in Denver! You scared the peanuts out of me!" She went to shove him again, but he was leaning over, hands on his thighs as he laughed even harder.

"I thought you were a bear or something!" She kicked at the ground, which was covered with the kibble that had sprayed out of the bag when she'd thrown it.

He closed his hand over her shoulder, holding her in place. His face was pale in the headlights but the broad smile on his face was brilliant. "And you what? Thought you'd ward off the bear with kitty kibble?"

She kicked more nuggets of said kitty kibble over his legs. Now that her silly panic was assuaged, she didn't want to acknowledge the smile struggling to get free. "I thought you were out of town," she repeated.

"I was." He was still cupping her shoulder and when he turned and gestured with his other hand into the darkness beyond the headlights, his arm just seemed to naturally slide around her shoulders altogether. "My truck's parked right over there. How'd you miss it?"

She shrugged his arm off before too many of her cells could remember how much they liked the contact. "Maybe because I was concentrating on feeding a cat that I don't even believe exists!" She let out a loud breath and tugged at the hem of her blouse that had escaped her waistband. "But now you're back, which means I am off that particular hook." She started marching back to her car.

"Oh, come on, Nell." Archer followed her. "Relax. Come on up to the house at least. I was just about to put a steak on the grill when I saw your headlights." He caught her hand as she reached for the door.

"It's late and I have things to do." She ignored the warmth streaking up her arm.

"What things? Fighting moths?"

She let out a frustrated sound. "It doesn't matter what things!"

"Then whatever they are can wait." He squeezed her hand slightly. Cajoling. "Come on. You can fill me in on Vivian's project. I worry about her."

The sound she let out then was nothing but pure scoff. "Vivian's the last person you need to worry about. She runs circles around everyone."

"Yeah." His thumb brushed a small, distracting circle over the back of her hand. "But she also has an inoperable brain tumor, so humor me."

It took a moment for the words to penetrate. "I… *What?*"

"She wouldn't appreciate me telling you, either. She prefers to choose who, and when, she shares that information with so try not to throw me under the bus next time you see her."

No longer in the line of the headlights, all she had to see him by was the light from inside her car and the proliferation of stars punctuating the sky overhead. She peered hard at him. "You're not joking."

"Not about that."

She let out a long, long breath. "A tumor."

"Yes, a tumor. Fortunately, it's small and hasn't caused any bad episodes in over a year, but there are no guarantees. It's a situation that could turn on a dime. Anytime. Anywhere. She has tests every few months, monitoring it."

Nell finally tugged her hand away from him and ducked into the car. She turned off the engine and it ticked softly in the sudden silence.

Her mother had died of a brain aneurysm.

No warning. No preparation.

She closed her eyes for a moment. The car engine ticked twice more.

Then she straightened again, closed the door and faced him. "I hope you have two steaks, because I haven't had a chance to eat all day."

Chapter Seven

"Could have pulled your car up to the house,"
Archer told her for the third time when they
reached the house after a fair piece of walking.
"It would have saved you walking all that way in
those plain Jane grandma shoes of yours."

She huffed. She'd chosen the shoes because
they were leather with chunky heels of a sensible
height that worked perfectly for an associate lawyer who usually was racing from one courtroom to
another. She'd owned them for years and had already had them resoled. Twice. "If I were wearing
shoes like *your* grandmother wears, I would have."
So far, Nell hadn't seen Vivian wear the same

shoes twice. They were all quite high-heeled, and they all screamed "designer."

"Yeah, she does like her shoes, doesn't she?" He took two steps in one as he vaulted up the wood stairs near the corner of the house.

She'd seen the structure only from a distance up to now, of course. She still hadn't seen a guest-house at all, which made her think he'd made that up just to yank her chain.

It would be typical Archer behavior.

She followed him up the steps to the wood deck lining the front three sides of the house, past a fancy gas grill that put the little charcoal thing next to the pool at the Cozy Night to shame, and through a door that opened into his kitchen.

It was hard not to gape a little, because it looked like a kitchen that actually got used. A lot.

Not because it was messy, though there were a few dishes stacked in the sink, but because the pots hanging from a rack over the stove looked slightly worn. Well used. Because there was a jug of utensils—mismatched ones—sitting next to the gas stove. The ones tucked inside a fancy stone container that had sat next to the stove in the condo she'd shared with Ros had all been carefully matched and had stayed that way for the simple reason they'd never been used.

A rustic loaf of bread sat on a scarred cutting board and the coffeepot—the real kind, not one of the fancy pod deals that she was used to—sat on a cast-iron stove grate.

There was a farmhouse sink, a doublewide stainless steel refrigerator and a sturdy wood table in the middle of the room. The counters were butcher block, the floors were slate, and the colorful modern painting hanging on one wall was probably an original.

She peered at the slanted signature in one corner below the swirl of squiggles covering the canvas. Soliere.

She'd never heard of the artist. But that didn't mean anything. She'd never bothered with art studies. She'd been more interested in passing the bar exam.

Feeling bemused, she set her car keys on the table. "This is, ah—"

He waited, eyebrows raised, and she felt her cheeks flush. "Is...what?"

"Nice," she finished a little helplessly.

His lips twitched. "Meredith would thank you."

Meredith. His stepmother. Ros's mother.

For some reason, it relieved Nell to know he'd had help with the kitchen. As if he, too, might share some of her kitchen incompetence.

"How *is* Meredith?" She'd first met Ros's mother when she'd been a teenager. But the last time she'd seen her had been at least a few years ago.

"Happily wallowing in grandparenthood." His

tone was dry. "Every one of my sisters is diligently practicing the 'be fruitful and multiply' thing these days. Well, except for Rosalind."

"Wouldn't be too sure about that," Nell murmured.

He gave her a quick look. "Ros is pregnant?"

"No." Then she shook herself. "Not that I know of, anyway." It hurt to think that as things stood now with Archer's sister, Nell would be the last one with whom Ros would share that sort of news. "She mentioned that her boyfriend was interested in starting a family. That's all."

Archer looked thoughtful for a moment. Then his eyes glinted as he rested his hand on the refrigerator door. "Interest you in something to drink?" He waited a beat. "Champagne?"

She gave him a look. She needed no reminder that her last interlude with champagne had landed her in his guest room. "Water is fine," she overenunciated. And had a flash of Montrose's face in her mind as a result.

Archer's smile twitched and he reached into a cupboard instead of the fridge. He filled the glass he pulled out with water from the tap and set it on the table next to her car keys. "There is something else I need to break to you, though." His voice turned serious.

Unease crept through her. Something worse

than his grandmother's brain tumor? "What?" Caution practically dripped from her voice.

"I only have the one steak."

Her shoulders sagged as unease trickled away. "You are—" she jabbed her finger into his shoulder "—impossible."

"It's a big one, though," he said as if she hadn't spoken at all. "One of those cowboy cuts."

She didn't know a cowboy cut from a finger cut. But she did know that her stomach was growling.

She rubbed her palms down the sides of her skirt. It had already been so late when she'd gotten away from Vivian's that she hadn't wanted to take the time to change before driving out here to feed the cat. "Is there somewhere I can wash up?"

He looked like he wanted to start laughing again. "Worried I don't have indoor plumbing?"

"If you don't stop laughing at me, you can start worrying what I might do to you if I get my hands on one of those pots hanging behind you."

"I don't laugh at you, Cornelia. I laugh with you."

She gave him a deadpan stare. "Am I laughing? I wasn't aware."

He chuckled and gestured over his shoulder toward a darkened doorway. "Second door on the left."

She went through the doorway and startled when a softly golden light automatically went on.

A farmhouse with tech.

Trust Archer Templeton to have it.

She found the bathroom and washed up, staring at her reflection in the oval mirror hanging above the pedestal sink. He obviously had a predilection for them. She didn't care how many pedestal sinks he had in however many bathrooms.

She just needed to remember she shouldn't have a predilection for *him*.

She returned to his kitchen, resolutely keeping her curiosity about the rest of his house under control. He was standing at the butcher-block counter wielding a knife, and for a moment she watched the play of muscles beneath his shirt.

She moistened her lips, hovering there, feeling warm inside. Why, *why* did he have to be the one to ring those bells?

"Don't just stand there," he said without looking around at her. "Salad makings are in the fridge. Tomatoes are on the counter in a bowl. In case you don't recognize them, they're the round, shiny red things."

She flushed and yanked open the refrigerator door. Her idea of preparing a salad was to tear open a bag of the premade stuff.

There wasn't any such animal in his fridge, though.

She pulled out a bunch of romaine from the crisper drawer and carried it over to the counter near where he was working. She had seen a cooking show a time or two. Or at least had flipped past a cooking channel on the hunt for something more interesting. She could fake it.

She peeled off the rubber band keeping the lettuce leaves contained and hesitated.

Archer stopped chopping and set a large, holey bowl on the counter next to her. He began chopping again.

Garlic. That she knew simply because of the penetrating aroma. And he already had a neat stack of thinly sliced onions.

She slid her gaze back to her own task at hand and separated one leaf from the rest of its pack. She was as unsuccessful at blocking him out of her peripheral vision as she was blocking out how enticingly companionable it felt to be standing there with him.

She focused even more attention on the lettuce, methodically tearing the leaf into bite-size pieces that she dropped in the bowl. She repeated the process with a couple of more crispy leaves and was feeling quite proud of the precisely sized results. Then she finally ran the bowl under the faucet and shook it as dry as she could get it.

In the same amount of time that she'd taken to tear up a few lettuce leaves, however, Archer had filled his cutting board with a huge mound of chopped vegetables.

His eyes crinkled with amusement when he caught her comparing her small pile with his. "Size doesn't matter."

She managed to keep her response contained to a bored, raised eyebrow. "That's what all men say."

He gave a soundless laugh and swiped half of his cutting board bounty into another bowl. He dropped a pair of salad tongs on top and handed it to her, then carried the cutting board and the rest of its contents, along with the enormous steak, out of the kitchen.

She pressed her tongue against her teeth and eyed the painting on the wall. The squiggly lines racing around the canvas might as well have been the pattern of her crazy heartbeat.

Afraid he'd come back in and find her standing there like that, she hastily dumped her lettuce pieces in with the rest of the veggies and flipped it all around a few times with the tongs.

It was the only kind of salad she really liked. One that was less green stuff and more chunky vegetables. He'd even sliced the kernels off a fresh cob of corn.

The man had probably never poured prepared salad out of a bag in his life.

She set the salad bowl in the center of the table

and then poked around the kitchen enough to find a couple of plates and flatware.

She set them out on the table and then, with no other reason to keep hiding in the kitchen, followed him outside.

He was standing in front of the grill. The sleeves of his shirt were rolled up to his elbows and his shirttails were hanging loose over his jeans.

She had a mad desire to slide her hand beneath the shirttail and run her palm up the length of his spine. To discover if his skin still felt as warm and supple where it stretched over sinewy muscle as she remembered.

She lifted her glass so fast to take a drink that she managed to spill water down her chin and the front of her blouse in the process.

"Having a problem there?"

She wanted to sink through the deck and the Wyoming earth beneath.

She swiped her chin and set the glass on the wide beam of wood at the top of the deck railing. The steak was sizzling on one side of the grill, sending up a delicious aroma that had her mouth watering. At least she hoped it was the primary reason behind that particular reaction.

Yes, Archer was insanely attractive. Always had been. But she flatly refused to believe he could actually make her mouth *water*.

"Want a taste?"

He was holding up a chunk of red bell pepper with grill marks on it and before she could even offer a yay or nay, he'd slid it past her surprised lips.

It was deliciously charred and terribly hot. She chewed quickly, gingerly, chasing it with the rest of the water in her glass. "Give a girl some warning," she managed when she finally swallowed. But then she ruined her protest by stepping closer to him and the grill. "Can I have another one?"

On the other half of the grill, he'd dumped the vegetables atop a thick piece of foil and was slowly turning them with the tines of a long-handled fork. He jabbed another chunk of pepper and handed it to her.

She carefully took it from the fork, holding it between her fingertips. While she waited for the morsel to cool a bit, she studied him from beneath her lashes. "When did Vivian discover she had a tumor?"

"Before she moved to Weaver," he answered immediately. "I think it's what prompted her to come to Wyoming. Feeling her mortality. Wanting to set things right between her and my father and uncle."

Because of the summer after her mom died when she'd accompanied Ros on her forced visitation with Meredith, Nell knew enough about his family to remember that his father, Carter, was a retired insurance agent and his uncle was a pediatrician. And that they'd lived in Wyoming for as long as Ros knew, anyway. "Why did things need to be set right?"

"Vivian wasn't always the philanthropic, kindly old lady you know and love."

Nell let out an abbreviated laugh. Vivian was, indeed, philanthropic. But in just the last week Nell had learned the woman was not at all the "kindly old lady" type. She was sharp, decisive and demanding. She also wasn't above manipulation when a situation called for it, which explained the cocktail party that she'd decided to throw.

"It's too early to love, much less claim to know her very well, but I *do* like her," Nell said. "She's a force, just like you said. Kind of hard not to be impressed by her."

"True enough." He adjusted the heat under the vegetables and leaned against the rail next to her.

She told herself it was just coincidence that his hand happened to land on top of hers where it rested on the smooth wood. Particularly when he moved it away again a moment later to fold his arms across his wide chest.

She quickly averted her eyes from the way his shirt tightened around his biceps.

"My father and uncle, on the other hand, find very little to admire about their mother." He

crossed one boot in front of the other in a casual stance. "They railed against their rigid up-
bringing. Blamed her when their father—Sawyer
Templeton—died. They had an older brother who
took off when he was still a young man and then
he died too, and that was yet another thing to
blame her for." He dropped his arms and selected
his own steaming-hot piece of squash, blowing on
it briefly before sinking his teeth into it.

She swallowed, looking down at the toes of her
shoes. A dim portion of her mind acknowledged
that they really were sort of unflattering.

The rest of her was humming along with the
internal tune of jangling bells.

"Anyway," he continued, "none of us even
knew Vivian existed until she showed up here
out of the blue one day. She'd buried another husband—"

"Dear Arthur."

He nodded. "Dear Arthur. And she said she
wanted to make things right. At first, Hayley was
the only one who'd have anything to do with her."
He shrugged. "Stands to reason, I suppose, my
sister being a psychologist and all."

Nell knew that Ros had always been less an-
tagonistic with Hayley than she was with Archer,
but then Hayley didn't go out of her way to antag-
onize their stepsister the way Archer did.

"Vivian even lived with Hayley for a while,"

Archer continued. "She's a good family therapist, but not even she was good enough to heal the rift between Vivian and my dad and uncle."

"Things got better, though. Right? Vivian talks about you and your sisters and cousins all the time."

"It got better with us grandchildren," he allowed. "My dad and Uncle David tolerate her because the rest of us have said they have to. But I doubt they'll ever be able to really let go of the past. Some things run too deep for healing."

"Seems sad to me. Your dad and uncle are missing out on knowing the person she is now."

"It's just the way it is. What would you do if your father suddenly turned up after all these years? If he offered an apology for the way he bailed on you and wanted everything to be hunky-dory again?"

The question hit her hard and she winced a little.

"Sorry."

"No." She turned to face him and the grill, though her thoughts were suddenly in the past. "It's a fair enough comparison." She chewed the inside of her cheek for a moment. "I'd be hard-pressed to accept it," she admitted eventually.

"There you go," he said quietly. "I'm not going to bust my dad's or my uncle's chops for feeling the way they do. Their relationship with Vivian is different than mine or my sisters' or my cousins'."

She angled her head, studying him for a moment. "You're pretty nonjudgmental for a lawyer. Maybe you should be a judge."

He chuckled. "No thank you. Too much politics to deal with for my taste."

"Yet you're dating Judge Potts." Her stomach churned a little.

"I date lots of women besides Taylor," he countered mildly.

"You're not getting any younger—"

"Flattery. Nice."

"—don't you ever think about getting married?" As nettling as she found her own curiosity, she couldn't seem to stop herself. "Settling down and doing the fruitful-and-multiplying thing yourself?"

"Despite the setups Meredith keeps trying to throw my way, maybe I'm not the settling kind, either."

She felt oddly tense. "You think *I'm* not the settling kind?"

"Are you?" His gaze slid over her face. "How many men have you ever let get under your defenses? And don't say Muelhaupt," he added abruptly. "He's a mouse compared to you."

She made a face. "What is *that* supposed to mean?"

He had the nerve to laugh. "Do you even know how impressively intimidating you are?"

She felt her eyebrows climb up to the middle of her scalp. "Intimidating! If I were the least bit intimidating why am *I* the one who has gotten herself basically banished from Cheyenne for daring to speak the truth?"

Her impetuous words rang out to be quickly absorbed into the night air. But not quickly enough.

And there was nowhere to escape the intensively close look he was giving her. "What truth is that, Cornelia?"

Her mouth ran dry. She opened her lips to say something, but her words failed her.

Telling him what Martin had done would only prove how gullible she'd been. And if she started getting pity from Archer Templeton, she wasn't sure she could stand it.

The sudden flare of fire that streamed into the air from the grill broke the spell and she swallowed, ridiculously relieved when he turned back to the food.

"Get me a couple plates from inside, would you?"

She quickly went inside, grateful for the opportunity to flee even if momentarily. In the seconds it took her to get two more plates and take them out to him, she'd scrabbled together a minimum of composure and he'd conquered the spitting fire.

She held the plates while he transferred the enormous steak to one and the vegetables to the other and then carried them inside while he shut down the grill.

When he found her still standing—hovering—at the table when he came in too, he frowned slightly as he pushed the kitchen door closed.

She almost wished she were somewhere else. "I wasn't sure which spot was yours," she said.

His expression lightened then. "They're all the same, sweetheart." He pulled out the chair closest to him and gestured for her to sit.

She slipped into the seat, but he didn't immediately join her at the table. Instead, he walked out of the room and returned a few moments later with a bottle of wine that he'd already uncorked.

He unceremoniously plunked a clean, stemless glass in front of her and splashed a generous measure of red wine into it. Then he repeated the process for himself and finally took the other chair.

He lifted the glass. "What should we toast to?"

She circled her fingers lightly around her own glass. "Do we have to toast to anything? We could just give it a pass."

"How long has it been since you and I sat down and had a meal together? And I'm not talking about the bar association's annual dinner."

If she really had to, she could calculate it right

down to hours and minutes. "A while," she allowed.

"All right, then." He waited until she lifted her glass also. "To old friends and nonexistent cats."

She gave him an incredulous look. "You cannot really be serious."

His eyes glinted, the green color seeming deeper than ever. "To old friends and unexpected bedfellows."

Her cheeks burned. "To old friends and nonexistent cats," she said crisply.

He smiled and lightly touched the edge of his glass to hers.

When she lifted the glass to her lips, she hoped she was the only one who noticed her hand wasn't entirely steady.

He sliced the enormous steak into two pieces and pushed one of the slabs onto her plate, then followed it up with half of the grilled vegetables despite her protest that she'd never be able to eat that much.

His eyes crinkled. "Sure you can."

And she did.

Afterward, when all of the dishes were empty—except the salad bowl, which was still full—they washed up and Nell gave up trying to stave off that sense of companionability. He poured her a second glass of wine while she dried the few plates they'd used and she sipped at it while he put them away.

And even though she knew she ought to make some move to leave, she kept putting it off.

He showed her around the rest of his house, consisting of three minimally furnished bedrooms—she barely allowed herself to glance into his—an office that was bigger than her room at the Cozy Night and lined with bookshelves crammed with books, a finished basement that housed a gigantic half-moon of a couch and a television that took up nearly an entire wall, the spectacular deck that surrounded three-fourths of the exterior, of course, and yes, even the guesthouse that did exist, after all.

The only reason she hadn't noticed it at first was because it was down a steep hill on the far side of the house, and reached by several steps cut into the hillside.

"Sun rises there," he said, gesturing in that direction. "Best view in the world. And you could still use it. No moths last time I checked."

She looked from the darkened windows of the small guesthouse to his face. "I don't think it's a good idea, Archer."

He made a soft *hmm* sound. "You promised to feed the cat."

"You're here. You feed the cat. You won't even be serious about whether he's real or not."

He dropped his arm over her shoulder. "I'll drive you back to your car."

She tried to refuse but he was adamant. Despite the brilliant moonlight and the bouquet of stars that looked close enough to pluck, it would be too easy to turn an ankle, he said. Too easy to cross paths with a wild animal.

The drive was short. In a matter of minutes, he came to a stop next to her car, right where she'd left it on the other side of the open gate.

She pushed open the truck door and slid out onto the ground. "Didn't see any wild animals," she told him drily, conveniently ignoring her scare when she thought he was one just a few hours earlier.

He draped his wrist over the steering wheel as he looked at her. "I don't want to chance you getting hurt."

Too late.

The words whispered through her mind and had nothing to do with turned ankles or wild animals and everything to do with him.

She stepped away from the truck. "Good night, Archer. Thanks for the steak."

Then she firmly shut the door, climbed quickly into her own car and drove away, grateful that she was the only one who'd ever know the way her heartbeat squiggled around wildly like lines on a canvas.

Chapter Eight

Nell pushed through the door at Ruby's Diner the next afternoon. There was the usual crowd of people waiting for tables alongside the door.

But the occupant of the stool at the counter whom she'd gotten used to seeing was not there at all and she was so surprised that she stopped right in the doorway.

And was promptly bumped into from the rear, and everything she was holding in her arms slid right onto the floor. Pages spilled out of her binder and her purse went sliding.

"Sorry, miss." The bumper crouched down beside her to help as she scrabbled her belongings to-

gether. "Didn't see your brake lights fast enough."
He gathered up a splayed pile of documents, hand-
ing them to her, and she flushed a little.

He was smiling, dark-haired and ridiculously
good-looking.

"It was my fault," she said quickly, taking the
pages and pushing them every which way between
the covers of the binder. She started to straighten
but he beat her to it and took her hand, helping
her up the rest of the way.

She flushed harder, more from knowing they'd
earned the attention of the diners all around them
than because of him. Though he really was attractive. Sort of like an engagingly cute puppy.

"I'm Nick," he said. "Nick Ventura."

His name surprised her even more. "You're
Vivian's architect! The one who's been design-
ing the new library." Her employer hadn't said
just how young her architect was.

His smile widened. "Guilty, I'm afraid. And I
hope one day the library actually makes it off the
page. And you are—"

"Nell Brewster." She adjusted her tenuous
grasp on her belongings again to stick out her
hand. "And I can tell you that she absolutely in-
tends for the library to make it off the page. Vivian hired me to manage the project."

He closed his hand around hers, smiling
warmly. "Then I'll have something more to look

forward to when she calls for design change five hundred and sixty-two."

Nell laughed. "She does have a strong opinion about things that matter to her. I've learned that much." Which was probably the reason why she'd hired an architect before she even had a confirmed location or approval from the town council. "But as it happens, I was going to call you this afternoon. Vivian is having a party this Friday and would like you to do a brief presentation if you're available."

"Have a feeling she'd want me to do it even if I weren't available," he said wryly. "But sure. Whatever she needs."

"Great. Are you here by yourself or—"

He shook his head. "I'm meeting my cousin— ah. Over there." He raised his hand in acknowledgment and Nell automatically glanced over her shoulder to look. A striking woman with graying auburn hair was sipping iced tea while a younger redhead with an animated expression was looking their way.

It was the red hair that caught Nell's attention. She remembered seeing the woman in the courtroom with Archer a few times.

She also remembered the way she'd felt inside witnessing the obviously comfortable way the two related to one another. She'd figured they were involved.

For all she knew, they still were. He'd said it himself. He dated lots of women. Just because Archer was romancing Judge Potts didn't mean he wasn't romancing someone else, too. He'd done it back when Nell had been in law school, after all. She just hadn't known about it at the time.

"Then I should clear the intersection," she told Nick lightly, stepping to one side.

"Why don't you join us? April won't mind—"

"No, no." She shook her head. "Thank you, but I don't want to intrude. And I'm just grabbing a bite. Working lunch, I'm afraid. I'll email you the details about the party." She patted her notebook and began sidestepping toward the counter. "I'm glad we bumped into each other."

"Best collision I've had all year."

She couldn't help but laugh. He was too friendly not to.

She was still smiling when she slipped into the spot between the cash register and Squire Clay's empty seat and dumped her notebook and its disheveled contents on the counter.

Tina immediately greeted her with a wave. "Be with you in a sec, Nell."

"No rush," Nell assured her. She had plenty to keep her busy. She flipped open the binder and began restoring order to it. She'd begun using the notebook to help keep herself organized. She already had sections for fundraising, for construction issues, for permits and approvals. She even had copies of the architectural renderings.

But the section right now at the front of her binder contained her checklists for Vivian's cocktail party being held the following day.

Two items remained unchecked among the dozens of others that were marked off.

A proper dress for Nell.

And a confirmed RSVP from Squire Clay. He was the only holdout from the entire council.

Which was the whole reason she'd come into the diner for lunch in the first place.

She fit the last page onto the binder rings and snapped them closed, then waited until Tina flipped over her coffee cup and filled it before asking about the man's whereabouts. "I thought Squire comes in every day."

"He does." Tina glanced beyond Nell's shoulder and dropped her voice slightly. "But not when she's here."

Nell raised her brows. "When who is here?"

"Gloria." Tina's voice dropped even more. It was nearly soundless. "His wife." She inclined her head an inch. "She's in the corner booth over there with her granddaughter, April."

The corner booth where Nick was now sitting alongside the older woman. A quick sideways glance confirmed it. Nell lifted her coffee cup and took a sip. "He doesn't eat here when his wife eats here?"

"Not since they separated," Tina said under her breath. "It's been the talk of the town all summer."

Nell felt a stab of sympathy for Squire and his estranged wife. She didn't like being the subject of "talk" in Cheyenne. She could only imagine how much worse it would be in such a small town like Weaver.

A peal of laughter erupted from the table in the corner and Nell had to control the urge to look over again. She quickly ordered one of the sandwich specials from Tina before the waitress had to tend her other customers, and flipped to the fundraising section in her binder.

Aside from several corporate donations that had already come in, there was a healthy amount of money that had been contributed by John and Jane Q. Public. But the amount raised still needed to be significantly higher, so in between refereeing the cocktail party appetizer selection battle between Vivian and Montrose, Nell had been looking into possible grant opportunities.

There was one in particular being funded by Swift Oil. And even though the CEO of the company had already made a personal donation—one of the first sizable ones, in fact—Nell didn't see why that should stop her from applying for one of the company's annual philanthropic gifts.

She didn't have a lot of experience with grant writing, but she was willing to try. Swift Oil was headquartered in Braden. The CEO, Lincoln Swift, obviously already recognized that the residents in his town would also benefit by an expanded library in Weaver. She had most of the statistics ready but writing the narrative would take some time. And time wasn't in great supply since the deadline for grant applications to even be considered was tonight at midnight.

She'd printed off the lengthy application on Vivian's printer and had managed to read through it once.

She believed she could get it done in time, but it would be close. And if the library were fortunate enough to win the grant, it would all be for naught if the town council still couldn't agree that it should even be built.

Tina stopped long enough to deliver Nell's sandwich and top off her water glass.

"Where does he—" Nell leaned her head toward the empty seat beside her "—go on days like today when he's avoiding the diner?"

Tina thought about it for a moment. "Honestly, I don't think he goes anywhere. He's probably at home."

"Where's that?"

For a moment, Tina looked surprised. "I keep forgetting that you're not from around here." She glanced toward the corner booth and lowered her voice again. "The Double-C Ranch," she said.

Nell had heard of the ranch, but that didn't mean much. She'd also heard of the Squawking Turkey, too, only to discover the apartment it had offered to rent was little more than a glorified chicken coop. "Can you tell me how to get there?"

"Sure." Tina pulled out a napkin and quickly swiped her pen over it, drawing a few intersecting lines. "Head that way out of town." She jerked her thumb to the left. "Be careful when you take the turnoff. The road is graded but it's still gravel. Once you're off the highway, you'll see the ranch entrance. It's huge. But you'll know you're on the right track."

"Thanks." Nell tucked the impromptu map in her binder and delved inside her purse for her wallet. "Mind wrapping up the sandwich for me, and adding a meat loaf sandwich, as well?"

In answer, Tina whisked away the plate and returned a few minutes later with the two sandwiches neatly packaged. She tucked them inside a paper bag that she handed to Nell. "I don't know why you're so anxious to see him, but good luck."

"Thanks." Leaving enough cash for the bill and tip on the counter for Tina, she gathered everything up and hurried toward the door.

From his spot in the corner, Nick caught her

eye but she didn't linger long enough to do more than return his smile with a quick one of her own.

Following Tina's instructions proved simple enough and before long she was driving though the Double-C entrance, while a cloud of dust billowed behind her in her rearview mirror.

When she finally reached a circular drive that fronted a long, rambling house, the dust clung to every inch of her car. Even though she'd quickly closed her car windows, she felt as if she had dust clinging to every inch of her, too.

With the bag from the diner in hand, she left everything else in the car and approached the massive wooden door at the top of several shallow steps.

She was quickly realizing that the Double-C Ranch wasn't just some regular old cattle ranch.

Not if the outbuildings she could see and the number of vehicles parked around them were any indication. They all bore the same brand that had been burned into the timbers of the ranch entrance.

She used the heavy iron knocker on the door because there didn't seem to be a doorbell. But she eventually had to accept that nobody was coming to answer.

Chewing the inside of her lip, she went back down the steps and started off toward the buildings with all of the vehicles parked outside.

When she reached the first one, she found it to be an office of sorts, with three young women sitting at computers. None of them knew where Mr. Clay might be.

She didn't want to admit defeat. But it was disappointing, even though she'd had no guarantee that he'd be at home.

She left the sandwiches with the girl named Melody, whose desk was closest to the open door of the office. "If you do see him, would you tell him this is from his seatmate Nell at the diner?"

"Sure." Melody didn't seem surprised by the request or anything else where Nell was concerned. She turned her attention back to her computer screen before Nell even turned to leave.

Rather than drive back into town, Nell went to Vivian's place. She parked in the courtyard as usual, but instead of going through the side door there, she circled around to the backside of the house and entered through one of the patio doors where she'd be less likely to run into Montrose.

In that, at least, she was successful. She made it up the stairs in the atrium to the second floor and slipped into the small office she'd taken over not far from where Vivian's was located.

Nell's office didn't look out over Rambling Mountain the way that Vivian's did. In fact, she didn't have any windows at all.

It was still nicer and more spacious than the

cramped quarters she'd occupied at Pastore Legal and there was even an elegant little powder room right next door.

She propped her elbow on the fancy wooden table she was using as a desk and cupped her cheek. She needed to stop thinking about what had been and keep her focus on what was.

A fine idea if she could only manage to follow it consistently.

The phone ringing at her other elbow was a welcome distraction. She answered it with one hand while she pulled a pen from the crystal bowl she'd pressed into service to hold a dozen pens and pencils. She was a little concerned that it might be Lalique or Baccarat crystal, but assumed it wasn't since it had been just sitting around in the conservatory—Vivian actually used that term for her plant-filled sunroom—holding a few cups of potting soil.

"Nell Brewster speaking," she said briskly, then winced a little because that was the way she'd answered the phone at Pastore Legal. And if the caller was a client, she'd immediately begun timing the conversation. Billable hours and all that.

"Thank you for the sandwich."

Squire Clay. Surprise made Nell sit up straighter. "You're welcome." So the sandwich actually had made its way to the man. Melody and her compatriots hadn't seemed overly concerned that it would. "How, uh, how did you know to reach me here?"

"Small town," he said as if that explained it all.

She spun her chair around to stare at the narrow span of wall behind her. There was nothing hanging on it. No artwork. No paintings. She might have repurposed the dirt bowl, but she didn't have enough nerve to commandeer anything else.

She doubted Vivian would care, but Nell wasn't so sure about Montrose. She had no desire to earn his wrath.

Archer's kitchen and his squiggly-lined Soliere drifted through her mind.

She closed off that thought. "I'm sorry I missed you," she told Squire. "But I'm glad the sandwich reached you. I hope it was good."

"Ruby's food always is. Question I've got is why you made that effort at all. Your boss lady's never stooped to sending a pretty filly along to do her dirty work before."

"There's no dirty work," she assured him, trying not to sound stiff. The only dirty work she'd ever been involved in had been because of Martin, unintentional on her part or not, and she didn't appreciate hearing the term now. "I was in the diner this afternoon and missed your company."

He made a soft sort of snort. "You wanted to convince me to show up for the dog and pony *soiree*—" the word dripped with scorn "—that the rest of my council brethren have been suckered into attending."

"I don't think Vivian plans a dog and pony show," Nell countered mildly. "She's only interested in smoothing the way for a new public library. Do you have grandchildren in this community, Squire?"

"Not as smart as you look if you don't already know the answer to that."

He was right. She should have done more homework where he was concerned. As it was, she'd felt a little sideswiped by the impressiveness of his ranch. "A new library only benefits Weaver and the surrounding region. Do you really disagree with that?"

"Only thing I disagree with is the woman you're working for. She doesn't do anything without an ulterior motive."

"I think that could be said of most anyone," Nell pointed out. "In my experience, people's actions almost always have a deeper motive than what is first apparent." She waited a beat, but he didn't reply. Nor did he hang up on her, which she chose to take as encouragement. "I'm no different," she continued. "The first time we met, I could have told you that I'd been hired by Mrs. Templeton. But I knew there was dissension between you when it comes to the library—"

"Not just the library, girl."

She hadn't done her research, so she let that pass, too. "And I was enjoying your company too much to want it ruined. I also realized that if you could get to know me a little before painting me the same color as you've painted her, perhaps you would also have a more open mind when it comes to bringing something really important to this town. You see? Deeper motive."

"Don't have to tell me what's important to this town, either. Been here a hell of a lot longer than she has."

"Yet another reason why it's so important that you exercise your support for it. Do you really think the existing library is adequate?"

He didn't answer that. "Is she going to fire you if you don't get me there tomorrow night?"

Nell winced. She ought to have been prepared for such bluntness. "I certainly hope not. I need the paycheck," she admitted, just as bluntly. Vivian had never mentioned Squire by name. She'd just said she wanted the council there. "But no. I don't feel like it's her intention to hang me out to dry."

"Pays to be cautious where you put your trust, girl."

How well she knew that, too. "And sometimes it pays to go out on a limb despite one's caution," Nell countered. She felt guilt fire in her face, because what limb had *she* ever gone out on? "Particularly when so many others will benefit as a result."

Her little speech was met with silence and she squelched a sigh. "I'm well aware that I'm the new kid on the block, Mr. Clay, and that it's not my place to shower you with platitudes. So let's just leave it that I am glad you enjoyed the sandwich. And I hope one day, I'll share the lunch counter again with you at Ruby's." She didn't wait for a response that she was certain wouldn't be forthcoming anyway, and hung up the phone.

She flipped open her notebook to her checklist and eyed the two incomplete tasks.

She'd struck out on Squire Clay.

That left acquiring a cocktail dress that Vivian Templeton would deem appropriate.

She pinched the bridge of her nose for a moment, then closed her binder again, took it and her purse and cautiously snuck down the staircase so that Montrose with his bat-like hearing didn't notice.

Weaver's current and only library was located in Old Weaver.

That evening, Nell found it easily enough and entered through the swinging glass door. It was the only fairly modern element that the structure possessed. Aside from that, the two-story structure just looked like an old, vaguely Victorian house. Considering she'd been in Weaver nearly a week, she should have done more than just drive by it by now.

Inside, she passed the circulation desk. The teenage boy manning it was engrossed in a thick novel and didn't even look up at her.

That was okay. She wasn't there to check out any materials. She wasn't even there to judge for herself whether the facility was too out of date for the town. The reason she was there was to escape the noise coming from the motel room next to hers while she worked on the Swift Oil grant application.

At the motel, Gardner's car had been gone, meaning that she was working the evening shift at Udder Huddle. Her three boys had been left to stay in the motel room where they'd been in fine form, whooping and hollering over the video game they'd been playing.

The noise had been clear through the walls. They hadn't been misbehaving. They hadn't been fighting. There'd been no reason for her to try to squelch their natural exuberance just because she'd found it difficult to concentrate.

Now that she *was* in the library, though, Nell couldn't stop herself from wandering the aisles, pulling out a book here and there. Paging through it. Lifting the book close to her face and just inhaling the smell of the pages.

She loved that smell.

It always reminded her of her mother.

However, she had a task to complete and wandering among the stacks wasn't going to get it done.

There were only two study desks that she found, and one had bright yellow caution tape strapped all over it because of a broken leg.

Fortunately, the other was not broken and she sank down on one of the hard wooden chairs surrounding it. She flipped open her binder and pulled out the application form, spreading it across the table in front of her. She uncapped her bright yellow highlighter. The instructions were lengthy. Detailed. She wanted to be sure she didn't miss a single thing, because she knew the quickest way to have an application tossed out was for it to have been submitted without every instruction followed.

She read through it once, highlighting the key elements with her marker. When she was done, almost the entire sheet was yellow.

"You always did have a heavy hand with the highlighters."

Nell stared up stupidly at Archer, who'd appeared seemingly out of nowhere to stand beside her table. She frowned at him. "Aren't you supposed to be cat-sitting somewhere?"

His eyes crinkled slightly and he dragged a

chair from the adjacent side of the table and strad-
dled it right there next to Nell. "What're *you* working on?"

She would have liked to produce some reason
not to tell him, but there wasn't one. Not a good
one, anyway. "Swift Oil annually awards a couple
major grants. This year they're both focused on
education. I figure the library fits the bill."

"That explains this." He lifted the edge of the
mostly yellow page. "But it doesn't explain why
you're doing it here." He made a point of swiveling
his head around at the stacks surrounding them.

"Three boys in the motel room next to me
who like playing video games. Very noisy video
games."

"Ah. Now I see." He reached across her to pick
up the first page of the grant instructions and his
arm brushed against hers.

She wanted to gnash her teeth.

She hadn't succeeded that day with Squire
Clay.

She'd failed to find a dress at Classic Charms,
because when she'd gone by, the small store had
been closed for the day.

And now, when she needed to be entirely focused on the grant-writing task at hand, all she
was able to focus on was him.

She had only a couple of hours before the library closed, and she needed to make the most of

them. Midnight was going to arrive in five hours whether she was prepared or not.

Doing her best to ignore Archer, she pulled out a fresh sheet of paper and clicked her pen a few times. She pondered for a while, then wrote out her first sentence, which was simple and straight-forward.

Weaver needs a new library.

She scratched it out, tossed down her pen and gave him an annoyed look. "What *are* you doing here?"

"Lawyers need libraries like flowers need rain."

She rolled her eyes. "You have a more than adequate library in your own house. You showed it to me last night."

He smiled slightly and brushed a lock of her hair away from her cheek. "Caught me. I was over at the sheriff's department. Saw your car parked here when I was leaving."

"So?"

"So, I thought I'd see how things were coming along."

"Nothing's changed since the last time you saw me. I haven't managed to raise the rest of the money we need."

He looked amused. "That would have been quite the accomplishment if you had. Vivian would feel compelled to give you a raise in pay."

"I also haven't gotten Squire Clay to agree to attend Vivian's cocktail party tomorrow. He's the last holdout on the council."

"Yeah, well, that's not surprising, either. Lot of murky water under that particular bridge."

She raised her eyebrows, waiting, but he didn't elaborate. Instead, he angled his head as he read through the second page of grant instructions.

If she didn't get to it, not only would the library close right around her ears, but she'd end up missing the deadline.

She picked up her pen again. "Weaver needs a new library," she wrote again.

She scratched out the second, identical line, which had only served to prove how singularly unimaginative she was.

Archer's fingers brushed hers as he slid the pen from her hand. "I'll help."

She stared. But then reason intruded. Of course he'd help. It wasn't Nell herself who'd prompted his offer. The library project was spearheaded by his grandmother.

And it wasn't smart to look a gift horse in the mouth whether or not her self-protective instincts urged her to keep him at arm's length. "Do you know anything about writing a grant proposal?"

"No. But I know Lincoln Swift at Swift Oil." He gave her a quick grin as he tossed aside her pen and crumpled her carefully highlighted pages into a ball. He nudged her chin when she opened her mouth in protest. "Don't say anything you'll live to regret."

"But—"

"My sister Maddie is married to him."

She blinked. And then she closed her mouth and quickly began stuffing all of her materials right back into the binder.

Chapter Nine

"Thank you *so* much. I can't tell you how much I appreciate your support."

Archer watched Nell pump Linc's hand and hid a smile. The only times he'd ever seen his imperturbable brother-in-law perturbed had been when he'd been caring for his little niece Layla a few years ago when she'd been abandoned on his doorstep, when Maddie had been in labor with their own son, Liam, and now, in the face of Nell's fervent appreciation.

"I'm glad to help," Linc was saying. He managed to extract his hand from Nell's. "I wish I could just tell you that Vivian's project could receive Swift Oil's grant, but I'm married to one of her granddaughters. That automatically excludes her project from consideration. But that doesn't have to stop me from putting the screws to my business associates who aren't related to her. They can dig deeper into their pockets, too."

They were at the stately house located squarely in the middle of Braden where Linc and Maddie lived. Only Maddie—who was a social worker with family services—had been called out on some emergency, which left Linc alone on Liam duty.

"Any and all support is really appreciated." Nell was beaming at Linc and it spilled over into the glance she gave Archer. He wondered if she even realized it. She'd never smiled that much when she'd worked for Pastore. "I really should have realized your connection to Vivian before now. I just—"

Linc shook his head, waving off her comment. "People who've lived here a lot longer aren't even necessarily aware. Don't worry about it." His attention perked when he heard a noise. "Just a sec." He strode from the room and returned a moment later with a cross-looking Liam in his arms.

At the sight of Archer, though, the toddler shoved at his daddy's hold, nearly launching himself into midair toward him.

Fortunately, Archer was used to the greeting

and was prepared for the catch. "Hey, bud," he said, smiling into Liam's little face. He held up his palm and Liam showed off his mouthful of stubby white teeth as he smacked his fist against Archer's hand. "Aren't you supposed to be in bed by now? It's after eight."

Linc looked chagrined. "And Maddie won't be pleased. She likes Liam down by seven."

"I know. Last time I babysat, she gave me hell for not getting him into bed on time. Said I deserved to have to watch him the morning after when he's cranky as all get-out because of it." Archer caught the bemused look on Nell's face as she watched him with the baby. "What?"

She lifted her shoulders, giving him an innocent look that he didn't buy for a second. "Nothing." She jerked back a few inches when Liam aimed his fist her way, accompanied by a stream of babble. "Just trying to imagine you babysitting."

"Hifi, hifi, hifi," Liam demanded noisily as he waved his arm again toward Nell.

"He wants you to high-five," Archer interpreted.

Her dark gaze swiveled to the baby and she lifted her palm just in time to meet Liam's next swing.

Liam chortled and squirmed in Archer's hold,

both arms outstretched as he threw his upper body toward Nell.

She looked surprised and delighted as she caught his torso, and then had to take a steadying step when she received the full brunt of the boy's weight. She quickly adjusted her grip though, and laughed into Liam's face. "Well, hello there, Liam. Aren't you a live one?" She caught his hand with hers and wriggled it. "How old are you?"

"I fi," he said giggling.

"You're *almost* two," Linc corrected wryly. "For some reason, five is his favorite word these days."

"You coory," Liam told her, patting her head with obvious glee. "Coory coory."

"Curly," Archer supplied.

"I am curly," Nell agreed. She touched Liam's smooth hair. "Is your hair curly?"

His forehead puckered. He shook his head. "No, I a boy."

Nell laughed. She shot Archer a sparkling look that made him nearly hurt inside before looking back at his nephew. "Sometimes boys have curly hair too, you know."

"Unh-uh." Liam was certain. "Hifi." He raised his fist again and she obediently tapped her palm against it. He pumped his fists up in the air and whooped.

Nell laughed again, and rubbed her face against the boy's head.

"You're watching too many basketball games on television," Archer told Linc. "Kid's starting to sound just like you."

"Come here, pal." Linc lifted his son out of Nell's arms. "Everyone is his best friend right now," he told her.

She was smiling, something soft in her eyes. "He's darling."

"Yeah." Linc rubbed Liam's head. "I think we'll keep him." He led the way from his downstairs office into the foyer, swinging Liam upside down over his shoulders.

The toddler squealed excitedly. "Daddy!"

"That'll help get him to sleep," Archer said drily. He reached around Nell to open the door. "We need to get while the getting's good. You do not want to see Maddie when she's on a tear 'cause her firstborn isn't in bed when he's supposed to be."

"I have a few tricks to calm her down," Linc assured him.

Archer shuddered. "I need to wash out my ears now." He started to nudge Nell out the door. "That's my baby sister you're talking about."

"Hold on." Linc opened a closet door and pulled out a black box about half the size of a shoebox. "If you're heading back toward Weaver, can you drop this off with your folks? Maddie borrowed these socket wrenches from your dad."

"Sure." Archer took the box. "What'd she need them for?"

"Putting together another crib." Linc winked and darted up the stairs, bouncing Liam up and down to make him squeal even more.

Archer was aware of Nell tugging his sleeve. "We going to stand here for a while or—"

He looked down at her. "Did he just say *another* crib?"

"Yes." She pursed her lips. "Is that his way of announcing another baby?"

"Yes," Linc said from the top of the staircase. Laughter was in his face. "But keep it to yourself. Maddie wants to tell your folks this weekend." He lifted his hand and disappeared along the landing.

"Great," Archer muttered as he followed Nell out through the door. "Drop some news like that on me even though I'm doing him the favor of returning the tools?"

Nell laughed. "Stop complaining. You're thrilled with the idea of another nephew or niece. I can see it on your face."

He dropped his arm over her shoulder as they began descending the dozens of steps leading from the street up to the distinguished brick house that sat high on a hill. "It keeps Meredith from looking too closely in my direction on that score," he allowed. "And don't remind me again that I'm not getting any younger. My ego still hasn't recovered from the first time."

"Please. Your ego is steel-plated."

He chuckled. It was better than letting on that she was the only one who had ever left real dents in it.

She skipped down several more steps, her hair bouncing like springs around her shoulders. He could understand his nephew's appreciation for her hair. It was even curlier than his stepmother's was, though nowhere near as long. Meredith's wildly curling hair reached almost to her waist. Nell's—on these rare occasions when it was actually down like now—bounced around just below her shoulders.

His dad had once told him that the first thing he'd noticed about Meredith had been her hair. The second had been her happy spirit, which, considering everything Archer knew about those days, said a lot about his stepmother's ability to rise above her situation.

Nell had noticeable hair, too. But until lately— until she'd left Cheyenne, in fact—the last time Archer had seen any kind of real happiness in her spirit had been when she was in law school. When, if she weren't studying, she'd been working in a dinky off-campus bookstore that she said reminded her of the one her mother had owned.

They'd finally reached the street where his truck was parked and he set the wrenches in the back seat. She'd already climbed in before he could open her door and he sighed a little inside.

Carter Templeton had raised his kids with some hard-and-fast rules.

One: you returned anything you borrowed, especially tools and money.

Two: men took off their hats indoors and held both chairs and doors for women, regardless of whether they were two or two hundred.

Three: you protected others. The people you cared about. The people who couldn't protect themselves. Even the people who didn't realize they needed protecting.

He got behind the wheel and drove across town to his parents' house. Nell was quiet, seemingly lost in her thoughts.

"You don't mind stopping at my folks' house, do you?"

"What?" She gave him a surprised look. "Of course not. I haven't seen Meredith in—" She was shaking her head. "I don't know. Too long to remember." She was silent while he drove through an intersection. "Braden's grown a lot since I was here with Ros."

"Lot of time has passed since then. Lot of changes. Fortunately, whatever Braden doesn't have, Weaver does, and vice versa. Folks around here may not have everything they want, but they pretty much have everything they need."

"Except a sufficiently large library."

He smiled slightly. "Except that." They passed a large darkened building with boarded windows. "And that." He jabbed his thumb at the window. "Movie theater. Closed at least a year ago."

"Free access to a public library is more important than commercial access to a movie house."

"Tell that to the people spending fortunes making movies." He turned a corner. "And people around this area who have to drive to Gillette or Sheridan just to see a movie in a real theater. Would be like someone in Cheyenne having to go to Denver."

She peered out the side window. "Is that building still your uncle's pediatrics office?"

"I'm surprised you remember."

She rubbed her arm. "He had to give me a tetanus shot that summer when I cut my foot—"

"—climbing the fence at the schoolyard with Ros. I remember."

"That leaves us both surprised, then." Her voice was light.

His, not so much. "I remember a lot of things, Nell."

He felt her gaze, but she didn't say anything.

And then he was pulling up in front of his parents' house. He parked and got out, retrieving the set of wrenches from the back seat. Nell was still sitting with her door closed and he pulled it open. The interior light came on, shining over the top of her dark head like some sort of halo. "Come on."

"It's late," she started to protest. "I shouldn't—"

"—avoid Meredith and let her find out about it," he said over her words. He reached in, and ignoring the consternation on her face, unsnapped her safety belt. He gestured. "Come on."

Nell's waist tingled where his arm had grazed it and she briefly debated whether it was worth taking him to task for undoing her belt without asking.

It wasn't.

When it came to debates with Archer, she rarely won. She finally huffed, swinging her legs around so she could slide out of the truck. She couldn't explain the reluctance she felt accompanying him inside his childhood home. "You could at least warn them."

"We don't need warnings in my family."

"I'm not your family."

"No matter what's going on between the two of you lately, you might as well be Ros's family, so that counts, too."

Maybe that was the problem. Seeing Meredith Templeton would bring home all over again the pain Nell felt where Ros was concerned. "You wouldn't say that about Martin."

"That's because he gives cockroaches a bad name." Archer took her arm and tugged her up the walkway toward the house. It was the same one she'd visited all those years ago.

Just a normal house. Not overly large. Not overly small. The kind of house that was comfortable and filled with family members who squabbled and laughed and always, always loved. Being here that summer after her mother had died had been a balm for Nell's aching soul.

And she couldn't believe how choked up she felt as he reached the front door and walked right in with only a loud knock and a "hello," to announce their arrival. The hand he'd kept on her arm now caught her hand, brooking no argument as he pulled her inside the house. "I brought a guest," he said as he walked across the foyer.

"In the kitchen!" a bright, feminine voice answered, and a moment later, a familiar face popped around a doorway.

Meredith Templeton's eyes widened at the sight of Nell and her smile widened even more as she hurried toward them, bringing with her the scent of lavender and patchouli and the faint jingle of bells from the bracelet she wore around one ankle. "Nell! Well my goodness, what a delightful surprise."

Nell caught the way Meredith looked beyond

her, as if she hoped to see someone else—namely her eldest daughter—accompanying them.

If Meredith was disappointed that she didn't, she hid it well as she lifted her cheek toward Archer's kiss. "I didn't even know you were back from Denver!"

"A few days now."

"You make it so difficult to keep up with you. If it weren't for the calendar Jennifer sends me, I'd never know where to find you." She lightly swatted his shoulder and turned in a brightly colored swirl of flowing fabric. She stretched out her arms. "Honey, what a treat this is."

Before Nell knew what was happening, Meredith—several inches shorter than her—had pulled her down into a tight squeeze of a hug.

Her eyes stung. "It's good to see you, too, Mrs. Templeton."

"Don't you dare call me that." Meredith pushed her back and peered into her face. "I'd heard that you began working for Vivian. She's the only Mrs. Templeton around here. And I have to say that Cheyenne's loss is certainly Weaver's gain." She twirled on her bare foot again, skipping slightly as she hurried over to a doorway. "Carter! Put down the book and come see your son." She practically danced back to them and she wrapped her arm through Nell's. "Come into the kitchen. I'm testing out a recipe for the women's wellness expo next month."

"Beware," Carter said as he entered the room and followed them into the kitchen. "This is her third go at it. She's been trying to bake chocolate brownies without using real sugar, flour *or* chocolate."

He stood as tall as Nell remembered—and looked just as stern and formidable, particularly now that he had more gray than brown in his hair. Carter offered a glimpse into the future of Archer's looks, because their handsome faces were nearly identical. His gaze rested on Nell and there was a faint smile in his eyes. "Considering you're working for my mother, you're looking well."

"She looks better than well," Meredith chided. "She looks positively wonderful!" She let go of Nell and pulled on an oven mitt. She opened the oven door and a strong scent of chocolate wafted out even before she withdrew the pan and set it on a trivet. When she was done, she tossed her oven mitt aside.

"Now." She turned once more to the accompaniment of soft bells and the swishing skirt around her ankles. "Tell me everything that's going on in your life. How do you like working for Vivian? Is Montrose behaving himself? Where are you staying?" Her bright gaze landed on her husband. "Oh, Carter, don't you wish she could stay here?"

Carter's expression when he looked at his lively wife was a combination of indulgence, bemusement and abject adoration.

It was as wonderful a thing to witness now as it had been when Nell was a teenager. And it was one of the realities that had most nagged at Ros—the fact that her mother was so deeply happy with her new family. A new family that hadn't really included Ros no matter how often Meredith reached out.

"I think she'd get a little tired of commuting between here and Vivian's house in Weaver," Carter told his wife with the same dry tone that Archer so often used. His gaze took in Nell. "But of course you are always welcomed here. We have plenty of empty bedrooms. Only times they're used these days are when we're watching one of the grandkids."

"Which is never often enough," Meredith admitted ruefully. "And because we don't have enough of them. Did you hear me, Archer?"

"I heard. You tell me often enough." Archer's amused gaze met Nell's for a moment before he turned away and pulled open a drawer.

Feeling a little overwhelmed, Nell looked from Carter to Meredith. "That's very kind of you, but—" She shook her head. "It *would* be a long drive every day." There were other reasons why she'd never agree—their son, Archer, being chief among them—but it was by far the easiest excuse.

"Of course it would," Meredith agreed. "Archer's place is much closer to Vivian's. You could stay with him."

Nell nearly choked.

"I tried telling her that." Archer gave a helpless shrug.

The problem with that, of course, was that Nell had never known him to be helpless for a single day in his life. "I'm looking for something to rent in Weaver," she said, hoping to put an end to the topic altogether.

She hadn't actually devoted any time to the endeavor in the last few days, but then again she hadn't actually had much time to do so.

"Meanwhile, she's at the Cozy Night," Archer informed his parents. He'd pulled a fork from the drawer and shoved it closed with a little snap.

Meredith looked dismayed. Carter's brows pulled together.

"It's *fine*," Nell said quickly. "There's a really nice woman and her three boys who have the room next to me and we've grilled out together by the pool and…and everything." Yes, it was an exaggeration, but under the circumstances, she thought it was a forgivable one.

"But it's the Cozy Night," Meredith protested

weakly. "It was closed down last year because of drugs."

"And it opened up again," Carter reminded her. "All cleaned up. Unless you don't believe Ali. She's the police officer in the family. She ought to know."

"Of course I believe Ali." Meredith looked at Nell again. "But surely there's a better solution while you try to find something suitable to rent. Vivian would certainly have room—"

"She doesn't want to live at Vivian's, either," Archer said. "All those years living with Ros must have rubbed off on her. Stubborn as the day is long."

The last thing Nell wanted was to get onto the subject of Rosalind.

"I'll probably be out of the motel in a week," Nell told Meredith with an optimism that she miraculously conjured out of nowhere. "And I'm hardly ever there anyway. I appreciate your concern but truly, there's no need to worry about me." She spread her hands and smiled. "I'm a little more grown up now than I was the last time I was here. I'm used to looking after myself."

Meredith clasped one of Nell's hands in hers. "And I know you're positively brilliant. Archer has said so more than once."

Nell's cheeks warmed and she couldn't help sneaking a glance at Archer. Fortunately, he was poking the fork into the contents of the hot pan so he didn't notice.

He lifted out a little hunk of brownie, blowing on it for a moment before gingerly putting the morsel in his mouth. He swore around it and swallowed quickly before sticking his mouth right under the faucet for water.

"Archer," Meredith chided. "Manners."

"Emergency measures," he said when he'd shut off the water and straightened. His expression could have belonged to Liam when he'd high-fived. "Hotter 'n hell." He grabbed the checkered towel folded over the edge of the sink and wiped his chin. "A little sticky. But they taste pretty good."

Meredith crossed her arms. "And why do you make that sound surprising?"

His laugh was rich and full and it curled right around Nell.

He dropped a kiss on his stepmother's head. "I adore you almost as much as my old man does, but even he would agree that not all of your kitchen experiments have been towering successes."

Meredith gave her husband an equally arch look. "Is that so?"

Carter's smile was slow. He crossed the room toward her. "Do you want me to say I fell in love with you because of your baking skills?" He closed his hands over her shoulders. "Or do you want me to tell the truth and say I fell in love with you for your—"

Meredith raised her hand. "That's enough," she warned with a musical laugh. But then she went up on her toes and caught his face between her hands, pressing her lips to his.

The kiss didn't last long. It wasn't some display of crazy-hot passion.

But the sheer intimacy in the look that passed between Meredith and Carter made Nell ache inside.

This. The word whispered through her. *This is what it should all be about.*

She found her eyes sliding toward Archer.

He'd hooked open the refrigerator door and was pulling out the milk jug. He poured himself a small glassful, sent an inquiring look Nell's way, and at her bemused headshake, returned the jar to the refrigerator. Then he scooped up another forkful of brownie and, this time, chased it with the cold milk.

"Definitely better," he said. "But if they don't have real sugar or flour in them, what do they have?"

"I've learned it's better not to ask these things," Carter cautioned humorously. He'd circled his arms around his wife's shoulders, holding her loosely against his chest. "Thought I'd taught you that, as well."

"You know me." Archer's gaze landed on Nell's face. "I like living dangerously."

Meredith's eyes sparkled with merriment above her husband's forearms as she looked toward Nell. "What are we going to do with these men?"

Nell managed a smile that she didn't feel. Neither of these men—Archer in particular—was hers with which to do anything. "You said you're preparing for a women's event?"

"I am, indeed." Meredith ducked out from Carter's embrace to begin cutting the brownies and scooping them onto a plate. "I'm very excited about it. Thanks to Vivian's financial support, we'll be able to bring in a few national speakers. We'll have free health screenings, a mobile mammogram truck, yoga sessions, art sessions, cooking, child care naturally. All sorts of things. It's a first, of course, but I'm hoping that it'll be successful and we can repeat it every year."

"Sounds great. If there's anything I can do to help—"

"Bless you, sweetie. There's always room for help." Meredith suddenly looked at Archer. "I bet she could help with your session, honey." Her head swiveled back toward Nell. "He's giving a workshop on navigating the legal system when it comes to child custody issues and child support." She clasped her hands, actually rising up on her bare toes in her enthusiasm. "It would be perfect! Women are often more comfortable talking to another woman about some things. Archer, you know that. You've talked about it so often. The two of you could be partners. Work as a team."

Archer's inquiring gaze caught Nell's and held it. "Well? What do you say? Do you finally want to be my partner?"

Her mouth turned dry.

He'd asked her that once. To be his partner.

It had been shortly after they'd slept together.

Shortly after Ros—who hadn't even known about her stepbrother and her best friend—had told Nell about the latest fling Archer was having with one of their professors.

Nell had been a month from graduating. She'd still needed to pass the bar exam.

She'd needed to remember that following her head never hurt the way trusting with her heart had.

She'd turned him down.

And chosen Martin instead. Martin, who'd been a mentor. Martin, whom Nell owed for having kept a roof over her head. Martin, whose approval Nell had wanted almost as badly as Ros had wanted his love.

"Yes," she said. Her head felt a little dizzy. As if she really were spiraling down into Archer's green, green gaze. "I'll be your partner."

Meredith clapped her hands happily and the

sound seemed to echo inside the warm, inviting kitchen.

Or maybe it was just inside Nell's head.

"This'll be *just* perfect," the older woman was exclaiming. "The two of you together? You know exactly what you're getting."

But now that Nell had agreed, and she realized that deviltry had entered Archer's eyes, she wasn't sure at all what exactly she'd be getting.

Chapter Ten

Meredith insisted they celebrate the decision with more brownies and coffee.

The coffee was welcome. Particularly when the sticky brownies dried out and turned hard just as soon as they were fully cooled and needed something to help wash them down.

It was close to midnight when Archer finally managed to get them out the door and on the road back to Weaver.

"Sorry about that," he said once they were actually driving away from the house.

Nell hugged her to-go cup that Meredith had sent with them. The hot coffee it contained was sweet and light, exactly as Nell liked. "About what? Getting saddled with me for your workshop at the women's expo?"

"If you didn't want to do it, you could have said so."

"I didn't say I didn't want to do it. I said *you*—" She broke off, shaking her head and looking out the window. "Never mind."

"Nobody saddled me with you. Not even Meredith. She had a good idea and I agreed with her. So are we partners or not?"

He was the one who sounded annoyed.

She decided pointing it out was not a smart route to take. "Yes," she said. "We're partners." Then she looked out the window beside her because the words sounded far more momentous than they ought to when all they were talking about was a simple workshop. The kind of workshop she'd conducted more than once for Sally Youngblood at the legal aid office.

She nervously rubbed her finger up and down the side of her warm cup as the lights of Braden thinned.

Just a workshop. Just a workshop.

Just. A. Workshop.

Finally, when the lights behind them had fallen away altogether, she felt brave enough to tackle the lingering sense that there was something amiss. "We were still talking about the women's expo, right? The workshop."

He waited a beat. Long enough for the skin on the back of her neck to prickle.

A lot.

Then it was just one word from him. "Sure."

She was not reassured.

But it wasn't as if he could commandeer her into becoming a real partner. She had a job now, anyway, working for his grandmother. At least temporarily until the library was truly underway.

And what are you going to do then?

There were so many thoughts circling in her mind, it was exhausting. She was glad she wasn't the one behind the wheel. Until she'd driven with Archer to see Lincoln Swift earlier that evening, she hadn't realized how the road became even narrower and more winding on the way to Braden once it passed where Archer lived. Considering how distracted her thoughts were, she'd be a danger on the road.

"Thanks for bringing me." She meant it, but mostly she needed to hush the noise inside her head. "To see your brother-in-law, I mean." Seeing Lincoln had been the purpose for the trip, but that seemed to have taken a back seat once Archer had pulled her inside his parents' home. "It was really nice seeing your folks again, too. It doesn't seem like they've changed a bit. They're so—" She broke off, hunting for the right words.

He seemed to understand, though. "I know. They fit. You look at them and you think, *this*."

She shivered and all of the busyness inside her mind went still.

This.

He shifted slightly in his seat and if he noticed her startled reaction, he didn't show it.

"If you had to pick two people who seem ideal for each other, you'd never think to pair a guy like my dad with a woman like Meredith. He's rules and order and always hedging against disaster. The only thing orderly about Meredith is her constant disorderliness. But together, they're like two halves of a whole."

He dropped his right hand down to his own to-go cup on the console between them.

Nell knew the contents would be the exact opposite of hers.

She rested her head against her backrest and studied him. His profile was little more than a shadowy outline. Not even the bluish glow from the gauges on his dashboard was enough to penetrate the utter darkness.

She could look her fill and he'd never be the wiser.

She fit her coffee cup into the holder molded into the console. She was very aware of his arm just a few inches away from hers. If she spread her fingers, they'd be touching his. "Ros always saw that, too. The way her mom and your dad were together."

"It's part of the reason why she didn't like having to come and visit."

"You knew?"

"Hard not to. Through no fault of her own, she got the short end of the stick."

She felt indignant on behalf of her friend who no longer even wanted to *be* her friend. "If you feel that way, why have you always been so at odds with her?"

"Calm down, Cornelia. Understanding her situation doesn't mean she wasn't a pain in the butt." He let out half a laugh. "Even under the best of circumstances, Ros is competitive as all hell." She felt his gaze. "Tell me I'm wrong."

She couldn't. Her indignation was dribbling away. "There's nothing wrong with having a competitive streak, though." Ingrained habit still made her defend Ros. "It makes us all strive to do better."

"Some people strive to do better just because they want to do better. Not because their life seems to depend on outrunning the person in the lane next to them." He lifted his cup for a drink and when he lowered it once more, his arm seemed to be resting even closer to hers. "Problem with Ros is that she's never understood she didn't have to compete for Meredith's love. She was always so busy trying to outrun us all that she couldn't see she was also running in the wrong direction. You know why Meredith left Martin?"

The abrupt question took her by surprise. She moistened her lips, feeling suddenly awkward. "Not, um, not really."

"For a lawyer, you're a crappy liar."

"I'll take that as a compliment since I don't have any desire to be a really good one!"

"You heard that she was having an affair with my dad when they worked in the same office. That's why you think they split up."

"It's none of my business!" She wished they'd never ended up on the subject. Meredith held a secretly special place in Nell's heart. She had done so ever since that long-ago summer. Whatever her history was, Nell had no intention of sitting in judgment.

"Martin beat her."

"What?" Shock slid through her with nauseating speed. "How do you know?"

"Because my dad had the pictures he took of her when he first realized what was happening."

Archer looked toward her, as if he expected her to say something, but she was too busy struggling with her dismay and after a moment, he turned his attention back to the road. "Ros was just a baby then," he went on. "When Dad first left the army, he moved with Hayley and me to Cheyenne. He went to work at the insurance company where Meredith was working part-time as a file clerk. That's how they met."

"If Martin was abusing her, how did he ever end up with custody of Ros? How—"

Archer closed his hand over her fingers and her words stuck in her throat as surely as Meredith's everything-free brownies. Nell would've reached for her coffee to wash the knot down but doing that meant moving her hand from beneath his.

"You know the position of authority an abuser holds over his victim." Archer's voice was neutral. "She was afraid."

Despite the neutral tone, though, Nell could tell there was a volcano brewing beneath the surface.

She'd never seen Archer truly angry. Over the years, in court and out, she'd seen him hypnotically charming. Contemptuously cold. And myriad shades in between.

But she wasn't sure she'd ever actually seen him angry. Really and truly, wrenchingly angry.

She wasn't sure she ever wanted to see that.

"Afraid," he repeated, squeezing her fingers tighter. "And more afraid than ever once my dad got involved."

She shifted in her seat, angling toward him even more. "Archer, you don't have to—"

But clearly he did, because he ignored her tentative attempt to stop him. "He started out just wanting to help her escape her situation. It hadn't been that long since *my* mom had died. Hayley was like three years old."

Nell felt his gaze slide her way again even though she couldn't actually see it.

"He tried talking Meredith into leaving Martin—for her own sake if nothing else—but she refused. She'd already tried to escape once and the slimeball had her convinced that she'd never see Ros again if she tried leaving him."

Nell couldn't stop a dismayed sound from leaking out. Even if she hadn't discovered his attempted collusion in the Lambert probate matter, Nell could well imagine Martin convincing Meredith of such a claim. He simply was that intimidating.

Nell knew Meredith didn't have other family. More than thirty years ago, she would have been so young. So alone.

"No wonder you can't stand him."

"That's just the start." The neutrality of Archer's tone edged into grimness. "Even though he now knew the truth, my dad couldn't stop Meredith from quitting her job. He couldn't force her to leave her husband. She doesn't talk about what happened during those few years that followed, but you can be pretty certain Martin didn't change *his* ways. People like him usually don't."

"No. They just get more entrenched in them."

Archer's fingers squeezed hers. "Anyway, Dad moved us to Braden. I don't know if it was because he wanted to put more distance between him and Meredith or not. My uncle was already there with his medical practice. So maybe it really was because of that. In any case, he started up his own agency and time passed. But eventually he ran into Meredith again. And this time, things got even more serious even faster, and she ended up pregnant with the triplets. Which put her really between a rock and a hard place. Protect herself and the babies she was carrying by leaving to be with my father, or stay with Rosalind, who was still just a toddler."

Nell pressed her lips together. Even though she knew how that situation had ultimately ended, she couldn't help feeling anxious. "What happened? What made her leave Ros with him?"

"She didn't leave Ros."

"But—"

"Martin discovered the affair. He tried to raise his hand against her again but this time she fought back. She ended up clocking him with a cast-iron frying pan. Knocked him out cold. Put him in the hospital, in fact, with a concussion. She bolted *with* Ros and went to my dad." Archer's voice tightened. "But a few days later, the cops came to arrest her for assault and they put Rosalind right back in her father's hands."

"But Martin was the abuser," Nell argued as if there was something that could still be done about it. "He was the one who belonged in jail. Not Meredith—"

"Use your head, Cornelia. This was more than thirty years ago. Laws then were even less perfect than they are now. You know that sometimes the bad guys win. He was already making a name for himself in legal circles. The people's champion." He made a disgusted sound. "He had people lined up vouching for his character. Attesting to what a good father he was. The best parent for Ros, certainly, since his wife was clearly unstable. How hard do you think it was for him to find a judge who gave him quick custody? Particularly with Meredith in jail for assault."

"Was there never a record of this?" It was inconceivable that Ros didn't know any of this, but if she *had* known, how much different would things have been for her friend? Ros wouldn't have worked her entire life to earn her father's love if she'd known he'd abused her mother.

"Officially?" Archer made a rough sound. "You worked with Pastore long enough to know his methods. The only records that exist show his magnanimousness in dropping the assault charges. He'd won, of course. He had Ros. And Meredith was still terrified that he'd disappear with her the way he'd threatened before. So Dad pulled out those old photos."

"He still had them!"

"Insurance," Archer explained.

"I'm surprised Meredith allowed it."

"I don't know that he gave her a chance to argue the point. But it was good that he'd kept them. Even as an abuser, Martin had been calculating. He hadn't been stupid enough to leave marks on her where a casual observer might see them, but he had been twisted enough to use a cigarette to basically brand his initials on her. The photos were pretty intimate."

Nell's stomach churned even more. She thought about the warm, loving woman experimenting with her brownies. And about Martin the last time Nell had seen him in his office. Sitting at his desk, arrogant and confident despite the evidence she'd all but thrown into his face. "That's revolting."

"It was. All along, Meredith had been adamant that the photos would never be seen. It's amazing that she'd let my dad even photograph her like that in the first place."

"She wanted help."

"Help that she ended up not even taking for another few years. But by then, she had more than just herself to consider. She was pregnant. How could she sacrifice one child to make sure the others who weren't even born yet were safe from Martin? She told me once that every step she took landed her deeper in the weeds until she felt like she was drowning in them. And that falling for my dad—right or wrong—was like finding air to breathe again."

"Thank goodness for that." Nell's eyes burned. "So what happened? I assume your dad used the threat of exposing the photos as leverage against Martin."

"Let's just say they came to an agreement."

"Martin had to keep Ros in the state where Meredith would have reasonable visitation," Nell concluded.

"He also had to get the assault charges dropped. And if he ever laid a hand on Ros the way he did Meredith—" He shook his head. "I think my dad would have ended up in jail for attempted murder."

"But once Martin was over the barrel, why not push for regaining custody altogether?"

"Because even when he's over a barrel, he has an angle. Meredith and Dad weren't the only ones who could go public. Martin could, too. Those photos were a double-edged sword. As much proof of their affair—remember, they'd been taken a few years earlier, even—as they were proof of Martin's abuse."

"Of course he had an angle," she said huskily. He'd had one with *her*, and she was chopped liver in the scheme of things.

"Meredith didn't care about her reputation, but she did care about Dad's. He had a new insurance business where reputations did matter. She didn't want any of her children exposed to Martin's vitriol. You know him. He would've made sure the scandal never died. And my dad didn't want Meredith to be humiliated that way, either. The scandal of it all had taken a toll on her. She'd already spent weeks in jail. He was worried about her health. About her pregnancy. So they took what they could get.

"I believe they intended to push for more at some point, but it never came to pass. Meredith never wanted Ros to know how treacherous her father had been."

Nell turned even more toward him, pulling one knee up beneath her. "But they told *you*."

"My father told me," he corrected. "Not until Meredith agreed to it first, but he was the one to tell me. And only so I could make sure Ros would always be protected where Martin was concerned in case something ever happened to them. Just because Martin never mistreated her once all the dust had settled after the divorce, it doesn't mean he wouldn't change his stripes again if he had the chance. Ros idolizes him. Always has. Does even now when she's a grown woman who should know better. But if she were to get on the wrong side of him?"

"How long have you known all this?"

"Since I passed the bar. Dad calls me up. Invites me out for a beer. Figured he was going to congratulate me. You know. All that." He shifted in his seat again, the only evidence that the subject was more disturbing than his steadily delivered explanation hinted at. "And he did congratulate me. But then he pulls out an envelope containing a half-dozen old photographs and—" He made a rough sound. "It's bad enough seeing something like that when it's a client. When it's the woman who has loved and raised you for most of your life—"

Nell turned her hand until her fingers slid through his. The glowing dials on the dashboard blurred. "Why are you telling *me* all of this? Ros is the one who needs to know the truth."

"Like she accepted whatever truth it was that had *you* moving away from Cheyenne?"

Nell's chest squeezed. Her situation with Martin was a water droplet in comparison with what he'd done to Meredith and Ros.

"As smart as she is, Ros is not reasonable when it comes to Martin. She's been drinking that Kool-Aid for too long now. Which leaves it up to someone else to keep a watch out for her interests even if she never knows it's happening."

"Yes, well, if she did, she'd be furious."

"Yes, well, chances are she won't ever know. Won't ever need to know." His fingers curled tighter around hers. "But Dad had his plan of succession by telling me. I have my plan by telling you."

She felt a sudden knot in her throat. "Archer—"

"—And I trust you enough to know you'll never breathe a word of it unless it's to protect my stepsister."

She blinked hard and looked away, but a tear still leaked from the corner of her eye, feeling just as hot crawling down her cheek as his palm felt against hers. "I don't know what to say." Her voice was husky.

"You don't have to say anything. You just have to believe what I've told you."

"You wouldn't lie about something like this." That was Martin's way. He'd twist words, twist situations. Always calculating. Always manipulating.

She stared at the console. At her hand clasped with Archer's. "Did you really want to go into practice together?" she asked suddenly. "You know. Back then. Or was it because we'd—" she swallowed and reminded herself that she was a grown woman "—because we'd slept together?"

"Yes."

She absorbed that. Then she frowned. "Yes, you wanted the partnership? Or yes, you wanted it because we'd slept together?"

"Yes," he repeated with exaggerated patience, leaving his answer still wholly unclarified.

Her breath escaped slowly. Noisily. "Obviously," she said, "you're just trying to annoy me." After taking the time to confide something so extremely personal, too. "Why?"

She realized their hands were still clasped when he rubbed his thumb across her palm. "Some habits are easier to break than others."

Then he let go of her and slowed the truck as he turned the steering wheel. A moment later she recognized the stone pillars beneath the wash of headlights.

Her nerves shot into another gear. She moistened her lips. "What are we doing here?" She was afraid of jumping to conclusions. Particularly when her thoughts were already skittering around like lines on a painting and bells were jangling inside her veins.

"It's late."

She swallowed. "So?"

"So it's been a long day and I don't want to drive any more tonight." This wasn't strictly true, since he did drive farther, at least until he reached his house where the exterior light washed invitingly down over the deck.

"Don't worry," he said as he put the truck into Park. "There are several bedrooms, including the one in the guesthouse, that you can choose from."

"I have a lot to do tomorrow," she argued, even though it was patently obvious that he wasn't going to budge. "Your grandmother's party is—"

He covered her mouth with his hand. Lightly. But the fact that he'd done it at all was enough to make her go rigid.

"Don't worry," he said in a mock whisper. "I'll take you into Weaver in the morning. Nobody'll be the wiser." He dropped his hand and shoved open his door.

She swallowed hard, watching him circle around the front of the truck. Moonlight shone down over his dark gold hair. He was so ridiculously beautiful it stole her breath. But it was the man inside who shined even brighter.

Would Ros ever know just how long he, and his father before him, had been watching out for her? Would she ever get over being kept in the dark about her father's true nature? Or would she deny the truth, even if proof were physically presented to her?

The door beside her opened.

"Well? Are you coming in or do I bring you a

blanket because you want to do something stupid like sleep in the truck?"

That, at least, spurred her to action. "I don't want to sleep in the truck," she assured him a little waspishly. What kind of prude did he think she'd become?

"All right, then." He held out his hand.

She didn't allow herself any time to think. She just took it and slid out through the door. But when she was standing firmly on the ground, she pulled her hand away and curled her fingers into her palm, holding on to the warmth that lingered.

He never needed to know. He was already leading the way up the steps of the deck.

She followed. "Which bed has the cleanest sheets?" Her voice was tart.

He turned and looked at her. "Mine."

Her foot nearly missed the next step. Her breath parked itself uncomfortably in her chest.

She peered up at him, wishing she could read his face. But he'd reached the top of the stairs and the light from the house was behind him, making his expression a wealth of impenetrable shadows. "Is that an invitation?"

"Do you want it to be?"

She felt her lips move, but no words would come. It was worse than when she'd made her first court appearance on her first real case. So many thoughts pushing inside her, all wanting to escape, and not a single one to emerge in anything remotely resembling a coherent statement.

She opened her mouth again.

A loud, yowling sound cut through the night, eclipsing the strangled sound she'd managed to emit.

She thought of bears again. Of mountain lions and who knew what else. "*What* was that?"

He chuckled suddenly as he turned and went over to the kitchen door and pulled it open. "That, sweetheart, is the cat."

Chapter Eleven

*T*he cat?

Nell looked over her shoulder out into the night as the yowl sounded again. Plaintive. Annoyed.

"And from the sounds of it," Archer added, "he's none too happy about missing being fed."

She turned and followed him quickly into the house. "That doesn't sound like any housecat I've ever heard. Are you sure we haven't been feeding a bobcat?"

He reached into a lower cupboard and came out with a plastic bucket filled with cat food. "It's not a bobcat," he dismissed. "Go find a bedroom.

I'll be back." He brushed past her on his way out the door again.

She watched Archer from the doorway until the night swallowed him. After everything, she still felt wobbly inside.

Do you want it to be?

She hugged her arms around herself and walked out of the kitchen. Once more, that same soft light automatically came on.

She walked down the hall, passed the powder room with its pedestal sink and stopped at the staircase. His study and a small bedroom were on the other side.

The bedroom possessed a bed. Not quite as narrow as a twin, but not as wide as her overly soft bed at the Cozy Night, either.

She chewed the inside of her cheek, looking toward the room and feeling her pulse throb.

Do you want it to be?

Upstairs, there were three more bedrooms. Not including his.

Even the guesthouse had a bed. He'd told her so.

That was the best choice. The wisest choice. Don't even stay the night under the same roof.

She closed her hand over the square newel post. Placed her toe on the bottom step.

What would the cost be if she went up the rest of the steps?

She took her foot from the stair again. Walked past the staircase. But instead of going into the bedroom with the narrow bed, she turned and went into his study, instead.

Bookshelves lined three of the walls. Not just any ordinary bookshelves, either. No, these started at the floor and went all the way up to the ceiling. A dark metal rail for a rolling ladder two-thirds of the way up ran continuously around the three walls, too.

She crossed to the closest wall. Ran her palm lightly over the wildly mismatched spines. He seemed to have a little bit of everything. Biographies. Political commentaries. Science fiction. Historical fiction. Satire. Thrillers. Poetry. Even—

Her trailing fingers stopped atop the sweetly familiar name. *Julia Brewster.*

She slowly pulled out the narrow book. The glossy dust jacket was pristine. She smiled slightly as she touched the familiar rotund little penguin on the cover. "Hello, Monty," she murmured. "What are you doing here in this house?"

"Keeping company with Seuss and Dahl."

She turned on her heel, clutching the book against her chest. She felt engulfed by Archer's green, green gaze. "It's one of my mother's books."

He was still holding the bag of cat food and he

set it on the corner of his unexpectedly cluttered desk as he approached her. "*Monty the Curious Penguin.* I know."

Her chest felt tight. "But why?"

"Why not? It's your mom's first book. And it's a good one. One of Layla's favorites, in fact. She's Greer and Ryder's oldest. She'll be three in a few months and she always wants to look at the pictures when she is here."

An image of him reading to a little girl filled Nell's head way too easily. It joined the memory of him holding Liam. And it caused an increasingly familiar longing deep down inside her.

"It's not for sale anymore," she said. He'd stopped only inches away from her and she stared up at him. "It hasn't been for a very long time."

"I know. You told me."

He'd either had it for a very long time or he'd put some effort into finding it. "There were twelve in all."

"You told me that, too." His voice was impossibly gentle. "Did you ever finish tracking all of them down? You had all but one."

"The tenth." She shook her head. "Is it a coincidence? You just happen to have a copy of this?" She held up the book between them. Almost like a shield.

"Is that so hard to believe?"

"Yes." She turned and slid the book into its

narrow space on the crowded shelf, then just hovered there, her blind gaze on the myriad titles. Her heart was beating so hard, she felt dizzy.

She forced herself to turn back. To face him. Because not facing him felt cowardly. And when it came to him—to the things he'd told her tonight—the last thing she wanted to be was cowardly. Her gaze caught on his strong, angled jaw for a moment before finally reaching his gaze. "And yes, I want it to be an invitation."

"I'm sensing a *but* in there." There wasn't a single spark of deviltry in those green depths now. If there had been, she'd have been able to resist his intense lure.

Her throat tightened. Her mouth was dry. Swallowing was nearly impossible. "But I'm afraid."

His hands settled lightly on her shoulders. Thumbs roving in small, gentle…distracting… circles. "Of what?"

Of everything.

"Making another mistake," she said instead.

Something in his eyes flickered. The distracting circles slowed. Stopped. The corners of his lips lifted for such a brief moment she almost missed it. Then his hands moved. Lightly cupped her face. He lowered his head and brushed his lips across hers in a kiss as faint as a whisper.

Maybe for that reason alone, it shook her all the way down to her soul.

Then he straightened.

His hands fell away.

"We're all afraid of making mistakes, Cornelia." And he turned and left her alone in his study.

She sagged against the bookcase behind her. Against her mother's first book that was sitting on his bookshelf.

Eighteen hours later, Nell still didn't know if she'd passed up the chance of a lifetime with Archer or if she'd escaped by the skin of her teeth.

What she did know, however, was that she still felt shaky. And it was extremely inconvenient, when she ought to have all of her focus on her final checklist for Vivian's cocktail party.

Which was probably why she nearly jumped out of her skin when a young woman suddenly breezed into Vivian's office at the mansion with a cheerful "Hi! You must be Nell."

Nell stared at the gamin-faced girl. She was wearing a short, glittering red dress that showed off her legs, particularly when she hopped up to sit on the side of Vivian's desk, knocking aside a stack of mail. "Yes," Nell returned warily. "And you are—"

"Delia."

Vivian's granddaughter-slash-assistant who'd been away, Nell realized.

She suddenly felt very self-conscious in her

black dress that was nowhere near as vibrant. It didn't sparkle. It didn't cling and it covered her knees. In fact it looked more like a shapeless sack, but since Nell hadn't made it into *Classic Charms* until the last minute, she'd had to go with what had been available.

The salesgirl had insisted Nell looked *très chic*, but at that particular moment, Nell felt anything but.

"I'm Nell," she said, and quickly shook the other girl's hand. "And it's nice to meet you. Though I think we probably did meet a long time ago. I spent a summer once in Braden with your aunt and uncle. And all of you came over one day for a barbecue in the backyard. You would have been just a little girl."

Delia smiled mischievously. "Fortunately I'm not little anymore. And don't be offended when I say I don't remember you." She swung her feet that were clad in ruby-red sandals with mile-high heels. "So how do you like working for our Vivvie?"

Nell almost choked. *Vivvie* was about the last thing she'd have dared to call Vivian. But then she wasn't one of the woman's grandchildren. "It's very interesting."

She moved over to the windows to look down at the patio below. It was so nice and warm, they would be starting off out on the rear patio. Montrose had been busy in the kitchen all day making his preparations. She hoped.

All Nell could do was trust that the chef would do his part, since he'd barred everyone from entering the kitchen after having one too many shouting matches with Vivian over the menu.

There were no trays of food on the linen-draped tables. But at least the florist was there, setting out several bouquets. They were fancier than Nell thought necessary, but they weren't quite as formal and ornate as Vivian had envisioned.

Nell could only hope the decision she'd made where the flowers were concerned would be more on point than her indecision where Archer was concerned.

After spending a sleepless—and solitary—night on the narrow bed in the bedroom next to Archer's study, he'd returned her to Weaver early that morning just the way he'd promised.

With no one the wiser.

Well, nobody except Gardner, who'd been trying to get her three boys corralled and into the car for their day at summer camp.

Archer, who during the drive into town had acted as if nothing important had or had not occurred between him and Nell, had given the single mom one of his trademark smiles before driving away.

Nell marked off the floral decorations on her

checklist and wished she could mark off Archer as easily. She glanced at Delia. "Your grandmother told me she wasn't expecting you back for a few weeks."

The girl lifted a shoulder. "I decided to come home early."

Another thing that Vivian had said about Delia. She was as spontaneous as a spring breeze.

"I imagine this is usually your job." Nell gestured at the tables down below.

"Organizing one of Vivian's boring little soirées?" Delia laughed. "Not likely. She doesn't trust my taste at all. Tells me I'm too prone to sequins and glitter." She stopped next to Nell and looked out at the patio, too. "She obviously trusts yours, though. Very…tasteful."

"You mean boring," Nell interpreted drily.

"It's not boring if that's what makes you happy."

Paying exorbitant amounts of money for out-of-season floral arrangements—even scaled-down ones—wasn't something Nell cared about at all. But Vivian did.

"How many people are on the guest list, anyway?"

Nell flipped to another page in her organizer and extracted the list. She handed it to Delia. "About thirty-two. Most of the town council and their husbands and wives. A couple others. Your grandmother's architect."

"Exciting." Delia's eyes looked mischievous.

Nell raised her eyebrows. "Maybe not, but you came."

Delia shrugged. "Vivvie's not the worst pain in my side. I figure it's the least I can do. I've learned a lot from her since I started doing the personal assistant thing."

Nell looked out at the empty buffet tables again. "Did you learn how to negotiate between Vivian and Montrose?"

"That's not a skill anyone can master."

Great. Nell squelched a sigh. "Well, everything on this list is taken care of. Except for the hostess and the guests arriving. And hopefully the food will materialize."

"There will be food," Delia assured her. "Montrose might act like a total prima donna, but in the end, he'll come through for my grandmother. He always does. And there's never a problem with the guests showing up. People around here are *always* curious to get a glimpse inside the Templeton mansion."

"I can believe that." Only then did she notice that Delia was eyeing her with an assessing look. "What?"

"That dress does nothing for you," Delia said bluntly. Then she spun on her heel and disappeared as abruptly as she'd appeared in the first place.

"Gee thanks," Nell said under her breath. If she had any illusions about herself, she might have been stung. Instead, she could think only that Delia was quite the young chip off her grandmother's block. "Vivvie" was equally plainspoken.

With a few minutes on her hands, Nell left Vivian's office as well, going down the hall to her own. There was nothing else she could do to hasten Montrose short of breaking through his barred kitchen door, so she might as well make some phone calls. Try to live up to her insistence that she'd soon be moving out of the Cozy Night.

In short order, she'd made three appointments to see one of the overly expensive apartment units near Shop-World, a two-bedroom house that was over in Braden and a room in a four-bedroom house being shared by two other people.

It wasn't an impressive start, but it was still a start.

"I wondered where you'd gotten to." Once again, Delia's abrupt appearance caught Nell by surprise. She was holding two dresses hanging on hangers in one hand and she tossed them over Nell's desk. "Either one is better than that thing you're wearing. And I brought some shoes, too." She was holding a pair of black shoes by the sharp, high heels in her other hand. "Size eight?"

Nell didn't know if she was asking about her

shoe size or her dress size. Only one would be right. "Um—"

"You don't have to tell me," Delia interrupted her hemming and hawing, "but I am never wrong." Her eyes were assessing but not unkind. "And they'll go with either dress." She turned on her own high heel with a shimmering sparkle. "Leave your hair down, too," she said before she reached for the door on her way out. "You have five minutes."

Bemused, Nell looked from the door that Delia had just closed to the dresses lying in an untidy heap atop her binder and lists.

She took them by the hangers and smoothed them out, intending to just move them out of her way. But then her gaze fell on the shoes, pretty confections of narrow, velvety black straps with just a hint of sparkle on the delicate buckle.

They were pumps, all right. Closed toe, which would cover her naked, unpainted toenails, but otherwise as different from her chunky-heeled plain Janes as they could get.

And they were a size eight.

She hung the dresses on the back of the door and then kicked off her own shoes, tossing them to the corner.

Then feeling oddly trepidatious, she stepped into the black shoes and worked up the little zippers on the backs, then fastened the sparkling buckles that held the straps wrapped high around her ankles.

She straightened. She wouldn't have had a single female cell operating inside her if she'd been unable to appreciate the shoes. They were beautiful. Sexy, without being anywhere near as flashy as Delia's ruby reds.

She brushed her hands down her shapeless dress.

Then she made an impatient sound and whipped it off her head. It landed in a heap atop the shoes banished to the corner and she turned to the dresses Delia had brought. They were both black. One had spaghetti straps and a slit that went up the thigh. The other looked like a tuxedo jacket, with a softly shining satin collar and buttons that ran all the way down the front of it.

She undid the buttons and pulled the lined dress over her shoulders, certain that it would be too tight. Particularly if it had come from Delia's own closet. The younger woman was shorter and smaller.

But when Nell buttoned the first button, it fastened easily. And so did the next. And the next.

She wished she had a mirror. But even without one, she knew the front of the dress was too low cut for her plain beige bra, so she quickly pulled that off, too. She yanked the elastic band out of her hair and raked her fingers through it with one hand while she began the task of rebut-toning with the other.

She heard the door open behind her and auto-matically took a few steps away so Delia could enter. "I can't believe it fits." She was bent for-ward a little in order to reach the bottom buttons near the thigh-length hem. "When you said you're never wrong, you meant it."

"I appreciate the vote of confidence."

She whirled, then nearly tripped herself on the unfamiliarly high heels.

"Whoa there, Nelly." Archer's eyes were glint-ing as he caught her shoulders, steadying her be-fore she landed against him. His green gaze ran over her from head to toe, leaving her feeling ex-tremely flushed in all the parts in between. "Whoa there, Nelly," he repeated, a lot more softly.

Her breath felt so uneven, she might well have just run up and down a few flights of stairs. With the additional height of the heels came a brand-new vantage point on Archer's face. Her eyes were almost level with his. "I thought you were Delia."

His fingers tightened against her shoulders. "As you can see—" his gaze dropped for a moment and her lips tingled "—not so much. I recognize her influence, though. You look…different."

A warmth centered somewhere in her midriff began spreading. Upward. Downward. The lining of the dress felt cool and slick against her skin.

Her bare breasts. It wasn't a familiar sensation. But it was one worth savoring. Particularly when he was looking at her the way he was.

She moistened her lips, knowing the answer even before she asked, but wanting to hear him say it anyway. "Good different or bad different?"

"What do you think?"

She thought that not sleeping on the cleanest sheets in his house the night before was one of the biggest mistakes she'd ever made. Bigger than any mistake she'd feared she'd make by doing so.

She leaned two inches closer and pressed her mouth to his.

She felt the fast breath he drew. Felt his hands go from her shoulders, down her arms, then up her hips to her waist. Pulling her closer while memories and sensation exploded inside her cells and he angled his head, deepening the kiss that went on and on and on.

She felt his hair sliding through her fingers. Cool. Slick. Felt the brush of his cheek against hers as his head dipped and he kissed her jaw. Warm. Rasping. Felt the linen weave of his shirt when she ran her palms down his chest. Crisp. Hot.

Her head was heavy on her neck and her fingers found purchase in one of his denim belt loops as she lowered her head over him and his head dipped even farther.

He kissed the pulse raging in her throat, the valley of skin just above the low-cut first button of her borrowed dress. His hands cupped her breasts through the fabric and she couldn't stop the moan rising in her throat. A moan that was his name. "Archer."

His mouth trailed fire up to her mouth again. "Cornelia," he whispered and kissed her again and she felt his fingers tangling in her hair and her mind simply blanked out anything other than him. Other than the warmth of him. The taste. The scent. The wonderful, wonderful feel of him. Again when it had been so, so very long—

Then she felt the hard, cold surface of her desk beneath her and sanity reared its head.

Vivian's cocktail party was waiting.

She couldn't be doing this with Vivian's grandson! Not when there were probably guests already driving up to the house. When Montrose was hopefully putting aside his arrogant sneer as he showed the guests to the patio and the not-quite-ostentatious flowers and maybe, maybe some food—

"Wait, wait." Gasping, she grabbed for Archer's hands.

And realized with a start that was fueled far more by thrill than dismay that those hands were on her skin.

Her bare skin.

Her borrowed dress was gone altogether. His shirt was unbuttoned, hanging loosely off his broad shoulders, his jeans undone.

When had that happened?

"Archer," she tried again. And then gasped because his hand was sliding over her, finding her center right through her panties. She was so wet and so empty and had been for so long, that instead of reason, she embraced the insanity. She held his hand even tighter against her as she shuddered and tried to bite back her cry while his breath sounded even rougher against her ear as he urged her on.

But even as pleasure racked her, it wasn't enough.

Not giving a thought to anything else, she kicked off her panties and slid her legs along his hips, dragging him closer, wrapping her hand around him. Thrilling at the hard, pulsing heat of him.

"Now," she managed throatily. Begging. Demanding.

Either way it didn't matter, because he was there, there where she needed, pressing, filling, and she surrounded him with her legs and her arms. His mouth was open against her throat, his breath just as ragged as hers, her name just as much a groan on his lips.

"So long." His voice was a deep growl that

stroked over her nerves as surely as he stroked her so deeply inside. "Too long."

Then she was beyond hearing anything because he was at the core of the world tightening inside her, tightening until there was no more room to give and every cell she possessed exploded outward in shimmering, brilliant perfection.

Afterward, she didn't know how long she lay there on her desk, Archer's head against her breast while their panting breaths finally quieted. While the bells inside her veins stopped jangling. The cymbals in her nerves stopped crashing.

She was vaguely aware of something sharp digging into her right shoulder blade. Of an ache in her left knee where it was still hooked around him.

"I may never move again," Archer mumbled against her. But he put lie to those words by cupping her breast in one hand and running his tongue over her nipple.

The shaft of sensation streaking through her was almost painful in her satiated state and she laughed weakly. "Don't. Torture."

He braced his hands on either side of her and pushed upward. His hair was messy and falling over his brow and his bare chest bore a sheen of sweat. And his eyes, so deeply green, were almost enough to make her pull him down to her all over again.

Particularly when the corners of his lips tilted in a wicked smile. "What's a little torture?"

"This was completely unprofessional." She winced a little as she unlatched her ankles.

He dropped a kiss on the point of her shoulder. "Then it's a good thing I wasn't looking for a professional."

She found enough energy to glare at him. "Funny."

"I thought so." He straightened a little more, too, then winced himself and swore softly. "Your dorm room floor was softer than the edge of this desk." He finally straightened all the way with a faint grunt. "I may never stand straight again."

"At least you haven't been tattooed by a computer keyboard." She dragged the offending object from beneath her shoulder blade and weakly shoved it aside. It was easier to keep talking than to let the momentousness of what they'd done sink in. "And I don't recall you protesting too much." She slid off the desk, only then realizing that she was still wearing those sexy tall shoes.

His arm hooked her around the waist and he pulled her up flush against him. His gaze held her just as certainly as his arm did. "Neither did you, sweetheart."

Her fingers curled against his chest and her skin prickled. "This, uh, this doesn't change anything."

One of his eyebrows went up. "Like what?"

She felt stupid for having said it. "I don't know. But it just, you know. Doesn't." *Brilliant, Nell. Just...brilliant.*

"You'll still feed the cat, then?"

"What? Why?"

He dropped a hard, fast kiss on her lips and gave her a decidedly inappropriate swat on the behind. One that caused an equally inappropriate zip of excitement to race right through the center of her.

"I need to be in Colorado for a few weeks. Maybe longer." He hitched up his jeans and leaned over to grab his shirt off the floor. "Have a couple cases coming to a head and I need to be there."

She felt a jab of unwarranted unease. His schedule had nothing to do with her. Nor did she want it to. He was Archer Templeton, for God's sake. Just because he hadn't said a word about clients needing him in Colorado the night before when he was busy making her his "succession plan" didn't mean he was making them up. "You don't have to explain anything to me."

The look he gave her was so mild it would have alarmed her if she'd been the alarmable sort. It was the kind of look that said he knew she thought he was making excuses.

She looked away and picked up the tuxedo dress from the floor. She would have much preferred to pull on her own dress still heaped in the corner, even though it was just as shapeless now as it had been when she'd purchased it. But she couldn't. Not with him watching her. So she pushed her arms into the long sleeves once again and began buttoning that long row of buttons.

She hadn't even reached her waist when he brushed her hands aside to take over.

She damned the need that clutched at her insides when his knuckles brushed against her bare skin.

He obviously knew it, too, because he seemed to deliberately slow the task, and devilment was glinting in his eyes again. "The only reason I came here this evening was to tell you I had to leave town."

"There's this thing called a telephone."

"Yeah." He pushed through the button right below her navel. "But think of the fun we'd have missed."

She willed the wobbliness out of her knees. "Your grandmother will be disappointed. She was expecting you here for her cocktail party."

"She has you. She'll be fine."

At any other time, Nell might have appreciated his easy confidence of that fact, but it wasn't any other time.

"You going to wear your panties?"

Her skin went hot all over. "Excuse me?"

He leaned over again and when he straightened, her plain cotton panties were dangling from his finger.

She snatched them away, then balled them in her fist behind her back when the door suddenly opened and Delia stuck her head in.

She looked surprised for a moment to see her cousin there. Then speculative as her gaze bounced from Archer to Nell and back again.

"Knew the dress would fit," she said, and closed the door again.

Archer laughed softly. "Good thing she wasn't here five minutes earlier."

Nell just covered her face with her hand and wished the world would swallow her whole.

Chapter Twelve

The cocktail party was in full swing when Nell finally made it down to the patio some time later. She'd freshened up as much as she could in the powder room next to her office. She was still wearing the tuxedo dress, but at least her hair was back up in its familiar knot.

There was no sight of Delia among the people on the patio. As for Archer, he'd escaped the mansion.

As long as Delia never mentioned seeing him, his grandmother would never know that he'd been there at all.

Fortunately, Delia had been correct about

Montrose. The buffet tables were positively glorious with their artful arrangements of meats and cheeses, fruits and breads. Wine was flowing. All of the guests were smiling and soft violin music—Vivian had been strangely specific about that—was coming from the speakers built into the covered patio. In the grounds beyond the patio, lights were beginning to shimmer among the trees bordering the sea of green grass, and Rambling Mountain's peak seemed to glisten in the fading light.

As beautiful a sight as it was, Nell couldn't appreciate the mountain. Not when it reminded her of how easily she'd let Martin manipulate her. And now, after Archer's revelations, how he'd manipulated Meredith and Ros, too.

She turned away and grabbed a bottle of wine, working her way around the guests, topping off glasses as she went. Vivian, looking elegant in a gold tunic and black palazzo pants, was capably holding court.

It was still hard to believe she had any health problems at all.

Wine bottle emptied, Nell returned to the linen-draped table for another, then smiled when she saw Nick Ventura stepping through the opened glass doors between the solarium and the patio.

The sight of the tall, iron-haired man following on his heels made her eyes widen, though.

Everyone else seemed to have the same reaction at the sight of Squire Clay walking onto Vivian's patio, because all the easy chatter suddenly died, leaving only the strains of Vivaldi from the speakers and the chirp of crickets from the grounds around them.

The elderly man pulled off his dark gray cowboy hat and gave them all an irksome look. "Put your jaws back on their hinges." His gaze seemed to land on Vivian, who looked genuinely shaken.

So shaken that Nell quickly went to her. "Why don't you have a seat, Vivian." There were dozens of them—fancy ironwork things with deep custom-made cushions. And only some were actually being occupied. "I'll bring you a small plate and Nick can get started on his presentation." It was earlier than they'd planned in their timeline for the evening, but it would be a good way to distract attention away from Squire's arrival. She pulled out the nearest chair. "Right here."

"I'm not an invalid," Vivian said with enough spirit that Nell's concern dialed down a few notches. But her boss did sink onto the edge of the seat cushion a little less regally than usual. "Tell Montrose to bring me a Tom Collins."

Then she looked at Squire and waved her hand imperiously toward the vacant chair across from her. "Do you have a cocktail preference, Mr. Clay?"

"Cut the bull, Vivian," Squire said tersely. He yanked out the chair and folded his length into it. "You don't want to drink cocktails with me any more 'n I want to drink 'em with you."

Vivian gave Nell a pointed look and she quickly went in search of Montrose to prepare Vivian's drink. They hadn't planned on a full bar. Just wine and beer.

The chef was in the kitchen scooping tiny helpings of caviar onto equally tiny but elaborate edible structures. He gave her a heavy-lidded glare when she entered his domain.

"Vivian would like a Tom Collins."

He sniffed. "I'll get to it."

"Now," Nell said firmly. "Squire Clay just arrived and—"

Montrose lifted his bald head and something that might have been surprise entered his supercilious eyes. He set down the minute spoon and the tin of caviar and opened a glass-fronted cabinet filled with bottles.

A few moments later, he handed Nell a tall, slender ice-filled glass topped with a lemon twist and a cherry, and returned to his caviar task. "Now please leave," he said haughtily.

With pleasure. "Thank you for the drink," she said and left.

When she reached the patio once more, at least the two individuals seated alone together at the table no longer seemed to be quite the focus of everyone else's attention. Particularly since Nick had his presentation projecting onto the white screen Nell had arranged for that purpose.

She set the cocktail at Vivian's elbow, then moved quietly around to the buffet table.

"So." Delia appeared seemingly out of nowhere and Nell nearly dropped the two plates she'd just picked up. "Archer."

Nell flushed. She jabbed several pieces of cheese onto both plates. She kept her voice as low as Delia's. "What about him?"

"You're not his usual type."

How well Nell already knew that. "I'm not interested in being anyone's type." She quickly added meats and two small arrays of crackers. Ignoring Delia, she returned to Vivian, placing one plate near the cocktail and the other near Squire. The two didn't seem to be doing much besides glaring at each other, and Nell couldn't help wondering what had made the water under their bridge so murky.

An old romance?

That particular pairing hardly seemed likely, but what did Nell know?

She'd at least stopped wondering about it by the time Vivian's soirée finally broke up several hours later. Delia had disappeared shortly after Squire's arrival and never returned. Vivian and

Squire spent the whole time locking nonverbal horns, which had left Nell and Nick to keep the others' interest on the intended topic of the evening.

She was back in her office trying and failing not to recall what had happened there as she jotted her notes from the discussions she'd had with the guests, when Vivian found her.

Not a hair was out of place on Vivian's head, but her face looked tired and wan. "I don't know how you succeeded in getting that man here."

Nell popped out of her chair like she'd grown springs. Even though she'd exchanged the tall heels from Delia with her own dull pumps, she still stood head and shoulders above her diminutive employer. "He's a council member. You wanted the council here."

"Yes, but I still didn't expect him."

"I'm sorry."

Vivian waved her hand impatiently even though she seemed to sway a little as a result. "You did your job. Don't apologize."

Nell pushed her chair around for Vivian. "Please."

Vivian's lips thinned, but she sat. She crossed her ankles and pinned Nell with a baleful look. "Who told you? Delia? Archer? They told you about this thing squatting in my head."

Nell leaned back against the table, straightened,

then realizing Vivian was watching her closely, made herself lean back again. "Archer," she admitted.

"It's not the tumor that is making me feel old tonight," Vivian said. "It's history." She brushed an invisible speck of lint from her palazzo pants. "The worst part of getting to my age is the pallet of regret I have to haul along with me. If it weren't for my dear Arthur, that pallet would be a lot heavier. People nowadays say to live without regrets, but who actually does it? I say get rid of things that you regret while you're still young," she advised. "Life is a lot easier that way."

The edge of the table felt hard and unyielding behind Nell. But did she really regret what she'd done with Archer?

"Where was Archer this evening?" Vivian asked, almost as if she'd divined the direction of Nell's thoughts. "He knew I expected him here."

She willed away a blush. "He had to return to Colorado."

"Boy needs to settle down," Vivian murmured and pushed herself wearily to her feet. "This is quite the little hole of an office you've made. You could have chosen any other space. Outfitted it however you like." She picked up the crystal bowl full of pens. "Still can."

Nell *really* hoped that bowl wasn't precious. "I don't need a lot of space." Her job was temporary. Once the library was a reality, it would be finished.

"You'll have time to think about it." Vivian set the bowl down again. "How do you feel about your first week here?"

Like it had been so, so much longer. "I think how *you* feel about it is a little more relevant."

Vivian smiled slightly. "You accomplished something no one else has."

Nell had to step away from the edge of the table again because it felt like it was burning into her butt.

"Squire," Vivian prompted.

Nell nodded a little jerkily. "Right."

"I did his first wife a terrible wrong a very, *very* long time ago when I was married to my first husband. She was his half sister, you see. Illegitimate. Back in the day when those things mattered. Trivial, you know. You find that out when you get old." Vivian pushed the chair up to the edge of the table. "If I can finally make that right, then maybe I can finally have some peace."

Nell frowned. "I'm not sure I like the sound of that."

"Now you sound like Archer. Don't worry. I don't plan to kick the bucket any sooner than the maker plans for me. I'm *reducing* my load of regret. Not increasing it." She startled Nell when she patted her cheek. "Good night, dear."

Then she left Nell alone in her office.

Alone to think about her own regrets. And to face the fact with absolute certainty that Archer wasn't one of them.

"I need a favor."

Nell pushed up on her elbow to stare blearily at the screen of her cell phone, then she fell back against her pillow and put the phone back to her ear.

"It's two in the morning," she told Archer. Her heart was jumping around all over the place and not entirely because it was his voice on the other end.

It had been nearly three weeks since the cocktail party. Since she'd last seen him.

But his absence hadn't meant she'd been able to get him out of her thoughts. Or her fractured dreams.

And it certainly hadn't meant she hadn't talked to him on the phone. Somehow, he'd developed the art of calling her at the most inconvenient of times.

When she was stepping out of the shower in the morning.

When she was in the middle of discussing site selections for the library now that the town council had finally green-lighted the project.

When she was sound asleep in her bed while dreams of Archer danced in her head.

He called to ask about the cat. He called to talk about the workshop they'd be conducting at the wellness event. He called to check on Vivian.

"The phone rings at two o'clock in the morning and you answer it because you think something disastrous has happened," she told him, not caring at all that she sounded cross. "Not because you think someone's calling for a *favor*. I'm already feeding the danged bobcat every day for you." An inconvenience that had tempted her more than once to give up her boycott of his guesthouse. Particularly since she still hadn't found better lodgings than the Cozy Night, where she didn't even have the engaging Gardner and her three boys next door anymore. They'd packed up earlier that week to head onward to whatever it was that had been calling them ever farther away from their Ohio origins. "What more do you want?"

He laughed softly. "Dangerous question, Cornelia."

She covered her eyes with her arm. She still couldn't blot out the image of him, sweating and breathless, moving against her.

It had been the main feature of the dream her ringing phone had interrupted, and her insides still felt shaky and hollow.

"What's the favor?"

"Judge Fernandez called for a status meeting for tomorrow morning for a client of mine. I'm still here in Denver. Have court all day and I'm not going to be able to make it. Need you to stand in for me. Should only take a few minutes."

Judge Fernandez was the judge who'd handled the Lambert estate.

Nell dropped her arm and stared up at the dark ceiling. Regrets, she thought.

Ever since the night of the cocktail party, the memory of Vivian talking about dragging around her pile of regrets had been haunting her.

"What time?" she asked resignedly.

"Nine o'clock in the judge's chambers."

"Client?"

"Matt Rasmussen. Drunk and Disorderly ninety days ago. Third one. He's been attending cessation meetings twice a week. Walking the good walk. He'll meet you at the courthouse."

"Fine." She waited a beat. "Anything else? Any briefs you need me to write for you, too?"

His laugh was soft in her ear. "Good night, Cornelia."

She muttered a cranky good-night back to him and swiped her phone silent. But she still could feel the smile tugging at her lips as she buried her face in her pillow once more, and she wondered if he'd be calling again in a few more hours, catching her naked and wet from her shower.

But her phone stayed silent.

And at 9:00 a.m. the next morning, she walked into Judge Fernandez's chambers alongside Archer's middle-aged client.

A few minutes later, after having reported on his progress in the last month, Matt Rasmussen walked out again.

But Nell stayed.

She reported everything that had occurred with the Lambert estate. She didn't spare one word, not even her own culpability for failing to report everything the moment she'd discovered it at the beginning of the summer—a cause for censure in and of itself.

It took hours. It took Judge Fernandez calling in a court reporter to get everything on record, and conferencing in members of the Professional Responsibility Board to figure out exactly how to proceed with Nell's complaints against Martin Pastore.

When Nell walked out again, she didn't know if she'd ever practice law again, but she did know that even if she didn't—even if Martin were able to wiggle out of this and succeeded in putting all the blame on Nell's shoulders the way he'd planned—she'd done the right thing.

It wasn't a cast-iron skillet upside his head.

But it was close enough, and her only regret

about anything was that Ros might once again be hurt in the fallout.

She might have been drawn into Archer's whole succession plan business, but that didn't necessarily mean she agreed with it. Ros should have had the opportunity to know just how hard her mother had fought to keep her.

But Meredith's secrets weren't Nell's to tell, either.

She could deal only with her own, and she was glad to have all of it off her chest once and for all.

Those particular chips would fall as they may.

The courthouse was near Ruby's, and even though it was nearing closing time for the diner, Nell went inside and slipped onto one of the round stools at the empty counter and returned Tina's wave. She was suddenly famished in a way she hadn't felt in a long time.

She was halfway through her meat loaf sandwich and hot fudge sundae chaser when Delia appeared. She had a *Classic Charms* shopping bag over her arm and she dumped it on the counter as she took the stool next to her. "Montrose told me you took the day off."

Nell dabbed her cheek with her napkin and it came away with a smudge of sticky chocolate. "Was handling some court business. What'd you buy today?" Since Delia's return to Vivian's, Nell had gotten used to the younger woman's penchant for shopping.

Delia reached in the bag and pulled out a navy blue sundress patterned with bright yellow polka dots. "I got it to wear to Meredith's wellness event. Cute, huh?" She didn't wait for Nell's nod before dropping the dress back into the bag. "He's afraid you're looking for another job."

"Who?"

"Montrose."

Nell stared. "He hates me."

"He hates everyone. But he is still afraid you're planning to leave."

"He told you that?"

"Oh, God no. But I can still tell."

Nell smiled wryly. "How? The same way you can tell what dress size someone takes?"

"Hey, don't knock my one skill."

"You've got more than one skill," Nell chided.

"Not according to some people." Delia folded her arms atop the counter, not looking unduly concerned by that declaration. She pinched one of the French fries from Nell's plate and gave her a side-long look. "Heard from Archer lately?"

Nell's nerves gave a reflexive little twitch. She wasn't likely to forget that Delia had nearly caught Nell and Archer together. "This morning. Part of the court business."

"The two of you go way back, don't you?"

Nell hesitated. "Sort of. We've known each other a long time. More than twenty years when it comes right down to it. Why?"

"Was it always?" Delia waggled her hand in the air. "You know. Like that with him?"

Nell polished off the rest of her sandwich, eyeing Delia more closely. She swallowed and wiped her lips with the napkin again. "Like what?"

Delia huffed. She rolled her eyes. "Were you always hot for each other?"

Nell was glad she'd swallowed or she would have choked. "Not when I was fourteen," she assured. "My mother had just died."

Delia frowned, quick sympathy entering her eyes. "How awful."

"It was. But I had my best friend. And a summer with your aunt Meredith. It helped." She reached over the counter to grab a clean spoon, then nudged her partially finished sundae toward Delia. She handed her the spoon. "Want to tell me what's really on your mind?"

Delia took the spoon and jabbed it into the melting ice cream. "Archer tell you I'm the screwup of the Templeton clan?"

"Of course not!"

Delia slowly sucked the ice cream off her spoon. "My brother's an honest-to-goodness air force hero. My sister is a doctor. Only thing I can do is guess other women's dress and shoe sizes."

"You've been Vivian's personal assistant for the last few years."

"You know Vivvie well enough by now to know she doesn't need a personal assistant. She figures out little tasks to keep me busy so I can earn a paycheck from her, which—despite the source—makes my dad happy. Which, in turn makes her feel better about the crappy childhood he had."

"I think you're underestimating yourself." Nell sucked on her own spoonful of ice cream. "So who's the guy?"

Delia grimaced. She dropped her spoon on the counter with a little clatter. "Nick."

"Nick?" Nell was a little slow. "You mean Nick *Ventura*? Isn't he—"

"Younger than me?" Delia nodded. "Four years."

"That's not the end of the world. What's four years?"

"He already has a master's degree." She propped her chin on her hand. "I'm a thirty-year-old with a high school degree." She twirled a finger in the air. "Whoopee."

"If you want more, go back to school."

"I don't want more," Delia said. "That's the problem. The idea of going back to school?" She shuddered dramatically.

"What about him? Does he know you're interested in him?"

Delia's lips twisted. "Unless he's been living under a rock. Which he has not." She suddenly twirled around on her stool, pressing her back to the counter and stretching out her legs. She was wearing shorts and a clinging T-shirt and could have easily passed for someone much younger than Nick Ventura. "So how serious is it with you and Arch?"

Nell automatically shook her head. "Archer's never serious about anyone."

"That's not exactly what I asked."

"It's not serious."

Delia didn't look convinced, but at least she dropped it and picked up her spoon again, and together, the two of them polished off the rest of the hot fudge and ice cream.

When they left the diner, they went their separate ways. Delia presumably headed back to Vivian's, where she occupied two rooms in what she lightly referred to as the West Wing.

Nell, though, headed out to look at another house for rent that had shown up the day before on the bulletin board at Ruby's. After having looked at more than a dozen potential places in the past three weeks, she wasn't holding out much hope.

Perhaps her lack of hope was the missing ingredient, though, because the small bungalow located not far from the Cozy Night was very nearly perfect. Oh, it needed a good scouring inside and out and the kitchen was ancient. But that still wasn't a deterrent for Nell. It wasn't as if she'd been gaining any new kitchen skills staying at the Cozy Night for the past month. The rental had two bedrooms, one bathroom that was slightly less ancient than the kitchen and an overgrown yard.

And it meant she could finally get the rest of her belongings out of the storage unit in Cheyenne.

She wrote a check covering the deposit and the first month's rent right there on the spot. She called around to the contacts that she'd been making since coming to town until she had a landscaper who could come and clear the yard the following afternoon and a cleaning crew who could be there even sooner.

She felt so energized by her progress that she went back to the motel and told the kid at the front desk—they were ever changing so Nell had never managed to learn any of their names—that she'd be checking out in the morning.

Then she filled the tank in her car with gas and, armed with an enormous cup of hot coffee in her console, she set off for the storage rental place in Cheyenne. By the time she rolled into town several hours later, her stomach was growling again and she stopped at a fast-food place for some dinner not far from Archer's house.

It had been only a couple of months since she'd woken up in his guest room bed there, but it felt like it was so much longer.

With both her stomach and her coffee mug refilled and knowing he was in Denver anyway, she turned down his block and trolled down his neat and tidy street. It was such a wildly different setting than his house outside Weaver and she wondered how much more different his apartment in Denver would be.

She'd never before considered that she might actually want to see it one day.

It was still light enough outside not to need the streetlights but inside houses up and down the street, lamps were beginning to come on in front windows and porch lights were beginning to come on by front doors. His house was no different. Golden light gleamed from the fixtures on either side of his front door, spilling down over the brick steps, and she smiled slightly because it was such a homey, charming sight.

When she saw a shadow move across one of the mullioned windows, she thought she'd imagined it. But when it happened again, she pulled right over to the curb and parked. She grabbed her cell phone and swiped the screen. Pressing the listing for her most recent calls, she heard clicks and a faint whir before it rang. Once. Twice. Three times.

His deep voice answered, and her stomach dipped, but it was just his voice mail message. "This is Archer Templeton, attorney at law. Leave a message. If it's an emergency, contact my office at—"

She peered through her windshield at his house, watching for another glimpse of someone inside while his voice reeled off his business numbers. "It's Nell," she said after the beep. "I'm in Cheyenne to empty my storage unit. Do you have someone staying at your house?" Then she hung up.

Crime wasn't exactly rampant in the town. But Archer, despite porch lights, was often gone for long stretches at a time. She waited for him to call for an interminable ten minutes, and when he didn't, she just exhaled and turned off the car engine. She crossed the street and skipped up the steps and walked across the porch, peering in through the front window.

The curtain panels on the inside were sheerer than she expected and easily afforded her a view of the woman standing near the fireplace.

Judge Taylor Potts.

And the man sprawled comfortably in his overstuffed chair. She could even see the cell phone clasped lightly in Archer's broad, long-fingered hand.

She jerked back but not quickly enough to miss

Taylor moving across the room to sit on the arm of his chair. To close her hand over his arm and lean closer to him.

Nell turned on her heel and darted down the steps. She raced across the yard. The street. Practically threw herself into her front seat and fumbled the car key into the ignition.

A moment later she roared down the block and around the corner, barely having the presence of mind to slow down because she was in a residential zone and the last thing she needed was a speeding ticket.

He'd told her he was still in Denver. That he had court all day.

Her fingers strangled her steering wheel as she drove to the storage unit. She should have known better. The man didn't make promises. He just kept moving on, routinely changing one woman on his arm with the next.

Never leaving anyone behind with hard feelings.

Except her.

Chapter Thirteen

"I've been leaving you messages for over a week."

Nell gave Archer a baleful look and turned away from him. She pointed accusingly at Montrose. "You said you'd warn me if he showed up."

His grandmother's chef and majordomo, wearing a white apron over his black suit, actually looked abashed.

It was unsettling enough that Archer felt mildly sorry for the way he'd bullied his way past the man when he'd opened the door at the small house where Nell had moved.

It had taken him a few days before he'd even been able to track down her address. It had been easy enough to find out that she'd moved out of the Cozy Night.

Not so easy to locate where she'd gone after that, particularly when his grandmother had abruptly departed for Philadelphia and taken Delia with her. Aside from his cousin promising him that it wasn't for health reasons and confirming that Nell *was* still in charge of the library project, he'd gotten no more information from that quarter.

Between Gage needing him to deal with Noah's latest situation and his caseload in Denver, he'd actually resorted to assigning Jennifer to the task of discovering Nell's whereabouts.

It shouldn't have been so hard in a small town like Weaver, but Nell wasn't exactly known for her talkative nature when it came to her personal business.

The way she'd kept quiet about Martin and the Lambert estate was a perfect example of that.

And now, the fact that Montrose was at Nell's at all was just one more reason why Archer felt like he'd landed in some alternate universe.

He followed her from the small kitchen where a pile of dough and flour was covering the only counter and out into a small, fenced yard. A rickety-looking picnic table was partially covered with a bag of potting soil and several plastic pots.

Even Nell looked different. She was wearing a sleeveless purple-and-green tie-dyed dress that looked as if it could have come right out of his bohemian stepmother's closet. The knit fit her as closely as a T-shirt, and when he realized he was focusing a little too hard on the swell of her breasts pushing against the fabric, he finally managed to look elsewhere. "You want to tell me what the hell is going on around here?"

She gave him a thin-lipped stare. "I don't know what you mean."

He spread his arms, encompassing the entire alternate universe around them. "You've been avoiding me for days and now...all this?"

"I haven't been avoiding you." She grabbed a spade and jabbed it into the bag of soil.

He snorted. "What do you call it, then? I've been trying to reach you since I heard about the ethics complaint you filed against Martin. And what is *Montrose* doing here?"

"Teaching me how to make bread," she said as if it should be obvious. She tossed down the spade in favor of crossing her arms over her chest, which plumped her breasts even more. "The real question is why are *you* here?"

He rubbed his forehead, trying to rid the feel and taste of those breasts from his memory, and paced around the cluttered table.

The fenced yard wasn't large. She had room for the rectangular picnic table and benches, a folding lawn chair—the lounge kind—and the stack of books that sat on the grass beside it. On the other side of the small square of grass was an ancient garage. The door was open and her car was parked inside it. "Where else do you think I should be?"

"I don't know. Maybe with Judge Potts."

He spread his palms. "Why would I be with her?"

Her expression tightened even more. "You were with her last week." Her voice was flat. "In Cheyenne when you told me you were in Denver, so you tell me."

He'd been in Cheyenne to talk to the governor about Noah Locke when he'd gotten a message from Taylor. "The only conversation I've had with Taylor Potts has been about *you*."

"She was at your house," Nell said in a flat tone. "I left you a message that I thought someone was there, but that someone was you! The two of you."

"Yeah, okay, so what?" In his present mood, he'd be damned if he'd tell her what he'd gone to the house to retrieve. Meeting Taylor there, too, so she could fill him in about the ethics case had been expedient. "You saw a conversation?"

"You told me you were in *Denver*!"

"When I called you that morning, I *was* in Denver," he shot back in a clipped tone. It wasn't often that he lost his temper but he was in danger of it now. He didn't like being accused of being a liar. "I had to go to Cheyenne because of a client."

"Right."

"Don't act like I'm the one who's been withholding information. I knew you didn't leave Pastore Legal because you hadn't made partner," he said. "But at first I figured it was your business. Same as whatever the hell caused your falling-out with Ros. Only thing I knew for certain was that Martin had to be at the center of it. He's the only thing she'd hold inviolate, even above your friendship."

He circled around her and her flinch as he got nearer added a finely honed edge to the mood that had been building in him for days now.

Ever since she failed to return the first message he'd left for her.

"But after everything I told you about Meredith, after everything that happened in your office at Viv's the night of her cocktail party—"

Her dark brown eyes darted to his, then she looked away just as quickly. But she looked as wounded as he felt.

"—after *everything*," he said through his teeth, "you still didn't give me one damn hint about Pastore's collusion. I had to learn it from Taylor. And now—" he spread his arms again "—now, you're finally out of that godforsaken motel and you come here!"

"Where else would I go?"

Archer was at his wit's end, and his voice rose, too. *"To me!"*

Her face went pale. "I don't understand."

"And you never have," he said, feeling a harsh pinch inside his gut. "You won't need anybody. You obviously don't trust me."

"I—" Her lips slammed shut at the look he gave her.

"Even all this." He flicked the bag of soil and one of the plastic pots tumbled off the table. "What is all this about? Cornelia Brewster 2.0?"

Color flagged her cheeks. "What if it is? I can't practice law right now even if I wanted to. Not until the state bar decides whether or not to censure me. Your grandmother's library is just a stopgap and one that's not even going to last all that much longer now that we've gotten the official go-ahead. For all of my adult life the only thing I have focused on is the law. I'm thirty-six years old. Isn't it about time I figured out if there's something else I might like to do?"

"For God's sake, Nell. Go work in a bloody bookstore. Or open one of your own. It's what you've *always* wanted to do. Or have you forgotten telling me that when you were a month away from graduating law school?"

She stared at him. Color rose in her face, then drained away just as abruptly. She suddenly pushed past him, bolting into the house. He hadn't taken two steps into the kitchen after her when he could hear the sound of her retching through the thin walls.

He shot Montrose a look. The man was sitting at the table, looking like he wished he were anywhere else. "Suddenly Nell's your best friend?"

"She doesn't take advantage of Mrs. Templeton," he said in his annoyingly pompous way.

Archer raked back his hair. "She doesn't take advantage of anyone," he muttered. "Has she been sick like this before?"

Montrose's lips pursed. Obviously he wasn't going to say.

Which actually said all that Archer needed to know.

Annoyed with the chef, annoyed with her and most of all annoyed with himself, he went to find her.

She was sitting on the floor of a bathroom smaller than a coat closet, resting her head on her knees. Her curly hair looked darker than ever splayed across her pale shoulders.

He had five sisters. Four of whom had babies.

"Are you pregnant?"

Her head whipped up. Her eyes were like saucers of hot fudge. Glistening. Brown. "Don't be ridiculous."

He flipped down the lid on the toilet and sat,

even though the room really didn't have enough space for the two of them. But it did mean she didn't have a lot of room for escape.

"We did get a little carried away that night." Understatement of the century. It was the only time in his life, except for the first time with her all those years ago, when he hadn't given a thought to protection.

She tapped her hand on her opposite arm. "I have an implant. The never-fail birth control because you never fail to forget it."

It took him a minute to identify the sensation inside him, because it should have been relief and it wasn't.

She'd lowered her head again to rest on her knees and he started to touch her curls, but drew his fingers into a fist instead and pressed it to his thigh.

"That's good," he lied. "Would've had to marry you."

She didn't look at him, but her scoffing sound was more than clear. "You're not the marrying kind."

"Maybe not. There's only one girl who ever made me consider it."

She finally raised her head. Her face was still pale, but at least it wasn't ashen the way it had been earlier. Her lashes were lowered, keeping him from seeing her eyes. "What happened?"

He shrugged. "She threw her lot in with some-one else. You're sure you're not—"

"I'm *not*. Besides, just because a man is a hus-band, it doesn't necessarily follow that he's a good father. My own is proof of that."

"Montrose says you've thrown up more than once."

She finally gave him a look. "Montrose would never."

"The fact that he didn't confirm it was confir-mation enough."

She maneuvered herself around until she could push to her feet, but had to use his shoulder as le-verage in the confining space. "You shove your career in a cement mixer for a while and see if it doesn't cause you enough stress to throw up a few times." She opened the crackled-mirror cabinet above the sink and pulled out a bottle of mouth-wash. She swished some in her mouth, spat it out and returned the bottle to its spot. Then without looking at him, she sidled around his legs again and left.

He followed her back into the kitchen, where the dough was now resting inside an oval basket. Montrose was wiping up the flour covering the counter.

"I think I can take it from here," Nell was tell-ing him as she tugged the cloth from his resistant hand. "Thanks."

"Once it's doubled, you punch it down and let it rise again."

"I know. I remember." Archer felt as if he was hallucinating when she tucked her arm through the other man's and maneuvered him out of the kitchen. "I'll bring you pictures tomorrow to show you the results."

"Bring the *loaf*," Montrose ordered. "I've made fresh jam to go with it."

Then he heard the door shut and a moment later, Nell returned to the kitchen. She picked up the cloth and started scrubbing at the flour still stuck on the faded pink-and-gray countertop.

"He has fresh jam."

"And I hope it's something pedestrian like good old strawberry and not weird like caviar basil or God knows what." She gave a quick shake of her head.

"I wish you'd have told me about Martin," he said quietly.

She didn't pretend to misunderstand. "And let you know how blind I was?" She had one hand braced on the counter as she scrubbed with the other, her springy hair bouncing around her shoulders. It was longer than it had been a few weeks ago.

"Why did you wait so long to report it?"

Her shoulders sagged and she stopped scrubbing. She angled her chin and looked at him.

"Ros."

She moved to the sink, a set expression on her face. "You're not the only one who protects her." She flipped on the water and rinsed her cloth. "For all the good it'll do if he's actually censured, too."

"You don't know for sure that *you* will be."

"I should be." She threw the cloth down into the sink and it hit with a wet splat.

He settled his hand on her back, right between her too-sharp shoulder blades. He felt her flinch but she didn't move away. He spread his fingers upward to the base of her neck, where her muscles felt as tight as his, and he turned her toward him into his embrace.

He'd expected resistance. But instead, she actually leaned against him. Her arms slid around his shoulders and she pressed her forehead against his neck. He could feel the sigh she gave throughout her entire body.

He kissed the top of her head. But he didn't dare do anything more because he'd already proved that he had too little control where she was concerned. "It's going to be all right. We'll get through this. One step at a time."

She didn't say anything. But her arms tightened around him. "I can't believe you remembered I wanted a bookstore like my mother's," she mumbled against him.

He closed his eyes. "I remember everything."

Her head moved, but only, it seemed, to burrow deeper against him. "I asked Greer to feed your cat," she finally said.

He smiled faintly and brushed a kiss against her hair one more time.

Nell stared at the plastic stick in her hand.

Two lines for positive.

One line for negative.

And there were absolutely two fat, pink lines.

The test she'd done the day before had given the same results.

And the one before that, also the same.

She lifted her arm to glare at the spot where she knew the tiny implant was located. "So much for you."

She dropped her arm and tossed the pregnancy test stick into the trash along with its two twins and eyed her reflection in the crackled mirror over her sink.

Did she look different?

Her face didn't. As long as nobody paid any attention to her breasts that seemed to have outgrown their usual cup size overnight, her body didn't look any different, either.

She pressed her hand to her stomach. "Not yet, anyway."

Her eyes suddenly stung.

It was an annoyance that had been happening with increasing frequency the last few weeks.

She'd gotten teary over the library site being finalized. Over her fifth failed attempt to bake a decent loaf of bread despite Montrose's tutelage. She'd even cried over the unexpected phone call she'd received from Gardner, who'd called to ask Nell for advice about the best way to protect her boys should something ever happen to her.

Her knees felt as watery as her eyes and she sank down on the closed toilet lid.

How was she going to tell Archer when not even two weeks ago she'd sat in this very bathroom insisting there was no possible way for her to be pregnant?

That's good. Would've had to marry you.

His words echoed inside her head.

As soon as he'd said them—before she'd even given any thought to the possibility that her implant might have become too old to be effective—she'd realized that the only proposal she would ever want from him was one *not* prompted by a baby in her belly.

She was in love with Archer Templeton.

And she feared she had been for a very, very long time.

Nausea clawed at her and she leaned over the sink, running cold water over the insides of her wrists until it began to subside.

They were supposed to be giving their workshop at the wellness expo that afternoon. He was picking her up because he was coming all the way from Cheyenne anyway after he'd spent the last few days in meetings at the state capitol building.

Considering the frequency of her bouts of nausea, she didn't know how she was going to make it through the drive to Braden, much less the afternoon-long workshop they'd be conducting, without him noticing.

That's good. Would've had to marry you.

She made an impatient sound and turned off the water. She mopped the mascara smudges from around her eyes, pulled on the soft pink biker-style jacket that Delia had talked her into buying at Classic Charms a few days earlier to go with her black jeans and left the bathroom just in time to hear a truck engine out front.

Her stomach lurched, but this time it wasn't because of nausea. It was simply pure nervousness.

She opened the front door to wave at Archer, then ducked back inside. She went into the second bedroom, where she'd set up a small table and enough shelves to house her collection of books, and picked up the stack of stapled packets she'd been preparing in her spare time for the workshop.

Archer had told her that his office in Denver could have taken care of it, but if she'd agreed, she wouldn't have felt like she was contributing anything to what was supposed to be their combined effort.

It was hard enough being ineffectual while waiting for the bar's decision regarding her future as a lawyer. She didn't need to feel useless where everything else was concerned, too.

She shouldered her briefcase strap and with her arms full of the packets, went back out to the living room. As usual, bells jangled inside her at the sight of him, tall and gold and crazily handsome, as he walked through her front door and set a stack of mail on the little table she'd placed there so she'd have a spot to dump her keys when she came in every day.

Like her, he was wearing black jeans. His white shirt was rolled up at the elbows and open at the neck. His jaw was clean-shaven and his hair was slicked back and if she hadn't vowed not to repeat the mistake that had gotten her into her latest predicament, she'd have been busily wondering if she possessed what it would take to seduce him.

But she *had* vowed, and she was not in the market to do anything such thing.

So she summarily dumped the packets into his hands. "I just have another box of handouts to grab." She frowned when he set the packets on the small table, as well.

There wasn't a single trace of amusement in

his deep green gaze. Not a hint of a dimple in his lean cheeks.

"What's wrong?"

He pulled a thin envelope from his back pocket.

There was no postage stamp on the corner and she recognized the seal on the front of it and felt her nerves pinch. "Have you become an official deliveryman now for the bar association?"

"They knew I was seeing you. Instead of making you wait for it to come by mail…" He held it out but when she went to reach for it, he tipped it out of her grasp. "I know you don't want to wait to see what it says, but there's something I need to—" He broke off and cleared his throat. "Just… just wait a minute before you decide to open it up."

She frowned even harder and her alarm grew. It was rare to see him looking so… She didn't even have a word for it. *Uncomfortable* wasn't quite right. Neither was *uncertain*.

"Why?"

"Because I…well, hell." He turned to the stuff on the table and sent the stack of packets careening onto the floor. He muttered an oath and if she weren't mistaken, a dusky tide of color was rising up his throat as he tried and failed to catch them.

She had to bite the inside of her cheek to keep from smiling, because as alarmed as she was feeling inside, it was seriously, *seriously* gratifying to see him have to fumble. Just once. Just a little.

She set down her briefcase and crouched next to him, gathering up the thick packets. Some had even landed outside the open door. She leaned on her hand and reached past him to get them, then sat back on her heels and dropped them onto the untidy pile he'd managed to gather. "Want to tell me what's going on here or should I start making guesses?"

"You wouldn't guess this." He dumped the packets back onto the table, then straightened and took her hands and pulled her to her feet. "Maybe you should sit."

Her mouth went dry. "Is Vivian all right?" His grandmother had returned from Philadelphia the week before without offering any explanations for her abrupt trip. Nell could only assume she'd been seeing doctors despite Delia's claim otherwise.

His brows jerked together. "Yeah. Yeah. She's fine."

Nell sank down on the edge of the couch. She'd bought it from Classic Charms. It was second-hand, but it was a pretty shade of blue and comfortable to boot. "Then *what*?"

"Martin's facing federal charges on bribery and extortion," he said abruptly. Bluntly. "He was arrested early this morning."

Her jaw dropped.

Archer crouched in front of her, his hands

clasping hers. "He might not pay the price for anything else, but he's going to pay the price for this."

"But how...what?" She could hardly comprehend it. "Does Ros know? Have you talked to Meredith?"

"Yes. And yes. I saw Ros for a few minutes before I started heading up here. Needless to say, the law firm's going to be picked apart before long. Investigations like that tend to spawn more. She's pretty shaken up."

Nell's eyes dampened. "I can imagine. I hope Jonathan is with her."

He made a face. "I think they already split up a while ago. Meredith and my dad are on their way to Cheyenne. I don't know if Ros will be all that ready to see them, but they're going to try."

Her eyes flooded with more tears. "I can't believe it." She swiped her cheek. "Where's the letter you brought for me?"

He took it back out of his pocket and set it beside her on the couch. "There's more."

"I'm not sure my nerves can handle more." She picked up the envelope and slid her finger beneath the sealed flap.

"What about your heart?"

She stared. "What?"

His throat had that dusky color again. "This is one of those when-it-rains-it-pours times." He got up again and went back to the table by the door, fumbling through the mess until he pulled out another envelope.

This one was thicker. Larger. And when he handed it to her, she could immediately feel that it contained a book.

"I should have given it to you a long time ago." He rubbed his fingers through his hair, looking oddly embarrassed. "I planned to. But things didn't turn out the way I thought they would, and—"

"Archer, what on earth are you talking about?"

"Just open it."

Her heart was suddenly chugging inside her chest, pushing up into her throat. She pulled open the flap and tipped the book out onto her lap.

The dust jacket was glossy. In perfect condition except for the small tear in one corner.

She traced a shaking finger over the fat little penguin on the cover. *"Monty Meets Mary,"* she whispered. Her mother's tenth book. The only one she had never been able to find.

A tear splashed on the cover and she slowly wiped it away.

"It was in a used-book store in Montana. Total coincidence that I found it." He shrugged, still looking uncomfortable. Uncertain. "I'd gotten in the habit of always looking for one of her books whenever I saw a used-book store. I was going to give it to you when you passed the bar. When I—"

"That long?" She swiped her cheeks. "You've had it that long? Why didn't you—" She broke off, because it didn't matter how long he'd had it. "It doesn't matter." She pressed the book to her heart. "Thank you."

"You didn't let me finish." He crouched in front of her again and took her hand and her heart lurched all over again at the realization that *his* hand wasn't entirely steady. "What I was saying was that I was going to give it to you when I asked you to marry me."

She went still. Her eyes felt trapped in his gaze.

He slowly reached out to draw a curl away from her face. "I didn't want you just to be my partner back then, Cornelia. You were the girl I wanted. The girl I wanted to be my wife. I still—"

"You were seeing someone else. One of the professors. Ros told me."

He looked pained. "You think she wanted to share her best friend with the stepbrother she couldn't stand?"

"I never told her about us!"

"I did."

"What?"

He scrubbed his hand down his face. When his gaze met hers again, his eyes were steady. "I know there's no point trying to whitewash my own behavior. I knew you wanted to join Martin's firm more than anything. Ros knew it, too, and she liked tossing that fact at me just because she knew how much it stung. So I told her about us just so she'd shut up."

"She never said anything to me."

"She wouldn't, would she?"

"So she lied to me about the professor?"

"It wasn't a lie. It was just information that was a couple years too old. And don't be mad at her for being foolish. We were all foolish then."

She was trembling. "You had an affair with one of the professors while *you* were still in school."

"Does it matter now? It was a long time ago. Before I fell in love with you."

She pressed the book harder against her breast, feeling his words quaking inside her. "I fell in love with you, too," she whispered.

"And now? Because you didn't let me finish again. I still want you to be my wife, Nell." He flicked his finger against the envelope lying on the couch beside her. "Regardless of what that says. I'm sick of pretending. Sick of waiting." He pressed his lips for a moment to the back of her hand that he still held. "Everything that's happened since you danced on that bar in Cheyenne and landed in my arms has made me face that fact. I want you as my partner. As my lover. And maybe—" His jaw canted for a moment.

When he spoke again, his voice was husky.

"And maybe one day you *will* be pregnant. Because you want to have my child as much I do."

There was a river of tears running down her face and she couldn't do a thing to stop it. She decided that was just what had to happen when a heart was too full.

She stood, still clasping *Monty Meets Mary* with one hand and Archer with her other. "Come." She pulled him into her spare bedroom and carefully slid the book into place on the shelf next to number nine. "This is number eleven." She pulled it out and placed it in his hands. *"Monty Marries Mary."* She kissed him slowly. "Yes. I want you to be my husband."

He started to reach for her but she shook her head. "Wait." She pulled out the last of her mother's books. "This is number twelve," she said huskily. "The final story." She slowly placed it in his hands, feeling herself sinking into his green gaze. *"Monty and Mary Have a Baby."*

His pupils dilated a little. "You want to have a baby?" He sounded disbelieving. "With me?"

She leaned into him and brushed her lips against his. "What I'm trying to tell you is that I am *having* your baby. With you."

His head jerked up.

His eyes searched hers. A sparkle suddenly glinted somewhere deep inside. "Really?"

She threaded her fingers through his and pressed them against her abdomen. "Really."

He dropped right then and there onto his knees and pressed his mouth against their joined hands. "I wish I had a diamond ring," he said fervently. No hint of disbelief anymore? "It would feel more official with a ring."

She suddenly felt like laughing. Because that's something a person also did when their heart was so full.

She threaded her fingers through his hair and kissed his forehead. His cheeks. His mouth. She had a vague thought about the workshop that they were still going to need to give. About the contents of the letter from the bar association. About Ros and how they were going to have to find some way to be there for her, too, because she was going to need them.

But for now, for at least these few minutes, and for the rest of their lives, they had *this*.

"You brought me *Monty Meets Mary*," she whispered. "And that, my impossible, beautiful Archer, is dearer to me than any diamond in the entire world."

* * * * *

COMING SOON!

We really hope you enjoyed reading this book.
If you're looking for more romance, be sure to
head to the shops when new books are
available on

Thursday 6th August

To see which titles are coming soon, please visit
millsandboon.co.uk/nextmonth

MILLS & BOON

MILLS & BOON

Coming next month

A WILL, A WISH, A WEDDING
Kate Hardy

'Miss Grey changed her will three months ago,' the
solicitor confirmed, 'and she was of sound mind when
she made her will.'

You could still be inveigled into doing something
when you were of sound mind, Hugo thought. And
Rosemary liked to make people happy. What kind of
sob story had this woman spun to make his great-aunt
give her the house?

'There are conditions to the bequest,' the solicitor
continued. 'Dr Walters, you must undertake to finish
the butterfly project, turn the house into an education
centre — of which she would like you to assume the
position of director, should you choose — and re-wild
the garden.'

The garden re-wilding, Hugo could understand,
because he knew how important his great-aunt's garden
had been to her. And maybe the education centre; he'd
always thought that Rosemary would've made a brilliant
teacher. But, if Rosemary had left the house to his father,
as her previous will had instructed, surely she knew that
her family would've made absolutely sure her wishes
were carried out? Why had his great-aunt left everything
to a stranger instead? And he didn't understand the first
condition. 'What project?'

'I'm editing the journals and co-writing the biography of Viola Ferrers,' Dr Walters said.

It was the first time he'd heard her speak. Her voice was quiet, and there was a bit of an accent that he couldn't quite place, except it was definitely Northern; and there was a lot of a challenge in her grey eyes.

Did she really think he didn't know who Viola Ferrers was?

'My great-great-great-grandmother,' he said crisply.

Her eyes widened, so he knew the barb had gone home. This was *his* family and *his* heritage. What right did this stranger have to muscle in on it?

'Miss Grey also specified that a butterfly house should be built,' the solicitor continued.

Rosemary had talked about that, three years ago; but Hugo had assumed that it was her way of distracting him, giving him something to think about other than the gaping hole Emma's death had left in his life. They'd never taken it further than an idea and a sketch or two.

'And said butterfly house,' the solicitor said, 'must be designed and built by you, Mr Grey.'

Continue reading
A WILL, A WISH, A WEDDING
Kate Hardy

Available next month
www.millsandboon.co.uk

MILLS & BOON

THE HEART OF ROMANCE

A ROMANCE FOR EVERY KIND OF READER

MODERN

Prepare to be swept off your feet by sophisticated, sexy and seductive heroes, in some of the world's most glamourous a romantic locations, where power and passion collide.
8 stories per month.

HISTORICAL

Escape with historical heroes from time gone by. Whether y passion is for wicked Regency Rakes, muscled Vikings or ru Highlanders, awaken the romance of the past.
6 stories per month.

MEDICAL

Set your pulse racing with dedicated, delectable doctors in high-pressure world of medicine, where emotions run high passion, comfort and love are the best medicine.
6 stories per month.

True Love

Celebrate true love with tender stories of heartfelt romance the rush of falling in love to the joy a new baby can bring, a focus on the emotional heart of a relationship.
8 stories per month.

Desire

Indulge in secrets and scandal, intense drama and plenty of hot action with powerful and passionate heroes who have it wealth, status, good looks…everything but the right woman
6 stories per month.

HEROES

Experience all the excitement of a gripping thriller, with an romance at its heart. Resourceful, true-to-life women and s fearless men face danger and desire - a killer combination!
8 stories per month.

DARE

Sensual love stories featuring smart, sassy heroines you'd wa best friend, and compelling intense heroes who are worthy
4 stories per month.

To see which titles are coming soon, please visit
millsandboon.co.uk/nextmonth

might just be true love...